LIGHTBRINGER

LIGHTBRINGER
K. D. McENTIRE

an imprint of **Prometheus Books**
Amherst, NY

Published 2011 by Pyr®, an imprint of Prometheus Books

Cover illustration © Sam Weber
Cover design by Grace M. Conti-Zilsberger

Inquiries should be addressed to
Pyr
59 John Glenn Drive
Amherst, New York 14228–2119
VOICE: 716–691–0133
FAX: 716–691–0137
WWW.PYRSF.COM

15 14 13 12 11   5 4 3 2 1

Library of Congress Cataloging-in-Publication Data

McEntire, K. D., 1980–
    Lightbringer / by K. D. McIntire.
        p. cm.
    Summary: Teenaged Wendy, who has the power to help souls cross over to their final destinations, falls in love with a ghost and discovers horrific, dark forces in the afterlife.
    ISBN 978–1–61614–539–2 (pbk. : alk. paper)
    ISBN 978–1–61614–540–8 (ebook)
    [1. Supernatural—Fiction. 2. Soul—Fiction. 3. Ghosts—Fiction.
4. Love—Fiction.] I. Title.
PZ7.M478454238Li 2011
[Fic]—dc23
                                                                                    2011028713

Printed in the United States of America on acid-free paper

For Jake.
You believed.

ACKNOWLEDGMENTS

This book wouldn't exist without a truly awesome group of people. I'd like to thank the amazing AgentJoe—aka Joe Monti—who was willing to walk a newbie through this whole process without once getting grumpy at me. I'd also like to thank the fabulous and mellow Lou Anders, editor extraordinaire and lover of all things geeky. Thank you.

Further thanks go to Nadia Cornier, who is the best sounding board ever, and without whom I probably would have tripped over my own plot holes. To my mother, whose timely help saved my work from going poof! And, of course, my Drafty Ladies: Karen Ramsey, Jennifer Day, Anna Hunt, Elly Hunt, and Christine Panus. You all humble me. Thank you.

Last but not least, thanks go to my husband Jake, and the teenage self he's willing to channel every time he picks up my work. Without you I'd never have time to write. Thank you.

PROLOGUE

When the last off-key strains of *Happy Birthday* trailed away, Wendy opened her eyes and blew hard. Twelve flames winked out and the waiter clapped politely before retrieving the candles from the cake, leaving the three of them alone with dessert.

The mountain of chocolate cake and ice cream in front of her was nearly the size of her head. Eddie, fork in hand, leaned forward to dig in when his father's fingers on his wrist stopped him.

"Manners, Eddie. Wendy gets the first bite."

Eddie grinned sheepishly at his father. "Sorry, Dad."

"It's okay, Mr. Barry." Wendy grabbed her own fork. "Race you to the plate!" Together they dug in and when the cake was demolished, Wendy tore into her gifts with equal abandon.

While the waiter cleaned up the mess of paper and plates, Mr. Barry helped Wendy clasp the locket her father had left for her around her neck. He patted her shoulder when he was done but Wendy did not miss the sympathy in his eyes. "It suits you."

"Yeah," Eddie agreed, spearing one last bite of cake off his plate before it was whisked to the kitchen. He wiped his wrist across his mouth. "It's pretty."

"You missed a spot," Mr. Barry said wryly, wetting a corner of his napkin in his water glass and gently wiping Eddie's chin. Eddie rolled his eyes and squirmed but Wendy caught the small smile he gave his father in thanks. She couldn't help a slight pang of jealousy at their closeness, but by now it was a familiar feeling and easily squashed.

Sensing her discomfort, Mr. Barry signed the bill quickly and rose to pull Wendy's chair away from the table. He held her jacket for her as she slipped it on and then offered her his arm. Wendy, feeling very grown up, took it. "When is your father due home again?"

"Next week." Puffed up and proud, she added, "Dad said that I can stay by myself tonight! I'm old enough now."

"But the twins and your mother will be back in the morning?" The doorman opened the door with a flourish and they stepped from the warmth of the restaurant into the slushy, drizzling night.

At her nod, he said, "Well, Wendy, if you decide that you don't like spending the night by yourself, you can call anytime and Eddie and I will come get you." He winked. "Or if you want Eddie to sleep over there, I think we can get along without him for a night."

Bounding up beside his father, Eddie grabbed Mr. Barry's wrist and tugged. "Really? You mean it?" Wendy grabbed his other wrist and danced a quick jig for joy.

Faced with their beaming smiles, Mr. Barry was lost. He threw his head back and laughed, hugging them both close with either arm. "You two were planning this, weren't you?"

"Thank you, Dad!" Eddie wrapped his arms around his father's neck and hugged tight.

Still chuckling, Mr. Barry held on for a moment and then stepped back, smoothing his son's ruffled hair. "But you have to behave yourselves," he warned, leading them toward the car. "Only one horror movie apiece. And if you call me at midnight scared out of your wits, I'm not coming over there."

Eddie sniffed haughtily. "We're not kids, Dad."

"Right," his father agreed gravely as they reached his car. A push of his key-fob unlocked the doors; it was Wendy's birthday so she sat up front while Eddie, plotting the rest of the night under his breath, slid behind her, sprawling across the seat on his back.

"Buckle up," Mr. Barry said to Eddie, cutting off his son's whine of protest with a pointed look. Eddie, scowling, followed orders. Wendy did as well.

The rain drizzling on the roof was soothing and Wendy, lulled by the swish of the wipers and the warmth of the heater blowing steadily across her face, quickly dozed.

Soon the car was too warm, however, and she uncomfortably shifted awake. The only noise was the hum of tires on pavement, the only light the hazy glow of the headlights barely cutting through the mist ahead of them. Mr. Barry was hunched over the steering wheel, craning his neck forward.

Groggy, she lifted her head and started to ask if she could turn the heater down, when a lurching shudder rocked the car.

"SHIT!" Mr. Barry's hand jabbed down, grabbed a lever nestled between the seats, and yanked. The car swerved violently left and right and Wendy heard the scream of tires drowning out her own tearing scream with their wail.

In slow motion the car slid left one lane, two lanes, three; Wendy threw her arms up over her face as a flood of fierce white light cut through the fog right in front of them. Dimly she felt the thump of Mr. Barry's hand slap against her collarbone as his outthrust arm protectively pinned her to the seat. A horn blared, filling the world with noise and the blinding white light.

Years or maybe only seconds later, Wendy opened her eyes.

There was a choppy *whirr-chunk* noise to her right and groaning to her left. Her whole body felt funny, tight and numb, and her mouth was filled with a taste like salt and metal. She spat twice and it helped somewhat, but it did nothing to ease the dreamy sensation of floating. Wendy blinked and realized, very gradually, that she was upside down. The seatbelt held her firmly in place and her hair, loosened from its band, brushed the roof of the car.

Slowly, marveling at the strange sensation of her hair catching on what could only be bits of metal and glass, Wendy turned toward the groaning. Her hand, moving of its own volition, stretched out in front of her, and stroked Mr. Barry's shoulder.

He, too, dangled toward the roof of the car, but there was something wrong. His cheek flapped open, wet and gleaming, torn apart in a wide swath at his chin. Mr. Barry's hand, studded with safety glass, rose up, took Wendy's hand in his own, and squeezed. The touch felt strange, his bones ground beneath the pressure of her fingers, but Wendy didn't let go.

"Light," he said, turning toward her so she could see the complete ruin of his face, the shattered nose, the misshapen lump of cheek and jaw. He deliriously hacked the words out one by one, stuttering and shivering as he spoke. The bottom curve of the steering wheel pressed into his sternum, cutting off his air. "Pr-pr-omise?"

Wendy nodded. He squeezed her hand again and she realized that his middle three fingers had been bent completely backwards, flopping over her knuckles loosely as he squeezed her hand over and over again, as he tried to soothe *her*, to comfort *her*.

"Eddie?" he asked. His words huffed out of him on a fine spray of blood and spit. "Is . . . Eddie?"

Craning her neck, Wendy felt the first stirrings of pain in her back and shoulders, but no matter how she twisted, she could not see. There was no guiding noise from the back, just the dying *kachunk* of the engine. "He's okay," she croaked, lying to calm him. She coughed, swallowed, and tried again. "He wore his seatbelt."

"Good." Mr. Barry's eyes fluttered closed. His lips moved but no sound came out. Wendy thought they might have formed "Eddie."

Long moments passed. His body sagged and Wendy realized that Mr. Barry must have passed out. Without thought she loosened her hand from his grip. His arm flopped onto the roof. Wendy, shifting until she could wriggle her leg to the left, kicked weakly at the dangling car keys, careful to avoid hitting Mr. Barry. It was better that he stayed unconscious until help came. On the fourth kick the engine gurgled to silence.

From the back she heard Eddie shift, groan, and mutter, "Dad?"

"He's sleeping," Wendy said, closing her eyes. In the distance she thought she heard the keening wail of an ambulance. Wendy relaxed, letting the seatbelt hold her weight. She felt herself drift again and welcomed it. "Let him sleep, Eddie. He needs it."

Time enough for Eddie to see his father broken and bloodied. *Let him sleep*, Wendy prayed silently to herself. *Let him sleep.*

CHAPTER ONE

Piotr hefted the newest box of loot and hauled it to the back of the mill floor, wrestling it into their makeshift pantry with effort. It had been good scrounging this week, their cubby was filled to overflowing, and Piotr was grateful to finally be done. On top of the closest box was a portfolio, battered but blank inside, and underneath a grocery bag bulging with Prismacolor colored pencils. Piotr collected the pencils and the portfolio, leaving the pantry. There was no light to turn off behind him.

It was late and the mill was silent. Poking his nose into various nooks and crannies, Piotr checked on the kids he was watching over. Snoring quietly, Specs lolled in his recliner, glasses askew, with a tattered copy of *The Hobbit* hanging from the tips of his fingers. As he'd done every night for over fifty years, Piotr saved his place and covered Specs with an army blanket, tucking aside the thick, black glasses on the windowsill.

The tangle of GI Joe blankets Tubs normally nested in was empty. Piotr found him asleep in Dora's corner; Tubs was curled under her blanket and an old duster Piotr had discarded months before. The soles of his footie pajamas were filthy and his chubby thumb was thrust in his mouth, lips smacking around it. Dora, still awake, glanced up as Piotr poked his head behind the beaded curtain that sectioned off her part of their den.

"Nightmare," she said, jerking her thumb towards Tubs. "How'd scavengin' go?"

"Decent overall." Piotr eased into Dora's room, careful to not jar

Tubs as he joined Dora at the warped closet door balanced on cinderblocks, which she was using as an improvised desk. Making a mental note to see if he could scavenge a better tabletop for her, Piotr set the portfolio and pencils on top of Dora's dwindling stack. "How's your landscape?"

"The bark ain't right." Dora held up a sketch of the overgrown courtyard outside the mill, skeletal branches of the lone tree yearning towards the sky. "It's junk! It's all just junk." Scowling, Dora tossed down her pencil and wiped a hand across her forehead, leaving dim charcoal smudges behind. "This pencil stinks."

It didn't. The Prismacolors were the best Piotr could scavenge, but Pandora's death had left her eternally at the age where every artist's block was a major disaster, and Piotr'd long since learned to ignore her hysterics. He mussed her hair. "Keep trying. It'll come."

"Yeah, yeah. You stayin' in?" Dora smoothed the ruffled strands of her white-blonde hair back behind her headband.

"At least for a while. I might walk the perimeter later."

"'Kay. Thanks for the supplies. I know they ain't easy to rustle up."

He grinned. "*Nezachto*. It was no problem. *Spi spokojno*."

She waved a hand. "Yeah, yeah. You too. G'Night."

Resisting the urge to ruffle her hair again, Piotr left Dora to her sketchpad and, rather than walking the long way around, gathered his will and drifted through the half dozen walls that separated her cubbyhole from his own. Some days, he thought, there were definite benefits to being dead.

Outside the night smelled of metal and salt, the scent drifting in through the rotting boards nailed over remnants of shattered windows. His corner was on the far side of the floor, away from the kids, giving them privacy. Piotr would have liked to be closer for safety's sake but he knew they needed their space.

Once the entire San Francisco area had been filled with little groups like theirs—ghost children, nicknamed the Lost, eternally protected by teens like Piotr—but now there were darker things preying the streets, and Piotr's makeshift family had become a rarity. It had gotten to the point that Piotr was considering leaving the dilapidated steel mill they'd taken as a home and relocating either north to the city or south into Silicon Valley. San Francisco was teeming with the living, however, as was the valley, and abandoning the relative safety of the mill was a very big decision; one Piotr was unwilling to make just yet.

Too tired to want to think further on the subject, Piotr stripped to his boxers and a tee shirt, crawling gratefully into his pallet. His window, one of the few in the deserted mill with glass still intact, gave Piotr a breathtaking view of the surrounding city and a hint of the bay stretching out beyond. Clouds drifted across the moon as Piotr sank into sleep.

Minutes or hours later, a shrill, high scream yanked him from uneasy dreams. At first Piotr thought he was in the living world again, where the sky was blue and bright and the sounds insistent, but the room was dark, and through his window clouds now rolled swiftly across the sky, obliterating the pale moonlight in shades of dark shale.

Stumbling to the window, Piotr scrubbed his eyes and squinted down at the street. Below, amid the trees, a luminescent figure, lean and white, loomed over a smaller shape, clearly one of the Lost. The kid screamed again and Piotr, snapped from his haze, shoved back from the window and pounded down the emergency stairs, leaping over rotted risers in bounds.

He was too slow. By the time he reached the ground floor both the Walker and the kid were gone; only the ice-frosted ground where the Walker had lain in wait remained. Panting heavily, Piotr glanced left and right, hoping to catch some flash of white, a telltale glimpse of the Walker's cloak to guide him in a rescue attempt.

Nothing.

Cursing, Piotr turned to go back inside . . . and found himself face to face with a second Walker. The Walker, hunched over and slavering, leaned in close so that Piotr could smell the rot of its face, the black decay eating away at the skin of its cheeks. "Rider," it hissed. "Meat."

Stumbling, Piotr fell back, his teeth clicking painfully together as he thumped to the ground. Foolishly he'd run downstairs without a weapon, hoping to snag the child and race to safety before the Walker knew what'd hit him. Walkers were lone wolves—Piotr never expected a second one to be waiting nearby.

Fingertips sharpened to brutal spikes arced across Piotr's upper arm, slashing his shirt into ribbons in four parallel lines of stinging pain. Hissing under his breath, Piotr grabbed his upper arm, and felt a gush of essence pour over his hand as he tried to stop the bleeding. The cuts were deep.

"Bastard," he groaned and kicked at the Walker's robed legs, hoping to at least push the monster back a few paces and give himself some space to scramble to his feet. Luck was with him. The Walker's knees buckled at his kick, slamming the monster face first to the ground. Lifting his leg as high as it would go, Piotr kicked again, aiming for the head, trying to ignore the wet rip of his heel breaking the thin layer of skin covering the Walker's skull. "Stay down!"

"Piotr!" Dora shouted from her window. "Here!" Balancing her hips on the windowsill, Dora leaned forward and flung her arm out in a wide arc. There was a whistling noise and a brief flash of moonlight on silver as a butter knife from the pantry clattered to the sidewalk mere feet from Piotr's outstretched and grasping hand.

"Fight to the death," Piotr grumbled, darting forward and snagging the blade with the tips of his fingers, "and she tosses me a dull knife. Great." Still, he knew what he was doing and even a dull knife was better than no knife at all.

The Walker, either sensing danger, or simply tired of the fight, flung a handful of pebbles and dirt into Piotr's face, blinding him. Cursing, Piotr swiped his free hand across his eyes, scrabbling to see, but the Walker had used his momentary blindness as a chance to flee. The courtyard was empty once again.

Groaning, Piotr struggled to his feet. He sniffed the air but his scuffle with the Walker had left a dense smell of rot clinging to his clothing. There was no way he could track the beast by smell alone.

Trudging back inside, Piotr hid a bitter smile. It looked like the decision whether to stay or go had been stripped away. Thanks to his clumsy fighting, the Walker had gotten away and now it knew where some Lost could be found. It would be back. They had to leave.

Inside, Piotr was met with anxious, pale faces. Tubs, clinging to Piotr's duster, huddled behind Dora, and Specs peered past splintery boards to the courtyard below. Piotr wanted to soothe them, to swear they were safe, but he didn't want to lie. Instead he remained silent.

The silence grew too long. Abruptly Specs turned from the window, pushing his round frames up on his nose. His hair, dark with grease, fell over one eye. "That was the third time this week, Piotr. We should pack."

"*Da*," Piotr sighed. "We should." He knelt down and Tubs flung himself into his arms, sobbing into his shoulder. Piotr stroked the back of Tubs' hair and let him cry.

"It spotted me," Dora said. "I saw it watchin' me."

"Most likely." Piotr stood, Tubs resting on his hip, and hugged the little boy close. Life seeped into Piotr from Tubs' skin in blue arcs, dulling his pain. The wounds on his arm began to slowly seal shut, itching like fire. "I am unsure but, yes, most likely."

"Perhaps we might bunk down with Miss Elle or Miss Lily," Specs offered, hesitant to bridge the topic of Elle to Piotr. "Or perhaps Mister James."

The thought of begging his fellow Riders for a place to stay made Piotr laugh roughly. "James? I'd rather leave you on your own." He set Tubs down and smoothed the wispy blond hair back from his forehead. "You okay now? Yes? Go wash your face."

When Tubs had toddled off, Piotr reached out and enfolded both Dora and Specs into a hug. Specs clung tighter than Dora, trembling lightly, the remaining unspent years of life flowing into Piotr in small, sharp spikes. The itching on his arm faded, replaced with smooth, blessed coolness.

Piotr squeezed them both and then stepped back, alert and wary, listening for intruders. "*Spaseebo.*" He gestured to his upper arm. "Thank you. For the aid."

Uncomfortable, Specs shrugged. "It is the least we can do, Piotr. You're welcome."

"They, the Walkers, are getting closer." Piotr crossed his arms over his chest.

"And smarter." Dora chewed her thumbnail. "Remember, Specs? When we saw one of 'em grab that kid right outta a tree last week? They ain't ever done that before."

"Do you think it's because of the White Lady?" Specs asked, pushing his glasses higher on his nose.

"White Lady or no, so long as you three are safe, I don't care the reasons why." Piotr ran his hands through his hair. He was still shaking, his mouth sour with adrenaline. The mill had been in a safe zone for years, but with the coming of the White Lady almost no place was safe anymore. The Walkers were everywhere.

"Honestly, I don't know what to do. Walker territory is spreading and the mill is stuck between them." Piotr leaned against a nearby wall, tilted his head back, and closed his eyes. They felt gritty with lack of sleep.

"We ain't strong enough to fight 'em." Dora drummed her fingers along the kitchen countertop. "Ain't stupid enough, neither."

"Since we are running, we should decide where to go," Specs said. "Which shall it be? Move closer to the bay or the valley?"

"I thought of that before, but there are too many of the living," Piotr said, rubbing his hands across his cheeks, feeling the light rasp of hair that would never grow past a certain point, brushed by calluses that would never fade. Piotr pushed away from the wall. "You should weigh in. What do you want to do?"

Hesitantly, after several seconds, Dora hunkered down into a squat and, wrapping her arms around her knees, murmured, "I don't mean to start no fuss, Piotr, but I wanna stay with Elle for awhile." Before Piotr could protest, she hurried to say, "I know we're safe with you, but there's been a lotta Walkers 'round lately and you can't be with us 24/7. We gotta be somewhere more, I dunno, more castle-like, you know? With a moat or somethin'. Def . . . dev . . . dependable."

"Defensible?" Much as he hated to admit it, Dora had a point. "Specs?"

"Staying with Miss Elle does indeed appear to be the best course of action." Specs took off his glasses and cleaned them on his shirt. Like Dora, Specs was too thin and gangly, caught in an early growth spurt by a death that had come too soon. Eternally eleven. "No offense."

Sighing, Piotr rubbed his hand along the wall, feeling the spots spongy with decay crumble away under his fingertips. Elle was not going to like this. "*Net*, there is none taken. Fine. Go pack up then and we'll go in the morning. Pandora, please pack for Tubs?"

"Gotcha." Dora and Specs drifted towards their quarters, leaving Piotr alone by the window. Lost in thought, he stared down at the empty courtyard and watched the swirling fog drift in from the bay. With a Walker down there somewhere, he knew there'd be no more sleep for him tonight. None at all.

Dawn came, lightening the sky to a pale grey, and Piotr carried Tubs piggyback as they made their way through the shriveled remains of the world. Picking a path through crumbling brick streets, they followed the whisper of surf breaking against the piers in the bay, leaving the mill behind. At first the going was slow; Piotr's turf was around fifteen miles from where Elle and her own Lost squatted dangerously near the tourist zone, amid the life and heat of Pier 39 and North Beach, wading through the press of humanity that eddied like the tides.

A steady pace brought them just inside Elle's territory by mid-morning. The idea of leaving the kids so close to the haunts of the living bothered Piotr deeply, but Elle was particular about her space, and likely wouldn't stand for another Rider on her turf for long—especially if that Rider were Piotr.

As if sensing his thoughts, an arrow speared the road inches from his toes, shooting shards of brick shrapnel in every direction. Piotr raised his hands high as the arrow quivered in the street, testament to Elle's skill. Raising his voice, Piotr glanced left and right, trying to determine from which direction the missile had flown. "*Dobraye utro*, Elle!" he called, striving to keep his tone light, cheerful. "Good morning!"

"How many times have I told you to stop with that foreign jibber-jabber?" echoed a reply, sounding both close and far all at once. Elle had picked her hiding spot well. "A simple 'Hi, Elle' will do me just fine."

Piotr bowed at the waist, struggling to keep his senses attuned to their surroundings, attempting to assess which direction the arrow had come from. "My apologies! Good morning, Elle. I see that you've gotten better at hiding."

"You haven't." There was a light tread behind him and Elle's hand firmly cupped the back of his neck, the strength in her fingers daring him to try something. Knowing the power of those hands and the muscles behind them, Piotr held still.

"Elle!" cried Dora, dropping her bags and flinging her arms around the slight girl holding him hostage. "I missed you!"

The hand squeezed sharply once, pinching, before dropping away. Elle turned to embrace the child. Freed, Piotr swiveled and dropped his hands cautiously to his pockets, hooking his thumbs just inside.

Dora had always adored Elle and the feeling was mutual.

Watching them hug was like watching a rainbow appear from the mist—all the darkness fell away and they were momentarily awash in happiness and light. Where the two of them touched, crackles of blue essence hummed, the years traveling from Dora into Elle and back to Dora in a circuit of joy. Dora was so pleased Piotr could taste her energy on the air itself.

Keeping her tone easy, Elle glanced up from rubbing her cheek along the top of Dora's head, and said, "I never'a thought a palooka like you'd show your mug around here. Didn't I give you the bum's rush last time?"

"Yes, well, times change." Piotr scratched his chin and glanced up at the brilliant silver sky. The sun shone with fiery white light, basking them in its dim warmth and faded glory, but in the distance thick black clouds churned above the sea. "The weather's looking foul. May we move this elsewhere?"

Elle rose from her crouch, muscles rippling. Her short, fringed tunic and thigh-high skirt left nothing to the imagination and Piotr politely turned his face away. Noticing his discomfort, Elle smirked. "Fine, ya wet blanket. What's eating you?"

"A Walker was poking around the mill last night."

Elle stilled and her blonde waves, silvery pale and close-cropped, trembled. "It sussed you out."

"Yes. And it escaped." Piotr shoved his hands deep into his pockets and hunched over slightly. "So I was wondering if you'd—"

"Of course." Elle turned fluidly, taking Dora's hand in her left hand and Specs' hand in her right. "This way."

Once, when they had been on better terms, Elle had confided in Piotr and shared some of her living memories like the jewels they were. She'd been a gymnast once, and rich, spoiled by parents with too much money and not enough time for their wild daughter. Archery, horseback riding, a separate tutor for every fancy. In the Never, these skills made her a handy ally but a terrible enemy. Piotr struggled to keep up as Elle sped through walls and past throngs of living men, their heat momentarily searing but fading the further they traveled. Confidently athletic, Elle raced along, never turning to note his pace behind.

It was early afternoon when they neared the pier and Elle's home. Unlike the mill, one derelict building among many where few humans bothered wandering, Elle's tribe squatted in an abandoned bookshop just off the main strip of Pier 39, the walls papered with droppings and overrun with nesting rats.

If he squinted, Piotr could just make out the words "Coming Soon" above the door. The letters were pink with age, however, and the floor inside was littered with the ghostly living shapes of sleeping rats huddled beneath overturned bookshelves and gently decaying easy chairs. Termites chewed the stairs, seagulls cooed in the eaves, and the floor was white and pebbled with decades of dried droppings. The living animal heat was mild however, easy to stand, and Piotr passed the rats with no problem.

The third floor of the bookstore was empty of furniture but sectioned into offices, the areas claimed by Elle's dozen or so Lost clearly marked with bundles of possessions and sectioned apart with piles of books that reached the warped and splintered ceiling. Elle led them here, leaving the kids to pick spaces of their own while she unstrung her bow and checked the arrows in her quiver.

Piotr, at a loss for what to do in this room once familiar but now alien, hovered near the door as Tubs explored the cupboard underneath the stairs and Specs unpacked in a relatively clean hollow in a far corner lined with the ghostly original copies of Yeats, Dickenson, and Blake.

Without pausing from her work, Elle said, "I have to hand it to you, Pete, you've done a good job with those kids. They kept pace pretty well."

Piotr crossed his arms over his chest and leaned against the doorway. He was surprised to realize that he was relieved. Elle was a good fighter, and smart. She'd keep his Lost safe. "That wasn't me. I still don't train them the way you do."

She snorted. "You oughta."

"*Da?* Well, I say let kids be kids." Piotr rubbed the bridge of his nose. It was warm up here, and close. He felt as if he could barely breathe. "As long as they want to be, that is."

"Whatever. You staying, too?" Elle glanced up from her task. Her voice was pitched low. "I don't see that excuse you call a bag."

"Have you forgiven me?"

"Never will." Elle returned to her task, her fingers flying nimbly over the arch of the bow, smoothing and polishing the grain of the wood. "But maybe I can forget for a bit. We can be copasetic for an emergency."

"Then I'm not going to impose." Ignoring the bittersweet pang at her words, Piotr sketched a shallow bow. "I owe you that courtesy." Glad to have the current state of their animosity sorted out, Piotr stepped away from the door and raised his voice. "I'm leaving."

"What?" Dora appeared at the door of a far office, pale-faced and scowling. "You ain't staying too?"

"Sorry, I can't." Piotr knelt down and opened his arms. Tubs trundled willingly in for a hug but Specs and Dora hung back, both frowning. "I need to go get the lay of the land."

Dora tried again. "But it ain't safe—"

"For you." Passing Tubs to Elle's waiting arms, Piotr rose and dusted his knees. "Walkers usually don't eat Riders, remember?" he teased, poking his bicep. "Our meat's too tough."

"Technically, you aren't a Rider anymore," Specs pointed out, pushing his glasses up his nose. When Piotr wouldn't drop his arms, Specs reluctantly stepped to Piotr's side and hugged him. When he squeezed, Piotr could feel Specs' ribs and the steady thrum of the years unlived just beneath his skin. "You quit, remember?"

"Teenagers, then." Specs stepped away and Piotr held out his arms. "Dora, please? I don't know when I'll be back this way again." He glanced out the window as he pleaded, noting the swiftly rising fog rolling in from the bay and the dappled clouds covering the shining silver sun. The storm was rolling in.

"I changed my mind." Hurrying across the room, Dora dropped
her backpack at his feet and flung herself at Piotr. Clinging power-
fully to his waist she cried, "I ain't stayin' here without you."

"Geeze, thanks," Elle muttered under her breath, and Piotr hid
a smile.

"It's safer here for you." Piotr knelt down and embraced Dora
tightly. "Elle is amazing at this. You know how good she is with her
bow. She'll keep you safe."

"But you ain't comin' back if I stay!"

"Pandora, my *malen'kaya printsessa*," Piotr groaned. He hugged
her tighter. "I promise. I promise that when I can guarantee there
aren't any more Walkers sniffing around the mill, I'll come back for
you three, yes? We'll go back home as soon as it's safe. *Da?*"

She sniffled, drawing back slightly. "You promise?"

"Cross my heart."

"'Kay." Pulling away, Dora knelt down and sorted through her
bag until she had her sketchbook in hand. She flipped to the last
page and ripped the tree sketch free. "Take it. You promised."

"I promise," he agreed, taking her sketch and tucking it away
before dropping a final kiss on her tousled curls.

Elle, balancing Tubs easily on her hip, followed Piotr down the
stairs. One-handed, she loosened a dagger from her hip and slapped
the flat of the blade against his upper arm until Piotr took the gift
and tied it at his side. Like all Elle's weapons, the dagger was honed
to a razor-sharp edge and curved cruelly.

"Offer's still open if you change your mind." Elle jiggled Tubs
until he giggled. "Isn't that right? Isn't it?" Tubs babbled happily
and the warm haze of his energy surrounded them in a sweetly
scented mist.

"Keep them safe." Piotr momentarily considered kissing Elle's
cheek but thought better of it. Dagger or not, she was still pissed at
him.

In the distance a trolley bell dinged, faint and faraway. The fog was starting to really move now, rolling across the streets in swift and steady waves, already up to Piotr's knees. Up the street the living thronged together, ignoring the fog and the dank smell of rotting fish rising from the sea. Nearby a woman screamed laughter; for the living it would be piercing, but Elle and Piotr were cushioned by the years of empty silence and could barely hear the cry.

"You keep yourself safe," Elle retorted. "Just cuz I hate you don't mean I want you pushin' up daisies. Again, I mean." She smirked.

"I'll try to do my best," he replied gravely and left, moving swiftly towards the shifting, eddying crowd.

"You always do," Elle sighed, waiting at the door until Piotr had vanished into fog and humanity. Then, fondly, she added, "Jackass."

CHAPTER TWO

The rising wind whipped flurries of debris about Piotr's ankles, lifting discarded shopping bags and candy wrappers into drifts like piles of autumn leaves. The brick streets beneath his shoes, warped into strange and twisted shapes by age and tectonic activity, were only the fading memories of the meticulously laid brick roads that had been before. Soon the remainder would crumble away, revealing concrete buckled by the California heat, already warped into rolling hills in the center, collecting water and spiritual debris with every summer storm.

Drifting along, letting the wind guide him as if he were as light as the trash spinning by, Piotr concentrated on the journey home rather than brood on what he'd just lost. It took all his will not to turn around and go back, to accept Elle's generous sanctuary and learn to move among the living like a shadow. He couldn't though, even if he wanted to. The sky had opened above him, rain poured down, and there were Walkers abroad.

Night was falling, brought in with the storm, and Piotr sped his pace, skidding down Highway 101's embankment, kicking aside flattened disks of soda cans and sodden cardboard boxes in his wake. The steel mill, their treehouse sanctuary, was still many miles distant, hidden amid the sprawl of industrial buildings and businesses that once thrived at the edge of the city, near the humid stink of the canal. Carefully maintaining his balance on the rain-slick grass, Piotr almost missed the sharp cry of pain amid the drubbing of rain and cracks of blue lightning across the sky.

He paused and it came again, a brief shout from the tangle of buildings just south of the highway, articulate with fear. Stepping up his pace, Piotr followed the scream, heart thudding in his chest and breath coming in short, harsh bursts.

Just south of the water treatment plant three figures fought, sliding through the fog and reflected highway halogens like skaters across ice. Two were long and lean and white-clad— Walkers—but the third, Piotr was surprised to note, was a short, dark figure he recognized: Lily.

What is she doing here, so far away from her own turf? Piotr thought, but then he spotted moonlit steel. Lily was backed against the building, left thigh torn open clear to the bone and leaking silver essence in rivulets like blood; despite her wounds, Lily gave as good as she got, twin daggers flashing.

"Lily," he cried, sprinting now, "hang on!"

Hearing him, Lily's attention wavered for a critical instant. One Walker was attacking her face-on, but the moment she paused the other swooped in from the side, clawing her deeply across the hip.

"LILY!" Reaching her side, Piotr slammed the second Walker into the wall. Up close he could see a line of jaw beneath the white hood, and the teeth of the Walker where they poked through the rotting holes in its cheek. Coarse black stubble rasped against his hand as Piotr slapped the Walker's head against the wall over and over again, curling one hand in the white cloak for purchase. A stench puffed out at him from the fabric, rot and wet decay, moist with a black stink like old sour dirt and albino, crawling things.

Then it laid hands on him, gripping him at the wrists, and Piotr was filled with cold.

The Walker's icy touch sapped him almost immediately, drawing the strength from Piotr's arms and chilling his fury away. He could still hear Lily's raspy cries of pain but they were distant, unimportant, and slowly, under the Walker's insistent pressure, Piotr's fist loosened and fell away.

Laying a palm flat against Piotr's chest, the Walker hissed in a slow and ragged language. Piotr felt a tug deep inside, a slow painful tearing like a hangnail peeling skin and nail away from the quick. He gasped for air but the pull lasted only a moment before the Walker drew his hand away in disgust.

"Too old," the Walker snarled, taking Piotr by the back of his neck and shaking him like a naughty kitten. "No years from you!"

"Sorry 'bout that," Piotr slurred and the Walker flung him away. Once outside the range of that intractable cold, Piotr could feel his will returning with the thawing of his limbs. Crawling on hands and knees, he made his way towards Lily, who'd collapsed in a heap only a few yards away. She appeared unconscious.

"No use," hissed Piotr's Walker. "No souls here. No life here. Only Rider filth."

"The White Lady will shriek," the other said, ignoring Piotr and nudging Lily with the toe of one white boot. "We should lick their bones in retribution."

"*Poshyel k chyertu*," Piotr cursed, reaching Lily's side and blocking her protectively. "And you can rot there, for all I care!" Forgetting Elle's dagger entirely, Piotr fumbled for Lily's bone knives, still clutched in her fists.

His hand was kicked away. Piotr stubbornly stretched for the knives again but the Walker's foot thrust down, grinding his wrist against the dirt. Skeletal fingers clad in loose gloves of their own rotting flesh pressed on his shoulders, pinning him to the ground. Behind him Lily moaned, eyes fluttering open.

"Piotr?"

"*Da?*" he gasped, trying not to breathe through his nose. The nauseating stench was all around them now, the cold seeping again into Piotr's bones and thoughts, slowing his reaction time to a crawl, and trapping him like a fly in molasses. Frigid molasses.

Her voice came at him from a million miles away. "Piotr? What's that light?"

Flush against his teeth Piotr's tongue felt numb and dumb, his lips frozen shut, forming garbled words in slow motion. "What . . . light?"

But he could feel it now, the odd warmth that tickled his skin, melting the cold of the Watchers away in rivulets of sharp white light. The pinning hands and foot were abruptly gone, stripped away, and Piotr took advantage of their absence, staggering to his feet. The area lit up in a corona, spilling around corners and through windows, shining with a fierce insistence across the dusty, hardpan yard. It stretched impossibly far, illuminating even the distant highway with bright, clean light.

"Whatever it is, it began glowing and they perked up like hounds scenting a bitch. They followed it." Lily's voice trembled. Groaning, she pointed in the direction of the southernmost building. "The Walkers left."

Puzzled, Piotr turned and squinted in the direction she pointed. She spoke the truth. "Maybe they weren't hungry after all?"

"Impossible." She lapsed into her native tongue, querying. When Piotr, uncomprehending, didn't reply, she switched to English with a frown. "The fox does not relinquish the hare so easily when the kill is moments away. Why would they leave like that?"

Piotr leaned down and scooped Lily into his arms. Though corded with muscle, his old mentor was still light as thistledown, slight, and easy to lift. "Who cares? Let's leave before they change their minds." Thankfully her leg was already beginning to mend, layers of effervescent tissue bubbling forth over the bone. Healing for their kind was slow without the touch of one of the Lost. Still, he was glad it had been just the two of them. A Walker scenting the Lost often went into berserker frenzy. Piotr couldn't imagine having to protect both Lily and a child against one Walker, much less against two of them.

They had to get out of there, NOW.

"Piotr, wait." Lily struggled in his grip. "I cannot leave. For many nights I have walked with the moon to track those monsters here."

"You . . . Lily, why? You're still camped out in San Jose, *da*? Why would you chase a pair of Walkers all this way?"

"The death dealers took Dunn. I will not leave without learning his fate." Her eyes were bright with tears that did not fall.

Sympathy welled in Piotr, coupled with abject horror. Losing one of your Lost was a horrible feeling, one no Rider should ever have to go through, but losing a child to the Walkers was worse. He ached for her loss. "Oh," he murmured. "*Zhal*, Lily. I'm so sorry."

"There is no sorry," she snapped, sloe eyes flashing. "Put me down."

"*Net*, I cannot." Piotr shook his head and started towards the highway. "They almost killed you and were going to chew on us to round out the evening. I won't let you serve yourself up for a second helping."

"Let me go!"

Firmly, he tightened his grip, careful of her wounded leg. "No, Lily," he said, careful to emphasize the English word. "I will not."

"I hope you rot, Piotr." Then, viper-quick, she punched him in the nose.

Without meaning to, Piotr dropped her, clapping his hands to his face as the tears streamed down. Piotr heard her limping quickly away, the scrape of her boots loud in the strange, still brilliance filling the courtyard.

By the time the dots had quit dancing in front of his eyes, Piotr had lost sight of Lily, but, unwilling to let her face the Walkers alone, he raced after, toward the light. Within moments crossing the distance grew difficult; the air had grown thick and syrupy, yet still comfortably warm, like wading through the midsummer surf, tidal in its intensity.

Just ahead Lily knelt, hands resting on knees, eyes cast forward. Further on by quite a distance the two Walkers cut their way through the air, moving rapidly toward a shining figure, lit from within. Even at this distance, Piotr could feel the heat the creature gave off, and the prismatic fire at its core was near blinding.

"Lily?" Piotr knelt beside her. "What is it? What's wrong? Are you hurt further?"

"Piotr," she breathed, "do you see her? Do you see *Awonawilona*?"

"Who?" Piotr touched Lily's shoulder. She was trembling.

"*Awonawilona*, Piotr. The bringer of light." Tears coursed down her cheeks, wetting the curtain of her thick black hair. "I've been here so many years, Piotr. So many years, almost as many as . . ." She hesitated then forged on. "My people, my shaman, I thought they were all mistaken. They weren't. *Awonawilona* does exist."

Shameless with joy, Lily cried and rocked back and forth on her heels, humming under her breath between words. Passionate and vivid, lit by the light, her voice had taken on a lyrical, musical quality, almost a chanting tone. "I had heard rumors of a creature made of light . . . but I never believed them. Yet here, now, in this forsaken place, in these grey lands, I've finally found the Light-bringer."

Dazzled and confused, Piotr turned to look again. The figure was small, but brilliant, lit up from within by the intensity of the light pouring from every pore. As he watched it raised two arms outward, seemingly embracing the oncoming Walkers. The faster one reached the figure, only the outline of its cloak setting it apart from the light.

Something about the sluggish way they moved struck Piotr as strange and wrong. The deadly grace of the two Walkers was stripped away, leaving only wooden puppets lurching toward the light like moths . . . like moths flying straight at candlelight.

"Lily," Piotr whispered harshly, scooping the young woman again in his arms, "it's time to leave, *da*? If that . . . thing . . . is a god, I don't know about you, but I don't want to be around when—"

Suddenly, from the depths of the creature, tentacles of light shot out, spearing the Walker through the chest, arms, and legs. They were horrific to look at—unnaturally long and quick, the fluidly shifting tentacles were spiky with light and energy, pulsing around the edges in a purple nimbus.

One after another more tentacles, over a dozen in all, burst from the Lightbringer's chest, stretched, and wrapped around the other Walker, downing it in a moment and dragging it kicking and shrieking forward. It fought, kicking and lashing with the sharpened finger bones, but the Lightbringer only shuddered under the onslaught, barely budging.

A smoky stench, sickly sweet and cloying, drifted downwind as the creature lifted the Walkers up, each impaled on the end of the long and thick tentacles. The scent was like leaves burning; the screams painfully shrill.

Then the first Walker started to flake apart before their eyes, cinders of its essence peeling from the core and floating in the light before burning crisply away. The second Walker doubled its shrieking but the tentacles never wavered, the screaming never stopped.

"No. No-no-no—" Lily gasped and, turning her face daintily aside, retched on Piotr's shoes. In the distance, after long moments, the shrieks finally wound down and the rich, thick smell of burning began to fade away.

Slowly the creature turned towards them and Piotr could feel a sinuous urge seep into him—he wanted to get closer to the light.

"I think," Lily said, wiping her hand across her mouth, "that perhaps that may not be *Awonawilona* after all."

"The Lightbringer," Piotr whispered, using all the willpower he had to take one stumbling backward step and then another. Turning his back on the creature, he closed his eyes to the light and concentrated on putting one foot before the other until they reached the highway and the urge to leap into the light miraculously subsided.

There, worn and weary, he sank to the earth, and it was Lily's turn to watch over him.

CHAPTER THREE

Half-sliding through her bedroom window, Wendy winced as the edge of her stocking caught on a splinter and ripped. Her book bag thumped to the floor and she froze, listening carefully for sounds from her father's room.

Blessed silence.

Shimmying the rest of the way inside, Wendy chucked her bag onto her bed and paused by the mirror to take stock of her appearance before her dad saw her. The rain had washed away most of her makeup, leaving her with raccoon-eyes and lipstick faded to a dull, smudged lilac. The temporary dye was almost gone; once again her hair shone coppery red at the roots and black at the tips, straggling over her shoulders in sodden hanks. Specks of mud dotted her cheeks and neck.

Tonight's search had been hard, even her nail polish was chipped, and she'd lost one of her sneakers hoisting herself over the treatment plant's back fence. The laces had caught on a snarl of wire and she'd pulled herself to the other side before realizing it'd slipped off her foot.

"Guess I'm gonna have to spring for boots after all," Wendy sighed, toeing off the lonely sneaker and tossing it in the trash. Downstairs the grandfather clock chimed twice.

Crap. It was late and she still had homework to do!

Stripping quickly, Wendy wrapped herself in her rattiest robe and tiptoed past her dad's door to the bathroom. Ten minutes in the shower and a quick visit to the kitchen later, Wendy settled down at her desk to tackle Algebra II. The problems were easy but she was having trouble concentrating. Patrol always left her edgy and after what she'd seen tonight, she had every right to be. Jabberwocky, the ghost of her mother's favorite Persian, was curled on the windowsill, eyes slitted closed and purring up a storm. Jabber had gotten a lot friendlier after he'd died. Before, no one but her mother could pet him, but now he spent nearly all his time in Wendy's room or just beneath her window, lounging in the tree.

Though the steady rumble of Jabber's purr was soothing, Wendy still couldn't focus. Setting aside her half-done work, she loosely grasped her pencil and stared out at the moon, mindlessly doodling on the back of her notebook. At first the lines were aimless, loops and swirls and hearts and stars, but then she drew a thickly lashed eye and followed with the curve of a slightly aquiline nose. Thick lips, sensitive at the corners, offset by high cheekbones, giving the face—his face—a faintly amused expression. Black hair waved over the forehead and past the chin, concealing all but a hint of the scar that puckered from temple to neck.

Picture complete, Wendy sat back. She knew where she'd seen these features before, but what she couldn't imagine was why she was bothering to draw them.

After all, they belonged to a dead man.

After the accident four years ago, it had taken the paramedics and firefighters half an hour to peel the car apart far enough to pull them out of the wreckage.

Between the two of them, Eddie had been the worst off—when they bustled him into the ambulance he was a bloody, bleeding wreck barely clinging to life. Hardly scratched and only slightly bruised, Wendy drifted through the rescue with barely a thought or word, barely noticing when the ambulance peeled away with sirens screaming, Eddie strapped inside.

Shock, the police officers said, and wrapped her in blankets, pressing a cool bottle of water between her fingers while they waited on a second ambulance to transport Wendy and Mr. Barry's corpse to the hospital.

Condition stable, Wendy sat halfway into the back of a police car and sipped water mechanically as adults eddied around her, asking questions and barking orders. Every inch of her skin felt calm and cold and distant, but far down inside her chest there was something expanding—like some strange, fierce fire, previously banked, had begun burning deep, deep inside.

It stung like nothing she'd ever felt before, but Wendy knew there was nothing wrong with her physically. The paramedics— including one or two she'd previously met while shadowing her mom at work—had already looked her over, so surely she must be imagining the pain. The fire blooming inside.

"I think," she said out loud, "that this is what going crazy feels like."

"*Da*, that is entirely possible," a gentle voice said and Wendy nodded, squeezing the bottle so the plastic crackled under her fingertips and the water sloshed against the sides. "But I think it is unlikely."

A figure knelt down beside her, hunkering so that his hands dangled between his knees. Unlike the others, his voice was kind but not sympathetic, very matter-of-fact, and he had a slight accent— not easily placed, unimportant just then, though years later Wendy realized it had been Russian.

He touched her wrist and his fingers were pleasantly cool. "Were you in the wreck?"

"Yeah," she said. Her attention wavered a moment, and she looked at his hand on her wrist. There was something not quite right about his gentle fingers, or about that moment altogether. Wendy tried but she couldn't wrap her calm, yet muddled, mind around the puzzle; couldn't figure out just what was different about this boy.

She looked up finally, taking in his scarred face, his serene eyes. He was older than Wendy but not by much, only a teenager. When he smiled, quiet and amused, it slowly dawned on her that she could sort of see through him. *Oh, that's what's weird. He's a ghost.*

Wendy was relieved to have pinpointed the oddity so quickly.

"I'm Winifred," she said because, despite his translucence, it seemed the polite thing to do. "But everyone calls me Wendy."

"Piotr," he replied, smiling gravely, and offered his hand. Wendy took it and marveled at how, when she concentrated, his skin darkened and became solid, firmer in her grasp. Thin steam rose from between their hands, curling into nothing only moments later. At first Piotr didn't seem to notice, but when he did, he frowned. "That is odd," he said. "Doesn't hurt, it's just strange."

Bluntly she asked, "Are you dead?"

"Do I look dead?" Unoffended, he released her hand and stood up, patting himself on the chest and arms. There were faint rustling sounds where he patted but, away from her touch, he'd faded back to his initial translucent state.

Wendy nodded and Piotr chuckled. "Well, I suppose I must be dead, then."

She frowned. "But I'm not dead." Tentatively Wendy rapped the window of the police car. It *felt* real. "Am I?"

"I can see you," Piotr said as he looked around the scene of the accident. "And it seems that they can see you. So I don't know, curly-haired girl." He reached out and gently brushed away the copper-colored curl hanging in her eyes. "Maybe *da*, maybe *net*, but my best guess is *net*. Doesn't look like you're dead to me."

Wendy couldn't help but smile. "Your accent's funny."

Piotr pressed one hand flat against his chest in mock offense. "*My* accent is funny? What about yours, *malen'kaya printsessa*?"

"What?"

"Little princess," he translated. "It is a very nice thing."

"Are you gonna take me away?" Her voice trembled.

"What?" He seemed horrified at the suggestion. "Curly, no, no, *net*. I'd never do that." Piotr knelt at her feet again and took her hands, gently rubbing her knuckles to soothe her. Again, where they touched, thin steam rose and drifted away. This time he didn't seem to notice.

"It is . . . it is just my job, you understand? To make sure you aren't lost, that's all. Sometimes, after accidents like this, children are shocked and scared and they can become . . . confused. Sometimes they wander off and are never found. I stop that."

"But only if I'd died?"

"Only if you'd died." He squeezed her hands one last time and stepped back. "You're a nice kid, Curly. Stay here and they'll take you where you need to go."

"Are you an angel?"

Piotr laughed and his fingers brushed his twisted scar. "*Net*, sorry to disappoint. I'm just a boy. But if I see one I'll certainly let them know you're on the lookout."

"That's okay." Wendy hesitated and then, shyly, "Will I see you again?" She couldn't help the waver in her voice, but so far Piotr was the only one who seemed to care more about her than about cleaning up the mess on the highway.

"Oh Curly, I hope not. Believe it or not, so do you." He glanced around at the chaos and sighed. "It's not strange that you're seeing me now, *da*? I promise. It happens every now and then. The shock of an accident like this one, it can open up the mind. It'll go away. Just tell yourself you dreamed it. And don't whisper to adults about me." He grimaced. "That never ends well."

"They'd think I was nuts," Wendy said. She understood about adults. "Or in shock."

"Crazy as a cuckoo, Curly." Piotr began walking away, fading rapidly into the mist, calling over his shoulder, "It's our little secret." He turned on his heel and waved when he reached the end of the clearing. "*Dasvidania, malen'kaya printsessa!*"

That had happened four years ago, and while Wendy never forgot Piotr's face, she never saw him again. Until tonight.

A quiet trill from her bedside table drew Wendy away from her desk to snatch at her cell phone. She had a message.

IKssBoiz&Grls: *U in yet, Crouching-Ninja-Hidden-Badass?*

Eddie had waited up for her. Smirking, Wendy flopped on the bed to reply.

EgonSpengler: *Nah. I'z in ur roomz, haunting ur butt.*

IKssBoiz&Grls: *Neat! What m I wearing?*

EgonSpengler: *Ur birfday suit. :P*

IKssBoiz&Grls: *Lucky guess. 4 real tho, how'd it go?*

EgonSpengler: *: - (*

IKssBoiz&Grls: *Aww. Nuthin?*

IKssBoiz&Grls: *Helllooo?*

EgonSpengler: *Sry. No sign of her. I had 2 reap 2 nosies tho & 2 others got away . . .*

IKssBoiz&Grls: *& what else?*

EgonSpengler: *Y u think there's more?*

IKssBoiz&Grls: *Cuz I've known u 4evr.*

IKssBoiz&Grls: *Sloths msg faster than u right now.*

IKssBoiz&Grls: *Ur stalling.*

EgonSpengler: *Fine. K, it's 2 weird. I saw teens.*

IKssBoiz&Grls: *& that's weird, y?*

EgonSpengler: *Been doin this 4 yrs & like 2nd teen EVAR.*

IKssBoiz&Grls: *4 real?*

EgonSpengler: *Yah. 2 of 'em. B & G. Far away tho.*

IKssBoiz&Grls: *Maybe they croaked 2gether. Romantic!*

EgonSpengler: *Right, cuz I'd wanna be 16 4evr. X-(*

IKssBoiz&Grls: *Live fast, die young, look hot 4 burial.*

EgonSpengler: *Sicko. Not funny.*

IKssBoiz&Grls: *U let ur job color ur outlook. B happy!*

The upstairs floorboards creaked and Wendy heard a rough cough from down the hall. Sliding off her bed, she hurried to her desk and pulled her Algebra book toward her.

EgonSpengler: *Dad's up. C u l8r. xox*

IKssBoiz&Grls: *Pick u up @ 7. Bai!*

Floorboards squeaked and there was a soft tap at her bedroom door. The door creaked slowly open. "Hey Pippi Longstocking, are you up?"

"Yeah, Dad." Wendy stuffed the phone behind her Lit book. Jabber, spotting her father, hissed and jumped to the floor, scooting through the dust ruffle to hide beneath the bed. "Polynomials are kicking my as— uh, butt." That little white lie stung somewhat; Wendy did quite well in math when she could find time to concentrate. Luckily, Mr. McGovern gave her leeway when it came to homework since she always aced the quizzes and tests.

"Ouch." Wendy's dad eased into her room, gingerly shutting the door. The edge of the door caught his robe and he had to tug it free, ripping the threadbare terry cloth in the process. "Damn," he cursed, pushing his glasses up his nose. He sagged so that even his plaid pajamas seemed dejected. "This's my favorite robe."

"It's cool, Dad." Wendy waved her hand at a pile of similarly mauled clothing in the corner of the room. "Chuck it over there and I'll get to it next weekend."

"That's an impressive stack." Her father neatly folded the robe and set it atop the teetering pile. "How do you manage to constantly ruin or rip up perfectly good clothes?" He held up the stockings from earlier in the evening. "Didn't we just buy you these last paycheck?"

"You know me," Wendy lied glibly, "clumsy, clumsy, clumsy." The clock chimed three downstairs and she held up her notebook. "Is there anything I can help you with, Dad? I have to be up before seven and I'm only half done."

Her father scratched his thinning red hair and settled on the edge of her bed. He leaned forward and asked, almost apologetically, "Actually, there is. When did you get in tonight, Winifred?"

Wendy paused for a brief moment, as if considering, and then shrugged. "I don't know, Dad. I didn't check the clock. It wasn't that late, though." Setting her notepad down on the corner of her desk, Wendy turned in her seat so that she was facing her father, and arranged her features into a mask of concern. "Why? Did I wake you?"

"No. You never wake me, honey." Her dad sighed and sat back and rubbed his hand through his hair again, a sure sign of distress. Her father had once had a head of hair as full and garishly auburn as her own . . . until her mother's accident. Now he was practically bald.

"Look, Wendy, I know you're sixteen and you're practically an adult and all that jazz, I understand that. And you've never gotten into trouble. After your mother . . . well, for the past six months you've been a super help around the house. I know the twins wouldn't cope as well as they do if it weren't for you." He hesitated.

Inwardly, Wendy snorted and thought: *Well-adjusted. Right.* If her father knew half of what was going on in their house, there was no way he'd be in such a big rush to hurry from assignment to assignment the way he did. On the bright side, his willful ignorance left her plenty of time to roam around town in the dead of the night, so she wasn't anxious to alert him to his misconceptions.

Wendy sat back and crossed her arms over her chest. "Yeah. But?"

"Wendy, sweetie, I'm just worried about you. You used to be a straight A student. You used to be in choir, you were on the student council. But now you and Eddie . . ." He waved his hand half-heartedly. "The two of you dye your hair black and paint your nails black and all those piercings can't be healthy. Don't even get me started on the ink your mother approved right before . . . well, you know."

Wendy's hand flew to her ears where, under her palms, seven studs marched up the curve from the lobe to cartilage on either side. "Hey! I like my ears."

"This isn't a joke, Wendy. You barely sleep, you barely eat, you're out at all hours, and your grades have been dropping all year. Since your mother landed in the hospital you look like death warmed over, and I'm getting sick of watching you screw up your life."

Offended, Wendy sat further back in her chair and crossed her arms over her chest, lips tightening into a thin line, eyes narrowing to slits. "Screw up my life? How so, huh?"

Point blank her father demanded, "Are you two doing drugs?" He crossed his arms over his chest, mirroring Wendy's posture. "Pot? X? Some kinda acid or pills, maybe? Speed? You're skinny enough for it."

Wendy, stunned, sputtered. She couldn't believe this. Her button-down, uptight father was accusing her of getting high? Sure she looked rough, but of all the people in the house to point a finger at, why did he pick *her*?

Ignoring her shock and anger, her father forged on. "I was sixteen once too, Wendy. I'll understand if you've been experimenting, but if you're on something really dangerous, I have to put a stop to it. I'm not going to let you fry your brain."

Finally she found some words. They weren't the right words, but anything was better than gaping at her father with her mouth hanging open. "I'm *sorry*, Dad, but *excuse me*? Seriously? I mean . . . seriously? What the fuck, Dad!"

"Wendy, honey—" Taken aback by her fury, her father dropped his arms and half-rose from the edge of her bed, confusion written all over his face. "Come on, kiddo. Language."

"Don't 'Wendy-honey' me, Dad!" Wendy knew her voice was rising shrilly, tottering on the edge of hysterical anger, but she hardly cared. "Look, I'm not a baby! There are all kinds of people selling at school and I could get high anytime I want, but I have this whole 'my-body-is-a-temple' thing and I'd really rather not. Hell, Dad, I don't even *drink*!" Wendy slammed her Algebra book closed.

"Keep your voice down! The twins are asleep!"

From beneath the bed Jabber began to growl, low and long. Wendy dropped her tone to an angry hiss, unconsciously mimicking the cat. "Whatever. I'm not pulling A's anymore, sure, but French sucks and English is boring and Algebra is hard, but since B's were good enough for *Mom* you really shouldn't give a shit!"

Horrified, Wendy's jaw clicked shut and she pressed her hands across her mouth as if she could choke the words back, shame coloring her cheeks scarlet.

"You're right," her father said, using the edge of the desk to rise. His shoulders drooped and he shuffled his feet, bunny slippers rubbing the carpet with a whispery sigh.

"D-dad," stammered Wendy, "I'm so sorry. I didn't mean to—"

"You did." He fumbled at his hips for a moment before realizing his robe was on the mend pile and there were no pockets to shove his hands into. "But that's okay. I believe you, and I'm sorry I brought it up. You finish up your homework and get to bed."

"Dad—"

"Hush. Come here." Her father drew her close and gave her a tight hug. Wendy could smell the traces of Irish Spring on his skin and the fainter smell of ammonia and bleach. He'd been to the hospital again tonight. He practically lived there when he was home.

"I don't do drugs, Dad." Wendy stepped back, slid into her desk chair. Her fury abated, she felt cold and tired and very, very sad. She shrugged, uncomfortable but feeling a need to say it once while she had her dad on the defensive, so that they would never need to have this sort of conversation again. "And, just in case you were wondering, I know what I look like, but I don't sleep around either. Really."

"Good to know, kiddo." He ruffled her hair and walked to the door. "Sweet dreams."

"Night, Dad."

He turned the knob, then paused. "Oh, Wendy? I've got a big contract coming up at the end of this week. I'll be gone eight, maybe nine days."

"Okay." Her mousy-looking father was a corporate efficiency consultant—a destroyer of jobs and dreams all in the name of profit—and his efficiency audits often had him on the road for weeks at a time. When he was gone, Wendy was in charge. "I have it all under control."

"Never doubted it for a moment." They paused, both aware of the irony of his statement, and then he slipped back into the hallway without another word.

Weary now, and wanting nothing more than to simply sink into her bed and sleep for a year, Wendy rifled through her Algebra text until she found the assignment again. A tear plopped onto the page, magnifying a variable, and Wendy wiped it away. Four hours until school, ten more polynomials, and an outline for her English Lit report.

"I can do this," she whispered, rubbing the heel of her palm against her eye as Jabber slunk through the desk to twine about her ankles. "I have it all under control."

CHAPTER FOUR

Due to Lily's injuries, getting back to Elle's was harder than usual, but Piotr was unwilling to walk away from their encounter without spreading word of the monstrous Lightbringer to the other Riders. The Lost were asleep when they arrived, huddled together under sleeping bags and stretched out atop beanbags. Specs, finger tucked most of the way through a *Lord of the Rings* omnibus, stirred when Piotr took off his glasses, but did not wake.

"You birds are all wet," Elle said as Piotr rejoined the ladies downstairs. "You're telling me some mook with a light show bumped off two Walkers with no problems whatsoever?" Agitated, she ran hands through her hair, mussing her fingerpicked curls every which way. "That's crazy!"

"It happened," Piotr said doggedly. "We would not lie to you, Elle."

"Yeah-yeah, I know you wouldn't beat your gums 'bout nothin' strong enough to take a pair of Walkers for a ride." Elle sighed. "Talk about your urban legends coming to life, though. I always reckoned that the stories of a ghost-killer were just a bunch of bull."

"The whispers among us sometimes tell tales true as well as false," Lily agreed, settling to the ground and carefully crossing her legs under her. Dora had been awake when they'd arrived; thanks to her, Lily's wounds were healed, but she would need Elle to help scavenge new clothing for her, or Lily would need to generate enough spare essence to repair her own. "It was some sort of creature." Fastidiously, Lily picked at the mud dried on a braid, scraping the dirt off and dropping it to the floor.

"Before it started shredding Walkers like paper, Lily called it the Lightbringer," Piotr said, moving carefully so the last stairs wouldn't creak under his weight and possibly wake the assembled Lost upstairs. "It's an apt name."

"Stop mixing your mud in with my dust," Elle grumbled to Lily, striding over to a nearby cabinet and retrieving a paper sack. She dropped it in Lily's lap then paused by a nearby window. Scowling, she peered outside. "Pick up the muck and chuck it. This joint ain't James' pigsty."

"He must be told," said Piotr, flopping to the ground beside Lily. Pressing the heels of his hands into his eyes, he groaned. "James and the rest of them. But I'll be damned if I'm going all the way to Half Moon Bay just to spread the word."

"Pipe down, flyboy." Turning away from the window, Elle leaned against the wall and tipped her head back. "It sounds like maybe we might have a situation on our hands. I'll send a runner out to James' at dawn." She paused. "Though I still ain't clear on why dusting two Walkers ain't cause to crack out the butts 'n beers." Elle pressed her fingers to her lips and sighed. "What I wouldn't give for a ciggy right now."

"Poison to the mind and body," Lily stated. "A brave needs not—"

Elle pushed off from the wall, hands fisted. "Oh yeah, Pocahontas? You wanna talk about poisonin' a good thing, then?"

"Hey, hey!" Piotr moved to stand between them, holding his arms out, fingers spread. "Ladies, ladies, relax. This isn't the time for us to be bickering."

Disgusted, Elle slapped his hand away. "Shoulda known you'd take her side, you piker." Scowling, she stormed over to the window again and planted hands on either side of the frame, glaring out into the murky fog.

"Elle—"

"These debates do nothing for us." Within moments Lily was on her feet and at the door. Hand on the knob, she surveyed the cluttered room imperiously. "My chance to retrieve Dunn is gone now, thanks to the Lightbringer. It ate the ones who took my Lost, leaving me no beast to track. If you will give me no succor, Elle, then I'll hunt blind."

Elle sagged against the window at the mention of the missing child. Piotr felt for her, he really did. Things were tangled between the three of them, words left unspoken for years now, and if this crisis didn't involve the Lost, she might not have even let them through the door. Elle might hate Piotr, but she outright loathed Lily.

"No, keep looking," Elle finally said, words pitched low and slow. "I'll send out scouts during daylight hours and keep a watch myself at night." She straightened and squared her shoulders, settling hands on her hips and raising her chin defiantly. "But when this thing is over we've got a conversation coming, you understand me, Pocahontas?"

Gravely, Lily nodded. "Understood . . . bitch."

Surprisingly, Elle threw back her head and laughed. Casually she pushed away from the wall and strolled to Piotr's side, dropping gracelessly to the floor beside him. "Yeah, yeah, fine. So, Petey, gimme the skivvy on this Lightbringer's mug so my boys can keep an eye peeled."

"Tentacles," Piotr replied, turning his eyes to the ceiling when Elle's skirt rode high on her hips. A soft rustle of fabric indicated Lily's return to the floor on his other side. "Tentacles of light. It was still so I could not gauge the speed, but it has—oh, I don't know what to call it. Some sort of pheromone. It makes you want to get closer to it."

"Phera-what now?"

"Like a flower that sings to the bee with its sweet odor," Lily explained. "Or the cat in heat that cries to every tom within range. That scent is difficult to resist."

"But you two pills managed."

Piotr glanced down and was glad to see that Elle had rearranged her short shift and was once again decent. "*Da*, but we weren't close. The Walkers were sucked in, moths to a flame. At the end, one fought, but . . . the call was strong."

"So it's a distance thing?" Elle shrugged. "I've got some spare bows. Me'n Pocahontas here can go pepper that thing full of holes right now." She smirked. "No offense, but your aim ain't exactly ducky, flyboy. We can gather up some folks, Riders and their Lost, get 'em all here to circle the wagons so to speak. Get a patrol going, maybe, and sort out some ammunition."

"A roster is needed," Lily agreed, fired by Elle's warrior intensity. "Perhaps we could arrange for a hunting party."

"That's a good idea. We don't want to jump in without knowing what we're up against," Piotr cautioned. "This thing . . . I've never even heard of anything like this before. I've already left my Lost here. I should be the scout."

Lily's hand, cool and dry, touched his. Her eyes were dark with apology. "No offense is intended, Piotr, but you are not the most reliable of sources for such matters. I do not believe you should be the one scouting. With his connections, James may be a better choice for this."

Offended, Piotr scowled at Lily and pulled away. "What's that supposed to mean? You think I can't handle myself, is that it? You think James might've heard something I haven't?" The words wanted to come out in Russian but he forced himself to speak slowly and form the phrases in English. "Because I know you two are friendly now, but James wasn't the one saving you from those Walkers, was he? And I'll have you know, I'm better at keeping my ear to the ground than *James* could ever be!"

"Now ain't the time—" Elle began, but Piotr cut her off.

"*Net*, I want to hear this." He crossed his arms over his chest. "Tell me. What's James got that I don't? How would James, Mr. Punch-It-and-It'll-Go-Away, be a better scout than me? What? Lily?

No answer? What about you, Elle? How's James better than me, huh?"

"Pete, you've been balled up for longer than I've been dead," Elle cried in exasperation, half-laughing, half-angry. "Loonier than a hen-house rat. I've known you for decades. Even way back when, you were a deuce or two shy of a full deck. A couple aces down, a couple marbles lost." Elle groaned and rubbed a hand across her face. "Listen up, jealousy, we ain't got time for one of your offended megrims, got it?"

Piotr clashed gazes with her, unwilling to let the suggestion that he might not be an asset to their team pass. "It's a simple question. I simply want an answer."

Elle slammed a fist on the floor. "Fine! You want to know the truth, Petey? Great, here's the truth. You're mostly right—even Pocahontas here is willing to admit that, kissy-face or not, James has himself one hell of a temper and under normal circumstances he ain't better than you at most things. But there is one mighty exception: that old memory of yours just ain't what it used to be, and James ain't in the habit of forgetting things. We need a scout we can trust, Petey, that's all we meant."

"My memory?" Piotr rolled his eyes. "That's what this is about? Everyone forgets things, Elle. I'm not alone."

"Things? Sure. Everyone misrecollects where they left the keys to the breezer now and then. But you don't just forget *things*, Petey. You forget a lot more than just little old things. This ain't about walking out with the stove on. And that's why Pocahontas here don't trust you with most of this operation, flyboy. Your head ain't exactly trustworthy all the time."

Brushing off Elle's mocking tone, Piotr shook his head. "My memory may not be perfect but I can remember what goes on. Better than you, that's for damn sure."

"Oh yeah? Fine." Elle crossed her arms over her chest and pursed her lips, eyes narrowing with the challenge. "Tell me about the day I died, Pete. Tell Miss Elle all about it."

"You died on . . ." he stopped, straining his mind for the important information. It seemed very close at hand, the date on the tip of his tongue, but muffled, as if the memory were wrapped and stored carefully away. "You were killed by . . . wait . . . *net* . . ." For several seconds he struggled. Finally, realizing the futility of trying to argue with them, he flushed and muttered, "You were wearing red."

"Got that right at least," she sighed. Then, teasingly, "My death was a doozy, though. Maybe I'll remind you about it sometime. Sit down and have us a little recollect."

Lily sighed. "This is not helping."

Elle smirked and flopped back onto the dirty floor, chuckling to herself. "Hush your mouth. Everyone needs to laugh at death a little, else all you can do is cry. Besides, it's funny the things a girl can have a chuck or two over, given enough time." She turned to Lily and made the shoo-shoo gesture again. "What about you, Pocahontas? Got any questions for old Pete, since we're toodlin' down old memory lane?"

Ignoring Elle, Lily gravely took Piotr's hand in hers and gently rubbed her fingertips across his knuckles. Like his, her hands were roughly calloused but her touch was soft. "Elle brings up a good point. This can be our test to see if you should indeed be our scout. Do you remember my death, Piotr?"

"Of course not," he scoffed, "you died ages ago, Lily." He laughed. "James said you lived in tents, made pots, that sort of thing." He shook his head. "I didn't believe him at first. It didn't seem real that anyone could be dead so long or have survived the Never like that."

"James," Lily said, "for all I love him, is a braggart and a fool. I made pottery with my mother, yes, but I lived in a pithouse." Her brows furrowed and she inched closer, eyes intently searching his face. "Can you really not remember all the times we have talked about this before? Do you honestly not remember when we met in the Sandia foothills? The reds and orange that stretched to the sky?

The mottled earth, the edges of the long grass-swept plains? None of it?"

This was utter nonsense. Piotr couldn't remember the days after his own death with such vivid detail, much less hers, so Lily was clearly teasing him. There was no test; they were having fun at his expense. Spending long hours discussing their lives was certainly something he'd remember with a girl as ancient and storied as Lily.

"*Net*. My apologies." Smiling now, calm at the realization that they must have decided to play some sort of joke on him, Piotr shook his head and let her continue on, enjoying the cadence of her smooth alto as she braided the joke into an elaborate tale. It was all fanciful nonsense but he had to hand it to her, she sure knew how to tell a story.

"Quit botherin' him, Lily," Elle finally grumbled. She smiled sharply and poked him in the ribs. "I think it's pretty clear that Petey never remembers anything, do ya Pete?"

"I was lost and wandering," Lily repeated, ignoring Elle and grasping at him, intent on keeping up the charade, "I could not find my way home. The floods had come, the antelope too, and my tribe had moved on, leaving only refuse behind."

Lily's fingers pressed tightly into Piotr's, blunt nails digging into his flesh. "Remember, Piotr? You took me by the hand and led me to safety. You taught me the ways of the Never—how to avoid the Walkers, how to find and gather the Lost, not only for their protection but for our own. How to keep them safe. You taught me all this, Piotr. You!" Her voice broke. "You truly don't recall?"

Elle snickered, unable to keep a straight face, and Piotr realized his patience was at an end for their foolishness.

"Lily," Piotr said, taking care to keep each word gentle but firm, "this joke's gotten old." He squeezed her fingers. "We've got more important tasks than trying to fool with me, *da*?" He took a deep breath and glanced at Elle. "Ganging up on me isn't funny. I'll be the long-distance scout and keep an eye out for both the Lightbringer and Walkers. Enough said."

"Atta-boy!" Elle agreed fervently, slapping her hands together. "Lily, we oughta quit beating our gums here. He ain't gonna buy our bull. Just give him the job already so we can move on to more important matters." She cleared her throat. "His noggin hasn't gone soft on us recently, anyhow. Maybe he's sorted himself out, yeah?"

Lily drew her hand away, took a deep breath, and nodded once. "Yes. This . . . jest was ill-timed, Piotr." She glanced past him to Elle and bit her lip, gnawing anxiously for a moment. Then, slowly, she whispered, "My apologies. I should have known better."

"*Nezachto*," he said, quick to smooth the tension away. "No worries." Outside, the dark was fading, coloring the sky dark purple. Soon the children would be up; they had to hurry. "Now, about the Lightbringer. We need to figure out a plan."

It took them some time to hammer out the details, but what they decided on was simple. Elle would remain with the Lost, guarding the bookstore and sending out runners to other parts of the city to spread news of the Lightbringer, inviting the other Riders to circle the wagons for safety. Lily would return to San Jose, collect her remaining charges, and then join Elle at the bookstore. Once they knew which Riders would stand with them, then they would decide what could be done about the new threat.

Piotr prepared to scout.

"Dunn liked to wander near his POD," Lily said, speaking of her missing Lost. "Your best bet is to search there first, to see if you can find any clues. They took him . . ." her expression twisted painfully as she forced out the words, "they took him intact rather than eating him, which is strange for a Walker."

"I bet you anything it's the White Lady," Elle muttered. "Rumors all over town chatting about more Walkers, fewer Shades. Everything's gone to hell since that dame came to town."

"Where is Dunn's place of death?" Piotr asked Lily, ignoring Elle, though he secretly agreed with her. Things had been a shade off normal the past six months and had been getting progressively worse.

"Mountain View, near Castro Street." Lily drew a map with her finger in the dust on the floor, tapping streets to indicate the direction he would have to go. "The actual place of death was a tenement building once, but it burned down. Now his POD is the diner that replaced it. He liked to sit in the empty booths and listen to the chatter."

Whistling low, Piotr shook his head. "Dangerous game to be so near the living."

"Dunn didn't care," Lily said. "He missed his family."

"Specs was like that," Piotr agreed, glancing over his shoulder at the staircase. "He haunted his house for years. Even now he tends to stay indoors."

"Yeah, we all got one or two who won't forget being alive," Elle grunted, pushing away from the window and strolling over to their huddle. She crouched down and tapped the map. "Do you even know what you're looking for, Pete? Besides this walking lightshow, I mean? Walkers? Some piece of Dunn he might've left behind?"

"*Net*, not really, but I'll know a clue when I see it." He smirked and tapped Elle's dagger at his hip. "Why, are you worried about me?"

Elle snorted and rose. "Not a bit. But the longer you hang around this gin joint, the more likely the Walkers are gonna start nibbling on Dunn's toes. You get the picture?"

"Indeed. Be safe." Piotr nodded towards the huddle of children, each lost in their own thoughts. "Watch my kids, Elle."

"Always."

CHAPTER FIVE

"**O**y, Sleeping Beauty! Rise and shine." A hard poke in Wendy's side jostled her awake.

Blurrily, Wendy squinted up at the figure hulking over her bed. Her head felt fuzzy, full, and her mouth tasted like a skunk had crawled in there and died in the night. The remnants of a horrible dream echoed at the edge of her waking thoughts. "Dad?"

"Already took off." Another hard poke, this one just under her ribs, and with it came the smell of bacon. "Come *on*, Wendy, get up! Eddie's waiting downstairs."

"Jon, come on, cut it out," Wendy grumbled at her younger brother, rubbing the grit out of her eyes. "Man, that was a crappy dream. Where's Chel?"

"Michelle is downstairs making breakfast," Jon said stiffly, taking a bite out of a truly gigantic breakfast burrito. He spoke around his mouthful with difficulty, holding up a hand to keep from spraying her with food. "There's eggs left, I think, if you want 'em."

"Oh for . . . are you two *still* fighting?" She flung off her comforter, checked her watch, and groaned. "He's early. Probably knew I'd sleep in." Stumbling to her closet Wendy grabbed tattered jeans, her favorite corset, and a sports bra to tuck in her bag. Today was Thursday, which meant gym. Wendy grimaced. She hated to sweat.

"Grab my boots from under the bed, will ya?"

Jon shoved the rest of the burrito into his mouth until he was

55

chipmunk-cheeked, hunkered down, peered under the dust ruffle, and pulled out a chunky lime-green platform. "These?"

"No, the Vietnam jump boots uncle Randy left. The ones with the red ribbons to lace 'em together."

"There's like three of them," complained Jon, sitting back on his heels and pushing his carroty mop off his face. "You are such a shoe fiend. Little more specific please?"

"Oh for . . . here, shove over. Watch." Wendy dropped beside her brother and stretched as far as she could, pointing to a set of boots way at the back. Jabber was under the bed but she had no worries about Jon noticing him—her brother couldn't see ghosts. "Those. Right there. Go get 'em, Stretch."

"Shut up," Jon muttered, blushing, but he obligingly buried himself under the bed to snag her boots for her. He'd shot up over the summer, going from the shortest kid in his middle school to the tallest freshman at MVHS. The Spartans wanted him on the team but, while he enjoyed shooting hoops in the backyard, he was miserable at actual basketball and had flubbed the tryouts.

Despite his two left feet and numerous double dribbles, Coach Cory had still offered Jon a second-string place and the opportunity to get better. But Jon was shy and bookish, hunched over and unhappy with his sudden height and sloping gut. He declined gracefully. Wendy would watch him some nights, though, playing Horse alone, and she didn't miss the longing there. Jon had recently begun eating half their weekly grocery budget by himself.

"You know," Wendy said, expertly slipping into the corset under her shirt while Jon sucked in his gut and struggled to reach her shoes, "Chel didn't mean half the stuff she said last week."

"Yes she did," came the muffled reply from beneath the bed. Her boots flipped out to the middle of the floor, and Jon wormed his way backwards from underneath the bed. He surfaced, red faced and dusty. "Just cuz she regrets it now doesn't mean that she didn't mean it then."

"Look, girls are weird," Wendy tried again as she fastened the last hook on the corset. "I know I was, freshman year." She grabbed her jeans and wiggled into them, inwardly cursing her stupid hips. Sucking in, she flopped backwards on the bed and forced the zipper up, buttoning quickly as soon as she was able. They'd soften and loosen over the day, but struggling into jeans in the morning was always the worst.

"Don't you dare tell her I said this, but they'll break up and then Chel'll be liveable again," she added. Fully dressed, Wendy slid her nightshirt over her head and threw it at her laundry hamper. It missed.

"Don't care," Jon muttered. "You gonna eat the eggs, or what?"

"Fine, whatever. I don't have time for this." Wendy pawed through her drawers for socks and a light jacket. She'd found getting away with corsets as a top at school was much easier when there was a jacket always on hand. "You two figure it out yourselves. Is there any toast?"

"Wheat, yeah. Is that all you want? No eggs?"

"Nah. Be the best brother in the whole wide world and grab me a slice? I got in late."

"I heard." The finality in Jon's voice caused Wendy to pause in the middle of pulling on her socks and look up. He was frowning deeply, pale and still. "Dad was asking us yesterday if we knew if you were up to anything, you know, skeezy."

"Great," Wendy muttered, tapping her tongue ring against the backs of her front teeth in irritation. "Thanks for the advance warning."

"I can't believe he'd think Eddie and you do drugs, and then he completely misses Chel's . . . you know." Jon threw his hands in the air. "You're the biggest prude I know. Dad's just been . . . weird, lately, you know? I mean, come on, *I've* had more dates than you."

"Okay, got your point, you can stop now." Wendy yanked on her boots. "Have you seen my makeup case? The black one?"

"Chel borrowed it. I think it's in the bathroom." Jon let her push past him and then ambled down the stairs. "Butter on your toast?"

"Please!" she called. "Hey Eddie!"

"Hey what?" he yelled from downstairs.

"How we doing on time?"

There was a pause as Eddie checked his watch. "Don't cake it on, princess, and we'll be right as rain!"

The bathroom was bare of her makeup and Wendy didn't feel like wading through the fashionista disaster zone that was Chel's bedroom. Muttering, "Hell, who needs lipstick anyway?" Wendy grabbed her backpack and rushed down the stairs.

"Perfect timing," Eddie crowed, planting a kiss on her cheek as she hit the last step. "You've chosen to go *au naturale*, I see. Daring, but elegantly done." He took her by the hand and bowed over it, brushing warm lips across her knuckles. She shivered faintly at the touch and quickly squelched the warmth pooling in her gut. "My lady, your chariot awaits."

"You're so weird," Chel said, bumping Eddie with her bag as she shoved her way out the front door. One of her poms dropped on the porch; Jon picked it up and she snatched it from him without comment. He took a large bite out of his second breakfast burrito in response.

"Ah, the buffy disapproves," Eddie said to Jon, clapping him on the shoulder as Chel threw her things in the back of his Cabriolet and slid into the back seat. "Luck is with us this fine morning. Like the groundhog not seeing his shadow or rain on your wedding day, a disapproving buffy means that all is right in the world."

"Toast, please," Wendy demanded, ruffling Jon's carrot-top with her free hand. He took her backpack from her so she could lock the front door.

The ride to school was quiet except for Chel's low-pitched chattering into her cell phone the entire way. Low squeals of "No, you stop!" punctuated by high-pitched giggles grated on Wendy's worn nerves fairly quickly. Every time she glanced in the side mirror she would catch glimpses of Jon's miserable expression.

"Chel!" she finally said, turning in her seat and glaring at her younger sister. "You'll see them in five minutes. Turn the damn thing off, or I swear I'm going to dump all your hair crap down the sink. Fast as your hair grows, you'll have roots in a week." She put on her best *I mean it* face and met her sister's furious stare unflinchingly.

"Excuse me, Marc, bitch alert. I'll see you in ten. Yeah, love you too. Byyyyeee." Snapping her cell closed, Chel shoved it deep in her purse, crossed her arms over her chest, and said snidely, "Happy now?"

"Very. Thank you." Wendy plopped back in her seat.

"You wouldn't have done it," Chel added, leaning forward. "Dad paid for my peroxide for my birthday. It's super expensive. He'd be totally pissed off." Her watch beeped. Smirking at Wendy, Chel reached into her purse, rifled until she came up with a bottle of pills, and dry swallowed one quickly, grimacing at the taste.

"Look, Malibu Barbie, no one here wants to hear about what your loser boyfriend had for breakfast, okay? You share that cell plan with Jon, so quit running up all the minutes. Text if you have to, but just be quiet."

"Like he has anyone to talk to," Chel grumbled under her breath. Her watch beeped again and she groaned. "Damn, I forgot my multi."

"You really ought to open a pharmacy out of your purse," Wendy said. "I bet you'd make a bundle."

"Eddie," Chel sneered, grabbing Jon's water bottle and chugging several quick gulps to wash down the vitamin, "why don't you just get in her pants already so she'll lay off the rest of us? Being that frigid just can't be good for her health. Also? Way annoying."

"Here we go," Jon muttered and sank as deeply as he could into the corner of the seat.

Wendy's jaw dropped and it took all her willpower not to slap her younger sister across the face. She turned in the seat and gripped the headrest so hard her knuckles turned white. "*Excuse me*, you little—"

"Hey, what-do-ya-know," Eddie broke in, pulling into the

parking lot and angling towards a space in the back row, "we're at school! Look everyone, an educational institute!"

"Thanks for the ride, Eddie," Jon gasped, grabbing his backpack and flinging himself over the edge of the car before it had completely stopped. Pulling out his wallet, Jon hurried towards the cafeteria doors, jogging in his haste.

"Get out," Wendy said tightly to Chel as Eddie parked the car. "Get out and get to class before I forget you're my sister." She turned back to the windshield, squared her shoulders, tilted her head back, and closed her eyes. Licking her lips, she ran over her schedule for the day in her mind. Meanwhile, in the parking lot, car doors slammed and students cat-called. The Cabriolet vibrated when Chel, pushing roughly past Eddie, made her exit, slamming his door as loud as she could. The engine cooled, ticking loudly.

Eddie shifted in his seat. "She's gone."

"I know." Wendy sucked the top of her tongue ring in irritation, rolling the ball at the end against the roof of her mouth.

"It's just a phase . . . I think."

"I know that, too."

He touched her shoulder gingerly, brushing a few of her curls off her cheek. "Wendy—"

"Don't. We've been over it." Wendy leaned forward, eyes still closed, and pressed the heels of her hands into her temples. "She has no idea what's going on. All she knows is Dad's not here and Mom's in the hospital and Jon can't get two words out around her without pissing her off. She's a nightmare and I'm getting to where I've had enough, you know?"

"She doesn't mean it."

"I know." Wendy took several deep, cleansing breaths, and sat back. When she opened her eyes Eddie was still there, hand on the armrest, fingers curled upward. Wendy settled her hand in his tentatively, and he gently closed his fingers around hers, as if she were a delicate creation he might crush if he held her too hard.

"You've always got me," Eddie reminded her.

She sighed. "No I don't. Not really. Not the way I need . . . someone. But not you."

"I do love you, you know," he offered, almost off-handly. Wendy glanced at him but his eyes were trained at thin clouds puffing across the sky. "You're totally hot. And my best friend. Two birds and all. Plus you're kinda awesome."

"We've been over this," she said again but it came out more of a question, hesitant and soft. "It wouldn't work, remember?"

Eddie slanted a look at her and Wendy's heart thrummed for just a moment, a quick staccato beat against her ribs. He was handsome, there was no doubt about that, with a quicksilver smile and even features, a wrestler's compact muscles and hair silky against his neck. Due to the most recent batch of dye, the black had faded to silver, giving him an ethereal look, and the few blond highlights that remained caught the sun like molten gold.

"Have we?" He squeezed her hand. He twisted so that he was facing her and reached out, stroking her right cheek with fingertips calloused from years of rough work in his uncle's garage. "You decided it wouldn't work and we've never even kissed. How do you know for sure?"

Chest throbbing, Wendy leaned her cheek into his touch, loving the warmth of him and the delicate way those talented fingers stroked a path from the cup of her ear to the curve of her chin, cupping her face and drawing her forward. His breath fanned across her lips, smelling of citrus and honey and Wendy trembled, hesitating on the brink of what she'd wanted for years.

"I can't," she mouthed and then, with more force, said aloud, "I can't."

"You won't," he corrected, sitting back. He seemed mellow though, unoffended at her refusal. "Not the same thing."

"Eddie, I go out and look for my mom's soul every damn night." She held up her scraped hand and the opposing wrist, exposing the deep scratch left over from the tussle with the two Walkers from the night before. "It hurts me, okay? I get hurt."

"Wendy—"

"This job, this thing I have to do, it's not fun or easy or romantic. What in the hell makes you think that a relationship between us would do anything but complicate my life?"

"First of all, I'm not asking for a relationship, you are." Eddie held his hands up to stall her reply. "And before you get on your high horse, it's not that no one wants to date you. Lots of guys totally do."

"Right, whatever." Wendy rolled her eyes, but felt the flush work up her neck. "Everyone wants to date the class freak. Sure they do."

"Oh please. Shut up. I'm making a point here."

"Oh yeah? And that point is?"

"The point *is* that you don't have to date, Wendy. This is the real world, right? There doesn't need to be some intense connection. You don't need to be wearing some guy's jacket or whatever to, you know, blow off steam, have a little fun. Especially not with me." He reached out, captured her fingers again, and squeezed her hand. "I am more than willing to consider less . . . permanent . . . options. For now."

"Blowing off something," she muttered under her breath as she sat back.

"I heard that, you perv. Secondly, maybe Chel's got a point. You're really wound up. I mean, okay, I'll admit, if you went for one of those losers I'd be jealous as hell, but . . . but it doesn't have to be me, I know that."

Wendy slouched in the seat, turned her face away. "Oh yeah? If not you, then who?"

"Please. You've got that whole bad-girl gothette vibe going for you, and some people—not me of course, because I myself am a goth god—but there are some dudes who find that vibe, likewise you, sexy as hell. They'd stick around even if shit got a little weird. Who doesn't like a little mystery?"

"Reaping. The. Dead. Eddie."

"So? They don't have to know about it."

"Right, like I'm supposed to Bruce Wayne my way through a relationship? I see a soul, maybe my mom's, and then I'm supposed to be all, 'Excuse me, honey, I just remembered that my house is on fire. Gotta go!'" Wendy snorted. "Not bloody likely."

"Do you have to go send every soul you see into the Light?" He slapped the wheel, exasperated. "I mean, can't you just let a couple of them slide?"

"I *do* let them go. I told you, I don't reap unless I have to now," Wendy snapped. "It's not like I'm in this for the glory, Eddie, and I don't want them noticing me any more than . . . any more than they want me noticing them, but sometimes . . . sometimes there's no choice. Some of them," she shuddered, "some of the ghosts aren't *right*. Some of them scare me."

Though she'd tried to explain before, Wendy knew she'd never have the words for the horrors Eddie couldn't see. He'd been in the operating room after the accident; he hadn't been there when she'd spotted her first Walker.

The ambulance came shortly after Piotr left her, shivering and lonely, hunched in the back of the police car. The paramedics looked her over and escorted her into the back, driving quietly to El Camino Hospital, where they left her in the ER to await medical attention. Her mother was an EMT so most of the ER nurses knew Wendy on sight. After she'd been declared bruised but intact, the nurses sat her in a corner bed and pulled the curtain, giving her privacy while she waited for her mother.

It was spooky sitting there, shrouded behind the green fabric. Wendy hopped down and opened the curtain a large crack before crawling back onto the table. Bored, she began watching ghosts wander by. Piotr had promised that the ability to see ghosts would fade but so far it hadn't. The shock of the accident had peeled back some protective layer in Wendy's mind, leaving her exposed to a different level of the world—a darker, colder place.

It didn't take Wendy long to figure out that only a small fraction of the ghosts seemed to realize that they were dead; they drifted from nurse to nurse, touching elbows and asking plaintive questions like "Where am I?" or "What happened?" They shuffled amid the staff, repeating their queries over and over again until Wendy thought she'd be driven mad by the soft, insistent questions. The rest just drifted, ignoring the living and the dead alike, lost in their own tragedies and oblivious to the world around them.

After awhile, she began keeping tally, wetting her finger and marking the paper beneath her legs when a specific sort of ghost wandered by. There were a very large number of elderly ghosts—men and women with wispy fly-away hair and age-spotted hands—most clad in hospital gowns or faded pajamas, and some sporting tubes in their noses or dangling around their necks, though the tubes faded into nothing just past their chests. There were fewer middle-aged spirits and even fewer ghosts in their twenties or thirties. She only spotted one child ghost, who was quickly swallowed by a wash of brilliant light as the orderlies rushed a gore-splattered gurney by her bed on the way to an operating room. There were no teenage ghosts in sight.

From the navel of each ghost dangled a thick silver-white cord, a twisted rope of pale, shimmering light; the cord hung between their knees and moved as they did, like moonlit seaweed shifting with the tide. The ends of some cords were severed cleanly, as if cut with a scalpel, while others broke off in ragged edges, thin and wavering as they shifted their weight. An hour into her stay, while Wendy watched, three spirits who'd come in from another car wreck faded before her eyes. Their cords had been neatly severed and they seemed glad to flee into the warm wash of light.

One ghost, however, did not wander in aimless circles. He moved through the ER rapidly, peering behind each curtain as if seeking someone specific. His middle was nearly bare—only the slimmest of cords dangled from his navel, black and sickly looking, rotted mostly through. Unlike the others, who appeared as paler, more transparent versions of the people they must have been in life, this ghost was bleached of color and stretched, thin and tall and hovering as he moved from curtain to curtain.

His face was a rotting horror.

This ghost in particular scared her, and when he approached her curtain Wendy instinctively ducked her head and buried her face in her hands.

Piotr, she thought desperately. *Piotr, help!* But Piotr was not there to hold her hand as he had before; she was alone. Wendy could feel the cold baking off this ghost in a shimmering cold-wave, like an icy version of summertime highway gridlock. The ghost hovered near her for several minutes, circling her like a jackal might circle its prey, wet snuffling noises filling the tiny space, before finally continuing its rapid progress through the ER.

No sooner had it gone than her curtain yanked back and her mother was there, arms wrapping tightly around her and the sweet smell of honeysuckle filling her nose.

"Oh Wendy, baby," her mother whispered, eyes tracking the ghost as it disappeared around a corner. "Don't be scared, sweetie. It's not a Walker yet. It can't hurt you. Shhh. You're safe. You're safe with me."

Startled, Wendy pulled away and searched her mother's face. There was sorrow there, and guilt. Her mother knew, Wendy realized, about the ghosts and the white man who, sniffing like a dog, had circled her bed.

Somehow her mother knew, and Wendy was no longer alone.

Eddie was oblivious to Wendy drifting off in the middle of their conversation.

"So leave the scary ghosts alone. You don't have to reap them. There's always a choice."

"No, Eddie, we've been over this." Wendy crossed her arms over her chest and glared at the tree they'd parked under. "If I see a ghost, that means it's trapped in limbo. *Trapped*, Eddie. Do not pass go. Do not collect two hundred dollars. Do not move on to your next fucking life! They stay there, rotting slowly, going batshit crazy or worse, for *centuries*, unless they figure out a way to move on."

"Or you help them move on. Like you used to."

"Key phrase there. 'Used to,'" Wendy said stiffly. "I try not to do that anymore. Not unless I have to." Her hand curled into a loose fist in her lap. "I don't have that kind of time."

"You could give up. Stop searching. It's not like you know for a fact your mom's out there somewhere."

"Yeah, well, maybe I don't want to be selfish and take that chance." She pressed her fingertips to her eyes and sighed. "Yeah, I might find her again. Or I might not. It's my mom, Eddie, I can't give up on the chance she's still out there somewhere." Turning to him, she reached out and squeezed his shoulder. "What about your dad, huh? What if he'd been stuck there and I'd turned away. How'd you feel then?"

Eddie jerked away sharply. "Okay, chat's done."

"Ed—"

"Pulling my dead dad into this discussion is about as tasteful as throwing down Hitler in a fight, Wendy. You just don't do it."

"Look," she whispered, "I'm sorry. I just wanted to explain why I can't have a normal relationship with you or with anyone. I didn't mean to upset you."

"Hell," he said and grabbed her by the shoulders, yanked her forward, and kissed her. His lips ground against hers for several seconds, but there was little passion in it. It was simple angry punishment in the shape of her best friend's mouth. Wendy, stunned by the onslaught, held still in his grip and slowly Eddie's touch softened, his kiss deepened, and she could feel a damp spot on her cheek, warm and wet against her skin.

When he drew back they were both breathing raggedly, Eddie's
chest hitching softly, and Wendy trembling.

"Well," she said, striving for lightness, "that was a jackass thing
to do."

"I know. I know! And you didn't deserve that," Eddie muttered,
shamed, pressing his forehead against the wheel. He pounded the
dashboard once, twice. "I'm sorry. I just . . . I—"

"I'm not mad about it," she said evenly, letting her galloping
heart slow before she dared open the door. "I said a shitty thing, you
did a shitty thing, but we're best friends. As far as I'm concerned
we're even. And stop beating up your car. Your mom'll kill you."

"Wendy—"

"Shush. 'Grrr, me Tarzan, you Jane, so shut up, woman' won't
cut it. I've known you since we were five and plus, it's totally not
hot. I'm not going anywhere, even if you did just try to cop a feel."

Eddie half-laughed, grateful for her easy dismissal, and shook
his head. The shock was fading from his eyes. "I only tried to cop a
feel? I thought I scored a direct hit."

"Whole lotta padding on this corset," Wendy replied blithely.
She knew she was letting Eddie off easy, but Wendy was tired of discussing it. Case closed.

"Darn, foiled again." He rubbed his hands along the steering
wheel. "My charms have failed. I shall have to soothe my wounded
ego with another."

Wendy rolled her eyes. "Please. You're so hard up lately that
you'd kiss a doorstop if it was halfway cute." She made a kissy face
at him and batted her eyes.

"True," he said, shrugging. "I am an equal opportunity sort of
Romeo." He grinned then, slightly reddened eyes twinkling and teeth
flashing in a heart-stoppingly dangerous way. "But we're okay?"

"Yeah, yeah. You're stuck with me. BFFs for life, yo." She patted
him on the shoulder. "I keep you from being bored, you keep me
sane. Also, yay, backrubs."

Eddie chuckled, amused at her posturing. "BFFs are a given. But don't you at least want to see what the fuss is all about?" He waved his hand between them. "I mean, romantically?"

"With you?" Wendy braced herself with a wide, bright grin, and then lied so hard it ached inside. "Nah."

Eddie shook his head. "Now who's pushing people away? You really need to follow my example and at least dip your toe in the dating pool . . . puddle. A dating teaspoon, even."

Gathering up her purse, Wendy snorted in reply. "Isn't dating a BFF's ex a major debacle? Anyone I'd like, you've probably already been there and done that."

"You wound me, dear. I'm not a total slut. Anymore." Eddie popped the trunk to fetch his bag and Wendy slapped the button for the soft-top to cycle closed, waiting until all the latches were in place to fetch the rest of her own things. The first bell rang and Wendy hurried off, leaving Eddie, as usual, to catch up.

Part of her loved Eddie and always would, but he didn't understand her situation. He'd already proven that he didn't get why she felt so guilty and torn. Wendy grimaced. Eddie thought letting her mother stay missing was a good thing.

Wendy knew, Eddie or no, that she had to find her mom.

She owed her that much.

CHAPTER SIX

Backtracking through the streets, Piotr let the wind guide him away from the city. Lost in his thoughts, it took him a while to realize that he wasn't going to get very far on foot; it was daytime and the trolleys were packed with living heat.

There were two ways an object could pass over into the Never: sheer luck and intense emotion. Dearly-loved possessions frequently worked their way into the Never. Though Piotr often found scavenging in San Francisco moderately easy, he still counted himself lucky to find a rusty bicycle with two good wheels abandoned beneath a tree in the park.

Listening to the creak and groan of the gears beneath him, Piotr pumped his legs and made for the 101. Grey daylight never seemed to last long lately, the afternoons were growing shorter; soon darkness would fall, and with it the Walkers would roam in greater numbers.

At times like this, doing something so intensely physical but essentially mindless, Piotr wondered if the sensations he felt were the same as he had felt when he was alive. Listening to the newly dead, still attuned to their physical shells, made him think that maybe what the dead did was close enough, but he wasn't sure. Even the simple act of running, of sprinting, legs pumping and feet pounding, seemed alien some days—like, if he wanted, Piotr could force his spirit to move fast enough that his legs wouldn't be necessary. Like if he just sped up enough, he could fly away. Like the only thing keeping him grounded was the living belief that gravity worked.

Concentrating on these musings passed the time; the miles melted away beneath his wheels. Piotr had passed into San Bruno when he smelled the smoke. Frowning, he slowed the bike and, on discovering the kickstand had rusted away, abandoned it at the edge of the highway. Sniffing the air, he followed his nose all the way down the embankment until he reached the edge of a twisted and warped tarmac. Piotr hesitated at the large, rusted sign declaring the buckled concrete to be the Mills Field Municipal Airport. There was a lot of activity on the living side—the heat here was sporadic but immense—but this place was clearly the source of the strange, sweetly smoky smell.

Still deciding whether he wanted to proceed, Piotr spotted a flash of white.

Walker.

It was crazy to sneak up on a Walker like this, especially since the previous few fights had been so close and the Walkers had evidently decided to start pairing up for their hunts, but Piotr was unwilling to pass up a chance to spy on a Walker when it didn't know he was near. With any luck, he might even learn something about Dunn.

Crouching down, Piotr dashed under the sagging hulk of a downed Bell P-39, hiding in the shadow of one wing. He briefly considered ducking into the aircraft itself and watching from the canopy but the plane was belly-down in the dirt, the landing gear long gone. A Walker would be able to spot him at eye-level for sure.

The flash of white came again and Piotr froze in the shadows, stunned into stillness. There were Walkers, yes, over a half dozen of them, but it was the woman clad all in white who caught his attention.

The White Lady.

It had to be her; Piotr couldn't think of another soul in the Never stupid or crazy enough to rub elbows with Walkers voluntarily. They certainly weren't attacking her. In fact, as Piotr watched, the White Lady paused at the edge of the tarmac and gestured.

Pushing aside the others, one particularly decayed Walker knelt down at her feet, knees on the tarmac and toes in the dirt, tilting its face up, allowing the White Lady to push back the edge of its hood, exposing the last tattered remnants of its cheeks and forehead to the light. Then, as Piotr watched, dumbfounded, she leaned down, hood sagging, and kissed the Walker full upon the ruins of its mouth.

A billowing cloud of white burst from the Walker's chest, accompanied by the sharp increase of the smoky sweet scent that had first caught Piotr's attention as far away as the highway. As he watched, the Walker stiffened, its limbs jerking spasmodically under the White Lady's onslaught, feet drumming up puffs of grit from the dirt. Piotr gagged, turning away, but not before he spotted the point of the painful kiss.

The rumors were right; the Walkers, at least these particular Walkers, were working for the White Lady now. She paid well. The longer the two of them remained lip-locked, the more of the kneeling Walker's ruined flesh grew back. By the time the White Lady released the Walker, most of the side of his face had returned. The flesh was pale white and fragile-looking, lined with thin blue veins, but certainly more substantial than the rotted horror it'd been before.

Stepping away from the Walker, the White Lady sagged. One of the Walkers at her side stretched out a hand, which she slapped away.

"Don't touch me," she snapped, the wind carrying her voice to Piotr a beat behind her movements. She gestured north. "Go." The other Walkers dispersed, leaving her with the newly healed one. She helped him to his feet.

"You're now mine." She smoothed the front of the Walker's robes. "Say it."

It bowed. "My lady. Always yours."

"You've been chosen, Daniel. I've got a special task for you." The White Lady took the Walker by the bony wrist. "This way."

They were too close and moving in his direction at a fast clip.

Piotr closed his eyes, waited for the cry of discovery, but none came. When he opened them again the White Lady was all the way at the far edge of the field and topping the rise, the Walker in tow. Intent on her goal, she'd passed him right by; they hadn't seen him crouched in the shadows.

Should he go back, tell Elle and the others about what he'd learned? Piotr knew they needed this new information, but he still had to investigate Dunn's disappearance. Lily would never forgive him if he failed her.

Lily could wait.

Piotr began to move after them when a large cadre of Walkers melted through the shadows and went the way the White Lady had disappeared. There was no way Piotr would be able to follow them for such a distance across the open space without being discovered.

Torn, but knowing that he had to follow through on his original mission, Piotr regretfully backed out of the shadows and hurried toward the highway, glancing once over his shoulder to make sure the Walkers hadn't spotted him. He would push himself to the limit getting to Mountain View and then speed back up to the city. The others had to know about what he'd seen, and Lily needed to know about Dunn.

He wouldn't fail them.

Though Eddie had claimed everything was fine, he wasn't at lunch, nor was he at his locker afterward. Brooding about what that might mean, Wendy worried her way through the rest of the day until gym, last period.

They had a sub. Instead of waiting to get picked last for basketball, Wendy found herself led to the back track. Most of the class knew that this meant an opportunity to lackadaisically lap the track and gossip, and Wendy originally intended to take it easy along with the rest, but as they lined up to begin she spotted a tell-tale flicker at the edge of the field. Wendy groaned. What *now*?

The sub stood at the start/finish line with a clipboard and a stop-watch. When the whistle blew, Wendy was the only one who took off running. Ignoring the giggles behind her, she sped around the track the required three times, barely noticing the surprised, "Great time!" the sub yelled as she crossed the finish line.

Assignment met, Wendy staggered over to the sub and, panting, asked, "Since I'm done, do you mind if I take the rest of class off?"

The sub's elated grin faded. "The rest of the hour? I can't let you do that. Are you nuts?"

"I'm not leaving campus," Wendy lied, keeping the spot where she'd seen the flickering light at the edge of her peripheral vision. "I just thought I saw a couple samples I can use for my biology project over there." She pointed toward the edge of the field with a prom-ising thatch of thorny bushes splashed with red and purple flowers. "It's just a little flower-picking. I'll be fast, I swear. You can hear that whistle anywhere near here."

The bulk of the class was coming, nearing the end of the first lap. The sub glanced at them, eyed the bushes, and sighed. "Fine. But stay dressed out. I've got my eye on you. Don't you think I'll forget, either. No funny stuff."

Skipping backwards toward the field, Wendy grinned and dropped a quick salute. "You got it, Coach!" Then she was off.

Under the patchy shade of the eucalyptus at the edge of school property, Wendy took a deep breath and glanced around. The flicker had faded while she was talking to the sub.

"Damn it, damn it, damn it," Wendy muttered under her breath, angling her head to make sure the sub was paying more attention to the last group of gossiping girls finishing their first lap than to her. The instant the sub's head dipped down to mark off the last stragglers, Wendy grabbed the edge of the fence and went up and over.

The dim flicker was gone. Wendy squinted and crouched down,

pushing through the thick, thorny bushes until the sounds from the school grew muted. The canopy overhead was thicker here, the shadows denser. Her mother had been great in the woods; it was as if she were a ghost herself, flitting through the trees easily. She always knew where to step, how to navigate. She never got lost. Wendy wasn't quite that good.

Resting against a nearby tree, Wendy hesitated; pushing on would take her out of the range of the sub's whistle. There was a chance the sub might not notice Wendy missing at the end of the day, but she'd seemed like one of those teachers who actually cared. It might be better to just not risk getting in troub—

There!

Catching the flicker out of the corner of her eye, Wendy pushed through the underbrush, scouring her shins and calves against thorny wild blackberry bushes. Longingly she thought of her thick jeans, neatly tucked away in her cubby back in the girl's locker room. Shoving through the dense patch, Wendy grimaced as her sneaker splooshed into a slurry of black rot and dank mud beside a rotted out trunk.

"So-so-so gross," Wendy groaned, making sure to look up and eye the green-brown canopy overhead. Her mother had taught her well—she could see a tangle of dead and dying branches hanging above, remnants from the storms of the previous week. Every one of them was at least seven or eight inches across, minimum. Widow-maker branches. Wendy eased back, making sure she wasn't beneath the heavy load. If the wind blew just right the whole mess would come crashing down, crushing anything unlucky enough to be directly beneath.

"Crap," Wendy muttered. She thought now she might have an idea where the flicker was coming from. Skirting the edge of the clearing, keeping to the thorny sides, she shoved deeper and deeper in until, just as she'd suspected, she found a dim shape hovering around a heavy fall of deadwood.

"I was wondering if anyone'd find me," muttered the ghost of the homeless man, clutching his tattered parka close. "Figures it'd be some kid playing hookey."

He leaned in, waving a hand right in front of Wendy's face and shouted, "Hey! You! Kiddo! You turn right around and you march up to your principal and you tell him what you found here! Do you understand me? You don't just leave me here!"

"I can't do that," Wendy said and hid a smile when the ghost jumped back.

"You can hear me? Really?" He grabbed Wendy by the shoulders and yelped, yanking back. "Shit! You're burning up, kid!"

"Yep," Wendy said. "Side effect. Sorry."

Waving his burnt palm in the air, the ghost eyed Wendy speculatively. "You ain't gonna tell no one about me? Really?"

"I can't draw attention to myself," Wendy explained, sighing. She knelt down and examined the pile of dead brush and the crushed form beneath, grimacing. "You were asleep when it fell?"

"Yep. Didn't feel a thing," the ghost said. "I guess I ought to be thankful, huh? Went to sleep cold and hungry and woke up . . . well, still cold and hungry but at least the weather don't bother me no more, huh?" He sighed. "So is this hell or something, kid?"

"Just the afterlife," Wendy said, swiping her foot across the dirt to obscure the place where she'd knelt down. "I can help you with that if you want." She stood back and eyed her handiwork. Her mom would've been proud. When the cops found the body, no one would know she'd been there. In theory, at least.

"Help me with what? You can't bring me back to life, can ya?" Despite his ragged state, he couldn't help the pitiful hope that crept into his voice.

"No." Wendy refrained from patting him on the arm, lest she burn him further. "But I can send you on. You're . . . where you are right now, the Never, it's like a halfway point. Limbo, sort of. I can give you a push to go to the next place. If you want." Eying the tree next to her, Wendy reached up and broke off a small, thin branch clustered with living leaves.

He cleared his throat. "You mean heaven?" His voice dropped. "Or, y'know, the other? Because if it's the other, I'll stay where I am, thank you very much."

Wendy shrugged and started back toward the school, making sure to swipe the fresh branch across her path and staying to the places she'd walked before. The homeless man kept pace with her easily, passing through the dense brush without dispersing. "Not my jurisdiction. I have no clue. But you won't be stuck in the Never until your soul rots. There's that."

"I'll rot? If I stay here?"

"Most souls do, yeah." Wendy glanced at her watch. "Look, I don't mean to be a bitch, but class is almost over and my coach is going to wonder where I got to. I had to lie to her just to get out here and try and find you. I didn't have to do that, I could've just ignored you." *I should've just ignored you*, Wendy thought bitterly. It'd been stupid to assume some random flicker might be her mother. Stupid and, seeing those tree branches, dangerous.

"So you're some sort of angel or something? Helping souls move on?"

"Something like that." Wendy stopped and tapped her wrist. They were almost at the first clearing and it seemed a safe place to drop her branch. "So what'll it be? Stay or go?"

The ghost squared his shoulders and, cringing like a child about to get a shot, said, "Do it."

Closing her eyes, Wendy opened the gates within and let the light pulse through her. It was over in a moment; the man cried out only once.

As the heat ebbed from Wendy's fingertips she heard the distant whistle. Trudging back to the track, Wendy kept her eye out for the sub but, despite all her admonitions, she'd already left. Wendy was halfway across the field before she remembered the flowers at the fence. She debated turning around to retrieve a handful—what were the chances of the sub checking up on her alibi, after all?—but decided it was better to cover her bases. Forcing her tired legs into a lope, Wendy hurried back to the fence and gathered up two handfuls of the blossoms, nicking her fingers on thorns in the process.

Bright yellow buses trundled down the road toward the pickup point and Wendy could hear the distant shouts of other students slamming lockers and pouring out the side entrances toward the parking lot. The sub really had forgotten about her.

It had, thus far, been a truly shitty day. Glancing down at her handful of blooms, Wendy realized that she was dirty and scabbed, sweaty and clutching the flowers like a tired little girl. When the memory hit it was like a punch to the gut.

The unexpectedly icy highway had taken many drivers the night of her birthday; now, a week later, the afternoon roads to the cemetery were thick with headlights. Her father stayed home with the twins while her mother escorted Wendy to Mr. Barry's funeral. When the wrapped coffin slid into the muddy hole at her feet Wendy dropped her armful of roses, turned, and buried her face in her mother's shoulder, inhaling the deep scent of vanilla and wood-smoke to center herself, to calm her tears. Easing her away from the mound of bruised petals, her mother hummed a little tune, so softly Wendy felt the vibration more than heard the song, and a blessed cool descended over her, easing the hot knot in the pit of her stomach.

"Soon, soon," her mother whispered for her ears alone. "Be strong, Wendy-girl. It's almost over." Her hand cupping Wendy's elbow was warm, her breath mint-sweet. Wendy, calmer, took the time while the mourners were tossing spades of dirt onto the coffin to pray that Eddie would be okay. He refused to sit shiva with the rest of his family and wouldn't leave his room, even for the funeral. Eddie was, simply put, a wreck.

Wendy and her mother drove home after—to collect more

flowers and food for the *seudat havrach* reception—and Wendy blew hot breath onto the window as the cold rain fell, drawing sad faces in the fog. Her mother ran into the house, returning with platters overflowing with deli meats and eggs, a small wicker basket of cookies, and a crockpot filled with hot lentil soup.

When they arrived Mrs. Barry hugged Wendy's mother close in the foyer. She was a large woman and the black of mourning did little to slim her figure. Wendy's mother was swallowed in Mrs. Barry's voluminous embrace, the tattered ribbon pinned to Mrs. Barry's chest poking her on the cheek. "Mary, I'm so glad to see you."

"I'm so sorry for your loss, Moira," Wendy's mother replied gently. Wendy hesitated in the foyer, startled by the warmth her mother displayed for Mrs. Barry. Her mother wasn't a harsh woman by any stretch of the imagination—she volunteered at homeless shelters up in the city and made a point of tithing regularly—but she rarely allowed anyone outside their family to touch her. She was protective of her personal space.

"Winifred," Mrs. Barry sniffled, drawing out a humongous linen handkerchief and honking loudly into it, "be a dear and go fetch Edward. He's being . . ." she hesitated, and Wendy felt the urge to turn away from the too-real grief etched across her face as she struggled not to cry in front of her guests. "He's been difficult this week," she finished. "If anyone can get him to come down, I know it's you."

Wendy glanced at her mother. "Go on, dear," Mary said, gathering the basket. "He needs you right now."

The staircase wall was lined with pictures: Eddie and his father posing with a Ringling Brothers clown, Eddie and his father posing with Goofy at Disneyland, Eddie and his father fishing, Eddie and his father at Dodger Stadium. The last picture was a formal family portrait of Eddie and both his parents posing in the park. Eddie was perhaps five at the time and his mother was thinner in the picture and happier, her mouth not so pinched and drawn. Only Eddie's father appeared ageless in the photo; the photographer had perfectly captured the perpetually happy grin he had worn all the years Wendy had known him.

"Eddie?" Wendy tapped on his door with one knuckle, eyeing the shrouded hallway mirror shivering in the upstairs draft. "Your mom told me to come get you, but I'll go if you want." She gently pushed the door open. The room was dark. "Eds?"

"I'm not going down," Eddie said from somewhere in the black. Wendy squinted and could just make out an Eddie-shape huddled in the corner under his bunk beds. The lower bunk had been pushed out from under the top and was against the wall; a trundle bed sat beside. Clearly, Mrs. Barry had guests sleeping in Eddie's room. It even smelled like old person in here, like Nana's perfume and moth-balls.

Wendy eased into the room and shut the door behind her, leaving them both in the pitch darkness. With the door closed the clink and quiet conversation from downstairs was pleasantly muffled, the room warm. Wendy edged around the detritus of the visiting relatives until she found the bunks and slid to the floor beside her friend.

"Any room under there for me?"

Eddie lifted the comforter without comment and Wendy wriggled until she was flush against him, shoulder to hip. She laid her head on his shoulder and they sat in the muffled silence for a long, long time.

"I'm not going to cry," Eddie said suddenly. He shifted and Wendy heard the scratch of his nails against the gauze still taped across his forehead. "Everyone keeps telling me that it's okay to cry, but I've tried and I can't. So I'm just not going to."

"My mom says it can take some time for the shock to wear off," Wendy offered. "That it's okay to not cry right away."

"You haven't cried yet?" Eddie sounded surprised. "Didn't you like my dad?"

"Dummy," Wendy replied kindly. "I loved your dad. He was

awesome." She gingerly felt around for his hand. The knuckles were bound in plaster. It was the arm he'd broken. "But it still isn't real yet, you know?"

"Yeah, I know." Eddie sighed deeply and switched his broken arm out for his good one. "Wendy?"

"Yeah?"

"I'm mad at him."

Wendy nodded. "It's a dumb way to die."

"He always got on me about my seatbelt but his didn't even save him."

Wendy nodded again. "Cars are dumb."

"Really dumb."

Eddie fell silent and Wendy scratched her knees; the thick hose her mother insisted she wear were itchy against her scabbed legs, her good shoes were too tight and pinched her toes. Eddie sighed and Wendy, moving on instinct alone, held Eddie's hand, humming her mother's favorite melody softly in the dark.

"That's pretty," Eddie said and laid his head against her shoulder. He may have slept, Wendy wasn't sure, but they sat still and quiet together, two children in the dark.

Hours passed, and when it was time for Wendy to leave she leaned forward and brushed a soft, hesitant kiss against Eddie's mouth. He inhaled and she knew he was awake; he tasted of soda and saline and salt. It was an apology and an entreaty and a promise of friendship.

It was her first kiss.

They never talked about it, even though Wendy knew it had been Eddie's first kiss as well. She never told him that she tasted his tears. She never told him that she'd lied about not crying yet herself.

They'd been damn near inseparable ever since.

Now, years later, when Wendy, freshly scrubbed after gym, thought she'd been forgotten for sure, she found Eddie waiting for her at her locker, book bag at his feet, earphones plugged into his ears. He took the flowers she handed him without question—merely popped open a leftover ziplock from some old lunch and slid the blooms inside— and, taking her elbow, escorted her toward the parking lot, bopping to the tinny music pulsing out a beat.

Jon was waiting for them at the car, demolishing the last of a bag of tortilla chips as they approached. "Finally! Where were you two?"

"Sub in gym," Wendy said glibly. "Held me after."

"Suck." Jon hopped in the back and plugged earphones into his phone as Eddie dialed the radio to the oldies station. They jockeyed to join the line of cars exiting the parking lot.

"I wasn't expecting you two to pick me up," Wendy said as Eddie, craning to see in the rearview, carefully maneuvered around a VW Bug. "You know, after everything from this morning. I figured on catching the bus home, give you time to chill."

"Like I'd let a little thing like that bug me," Eddie snorted. "Some friend I'd be."

"You weren't at lunch. I thought you were mad at me after all."

"Had stuff to do." Eddie glanced sideways at her. "Missed me, huh?"

"You," Wendy sniffed, "owed me lunch." She held up a wrist and sucked in her cheeks. "Do I look like I can afford to lose weight?"

"Uh huh. Well, how about I get you tomorrow, 'kay? All the pizza you can eat."

They reached the front of the line and Eddie turned left. Wendy frowned. The way home, or to their usual after-school haunt, was right. "Where are we going?"

"Eddie's taking us to see Mom," Jon said. "I asked him to."

"Yeah? I thought we went last week."

"Yeah," Eddie said, punching the gas as the lights behind them flashed and the Caltrain whizzed by. "You went, but Jon didn't. Remember?"

"Right." Wendy sank back into the seat and closed her eyes, letting the Supremes wash over her in a harmonic wave. The afternoon heat was pleasant on her cheeks, the faint breeze sweet. Once they were on the highway, Eddie reached over and brushed a stray hair off her cheek and gently squeezed the back of her neck.

Assured that Eds wasn't angry with her, Wendy relaxed and let her thoughts turn circles, brooding over the ghosts she'd spotted the night before. They had slipped away before she could ask if they'd seen her mother. Not that she could blame them; the Light under her control had taken down a pair of Walkers. It was unlikely any spirit would be willing to help her . . . but she had to try.

CHAPTER SEVEN

Sometimes Jon liked to visit with their mother alone. While he went inside, Wendy reclined the passenger seat and counted in her head, breathing in on the even beats and out on the odd. She was just sinking into a zen place when Eddie pounced.

"So what happened in gym?" he asked, zipping open his backpack and checking his cell.

Her breath hitched. "What makes you think anything happened in gym?"

"I know you. You prefer to shower at home unless you're really gross. The sub only had us walk the track, so I know you couldn't have broken a sweat there."

"I ran the track, thank you very much," Wendy replied stiffly. "New personal record."

"And?"

"And . . . I jumped the fence." Wendy glanced over at Eddie and winced. "What? I saw something. I thought it might've been my mom, I went to go check it out."

"What, are you stupid? Wendy, those woods are full of eucalyptus and there's a lot of wind today. You know better than that." Eddie tucked his cell away. "You could've been hurt."

"Hey, after all those accidents last fall I thought they cleared out all the eucalyptus!" Wendy protested. "But you're right. There's a guy back there." She grimaced. "It's gross."

"And you didn't do anything about it?" Eddie straightened and slapped the dashboard. "Wendy, that's probably illegal or something!"

"Hey, I took care of him!"

"You mean that you took care of his soul. Not his body. Right?" He glanced at her face and shook his head, disgusted. "Of course you didn't. Shit." Eddie sighed. "I thought you weren't going to go around just reaping any ol' soul anymore. Didn't you say that you have more important shit to do now?"

"I do." Wendy sighed and rubbed her eyes. This entire day had left her exhausted and it wasn't even over yet. She longingly considered skipping the evening patrol, but knew she wouldn't. She couldn't. "Look, I'm tired, I had a crappy night last night and a crappy day today. I saw a ghost and I wasn't exactly thinking straight. Mom took me training in those woods more times than I can count. I just figured that maybe it wasn't out of the question that if her soul got lost, it was wandering around there, okay? Lay off."

"Sounds like your mom was the one who was nuts," Eddie said. "She trained you out there? I mean, it's not exactly grizzly central, but there are snakes and shit, yeah?"

"I may have seen a snake or two," Wendy conceded, "but it's not like we did *all* our training out there. The woods behind the school were just a good place to learn how to climb and jump and run. They weren't that big, so there was little chance of me getting lost, and if I messed up there no one would see. I could get up and try again."

"Huh. I guess I just figured you did it all in graveyards." Eddie shook his head.

"Let me tell you a trade secret, Eds." Wendy leaned conspiratorially forward and pitched her voice low. "Ghosts hate graveyards. Unless it's right after a funeral, the chance of finding a ghost in a graveyard is nil. Vampires, on the other hand . . ." Laughing, Wendy ducked the playful punch Eddie sent at her shoulder. "What? Don't you believe in vampires?"

He snorted. "With you around, I'd believe almost anything, but I draw the line at vamps." He glanced up. "Oh, hey, there's Jon. You ready?"

Wendy grabbed her backpack. "Let's go."

As they passed through UCSF's Neuro-ICU doors, Wendy took a deep breath and squared her shoulders, wishing that she had just caught the bus home after all. A new nurse was on duty. She was stricter than the nurses normally were and wouldn't let them onto the ICU floor until both she and Eddie had signed in and she'd jotted down the addresses on their driver's licenses.

Eddie returned his wallet to his back pocket and waited until they were well away from the nursing station to whisper in Wendy's ear. "A little power-hungry, methinks."

"Shh," Wendy whispered, stepping past him into her mother's room. The neighboring bed was surrounded by baskets overflowing with pansies and roses, marigolds and cheerful carnations. Cards and stuffed creatures cluttered the bedside table and the window was open, the curtains parted. A fresh breeze scudded the aroma of fresh-cut greens in thick clouds across the room. Behind her Eddie coughed and waved a hand theatrically in front of his face.

On the other side of the curtain, her mother's side of the room was empty of furniture except for the bed, the table, and two plastic chairs stacked against the wall. Eddie navigated various beeping and wheezing machinery to unstack the chairs as Wendy leaned over her mother and pressed a gentle kiss to her forehead. "Hi Mom," she said and took her mother's hand. The skin was loose across her knuckles and the bones under Wendy's fingers felt delicate, breakable.

"Hi," Eddie echoed, nudging the chair against the back of Wendy's thighs. She settled on the edge of the chair and he sat beside her, quiet for once.

Wendy sniffed and squeezed her mother's hand again. "So," she said, "I think you're looking better. Isn't she looking better, Eds?"

"Much better," he agreed easily. "Up in no time."

"And Dad came by yesterday," Wendy continued, as if Eddie hadn't spoken, "so I know you're not getting lonely over here. You've even got a new neighbor, right?" She glanced over at the curtain separating the beds and was unsurprised to note the young woman in a gaping hospital gown peering around the edge. The silver cord dangling from her navel was thin and brittle, worn away in places, literally hanging by a thread in others. The woman, no more than twenty or so, seemed tired and weak, and her shape drifted away into nothing at the knees.

"Though," Wendy added in a softer tone, "not for that much longer, I guess."

Eddie, catching her glance at empty space, winced. "Bad accident?"

"Looks like. She's hardly there. She's gonna fade pretty fast."

A brusque rap on the doorframe made them both jump. Wendy dropped her mother's hand. A young doctor, one of the few Wendy didn't know, lifted the clipboard off the wall beside the door, sweeping aside her strawberry-colored braid to rifle the papers. Even in scrubs she was tall and elegantly put together, the sort of long-legged, cool-eyed beauty you'd expect to see strutting a catwalk instead of perusing charts. Beside Wendy, Eddie shifted uncomfortably, and Wendy felt a flash of irritation. Just that morning he'd been declaring his undying love and now he was shifting so the long tails of his overshirt covered his lap. Wendy snorted.

The doctor's eyes flicked over the room, pausing a moment to consider the neighboring side, and then she smiled apologetically. "Sorry to interrupt, but I'm here on my rounds."

"No problem," Wendy said, rising. It didn't seem as if the doctor had overheard them, but the last thing she wanted was another person thinking she was crazy. "I'm Wendy." She glanced at the bed and the emaciated shape of the woman beneath the sheets. "This is my mom."

"Oh, you're one of Mary's daughters?" The doctor crossed the room in three quick strides and offered her hand. When Wendy took it she pumped brusquely twice and dropped it. Her palm was hot to the touch. "I'm Emma Henley. I'll be assisting Dr. Shumacker on your mother's case during my residency."

"Nice gig," Eddie interjected. "Liking it so far?"

Emma looked coolly down her long nose at him. "Yes."

"Don't mind Eddie," Wendy said. "He's an old family friend, and my ride out here. Dad leaves me the car, but I don't like driving around the city and Eds is good company."

"Yes," Emma said, glancing at her clipboard and moving to the side of the bed. "I met your father yesterday. Very nice man. He's well-liked around here."

The soul of the woman in the neighboring bed drifted closer and peered at the clipboard. "Where are my charts?" she asked, waving her arms wildly. "Where is my boyfriend? He was driving. Is he here? Can I see him? *Why won't anyone talk to me, damnit?!*"

One of her flailing hands passed through the clipboard. Wendy tensed; sometimes the living could feel the cold when the dead or dying were near. The doctor, concentrating on the papers in front of her, didn't seem to notice anything amiss.

"Well, that's Dad, you know," Wendy said brightly. "He's always been, you know, super friendly." She paused, struggling for a way to answer the soul's question without appearing morbid. "Looks like there's a new neighbor for my mom, huh?"

"Hmm?" Emma glanced up. "Oh, yes. Things were busy in here for a few days, guests coming and going."

"Car accident?"

Emma raised one slim, perfectly manicured eyebrow. "I really can't say."

"Right, right," Wendy agreed. "Silly me. It's just, uh, I got a look at her and it doesn't look like . . . it just looks like an accident." Beside her the soul sobbed softly, tangled blonde hair dangling into nothing as she wept, over and over: *Please-please-please.*

"Accidents happen," Emma agreed and slipped to the left to examine a read-out on one of the beeping machines. "All too often, I'm afraid."

"That's life," Wendy said, giving up any attempt at subtlety.

"Look, I know you can't tell me anything, and I know this is going to sound so very grotesque, but can you tell me if her boyfriend survived? Whatever accident it was, I mean?"

The doctor stiffened and for a moment Wendy was certain she'd gone too far with her questions; Dr. Henley was going to order her out of her mother's room or perhaps call security to escort her off the premises. Then the doctor sighed and rubbed the bridge of her nose.

"Wendy," Emma said slowly, "why do you care? Do you know Lauren?" She winced. "The patient, I mean?"

At the sound of her name the soul wept harder, shivering from the effort.

"No," Wendy replied carefully, "but if I'd been in a big accident like that, one that landed me in a coma, Eddie'd be here every free moment, like my dad is for my mom."

"And how do you know that she doesn't have people in here every evening?" Emma crossed her arms over her chest. "School's only just let out for the day. Most working stiffs don't get off at three, you know."

"The chairs were over here," Wendy said simply, amazed that the answer came to her so easily. "I know Dad and Nana were here yesterday, and Dad always stacks them when he's done. There's no guest chair on her side of the room."

The corner of Emma's mouth twitched. "You're observant."

"I'm here every week or so." Wendy shrugged. "You learn how things work."

"I shouldn't be telling you this," Emma said, relenting. "And if you tell anyone that you got this from me, I'll deny it. Get it?"

"Got it."

Collecting the clipboard off the bedside table, Emma made a note in the bottom corner. "Good. Your instincts were right. The boyfriend was driving and he was D.O.A. They had to work all night to keep her going."

Dead On Arrival. Wendy winced as Lauren's sobbing ratcheted

up several levels to an almost earsplitting decibel of anguish and pain. "Oh man." She surreptitiously glanced at the soul beside her and sighed. "So she's not going to survive, then."

"There's no proof of that," Emma said stiffly. "She could pull out of it any day now."

"None of my business. I got it." Wendy reached down and squeezed her mother's ankle. "Thanks for being cool about it. Anyway, how are things looking here? Same old, same old?"

"Yes. I'm sorry." Emma patted Wendy on the shoulder and once again Wendy was struck by how warm the tall, thin doctor was. The hospital itself was kept at a comfortably cool temperature but Dr. Henley was baking. Wendy wondered if she should mention it. "That's nothing to worry over though, I promise. I don't want to get your hopes up, but one day I'm positive your mother will pull through." Emma winked and smiled. It was obvious that the expression was meant to be comforting, but it fell short. Still, her eyes were kind, and the fingers on her shoulder were gentle. "Call it a good feeling."

That tight smile ended Wendy's inner debate. "That's good at least. Hey, look, this is going to sound strange, but you're so *warm*. Are you feeling okay?"

"Am I?" Emma pressed her wrist to her forehead. "I guess I am. Must be picking something up; I'd better stop by the nurse's station and grab an Advil." She laughed. "Word to the wise, Wendy, don't go into medicine unless you've got the constitution of a bull. Being around ill people will knock you out every time." The pager at her hip beeped and Emma set the clipboard back in the plastic holder beside the door. "I've got to get that. It was very nice meeting you, Wendy."

"You too," Wendy said.

Once Dr. Henley was well away, Eddie patted the seat beside the bed. "Jon can wait a little longer. Come, chill for a few."

"I'm so tired," Wendy admitted. "I'm just not sleeping right, Eds." She settled onto the seat again and stared at her mother's face.

"You know, to be honest, I don't think it matters how long I scour the city or how many . . . how many souls I reap along the way. I don't think I'm ever going to find her."

In the corner, Lauren had finally quieted. The bad news had been a blow; she sat with her back against the wall and her hair dangling into her lap, forearms resting on her knees. Wendy's heart went out to her but the translucency of her soul spoke volumes—Lauren wouldn't need help crossing over. "I just wish I knew why Mom's different than the others." She sniffed and scrubbed her cheeks aggressively. "DAMN! I mean, this sucks. This just sucks. Mom knows this stuff backwards and forwards, Eddie. I'm still just in training. I can't. I can't. I can't do all this by myself anymore, you know? I'm only reaping the ones who get in my way and I'm still struggling to get by. I don't know how Mom did it; she must have been a frickin' superwoman. I need help." She hung her head. "I need help finding her soul before she ends up like *that*."

Eddie glanced into the empty corner Wendy was glaring at and shrugged, uncomfortable. Their talk that morning had left both of them a little raw but Wendy was opening up, something she hadn't done since her mother's accident. He reached over and took her hand in his, saying nothing, rubbing her knuckles with his thumb. It seemed like the best course of action.

"You're a good friend, Eds," she sighed, and slumped against the chair, leaning so her forehead rested against his shoulder. "The best friend a girl could have."

Eddie tensed and then sighed, relaxing. "Thanks, Wendy," he murmured, pressing a chaste kiss to her temple and bundling her close. "I'm glad to hear that."

It was their habit, after school, to go to the Dew Drop Diner for dinner and wait for Chel to get off from cheerleading practice. The trip up to UCSF hadn't taken that long but the diner was packed by the time they arrived. The smells of hot coffee, sizzling bacon, and crisp seasoned fries were rich around them as Eddie slid into their regular booth, hogging up an entire side. Wendy nudged Jon's bulk over and tried not to notice as Eddie gleefully ogled a couple three booths behind them.

"I thought you were taking time off?" she asked archly. "First the doc and now this?"

He dismissed her question with an airy wave. "The doc was just eye-candy and besides, I'm sure she's, like, twenty-two. Way too old for me. No, no, those two are the true shame. It must be a sin for people that hot to be together," Eddie mourned, sinking down. "Then I can't date either one."

"Think of the babies though," Wendy said, sneaking a peek. The boy was feeding his girlfriend ice cream, following it with a steamy kiss that reminded her uncomfortably of that morning in Eddie's car. "Genes like those practically guarantee moviestar quality. Aw, first love."

Jon glanced over his shoulder and snorted. "First love? Uh, no. They're in my class. She's not his girlfriend. That's Mike Anderson, right? His girlfriend's Sue Larson, on the—"

"Cheerleading squad with Chel," Wendy remembered, flopping back in her seat. "Which is practicing as we speak. Huh. Wow."

"Juicy," Eddie agreed, wagging his eyebrows. "I'm clearly behind on my gossip."

"You three are later than usual. Two cokes, one no ice, and a water?" their server asked as she approached their table. Lucy had been waitressing there since Wendy's mother had started bringing her for Sunday breakfasts when she was small. By now Lucy knew their order by heart and kept her pad tucked in the apron slung low around her hips. Smiling, Wendy shook her head. "Coke for me too, Lucy. I'm feeling festive."

Tapping the table twice to show she'd understood, Lucy spun on her heel to fetch their drinks. They never ordered dinner until Chel arrived, but homecoming was just around the corner, and her practice stretched longer every night. Wendy didn't mind. It was the one time of day she could let go and force herself to relax. Chel would join them soon, but in the meantime it was just the three of them and the busy restaurant, each lost in their own thoughts.

Eddie made space for their backpacks on his side of the booth, pulled out his reading assignment—*The Stranger* by Camus—and dived in. Jon, following his example, began puzzling over his Spanish homework, leaving Wendy alone without something urgent to do. Wendy thought about starting her homework, but after her long day she didn't feel like it. Lucy brought their drinks and two baskets brimming with fries. One sat before Jon, the other was for Eddie and Wendy to share. Jon absently began devouring his fries by the fistful.

Wendy sighed and tried not to think about their afternoon visit to UCSF or the lonely soul in her mother's room. Every room in the Neuro-ICU had a soul like Lauren's—souls trapped near their bodies by the last minutes of their lives, hovering somewhere between life and death. Until their connection to their bodies snapped, they weren't alive and weren't dead; hovering spirits waiting for the moment they either woke up . . . or died.

As much as it killed her to admit it, until they were dead Wendy could do nothing for them. They were beyond her reach. Still, despite that terrible limbo, it would have been a relief to see her mother's soul there among the others, even if her body grew weaker by the day. It would be proof that some part of her still existed.

But her soul, unlike every other soul Wendy had seen in such a state, was gone. Her mother's soul was missing and Wendy couldn't rest until she'd found it.

When night fell she'd go out on patrol, taking Caltrain closer and closer to the city, walking the streets every night until she was certain each section was empty, that her mother's lost and wandering spirit hadn't somehow taken up residence there.

Until sunset, though, Wendy could take a breather. She thought of her patrol the night before and the picture on her notebook. She thought of the kiss she'd shared that morning, how she'd pushed Eddie away. It had hurt at the time, but after all his over-the-top ogling and staring this afternoon, Wendy knew she'd done the right thing.

Maybe Eddie was right. Maybe she should've called the cops for that guy in the woods. It wasn't like she'd be the first kid to jump the fence; she couldn't get in too much trouble for it, right? But old lessons stuck and Wendy's mother had rules about encounters like the one she'd had.

Always cover your back. Her mother's words had been pounded into Wendy so often over the years that it was as if Mary was in the room with her, whispering them in her ear. When it came to reaping, her mom was all business, all the time. Especially in the early days, after Wendy had woken to the Light.

Her mother had waited until they were in the car to begin. "You and Eddie didn't come downstairs. I thought we told you to fetch him, Winifred."

"I tried, Mom, but he didn't want to." Wendy pushed back in the seat and scrubbed her palms across her cheeks. She wanted to explain further but she knew her mother's tone when she called Wendy by her full name like that; Wendy didn't want to push her luck and end up grounded.

"Bereavement rituals are important for the living and the dead." The car slid backwards into the street, engine purring. Pulling to the end of the street, her mother clipped the end of each word; her knuckles were white on the steering wheel. "Some dead stick around only for the funerals, Wendy. They won't pass into the Light on their own if they think the rituals weren't followed just so."

The guilt was sour in her mouth. "Was Mr. Barry angry at me?"

Her mother sighed. "Unless you spotted him, he wasn't there,

Wendy. But my point is that he could have been. They frequently are." She looked left, then right. "We're not going home right away. I can see now that I need to start your lessons sooner rather than later."

"But Dad—"

"Can wait. He's used to it." Her mother punched the gas and the station wagon darted forward into traffic. They drove up to the high school and parked in the principal's spot. The engine was barely off before her mother was out of the car and on the move, Wendy scrabbling to unbuckle her belt and follow. "Mom! Mom, wait!"

Tearing her skirt in thorny bushes, Wendy pushed on after her mother, trying to put her feet where her mother did, trying to slide through the gaps as neatly as her mother did. Her legs weren't as long, though; nor was she tall enough to push back the branches her mother could. When she finally caught up with her mother she was scratched from head to toe, her hair tangled and sweaty, her cheek cut and stinging from a stray branch. "Mom," she panted. "Why didn't you slow down? I'm bleeding."

"Wendy, darling, in our line of work you just have to get used to it," her mother said, but her words were gentle. She wasn't looking at her daughter, but instead staring intently into a backyard butting up against the edge of the woods. The chain link back here was only hip-high on Wendy, easy to jump if she needed to. A small girl, no more than three or four, was swinging on the backyard swing set. She wasn't pumping her legs; strong hands pushed her higher and higher. She squealed happily. "Higher Grandma! Higher!"

"But . . . she's dead. Right?" Wendy blinked and rubbed her eyes, thinking that perhaps the rapidly expanding twilight was playing tricks with her. "How can she do that? And can the kid see her? She can, can't she?"

Her mother sighed. "I don't have all the answers, Wendy-girl. But this much I do know . . . she died last week. I was here, picking up the body, but I couldn't do anything then." She pushed aside a branch and glanced around the yard. "Other than the two of them it looks all clear, but I'm not willing to risk it. It would look very strange, me showing up here like this. So you get to do it instead. Who's going to suspect a little girl?"

"Do it?"

"Send her into the Light."

"But, Mom, I don't know how," Wendy protested. "All I can do is see them!"

"You'll figure it out." She laid a hand on Wendy's shoulder. "But remember, Wendy-girl. Cover your back. I had to."

"What do you mean, you had—ow!" Wendy stumbled into the yard, her mother's shove pushing her far enough past the bushes that she had nowhere to hide. The girl's swing slowed; both the spirit and the little girl had spotted her immediately.

"Hi!" the little girl chirruped, jumping off the swing at the low point, stumbling when she hit the ground but catching her balance quick enough. "Do you want to swing?"

"Lacey, no," the old lady hissed. "Stranger danger! You don't know her name!"

"I'm Wendy," Wendy said quickly. She swiped her hand against her cheek, feeling the hot smear of her blood against her palm. "But your grandma's right, I don't want to swing."

"You . . . you can hear me?" The old woman hurried forward and grabbed Wendy by the shoulders. "You have to—ouch, girl! You're hot!"

"I am?" Wendy put her wrist against her forehead. She didn't feel any different to herself, not like she was running a temperature. Wendy shrugged. "Sorry? I can't control it."

"No matter. You have to go. You can't stay here."

"Why not?" Wendy knelt by the younger girl. "Lacey? Maybe you should go inside, okay? It's getting awfully dark and cold. You should go wash up."

"No!" The ghost waved her arms widely but Lacey, yawning,

toddled off toward the patio door. "Lacey Marie, you come back here! Lacey!" She turned on Wendy and wagged a finger in her face. "Young lady, I know you think you're doing the right thing, but you're an idiot."

"I just . . . I didn't want her to see this."

"See what?"

"See me . . . see me sending you into the Light." Wendy winced.

"Sending me into the Light? Child, I turned my back on that nonsense a week ago. You think I'm going to just let you shove me into it now? Especially when there's no sane person around to keep an eye on my granddaughter? Absolutely not."

"But . . . don't you want to go to heaven? Or whatever?"

She laughed mirthlessly. "You don't have the slightest idea what you're doing, do you? Look, young lady, I didn't believe in a god when I was alive, I'm hardly about to start believing in him now. Now if you'll excuse me—"

"Hey!" Wendy snapped, inexplicably angry with the stubborn old ghost who should've had the sense to go into the Light when it'd been offered the first time. If it hadn't been for her, Wendy would be home right now, safe in her warm bed, thinking good thoughts about the kiss with Eddie, not bloody and shivering at the edge of the woods while her mother skulked somewhere in the shadows and watched her argue with a ghost. "My name is Wendy! You wouldn't want me to start calling you 'old fart,' would you? And . . . and . . . okay, you don't have a choice. Right? If you need to go into the Light, you just go, okay? Or else you're stuck. The Light doesn't stick around forever, you know."

Wendy crossed her arms over her chest and scowled. She was making a huge mess of this, she could tell. Strangely, standing there with the anger bubbling was sending an odd feeling coursing through her body; an acid-tummy sort of feeling, but stronger, hotter. It was as if she could suddenly feel the heat the old woman had been complaining about. She felt unexpectedly flush and warm, her eyes drying in their sockets as if she were baking with fever. The ghost shimmered before her; Wendy blinked rapidly to keep her centered in her sight.

Her tone changed, softened. "Please . . . Wendy. I don't know what you are, but please, please, don't do this. Please. I need to stay."

"I can't," Wendy whispered, marveling at the bizarre heat pooling in her gut, straining to expand. Controlling the heat was incredibly difficult; Wendy felt her tongue begin to dry, making her next words clumsy and hard to say. "I don't know why but I can't stop." Wendy bent double, the heat throbbing out through her chest and belly now, insistent and fierce. "I'm really sorry."

"Then do me a favor," she said urgently. "You have to get Lacey out of here." The ghost pointed to the house. "I was the last blood relative Lacey has left. Her stepfather isn't a very nice man, he . . ." she stopped short, blushing. "How old are you?"

"Old enough," Wendy snapped, uncomfortably aware of the direction the conversation was turning. Her palms felt like they were blistering. She dropped to her hands and knees on the cold, muddy ground, feeling the earth beneath her knees simultaneously squelch and bake under her heat. It was as if the backyard were shining through some dark prism—one moment, the world was light and sweet, the backyard small but well-kept, and the next it was decaying in front of her face, the neat late-season roses lushly over-grown and rotting on the bush.

"The Never," Wendy whispered. Her mother had described the world of the dead to her, but this was the first time she'd seen it for herself. Wendy held up one hand, marveling at the tiny buds of Light beginning to illuminate the tip of each finger. "You want me to call the police."

"Please."

"Okay. Done," Wendy whispered and the Light unfurled within.

When she opened her eyes again, the old woman was gone and a pair of scuffed up boots were in front of her at eye-level.

"Kid, I'm giving you thirty seconds to get off my property," slurred the man standing over her. He had a beer in one hand and a baseball bat in the other. "And if you come around here jumping my fence any more, I'm calling the cops, you hear me?"

"Yes sir," Wendy murmured, pushing off the ground and staggering towards the woods.

"Hey! Idiot!" The man grabbed Wendy by the shoulder and spun her sharply around. "You can't walk through those woods. Not at night. Go by the street." He shoved her toward the side gate and Wendy, embarrassed, let him push her onto the sidewalk.

It took her an hour to find her way back through the winding neighborhood to the high school. "It's done," she said, sliding in the passenger seat.

"What did she make you promise?" Her mother wiped a hand across her mouth and Wendy realized that she'd been drinking.

"To call the police on the little girl's stepdad." Wendy reached for her mother's cell.

"Oh, hell no." Her mother snatched the phone out of reach.

"But, Mom, I promised."

"What did I say, Wendy? I said 'cover your back,' didn't I? Or did I imagine that?"

"Yeah, but—"

"NO BUTS, WINIFRED!" Her mother pounded the steering wheel. "We don't owe that family anything, you understand me? How would you explain yourself to the cops, huh? 'A ghost told me to call?' No. Absolutely not. That's not how we work."

"But—"

"Wendy, you listen to me." Her mother swiveled in her seat and grabbed Wendy by the face, squeezing her cheeks painfully. "You listen to me and you listen good. Okay? Are you listening? What we do? What we do is the ultimate sacrifice for these people. Those ribbons of light that come out of your fingers, out of your chest? Every one of those is a second of your own life. You are *giving up your life to help them*, to send them on. You are wrapping up a ticket home with your own life for these people. So if even one of them asks for anything more, you tell them *no*. Do you understand me? You tell them NO, Wendy."

"I can't," she cried. "I can't not help that little girl."

When her mother's slap cracked across her cheek, Wendy sank against the passenger side door and wept.

"You gave that woman a gift tonight, so that's my gift to you in return. That's your reward," her mother breathed, looming over her. "You're a Reaper now. Neither one of us wanted it like this, but what's done is done. It took the death of your best friend's father to make you this way. I love you, but the coddling is officially over!"

"Momma—"

"No. No. I'm done arguing. You aren't putting our family and everything I've worked for in danger by reporting that man. I don't care what the ghost said. I can't risk my cover for some stranger's kid. I'm sorry, I really honestly am, Wendy, but I can't."

"Then I don't want to be a Reaper," Wendy whispered, wiping her tears away. "I quit."

Her mother snorted. "Good luck. You think I didn't try that, too? You can't quit being a Reaper. It's who you are now. The best thing for you to do is learn how to do it right, how to cover your back in the living world, and how to keep yourself safe. You will be trained as my grandmother trained me, the same as her grandmother trained her. You will reap when I say to reap and you will do it over and over again until I've seen that you've done it right. As of this moment you're an adult; it's time to start acting like it."

Wendy thought she was heartless. They didn't speak on the way home and her mother said nothing when Wendy pounded up the stairs to her room, slamming the door behind. But later that night, while her mother was on her cell talking to Nana, the kitchen phone rang. Wendy answered; it was her mother's boss.

"Winifred, hi honey, is your mom there?"

"No, she's on the other line. Do I need to go grab her? Is she on call?"

"No, honey, nothing like that. I don't have time to talk right now anyway. You just tell her that I got her message and I pulled some strings. The SFPD already sent a unit out to fetch . . . well, they got someone out of a bad situation. That's all you need to know to let her know, that it's all been taken care of, okay? That's all, and you write it down if you need to. Quote: 'It's all been taken care of.' Unquote. I'll talk to her next week. G'night, honey."

Wendy wrote the message down, heart in her throat. She never brought it up again, but the next time her mother wanted to go reaping, Wendy went without comment and listened carefully to every instruction she was given. She owed her that much.

Pulling away from the memories before she started tearing up, Wendy grabbed her soda and gulped it down. The carbonation burned enough to clear her mind and she fought back a loud belch, pressing her hand flush against her lips and letting out a series of tiny burps instead. Setting down the glass, Wendy let her eyes wander around the restaurant, seeking anything to take her mind from her mother, her duty, her life.

CHAPTER EIGHT

L ate afternoon found Piotr hesitating in the bushes outside the Dew Drop Diner. The living heat within was immense, baking through the brick as the dinner rush built. Inside, waitresses twisted through the crowd with beautiful confidence, serving coffee and ringing up orders with an efficiency he envied. The bustle of life was intoxicating . . . but painful.

Still, there was nothing to do but get the job done. This was the last place Dunn had been seen. *Dora, Specs, Tubs*, he thought to himself, drawing courage from the thought of them taken like this, from a place they felt safe and comfortable. He had to find a clue, any clue, to help Dunn, and he had to do it now! There was no room for fear here.

Taking a deep breath, Piotr centered his will and stepped through the wall. When he entered the diner, Piotr was expecting a mess—Walkers in feed were like rabid wolves; if Dunn had been devoured, the walls would be dripping with his essence—but everything was clean.

"What the—" he wondered aloud and dropped to his knees. "What happened here?"

Since her thoughts had been so recently centered on Piotr, Wendy was certain Piotr's appearance was her imagination. She rubbed her eyes brusquely, sure he would vanish, but he was real. Or as real as a ghost could be, anyway. Her fingers itched to open her backpack, dive into the contents, and pull out her binder to compare her sketch from last night to the slim ghost now crawling across the restaurant, his hand gripping a table for balance.

Wendy's memories of him didn't do Piotr justice. She'd thought that the fall of hair, the dark eyes, even the scar that twisted from temple to neck half-hidden by his hair had been branded into her memory, but those pale images came up short of what he really was. Had any spirit she'd ever seen glowed so bright, so fiercely? Barely transparent, Piotr looked almost real, crouched on the linoleum. He looked alive.

Piotr, she said to herself. *Piotr*.

He was searching for something. Every few feet he leaned forward, peered underneath the booths, and then continued on; his counter-clockwise circuit of the diner would bring Piotr to Wendy's booth within moments. Eddie would understand if she did her thing, of course, but Jon wouldn't and neither would the other customers. The diner was packed, so there was no way to discretely step into the Never to talk to Piotr face to face on his own turf.

Torn, Wendy hesitated, not sure what to do.

While the heat of living bodies was immense, Piotr found it bearable if he kept his mind clear and concentrated on the task at hand. Being dead was all about willpower; you had to have the will to keep yourself coherent. Otherwise, eventually, you'd fade away until you became a Shade, a memory of a soul. It was a terrible, horrible way to go—deaf and dumb to everything, even the Never, drawn back to the place of your death and trapped there until you were a wisp, eventually extinguished.

Dunn wouldn't have become a Shade, Piotr reminded himself as he peered under a table. He had died too young, too strong. The Lost had too much willpower, too much energy, too much life left in them when they died. Dying a brutal death turned the Lost into batteries, going on and on and on without end, rudderless in a world that quickly forgot their short time on it. It made them a target for Walkers.

Cannibalism. Eating a young soul. It was the only way for an adult ghost to permanently stave off the centuries and the constant need to be vigilant and alert, to will themselves to remain whole. To continue to exist. Of course, there was a price: every Lost destroyed ate at the ties a soul kept to the Never until the cord was gone, until the salvation of the Light was impossible.

Eventually the Walkers became monsters, shadows creeping at the edge of the abyss, silver cords obliterated; mere shells of their former selves. Some of the Walkers deemed their damnation a fair trade for the certainty of existence. The Light was a terrifying mystery. The Never was just a darker sort of life.

For Piotr, there'd never been a question of what to do. The choice had always been simple. Seek out the Lost. Keep them safe. Repeat.

Protecting the Lost gave him the will to keep going on, as it did for all the other Riders. Over the years Piotr had lost a few of the Lost—some to the hunger of the Walkers and a couple who preferred other Riders like Elle or James—but most of his Lost eventually found peace on their own.

It took time, forgetting your own death and moving on, but when the Light came, Piotr was always there to help his Lost enter. It could take decades but, over time, the Light almost always came for the Lost Piotr protected. Only Dora had been with him so long he'd forgotten when he'd picked her up. He knew that, given enough time and attention, she too would one day enter the Light.

Secretly Piotr hoped that this was what had happened to Dunn.

It wasn't that Piotr didn't trust Lily's word—she was intelligent and her instincts rarely led her astray—but if he could find proof that Dunn had simply stepped into the Light, that the Walkers hadn't dared a restaurant full of living, searing human souls, then Piotr would rest easier.

It was a best-case scenario, but he was desperate for good news.

Now, kneeling on the floor of a diner stuffed with living people, their burning hot legs scissoring through him, clipping his hip, his thigh, his shoulder, Piotr moved as quickly as he could among waitresses who poured coffee, chatted, and made change. On hands and knees he crawled, seeking the charred circle that would indicate the presence of the corridor of Light, searching for proof that something might still be going their way.

So engrossed in his task, Piotr didn't pay attention to the living in the booths. Normally the living felt a chill when the dead were near, a pocket of cold air most noticed only as they were passing through. Most of the dead had the good sense to be still when the living were near—humans tended to pass quickly by, repulsed by the icy cold—so there was less chance of injury for the dead.

Searching closely for clues, Piotr left a wake of shivering humans behind him. Several called for their waitresses, complaining about the vents. More reached for jackets or sweaters, or cuddled against their booth-mates, seeking body warmth.

It wasn't until he was resting his hand on the table on the window side of the room that he noticed the girl. Unlike the others, no gooseflesh popped up on her skin at his proximity; she did not shiver or pull away. Piotr would have dismissed this—perhaps she was used to cold—except for the rigid way she held her body, stiff and still but breathing elevated, rapid. He could feel her heat thrumming, more intense than the others, a warmth like banked coals in a pocket nimbus of heat.

Piotr paused, looking her expression over closely. The girl tensed and her eyelids swept down, the thick concealing lashes feathered across her cheekbones, but underneath Piotr could spot the gleam of her eyes. Testing a theory, Piotr shifted his weight and her gaze, nearly concealed by her eyelashes but not entirely, followed his movement. Piotr frowned, shifted again, and again her eyes tracked him.

"You can see me," he said, wonder drying the saliva in his mouth, leaving his tongue thick and furry with excitement. A tingle began in his gut; working outward and leaving the edges of his body alight with a fierce pins-and-needles sensation. "You can see me."

The accusation was quiet, no more than a whisper, but the girl's breath hitched and she flushed; licking her lips, she turned away and glanced around the restaurant as if searching for a savior. There was no one.

"I have to get up. Excuse me," she told her two boothmates and rose, brushing by Piotr but not touching him, moving swiftly for the door. Piotr followed, heart hammering in his chest, and melted through the wall in time to spot her turning the corner and hurrying through the parking lot, chin tucked to chest and looking neither right nor left.

The girl was athletic, he noticed, lithe and well-muscled but small in stature, padded in all the right places. Her hair, brilliantly red at the roots and faded black at the tips, had been allowed to grow wild, tumbling down her back in a riot of curls. The clothing she wore wasn't immodest exactly, Elle often wore much less, but the cut of it and the way it clung left little to the imagination, granting the girl a fluid mobility Elle would certainly admire. Oddly enough, she was pierced and tattooed, intricate tribal designs worked around her wrists and collarbone in patterns that hurt Piotr's eyes when he looked at them too long.

Only her face, rounded like a child's, with large brown eyes and full lips, looked innocent. The rest of her whispered *danger*. But a living girl had seen him, had recognized him for what he was, and that was a siren call Piotr was unwilling to resist.

The girl approached a blue car, some new model Piotr didn't recognize, and dug through her pockets. Then, as if it were the most natural thing in the world, she opened a cell phone and pressed it to her ear.

"Hello?" she said aloud, glancing left and right at the empty parking lot. She settled on the back of the car, her weight barely dipping the trunk down. "Yes," she said, tilting her head towards the main road, studiously not looking at Piotr. "I can see you."

Confused, Piotr moved to stand in front of her so she would not be able to look away. "Are you insane? What are you doing?"

"Well," she said, meeting his eyes at last but still pressing the phone to her ear, "I've found that I look less crazy this way. You know, talking to myself."

"I see," he said, and he really did. He'd heard of people like her, the soothsayers and fortune tellers who actually had a touch of the Sight in their blood, Seers that a soul could turn to for aid if they were willing to pay a price. In years past, many of those women had been burned as witches. Some, at their death, came to live in the Never, promising rich rewards to the unwary and unwise. This Seer was young, though, and soft around the eyes. Perhaps this was all new to her, or perhaps it had never occurred to her to charge for her care. Most Seers he'd known wouldn't even talk to a spirit unless there was something in it for them; she seemed to be an exception.

"I am Piotr," he began, unsure what else to say. He tingled from head to toe now, heart hammering against his ribs, waves of jumbled emotion rocking him with unbelievable force. He cleared his throat. "And you?"

"Wendy," she replied shortly, meeting his gaze and giving him a long searching look. Piotr, unsure as to why she was staring at him so hard, broke the contact after a few moments. Wendy's expression was painfully intense; he felt as if he'd failed some vital test. "It's short for Winifred?"

When he looked back he realized that her lips had thinned into a straight, taut line. She wet them several times, as if tasting her next words. Long moments passed before she sighed, shook her head, and laughed brusquely.

"You don't recognize me." Wendy rubbed the side of her hand against her forehead, leaving a pink mark behind. "I guess I shouldn't be so surprised. I'm just me, right? Just Wendy."

Startled, Piotr stepped back, taking her in again, carefully this time. Wendy stared at him in turn, eyes tracing his face with something like wonder. He realized that she truly did know him in some way, though she was a mystery in return.

"*Net*, I'm sorry." Nervous now, taken aback, he clasped his hands and rocked back and forth on his heels, a child taken to task for an unremembered crime. Elle's taunts came back to him: *that old memory of yours just ain't what it used to be.* Annoyed, Piotr shoved the mocking voice away. "Should I?"

"Curly," she replied and laughed again. The bitterness was gone now and the warmth had returned to her smile. Wendy rolled her eyes. "You called me Curly."

The nickname was familiar but it took Piotr several seconds of actively casting back, thinking hard, before the image of the girl came. Blood-spattered and smoke-dusted, she'd been a tiny thing, eyes dilated in shock from a terrible crash and skin greenish-pale as curdled cream. It had been a car wreck, one dead, and the song of the Light fading away in the distance when he'd rode on the scene.

"*Da*, now I remember you," he said, marveling. "The highway . . . there was bad weather on your side . . . the living side, yes?" Without thought his hand stretched forward as if to touch her but he truncated the movement, embarrassed to show wonder at the reunion.

"Got it in one." The girl, Curly—no, Wendy—kicked her chunky boots and tilted her head back, staring up at the late afternoon clouds as if willing them to drift down and envelop her, stealing her away. "I thought I was seeing things, but you said I wasn't." She straightened and drew one knee up to her chest, resting her chin upon it. "In case you didn't remember."

"*Net*, I remember," he said again, at a loss for what to say, and uncomfortable.

Her smile was swift, bittersweet. "Yeah, you seem to, now." There was a clicking noise, faint but precise, and Piotr realized that Wendy had a metal rod through her tongue that she tapped thoughtfully against her teeth. He stared at it, fascinated. Why would someone do that to themselves? It boggled the mind.

"So, Piotr," she said at last, "what were you doing in there? Don't the dead usually avoid the living? Or am I just an exception for you?" Her chuckle was light and sweet.

Piotr's heart lurched and he felt like a fool, imagining what it would be like to get real, honest laughter out of this girl. Seers were by their very nature dour people. If time and contact with ghosts hadn't soured her against the dead yet, it would. It always did.

Still, Piotr decided, there would be no harm in telling her. Wendy was, after all, able to see his kind and might, if fate was kind, have been a witness to whatever happened to Dunn.

"Looking for clues," Piotr began, choosing his words carefully. He liked this girl and he didn't want to upset her unduly, but the situation merited a need for a certain amount of detail.

In the end Piotr outlined the bare bones of the situation, leaving out the horror that was the Lightbringer and the nightmare that was his recent encounter with the White Lady, stating only the rumors that the White Lady was ultimately behind the unrest among the dead and the recent rash of kidnappings. He told her about Dunn. Wendy listened in attentive silence, nodding her head at the right moments and clicking the bar against her teeth at others.

"So what you're telling me is that the Walkers," she said the word far easier than Piotr had anticipated. It slipped easily between her lips, as if she had practice, "are kidnapping the souls of little kids all over town?"

"We call the children 'the Lost,' but *da*, this is correct. Before . . . before, the Walkers always devoured the Lost," Piotr confirmed. "As soon as they got claws on them. But now . . ." he left the sentence unfinished.

"They're acting weird, traveling in packs. Grabbing instead of chowing down." Wendy switched the phone to her other ear. A car pulled into the space beside them and Wendy nodded to herself, muttering, "Uh huh, okay, I get it," until the passengers had turned the corner to the diner's entryway.

"*Da*! You understand, but . . . you've . . . had experiences with them?" Piotr knew he shouldn't be surprised at this, but the dichotomy of the thin, shocked girl huddled by the highway and this young, powerful woman was still fresh and startling to him. He supposed he would have to adjust.

"I've met the Lost before. Not often, but every now and then. Once I even spotted a Walker, uh . . . feeding." Wendy paled and she wrapped her free arm around her stomach, hunching over. "It was . . . it was horrible," she said. Piotr ached for her but didn't know how to comfort the living over the obliteration of the dead. "Nasty."

"So you know. You have seen."

"Well, yeah. I've been spotting Walkers wander all over for weeks, but I didn't realize it was this big a deal. And you think they're taking their marching orders from this White Lady chick? But why? Aren't they the ultimate evil on your side of the line? They've clearly got you and yours on the run."

"The White Lady can give them something no one else can," Piotr admitted. "Flesh. Before now, the Walkers would look out only for themselves. Then the White Lady came. Somehow, with her touch, she can reverse their deathrot. It was a mark of their darkness, the rot. It showed us that they fed on the young. To so casually reverse the marks of such blasphemy . . . she's *zloj* . . . evil."

"Gee, ya think?" Wendy sighed, rubbed a knuckle against the bridge of her nose, and tilted her head back, scowling up at the endless expanse of sky. "Great. Just what I need right now. An army of undead cannibals on the warpath."

Piotr searched for a tactful way to express his surprise at her reaction. "Why would this concern you? You are alive. The worries of the dead, surely they are nothing to you?"

"You'd be surprised," she replied shortly. "The concerns of the dead are sort of a big thing to me right now." Her expression softened. "In more ways than one, apparently. Count me in."

"You wish to help me?" Piotr was flabbergasted. "But why?"

Rubbing her eyes with the back of her hand, Wendy shrugged, flushing. "Couple of reasons, I guess. One, I don't care if they're alive or dead, no one should be messing with kids. Secondly, you were the first ghost I ever laid eyes on, so I sort of feel like I owe you. You know, for keeping me company when I had no clue what was going on. And finally, well, I've got my own selfish reasons, okay? I scratch your back, and vice the versa. I help you out, maybe you'll think about helping me with a problem I've got going on."

"It is a deal," Piotr said, marveling at his luck. A Seer could go places a regular spirit like himself could not; she was living, after all. "What aid may I offer, Wendy? How can I help?"

"You want to know now?"

"It is as good a time as any, *da*? Is it a question? Perhaps I have the answer already."

"I . . ." Wendy swallowed thickly. "I was wondering if you'd heard about a ghost wandering around town."

Piotr raised an eyebrow and dared a smile. "I see many ghosts. It is my luck."

"No, I mean . . . a specific ghost." Wendy chewed her lower lip and suddenly brightened. "Wait! I have a picture, here." She pulled the phone away from her face and pressed a few buttons in rapid succession. Piotr peered over her shoulder as she pulled up a picture of a slim red-haired woman with dark, kind eyes and a tired smile. Like Wendy, she sported a ring of intricate tattoos around her collarbone.

"This woman, she looks something like you," Piotr said. "A sister?"

"My mother."

"Ah," Piotr sighed. "She has recently died and you wish to know if she's still in the Never, *da*? Or if she's moved on into the Light?"

Wendy gaped. "You can find out if a spirit's gone into the Light? Seriously?"

He laughed. "Of course! You think the Light leaves no mark in our world? If you find a place where the Light has been, it is special, sacred space until the marks of the Light fade. Some even worship there, hoping the Light will return."

"Really? Why?"

"To find your Light is a great blessing in the Never." Piotr laid a hand against his heart. "It is an end to pain and suffering. Many think it is to go home again. For one at the end of their rope, essence worn thin . . . anything is better than fading away, *da*? And who knows? The Light might return to that spot, taking any other ready souls with it."

"Is that really what you think?"

Piotr shrugged. "Me? I do not know much about it. It is peaceful, I think, going when you are ready. The Light comes for them and my Lost, when they go, they always smile. I like that."

"That's nice," Wendy said. "I've never seen a ghost enter the Light on their own."

"Maybe one day you will, *da*?" Piotr leaned over her shoulder again and frowned at the picture on her cell phone. "But I do not think I have seen this woman, your mother, Wendy. *Yzveenee*, my apologies. I can keep a lookout, though. If you wish."

"I do," Wendy said, closing her cell. "I really do."

"Then I shall help you," Piotr promised. "You have my word. But . . ." He hesitated.

"But?" Wendy prompted.

"It is nothing." Piotr waved a hand. "My friend Lily says I am like an old woman. I worry too much."

His friend Lily? Wendy was startled by the jolt she felt at the mention of the name. After all, it wasn't as if Piotr existed only in the vacuum of her memories. Of course he'd have friends among the dead. "If you've got a 'but,' I want to hear about it," she said. Then winced. "I mean, what's got you worried, Piotr?"

"How long has it been?" Piotr asked. "Since your mother—"

"She had her accident in February," Wendy interrupted. She didn't know why, but she didn't feel comfortable admitting to Piotr that her mother wasn't dead yet. Perhaps because every other comatose soul had the good sense to remain tethered to their body and her mother . . . well, hadn't. "So it's been about seven months."

Peter's expression was grave. "That is long enough for a soul to find the Light on their own, Wendy. Or, if she didn't have the willpower to stay . . . she could have faded, become a Shade, is what I'm trying to say. You have met a Shade before in your wanderings, *da*?"

No shit, Sherlock, Wendy thought. After her first reap but before her mother's accident, Shades had been all Wendy had been allowed to reap. The lost and lonely souls had forgotten themselves so far that they wouldn't have recognized their Light if it'd burst into being right in front of them. Shades were their bread-and-butter, the meat of her duty as a Reaper. They were the souls she had to hunt down and the most important ones to send on. Otherwise they'd continue to fade, to pale, to vanish . . . into nothing. Souls lost and gone.

"Yeah," she said, disturbed by the realization that when she'd sworn off reaping last spring that she'd also left a city full of Shades to their own devices. How many helpless souls had been suffering through the long and drowsy summer while she'd searched only for her mother? "I've met a couple."

"I'm borrowing trouble," Piotr soothed. "This is unlikely. Seven months is not long. We will find her if she can be found. My word on it."

"Thank you," Wendy said. "I appreciate it."

"It is nothing," he swore and bowed slightly, clicking his heels together. "Now then, I must take my leave of you."

"What? Why?"

Piotr gestured to the diner. "I have work yet to do. Dunn was taken here."

Wendy straightened, her color returning. Her weary concern was replaced by a steely-eyed determination Piotr found fascinating. "Here? In the diner? But being so close to the living hurts you, right? Yet you wanna go back in and look for the kid?"

"*Da*." Piotr said. "I had hoped he had just gone into the Light, but there is no scorching in the Never. There is no essence, either." He saw her confusion and explained, "Essence is like flesh and blood to the living. It is a mystery." He sighed. "I had hoped, before . . . you weren't in the diner when he was taken? A few days ago, around noon?"

Sympathetic, Wendy shook her head. "No, I'm sorry. The food's awesome and I'd live here if I could, but that whole school thing gets in the way." Brightening, she added, "But maybe your first guess was right? Maybe the kid just moved on into the Light? You didn't get a chance to check under all the booths, after all. I got in your way."

"It is possible, but unlikely."

Kicking at the dirt, Piotr examined the Never terrain around him with a critical eye. The fire had scoured away the spiritual remains of the tenement building that had once stood on this ground, leaving only the solid diner in its place. He'd told Wendy the truth. There was no new residue here, he could see that now, no charred traces of Light that clung to walls or seats or doors.

Closer inspection proved that the boy hadn't passed into the Light. Lily was right. Dunn had been taken, most likely by the White Lady's Walkers.

"Going in there hurts you," Wendy said matter-of-factly, spying his troubled expression.

"*Da*."

"But you have to see if there's anything that'll point you in the right direction. A clue."

He nodded.

"Okay then." Determined to help, Wendy hopped from her place and strolled towards the diner. "Stay here."

"Wait . . . what?" Piotr hurried after, reaching for her shoulder. He drew back when he realized the folly of trying to grab her. Wendy was living; not only would his hand pass right through her, but he'd burn himself in the process. Speeding up his pace, he hurried to step in front of her, cutting her off. "I do not understand."

Amused, Wendy stopped walking and gestured to the building.

"Piotr, I can help you. It hurts you to be in there, right?" She waited for his nod. "Okay then, well, it doesn't hurt me at all, and I can see everything you see."

"You . . . can see the Never?" Stunned, Piotr stepped away from her and shook his head. He'd never heard of such a thing before, even from other Seers. Most could hear the dead, some could even make the dead out—dim shapes they'd describe to paying customers—but none that he'd known had ever admitted to seeing the landscape of the Never itself. It was mind-boggling to even contemplate. "Not just me, but my world?"

Wendy pointed across the street. "Remnants of a four story hotel layered over that Burger la Hut," she stated cheerily in a tour-guide falsetto, giggling every third word and bobbing her head left and right. "Next to the genuinely ghostly hotel, look south! In that sup-posedly empty lot is the remains of a fabulous fifties soda fountain with be-bop, soul hop, and rock and roll to soothe your soul! Don't worry kiddies, though the Big-Bopper-Drive-In has nearly faded away, the fifties will never die!"

Dropping the bubblehead act, Wendy jerked her thumb towards the diner she'd just been sitting in. "Not too long ago, there used to be an apartment building layered over that building, but the last of it faded away last May. I think it burned down, what, in the sixties?"

"*Da*," Piotr whispered, stunned. She was the most thorough Seer he'd ever met or even heard of. The strength of her power was stun-ning, and not a little frightening. "You have it."

"Let me help you," she urged. "Don't hurt yourself over this when I can do it for you."

This strange girl would be the undoing of him, Piotr mused silently, before nodding. She hurried away and he sank to the earth and closed his eyes. He had to bring her up to the others, he realized. Lily was wise; Lily was old. She would know what to do.

Because Piotr was at a loss.

CHAPTER NINE

Eddie was waiting for her when Wendy returned. She slid into the seat and said, "I needed some *personal* time." She flicked her gaze toward Jon, who had finished his fries and had started on Eddie's. Eddie, catching on, pursed his lips and nodded.

Casually, Wendy set her glass on the edge of the table. Then, just as casually, she elbowed it. The cup toppled off the table, hit the linoleum, and shattered, sending shards of glass, ice, and a splash of soda across the floor.

"Crap!" Wendy grabbed a handful of napkins and dropped to her knees, furtively glancing around the room. Most of the other customers were staring at her—a few clapped and whistled—but within seconds most had returned to their own conversations and meals.

"Oh honey!" Lucy exclaimed, dropping to her side bearing a towel and a dustpan. "Don't mess with that glass, Winni-girl, you'll cut yourself."

"I'm so sorry, Lucy," Wendy apologized, grabbing the towel from her. "I won't touch the glass, but let me get the Coke, okay?" Out of the corner of her eye, she spotted something faint and glowing under the booth next to her. Crawling to the empty booth, she mopped several pieces of ice back towards the pile Lucy was brushing up.

Beneath the table, half hidden by the table leg, was a ghostly Mets baseball cap. It was battered and ragged in several places—not just thin, the way ethereal objects got when their real-world counterparts had faded away, but covered in precise dime-size circles.

Wendy was reminded of the movie *Aliens* and the acid-holes left behind wherever the creature wandered.

Quickly, so no one would see, Wendy snatched the hat from under the table and backed out. Not looking where she was going, she suddenly hissed in pain. A piece of glass, about the size of her knuckle, was embedded in the meaty bulge beneath her thumb. "Ow."

"See what I mean?" Lucy reprimanded Wendy, kneeling beside her and taking her hand gingerly. "Oh poor thing. Let me see." She plucked the glass free and squeezed the wound to loosen any remaining particles. It hadn't gone in too deep; the cut bled only sluggishly.

"I've got it, Lucy," Eddie interjected, extracting a miniature first aid kit from the side pocket of his backpack. "She's always bumping into stuff."

"Well, at least go wash it in the ladies room," Lucy sighed, releasing Wendy. Half a dozen swipes later and the last of the mess was piled in the dustbin.

"Gimme that," Eddie ordered, ripping an alcohol pad packet open, and swabbing the cut. Jon, uneasy at the sight of blood, hunched over his homework, refusing to glance up. Eddie tsked. "That's not bad at all."

Wendy sat through his ministrations until he tried to bandage it. "A band-aid will just come off," she insisted, pulling her hand free. "It'll scab over. Thank you."

"But—"

"I think I need a breath of fresh air."

Now that the gore had been cleaned away, Jon was willing to rejoin the conversation. "Again? But you just got back."

"I'm tired and I just sliced my hand open," Wendy snapped. "Lay off."

Realizing that she was being too sharp with him, Wendy squeezed Jon's shoulder as she rose. "Sorry. Bitchy-me is gonna take a walk. I'm just super edgy for some reason, tonight. Call when Chel gets here." She shot Eddie a look—*I will explain later*—and he nodded, waving her off as he reached for Camus once more.

Piotr was waiting by the car. Wendy held the cap by the bill and passed it to him, conscious of the fact that even being in proximity to her must be unpleasant for him. Under normal circumstances, before her mother's accident, Wendy would have already dug deep inside and called upon her power to reap Piotr, to set him free.

But now? Since her mother's accident Wendy had sworn off reaping all ghosts, even the Shades, unless absolutely necessary. The accident had proven just how unprepared she was for the duties of a Reaper—reaping was too dangerous, impossible to control. But if someone deserved to be sent into the Light, wasn't it Piotr? He protected children, watched over them, kept them safe. He'd told her about the other Riders who were watching his own Lost. They were in good custody, weren't they? No one would miss him, and she knew it would be the right thing to do.

I think I really intend to do it, she mused. *I think I'm gonna reap Piotr and set him free.* But not yet. Piotr still had a job to do and Wendy, surprising herself, realized that she intended to help him do it.

When this is all done, she promised herself, *I'll release him. Protecting children. Waking me to my own abilities. If anyone deserves to be sent on to the afterlife, it's this guy.* Wendy ignored the increased thump of her heart and sickening tightness in her gut at the thought. Piotr was dead, she was alive. Cute or not, Piotr was long meant for the land beyond the Never's eternal limbo.

"*Blagodaru vas*," Piotr said, turning the cap around in his hands. "Thank you, Wendy. I owe you much. Was there anything else?"

"I didn't get much of a look, but that seems to be it." Careful not to get her hand too close lest she injure him in some way, Wendy pointed out the dime-sized holes peppering the bill. "Have you ever seen this before?"

After a surreptitious glance around the parking lot, Wendy settled herself on the curb and, remembering her cover, pulled out her cell phone again. The lot was empty of people beside herself and Piotr, but Wendy was unwilling to appear to be talking to herself, especially if Jon or Chel might see. With her luck, they'd run to Dad and tattle; then he'd slap her into counseling for acting crazy in public.

"*Net.*" Piotr raised the cap up to the sunlight, peering through the holes, and Wendy wondered what the world looked like on that side, if there were colors and textures or if everything was as washed out and grey as it appeared to her. "I must bring this to the other Riders and see if perhaps they've seen this sort of thing before."

"If they've seen a hat?"

Piotr flapped the cap. "This hat is made of Dunn himself. His essence. If he were gone—into the Light or eaten—the cap would vanish too, *da*? But it's still whole. Which means Lily was correct; Dunn is a hostage." Folding the cap as tightly as he could, Piotr stuffed it into one of the pockets in his cargo pants. "This complicates things."

"I'll say." Wendy shaded her eyes against the late afternoon sunlight, admiring him out of the corner of her eye. "So what now?"

"Nothing for now." Piotr frowned and gestured with the cap. "I must take this to the others. The word must go out."

"That's it? All that and you won't even tell me what's going to happen next?"

"You know everything I do." Piotr rubbed the bridge of his nose and sighed. "The cap, it is a mystery but it is enough proof that the Lost was taken. Where? Who knows? It is a place to start. Now I go north to tell the others. Again, *blagodaru vas*. My thanks." He turned away.

"Wait!" Caught up in the moment, Wendy forgot herself and reached out to grab his hand. Wendy didn't think about the action. If she had, she wouldn't have touched him for fear of what her powers would do. She simply reached out and grabbed for him, hoping to stall him long enough to at least let him know how to reach her.

Just as before, his hand smoked where she touched him, but the smoke dissipated quickly and appeared painless for Piotr. For Wendy, it was another story.

Her memories couldn't do justice to the strange feeling touching him wrought. Wendy had encountered other ghosts before, so many she'd lost count, but never had she been able to feel them as anything more than a sweep of chill air while she was not using her powers. There was a momentary sense of air pressure, a yielding, but nothing more. When she was in her other state, the touch of a soul was like grasping dry ice in her bare hands, and she kept her encounters as swift as possible to minimize any pain—both for them and for herself.

Touching Piotr shocked her into stillness. His flesh was cool but not icy, almost as firm as real skin under her fingers, and where her palm pressed into the bone of his elbow a sharp jolt ran up her arm to her shoulder, a tingling wave like static electricity. The shock left the muscles of her arm jumping and twitching in its wake.

"Wendy?" Piotr pulled his elbow out of her grip, breaking the connection that bound her silent and still. "What—"

"I didn't hurt you, did I?" Wendy gasped. "Just then?"

"*Net*," Piotr shook his head. "I am fine. But that . . . what was that?"

"I don't—I don't know." Wendy licked her lips and rubbed her hands together. Every nerve in her body felt pleasantly tingly, as if she'd passed through the eye of some electric tornado and come out the other end uplifted and unscathed. "I've never felt that before. Not even last time. You know, when we met."

Wendy closed her cell phone and slid it into her pocket. This moment was more important than a masquerade for the living. Inside the diner Eddie and Jon were eating fries and tick-tocking their way through their normal lives; out here was insanity too immediate to be denied.

"Are you hurt? Did I . . . ?" Piotr ran his hands wildly through his hair. "How do you feel?"

Her laughter came out a touch crazier than she'd intended it to; even to her own ears it sounded edgy and rough; high, sharp and broken. Wild. "Fine, I guess."

"Should we . . . ?" Piotr held out his hand, fingers splayed. An invitation. When Wendy nodded and held out her own hand in kind, he stepped closer. This time it was Piotr who reached for Wendy, threading his fingers through hers, cupping her hand in his. Wendy was helpless to stop it. Crazy electric sensations or not, she wanted to feel the intoxicating coolness of his not-quite-flesh pressed against the skin of her palm.

"This is amazing," Piotr murmured before breaking off, bewildered smile fading. Hand in hers, his not-flesh sizzled faintly but only for a moment, and the smoke was gone in a breath. "How do you feel?"

"Alive," Wendy whispered. "I can't . . . it's like . . . I can't describe it. I don't know." She closed her eyes. "It's nice. It hurts at first, and it's kinda cold to the touch, but it's only, like, a second of pain and then . . . whoosh! Every nerve lights up. I feel like the Energizer Bunny, Piotr, like every hair should stand on end." Wendy bit her lip. "What's it like for you?"

"It hurts, *da*, but the hurt is a blink. Then . . . I am calm inside? Quiet? It is very nice, very relaxed. I feel . . . peaceful." His fingers squeezed hers again and a pleasant warmth filled Wendy's chest at the gentle pressure. Dead or not, scarred or not, Piotr really was sort of attractive and he carried himself with such earnest conviction that even cynical Wendy found herself moved by his pleasure. She leaned in close, wanting to press her hand to his cheek when he casually added, "It is beginning to burn."

Horrified, Wendy snatched her hand away, cursing herself for ten kinds of fool. "I'm so sorry! When it didn't keep hurting me I just . . . did I hurt you? I'm such an idiot! Are you okay?" She started to reach for him, to soothe her touch, and then realized what a foolish gesture that would be. She tucked her hands deep in her pockets to quell the urge.

"I am fine." He held up his hands, turning them palm out to her. "The burn is fading." Piotr trembled, whether in joy or fear she couldn't tell. Perhaps, Wendy reasoned, it was like stubbing your toe or picking up a splinter; it hurt more after you realized you were hurt. Either way, Piotr seemed in no pain now.

The threat of future pain didn't slow him down for long. Marveling, Piotr reached tentatively forward, fingers hovering several inches from her cheek. "May I?"

Wendy closed her eyes and nodded. Feather-soft, his fingers brushed along her cheekbone and down the side of her neck, running through her hair and lifting the curling strands off her jaw with a whispering touch. When he ran his hands along each row of ear studs the metal cooled quickly, the posts growing painfully cold in her cartilage. Otherwise, his hand on her flesh was cool, pleasant and sweet.

Gonna have to get an acrylic barbell, Wendy inwardly mused then flushed with the realization of what her errant thought implied.

Slowly, feeling her way, Wendy reached out and mimicked his movements, brushing fingers across his eyebrows, down his nose, across his cheekbones. His lips were full and soft beneath her fingertips and the line of his jaw was firm. Everywhere she touched him, she tingled, the electric current running feverishly just beneath her skin. Inexplicably she felt sweaty and hot. Her corset was binding her torso close, and the jeans stretched across her thighs were suddenly too tight.

"This is crazy," Wendy whispered at last, drawing her fingers away, dulling the strange, fierce tingle that turned her muscles to jubilant jelly. "This shouldn't be happening."

"Insanity," he agreed and folded his hands in his lap, hunching over and shifting so she saw only his profile.

"Piotr?" Forcing her traitorous fingers to remain still, Wendy held back the urge to reach out and touch his shoulder. "Are you okay?" She was almost positive that none of the light inside had leaked through her skin when she'd been touching him, but the sensation of interacting with a ghost without reaping it was so fresh and new.

"I am fine." He grimaced and then shook his head, chuckling at some private joke. He shifted awkwardly, which seemed unusual considering the grace that Wendy had already seen him possess. "Just . . . overwhelmed."

"There are so many questions." Wendy crossed her arms over her chest, acutely aware of his proximity. After this crazy discovery, part of her knew that she ought to be reaping him right now, this second. Another part though, a deeper part, simply wanted to know why this dead boy, out of all the ghosts she'd ever encountered, was different. "Maybe your . . . this friend of yours will be able to help us figure all this out. Lilah?"

"Lily is wise and she may have theories about Dunn, but I doubt she's heard of *this* before." Piotr held up one hand and stared at it as if the fingers themselves held the answer to all the fresh questions he had. Wendy's eyes followed the movement and Piotr forced his hand to his side, baring his teeth in a pained half-smile. "It is unlikely."

A convertible swerved into the parking lot, overflowing with bleached blondes and pounding out rap with deafening bass. Chel scrambled out of the back, retrieved her bags, and waved as the convertible sped away. Bouncing with each step, she sashayed around the corner of the diner and vanished, presumably joining Eddie and Jon inside.

"My sister's here. I have to go."

"She doesn't look like your sister."

"Bleach." Wendy shrugged but was acutely uncomfortable. Chel's predilection for normal and average was still very disconcerting to her. God help her if she ever laid eyes on one of the dying. She'd go crazy.

"She's not as pretty as you." Piotr's lips quirked in his half-smile and Wendy jerked as if he'd touched her once more. Her knees, already weak, threatened to spill her on the ground.

"I . . . I have to go." Wendy rose, hands trembling, and ran her fingers through her hair. The interlude had left her empty and shaky, as if the first brush of his hand had stripped some core strength away. Wendy refused to entertain the idea that it might have been his words, not his touch, that left her so flustered and on edge. There was no way he was flirting with her. It was impossible. He was just being kind.

Still, she mused, the possibility of it wasn't unpleasant, just bizarre. Heart thrumming in her chest, Wendy desperately wanted to brush her hand against his cheek again, to touch his wrist, to say goodbye, to assure herself that this really was real. Part of her was scared that if she walked away now she would never see him again, that he wouldn't find her, or that the meeting itself was some crazy fluke never to be repeated. She'd spent the past five years dreaming of Piotr, drawing him, thinking about him and wondering how he was doing. Was she really just going to let this strange twist of fate end?

"I understand. Be safe," Piotr said and turned away.

Crushed, Wendy turned to go back inside and was ten steps toward the diner before she realized what she had to say. Quickly she turned, hoping to catch him before he got too far. Luckily, Piotr was still at the edge of the parking lot.

"Piotr! Wait!" Wendy hurried to join him, ignoring the strange looks of passing bicyclists as she reached to grasp thin air. "I live off of the corner of Montecito and Farley, not far from here," she said in a rush, fear tumbling the words from her lips in a tangled torrent. She forced herself to slow down and enunciate. "There are some town homes—"

Studiously not looking at her, Piotr made a hurry-up twirling gesture with his hand, expression inscrutable. "I've been there."

Forging ahead, Wendy said, "My bedroom's upstairs at the back of the house, the one with the bench in the side yard. If you . . . if you need me that's how you can find me, okay?" The irony that the first not-Eddie boy she was inviting into her room was dead was not lost on her; Wendy flushed and clasped her hands together to keep from twining them nervously through her curls. "It's the pink room.

Punk pink though, not like rah-rah girly-pink. And black. Pink and black." She swallowed heavily, babbling now. "But it's my room, you know? I like it."

"I understand." Piotr glanced at her out of the corner of his eye. "And if I do come visit you soon, Wendy? When do you want me to enter your home?"

"I dunno, whenever, I guess. Friday. We can talk that night. There's a tree. Can you climb trees? Anyway, there's a tree near the roof. It's an easy jump. Do ghosts have to jump? I don't . . . I don't have a lot of experience with this."

If Piotr noted her discomfort, he gave no sign. Instead he smiled and took her hand a final time, tracing a gentle circle on the inside of her wrist. Wendy's knees felt trembly at the touch, the cool brush of his skin obliterating her nervous energy in one fell swoop and leaving her aching and breathless.

Oh yeah, she realized, *I got it bad-bad-bad*. Eddie would never let her live it down. Wendy the Reaper, scourge of spirits, had a *crush*. And on a dead guy no less. What next?

"I understand," Piotr murmured, releasing her wrist and stepping away. He smiled, and that quirky grin, that twist of lips that was as familiar today as it had been five years before, was enough to make Wendy quiver from head to toe. "I will find you. Thank you."

Nodding once, Wendy turned and strode toward the diner. She refused to look back. *He's a ghost*, she told herself. *Just a ghost, no one special*. But her heart, thudding against her ribs, spoke an entirely different tale.

If she'd turned, just for a moment, she would have seen Piotr staring after her, expression wide open and eloquent with longing. Instead she flipped open her phone and dialed 9-1-1.

"Hello?" she said as the operator answered, "I'd like to report an accident in the woods behind the MVLA High School." She put her hand on the door and pulled. "You see, I was skipping last period, and—"

CHAPTER TEN

Unlike most of her peers, Wendy didn't get a cell phone until she was fifteen. It was a birthday gift from her mother and was strictly for the *family business*. Her father wasn't supposed to know about it. Dutiful daughter that she was, Wendy still kept it a secret even though she doubted he'd care about it now.

Though she and her mother had been close once upon a time, the death of Mr. Barry had changed things between them. Her mother began trusting Wendy more, especially with the twins, and going out more often when Dad was on assignment. If her mother had been any other woman, Wendy would have thought she was having an affair. And in a way, she was. The love of her life wasn't George, Wendy's father. Her mother was in love with her duty as a Reaper.

The night of her mother's accident started out typically. It was late February and the beginning of the rainy season. Wendy was studying at Eddie's when she received the call from her mother. The cell, tucked away in her bag, trilled once before going to voicemail. Wendy, deep in the middle of a tricky word problem, was unwilling to stop her homework yet again just because her mother expected her to jump at her beck and call. She barely glanced at her backpack before going back to work. Shades generally stuck to the same area; whomever her mother wanted her to send into the Light would most likely be there tomorrow. The reaping, Wendy decided, could wait for once. It was a decision she'd soon regret.

An hour later she filed her books away and remembered to check her phone. She pressed 2, the speed dial for her voicemail. She expected her mother to have left a list of boring reaping assignments to knock out before Wendy could go to sleep. Maybe there were Shades hovering around the Tiny Tot playground or a ghost wandering down Castro.

The voicemail turned out to be something much more important than that. Eddie, munching on popcorn, watched the smile slip off Wendy's face, replaced with a look of horror. He set the bowl aside.

"What's up?"

Wendy snapped her phone closed and shoved it in her pocket. "I need to borrow your car."

"Whoa there, hotshot, you've barely got your license."

She wouldn't meet his eyes as she gathered up her things and stuffed them haphazardly in her bag. "Ed, I need this. I gotta go."

"Then let me drive you." Eddie staggered to his feet, legs half-numb from the time spent on the floor, and grabbed Wendy by the upper arms. "Wendy, what's wrong? Is someone hurt? That was your mom, right? Is she okay?"

"You wouldn't believe me if I told you," Wendy snapped, yanking away.

Quickly, Eddie set himself between Wendy and the door, crossing his arms and tucking his compact wrestler's body firmly against the door. There was no way she was moving him without a fight. "I'm your BFF, Wendy. Why don't you try me?" When she hesitated his expression softened. "Give me a chance," he pleaded. "Please?"

Torn between her duty to her mother and the vow of secrecy her mother had made her swear, Wendy hesitated . . . and told him. She told him about the ghost she'd met the day his father had died, about the rotting Walker-to-be in the hospital, and about her mother's calling—now her own—as a Reaper.

"So now that you think I'm crazy," she finished, turning her face away so Eddie wouldn't see her fear for their friendship, "may I please borrow your car? You can listen to my voicemail. My mom needs my help. I really gotta go!"

"I don't think you're crazy," Eddie rebuked.

"What?" Wendy's head snapped up. "Of course you do. Didn't you hear a word I just said? Ghosts, Eddie. Dead people. You know, boo!"

"Wendy, look, you've always been a little weird." He laughed, shaking his head in amazement. "To be honest, it's a relief to, you know, have a reason for it. Why you're so strange. This seems as good a reason as any."

"You believe me?" Wendy could hardly believe her ears. "Serious?"

"I sincerely doubt that you of all people would lie to me," Eddie said, scratching his ear. "Not after everything we've been through. So if you're not lying, well, I guess that means you're telling the truth. I guess there's only one way to find out, huh?" He drew his car keys from his front pocket. "Let's go."

It took twenty minutes to reach Redwood City. When they spotted the gigantic pileup it took immense self-control for Wendy to keep her dinner down. Her mother's ambulance was at the back, parked beside the overturned school bus half on the highway. Most of the police were at the front of the wreck where a U-Haul lay on its side, the side torn open and its contents strewn across the lanes of traffic. A twin mattress lay haphazardly across the divider, sodden and bent double from the rain.

Eddie pulled to the side of the 101, tucking his car as far into the breakdown lane as he could—and as near as he dared without attracting notice from the cops. The storm opened up, rain pouring buckets upon buckets across the windshield so hard and fast that Wendy had to squint to make out the front of the accident.

"Oh my God," he whispered, thunderstruck. "What happened?"

"Who cares? There're kids out there," Wendy moaned, spotting the wandering hoard of Lost milling around the crushed remnants of the yellow school bus. Her eyes skipped over the garish splash of red splattered across the inside of the windshield. Apparently the driver hadn't made it either. "Normally Mom doesn't let me reap kids. All I've ever done are adults! Shades! Maybe a Walker. Once. But never kids!"

Eddie passed a hand over his mouth. "It looks like the U-Haul must've skidded. The semi couldn't stop and the bus ran into the semi. Those cars got crushed in between. Oh my God, this is . . ." he swallowed rapidly and wiped his mouth again. "You've seen shit like this before? How do you keep from being sick?"

"You take a deep breath and remind yourself that the body is just a shell." Wendy started scanning what she could see of the wreck. "Come on, Mom, where are you?"

"Can you do it without her? Reap them?"

"I guess, maybe, but kids are supposed to be way, way harder. I'm not supposed to; Mom'll kill me if I do and she didn't want me to." Wendy buried her face in her hands, torn with indecision; she could go ahead and help with the reap and catch flack for it later, or sit like a good girl and wait for her mother to spot the parked car and fetch her. Despairing, Wendy cried, "What should I do?"

Eddie took a deep breath and stared straight ahead, frowning at the swirling red and blue lights. "What's your standard operating procedure? For car wrecks, I mean?"

"Reap any souls that don't go into the Light on their own. But . . . kids . . ." Wendy plucked at Eddie's sleeve, trying to convey her terror at the potential job before her. Her mother was nowhere to be seen. Eddie, still staring at the chaos in front of them, didn't move. "Okay, Wendy," she muttered under her breath, "you can do this. Mom's obviously got her hands full or she would've been done here by now. Just . . . just do this."

"Wendy," Eddie said, voice flat and dull as he examined the site of the accident, ignoring her loosening hold and low pep talk. "Did you reap my dad?"

"Now's not the time, Eds." Wendy reached for the handle but before she could pull it the locks snapped down.

"Tell me, and I'll let you do your thing." Eddie wasn't looking at her, simply staring out past the windshield, hectic color in his cheeks. He reached out and grabbed her wrist, fingers digging in. "Did you? Did you reap my dad?"

Despite her worry for her mother, despite the steady pulse of the emergency lights and the throng of child-ghosts stumbling about right before her eyes, Wendy felt a tug of sympathy. Mr. Barry had been Eddie's world, she remembered, he had been Eddie's everything.

"No, Eddie," she said, her voice almost drowned out by the rapid swish of windshield wipers, the punishing rat-tat-tat of rain on the roof of the car. She remembered the scarred boy holding her hand, the way the two of them had looked out at the wreckage before Eddie had passed out. There'd been no ghost there but the boy who'd held her hand and comforted her, no other souls around.

"Your dad went into the Light," Wendy soothed. "He made me promise to watch over you and when he knew you were gonna be okay he just . . . let go. I never saw a ghost before that night; I couldn't have reaped him even if I'd known I needed to. But he didn't need it."

Eddie nodded, released her, and the locks snapped open. Wendy fled the car and his tortured expression, welcoming the familiar burn in her gut as the heat of the Light washed through her.

It was as if her arrival opened some small riptide in the hole of the Never. Rays of Light began spilling from the storm-shot sky, brilliant shoots of blinding warmth that drew the dead and dying toward them with near mindless yearning. Wendy had to do nothing for those that could find their own way; she stepped aside and let them travel on. Soon only a handful remained, a dozen or so ghosts, huddled together and crying. A woman, pale white and flickering, hung at the far edge of the accident, wiping her hands over and over again on her white slacks. From the look of her, Wendy guessed that she had been the driver of the U-Haul. The side of her face had been ripped apart.

"A deer," she moaned over and over again, the gaping maw that was her face flexing with her cries. "It was a deer! The streets were wet and I couldn't stop!" She grabbed one of the little ghosts and shook him. "You saw the deer, didn't you? Didn't you? It wasn't my fault!"

As Wendy approached, the woman in the white slacks backed away. "I've got to find the deer. I've got to! I'll prove it was an accident. Just wait here. You wait right there!" She turned on her heel and pushed past the little boy, hurrying over the edge of the highway and into the ditch where she quickly vanished from view. Wendy could have gone after her, but she knew that her mother would be able to capture the ghost far faster than she ever could. Her mom could get the driver; Wendy just had to find her and let her know what happened.

In this form Wendy walked the space between life and death. Paramedics were offloading bodies from the bus and the semi and the two cars at the back of the wreck but here, at the edge of the accident, she was a whisper of a being, a flickering creature made of shadow to the living and light to the dead. In the downpour and chaos of the accident, no one noticed her . . . except the ghosts.

"We didn't mean to," sobbed one ponytailed girl as Wendy brushed her with the ribbons of Light, "it was an accident."

Wendy, assuming the child meant the car wreck, kissed the girl's cheek and sent her on. There was a deep tug inside when she did so, a tidal pull like menstrual cramps, but fiercer, darker. Wendy, thinking that this was what her mother meant when she said that child-spirits were dangerous, relished the tug of pain. Her mother must be busy elsewhere, she thought to herself, sending a second child on, or perhaps she missed this group?

Each spirit sent into the Light made her weaker, set the pain in her gut a little higher until her lungs were burning and her eyes were watering. Every breath was torture. It was the worst pain she'd ever felt, the worst stitch in her side multiplied tenfold. Wendy, struggling to finish the job, sent the last of the children on and sank to the ground. Her Light flickered and dimmed, leaving her wholly human again.

At first Wendy thought she was inadvertently touching one of the corpses; perhaps a driver thrown free of the wreckage only to break their neck at the edge of the accident. But then her eyes spied the dark blue jacket of her mother's EMT uniform and the coppery wash of sodden hair. "Mom?" Wendy whispered, horrified. "MOM?"

Her mother did not answer and Wendy began to scream.

Now, seven months later, Wendy was still screaming . . . only now the scream was on the inside. She'd stopped reaping Shades in the days following her mother's accident. It hadn't been a conscious decision at first, merely a matter of convenience. Her father was a wreck and the twins needed someone to pick up the slack in the mothering department. Wendy had been doing most of the chores for years now so she had that part of the routine down, but she had to hide how adept she was at laundry and cooking from her father. Dad had no idea that Mom had been depending on Wendy for as long as she had.

She needn't have bothered. Now her father took Wendy's efficiency around the house for granted and only noticed when she slacked off. Sure, there was less reaping, since Wendy only took the souls that got in her way while she was on patrol, but covering the city section by section on foot was time consuming and tedious.

At first the lack of reaping had been a convenience thing, but it had stealthily grown into something more. The few times she'd tried to reap a Shade that summer, she'd failed. Her palms would grow sweaty and her vision would double; it felt like a vise had wrapped around her chest and was pushing the air out of her very pores until she backed away from the ghost and fled home. Her mother would have said she'd lost her nerve, if she'd ever had it in the first place.

Piotr's words had shaken her up, though. She couldn't stop

turning the numbers over in her head. Before her mother's accident Wendy had sent (on average) three or four souls a week on to the afterlife. It was something she hardly had to think about. Do the dishes, reap a Shade, go grocery shopping. It was rote. Over the course of the five years she'd been helping her mother send souls on, she must have reaped at least a thousand souls—or more!—all by herself.

How many souls had she left in the Never over the past seven months? And with her mother gone, how many of the day-to-day souls that she'd encountered at the hospital, at accident sites, even in people's homes . . . how many of those were left there, weeping into the stillness of a world that didn't even know they existed anymore?

Chel and Jon went their separate ways as soon as Eddie dropped them off. Wendy waved goodbye from the front porch and drifted upstairs, hardly noticing Jon puttering in the kitchen or the lights spilling out from the shared upstairs bathroom. Chel shut the door with her hip as Wendy passed, Wendy's makeup bag clutched in her left hand and her cell phone pressed to her ear in the right.

Wendy didn't bother turning on her lights. The rumpled bed looked too comfortable to resist. Pausing only long enough to toe off her boots, Wendy crawled under her covers and hugged her pillow against her chest. Her eyes drifted closed. She dreamed.

In her dreams, Wendy walked and walked, an endless beach stretching out before her, with foamy waves licking her toes and shells crunching beneath her bare heels. A person walked beside her—sometimes her father, sometimes Eddie, but most often Piotr—and when she grew tired of walking Wendy held out her hand for her companion to grasp. The hand in hers was warm and firm, the grip strong and reassuring. Holding this hand, Wendy felt safe, secure. His hand in hers, she was afraid of nothing. Fingers intertwined, they continued walking down the beach until they reached a door in the sand.

The door was made of millions of shells sunk into the firm, hard-packed sand at their feet. No two shells were the same, though each shimmered with a radiant and subtle rainbow. When Wendy looked on the door long enough, she realized that there were words written in the reflected light. Squinting, she concentrated, but could only make out a word here, a word there. Wendy turned to ask if he could make out the words, but the hand holding hers was gone.

"Dad?" Wendy called, shading her eyes against the grey glare of the sky and twisting to squint up and down the beach, hoping to catch sight of him. "Eddie?" There was nothing, not even his footprints in the sand; the dream had erased him.

Confused, but more curious about the door than her companion's disappearance, Wendy knelt down and ran her hands over the shells, finger tracing the mystery words like a child first learning to read. For a time the door grew brighter, almost bright enough to make out the words, but then a horrible thing occurred: every place her fingers touched, the shells grew black and cold. They crumbled as she watched, horrorstruck.

The words faded, became ghosts of themselves, and a wave washed across the beach, taking the blackened shells with it. The sand underneath these holes in the shell door was black as pitch, sticky to the touch, and foul smelling—a ripe, turgid scent like old mushrooms grown in rotted hollows that have never seen the sun.

Wendy drew back, stared avidly at her hands. Her fingers were trembling, sure, but her hands were as they should be—ten roughened fingers tipped with ten blunt and ragged nails. Silver bangles at each wrist jangled together, and two silver rings—one at each thumb—glinted in the pale, grey morning light.

Tipping her head back, Wendy looked up at the sky. The expanse was uniformly grey as far as the eye could see. A crowd of ramshackle huts crowded the shoreline, set far enough back from the beach for safety, but only a few dozen yards from the cool expanse of sea. Gulls cried and circled overhead, but no feathers clung to their outstretched wings; they were floating, darting skeletons dancing on the breeze.

As Wendy watched, one bony gull swept wings back and dove straight down, breaking the waves with a writhing creature grasped tightly in its beak. Squinting, Wendy could make out the shape of a fish being gulped down almost whole, but it was a fish nearly out of a cartoon, all spiky bones and eyes, extended from a scaly but flesh-less head.

"I'm dreaming," Wendy said aloud, realizing it for the first time. "This is a dream."

She pinched herself. "Wake up. Wake up, Wendy, wake up."

Though she pinched until her wrists and arms were tender, Wendy found herself no closer to waking than before. At a loss for what to do, Wendy examined the stretch of beach on all sides. The houses were gone now, swallowed by thick white mist rolling in from the ocean. Some miles distant, probably far out at sea, Wendy heard a foghorn boom across the water and the answering call north of her position, a mournful reply that split the silence in twenty-second bursts.

As Wendy examined her surroundings the mist finally reached her and enveloped her. A faint breeze pushed the mist against her face, tickling her neck and cheek like warm, wet kisses, dragging her curls down so they hung lank against her shoulders, sodden and dripping.

"I know this place," she said, and she did. With the mist had come the memory of a mother-daughter trip to Santa Cruz for break-fast on the beach years before, in the early months of her reaping. The sun had burned off the mist after only a few hours, but the memory of her mother sitting beside her, the cool morning air, and the world dressed in clouds, had always stayed with her. For a moment Wendy imagined that she could smell her mother's per-fume. Her eyes filled with tears.

Swathed in the white and blinded by her memories, Wendy

turned and turned, at first seeking some escape from these memories-within-a-dream, and then seeking even the faintest hint of a direction. The sound of the sea surrounded her, the foghorn boomed all around. The warm feelings disappeared in a rising wave of panic.

This isn't that beach. Mom is gone and I'm lost, I'm lost, she thought desperately. Wendy knew she was still at the edge of the sea—cool waves rushed around her ankles, the sand sucking greedily at her toes—but she could make out no outcropping of stern rock or figure out from which direction she'd come. *I can't do this anymore.*

Eyes straining against the white, Wendy believed at first that the figure floating towards her was her imagination. It bobbed in slow synchronicity with the swells around her ankles, drifting closer and closer through the mist, but it wasn't until Wendy heard the rhythmic thump of waves against a hull that she put two and two together. The figure, whoever it was, was approaching in a boat.

Glad for the company in this spooky expanse of dreamland, even if it was unexpected, Wendy stepped backward, away from the shifting shadow in the mist. The bow scraped sand and the figure, lean and lithe, leapt nimbly over the side with a little splash and guided the tiny sailboat higher onto the shore.

"Mom?" Wendy asked. The figure was slim like her mother, and about the right height. But then she spoke and the raspy voice told Wendy that this woman was not, could not, be her mother.

"A little help?" Up close, most of the figure's face was obscured by a deep, heavy hood, but the shape of her body was feminine, and she was only slightly taller than Wendy herself. The waves tugged at her cape and the shift beneath, pulling the sodden fabric toward the sea.

Wendy's heart sank. Dream or not, some small part of her had been hoping that it was her mother. Even dreaming her face was better than the pain of the real, waking world.

"Um, yeah, sure," Wendy surprised herself by saying, and helped tug the boat free of the sucking waves, leaving them both all foam and damp from foot to knee. The act of hauling the boat in had cleared her head, however; Wendy felt calm, in control once more, and grateful to the newcomer for the distraction.

"My thanks," the woman said. She had a knapsack slung across her chest, hanging loosely from shoulder to opposite hip, and she reached into it almost to her elbow, searching until she found a largish silver flask with a deeply tarnished edge. The woman spun off the top and drank deeply, wiping her mouth with the side of her hand when she was done. Then she offered the flask to Wendy. "Portable heat," she said. "The wind is cold; it eats my bones."

She was right, the seashore was icy, but accepting felt strange. "No, thank you."

The woman shrugged. "Suit yourself," she said and began slogging through the mist and away from the ocean. Wendy followed.

Keeping the line of the boat in sight, they moved until they'd reached the tide line before the woman sank to sand and tucked her feet beneath her. Patting the space beside her, the woman did not relax until Wendy settled by her side. They were, Wendy realized, seated not far from the remains of the door in the sand. The surf rumbled, the mist eddied, and they sat in silence, listening to the fading boom of the foghorn and occasional cry of a distant gull.

"I think," the woman said when the flask was done, "that it's time we had a talk."

"So talk," Wendy said, wishing that it were her mother sitting beside her. The quiet contemplation had cleared her mind until Wendy felt pleasantly light, open and airy, but lonely and very, very young. The sun was either rising or setting on the horizon, burning away some of the mist and setting the rest to glowing; infinitesimal rainbows refracted and shivered at the edge of Wendy's concentration, distracting her. "We can chat about anything you want."

"It's best if *you* begin with a question. That's how these things are done, I'm told." The woman scooped a handful of sand high in the air, tilted her hand, and let it fall in a steady stream. The sand hitting sand made a subtle swooshing noise. She brushed the crumbling beach off her hand and waited.

"Me? But this is a dream. Hello, why would I have questions? Especially from some chick I dreamed up?"

"Is it, now?" The woman wrapped one arm around her knees. "Or is this space something more?" She chuckled. "Even if this is a dream, ask anyway. Call me the genie in the lamp. The mysteries of the universe are yours for the asking."

"Right. Okay, fine, a question, a question . . ." Wendy couldn't imagine anything that she'd want to ask this stranger. It was a dream, nothing more. Then she realized that there *was* one thing she was curious about. "Why're you wearing a hood?" Wendy demanded. "Let me see your face."

"I don't think so," the woman replied, tugging the hood further forward. "I had an accident when I crossed over and my face isn't—" here she laughed unexpectedly, "pretty to look on."

"Crossed over?" Wendy snorted. "This isn't the Never. I'm only dreaming . . . aren't I?" The light, dizzy feeling left in a rush, leaving Wendy chill and tense and wishing her male dream companion from before could have maybe stuck around a little longer. *"Aren't I?"*

"'*Iam vero videtis nihil esse morti tam simile quam somnum*,'" the woman replied, drawing her knees up and resting her chin upon them. "Cicero's *De Senectute*." Her head inclined towards Wendy. "Roughly translated, it means, 'Now indeed you see that there is nothing so like death than sleep.' An apt description, wouldn't you say?"

Cold chills danced down Wendy's spine. "Do I know you?"

"No," the woman replied. "But I most certainly know you. You are the scourge of the Never, the one who walks at night." She sighed. "I hear quite a lot from where I sit. Quite a lot. And not all of it, I'm sad to say, is good news."

The woman straightened and turned so that she faced Wendy head on. All Wendy could see of her face was the bottom of her chin and long, lean line of her neck. When the woman spoke, the cloak shifted aside for a brief moment, revealing a crosshatched scar lining the edge of her collarbone, the remains of the puckered flesh dipping under the neck of her shift.

"You've been meddling in my affairs. Poking your nose where it shouldn't be."

"I don't know what you're talking about," Wendy protested. "I don't even know who you are. I'm dreaming this. I've got school—"

"Time is short here," the woman interrupted. "Though the hours seem long. A pair of very special Walkers went missing recently, a matched set, and I can't say that I like that one bit. I've got eyes and ears everywhere—seems some folks would like to join in on my pretty party—and the whispers say that you're the one to blame for my recent troubles. Riders I can handle, they're just a gang of arrogant kiddies, but someone like you? You need to be dealt with."

"Who the hell are you?"

The woman sighed. "They call me the White Lady." Her fingers plucked the crosshatched scars like a harpist strumming strings and her voice dropped low, insinuating. "Heard of me?"

Cursing, Wendy shoved away from the woman and leapt to her feet. She tried to unravel the Light but the fire was dead inside, black coals and dust. She could not even find the smallest flame to fan into a blaze. Wendy pounded her fists on her thighs. "Why won't it come?"

Amused at Wendy's display, the White Lady shook her head, hood swaying from side to side, and tsked. "Dreams may be like death, my dear, but they are still ages apart. Do you really think I'm so stupid as to approach you in the Never?" She sighed again, as if disappointed. "You've just proven that you can't be trusted; you'd reap me then and there, if I were to call for a palaver."

"What do you want?" Wendy asked flatly, ashamed of her outburst. She crossed her arms over her chest, keeping well away from the woman.

"A truce." The wind blew in a harder gust; Wendy was downwind of the White Lady and nearly gagged at the rich, thick scent of rot that filled her nose and watered her eyes, filling her mouth with the strong, sour taste of bile and coppery salt.

"You want a truce?" Wendy spat, trying to clean her mouth of the foul taste. She could hardly believe her ears. "What kind of truce?"

The White Lady threw up her arms in disgust. "The kind where you and I call a cease-fire. You don't attack my Walkers and I don't have them attack you and yours for interfering in my business. Truuuuuce. It's a simple enough word, haven't you ever heard it before?"

"I'm not stupid," Wendy snapped.

"Hmm, I wasn't so certain." High above them seagulls cried, their noisome calls bouncing off the jetty and echoing around the cove. "Excuse me a moment," the White Lady said, and stood, hem whipping about her feet. She gathered up a handful of sand and shells and rolled the damp mess in her hands until it was firmly compacted into a lopsided sandball roughly the size of her palm. "I do hate gulls."

"They're too far," Wendy pointed out. "It'll never make it."

"That, my dear, is the beauty of dreams," the White Lady said serenely and flung the ball hard in the direction of the seagulls' calls. It soared up and out, traveling impossibly far, retaining its firm shape as far as Wendy could see. The call of the gull broke as if severed, ending in a strangled cry followed by a sickening wet thump far distant down the shore.

The White Lady wiped her hands free of the last clinging grains.

Wendy turned her face away, sickened. "You're foul."

"No, just practical. They do make *such* a noise. A lady can hardly dicker for peace with a ruckus like that going on in the background," she said, rucking up the arms of her cloak to the elbows and holding out hands with palms turned up. "So how about it? Let's make a deal."

"I don't deal with the likes of you."

"The likes of me?" The White Lady pressed mottled and rotting fingers to her chest in a gesture of dismay. "And just what is that supposed to mean?" When she moved her hands the skin began flaking away from her bones in a shower. Wendy could spy yellowed sinew and slim cords of tendon holding her bones together.

"I don't deal with ghosts," Wendy said. "I don't deal with cannibals like Walkers. And I definitely won't deal with a ghost who's got Walkers taking orders from her."

"A little high and mighty, aren't we?"

"They're foul. They eat children. And I don't know how you're healing them, but if you were any kind of decent human being when you were alive, you'll stop helping them out."

"Ah, teenagers," the White Lady sneered. "You all think you know everything. Look, dear, let me tell you a little something about the real, *adult* world. You work with whoever you have to, in order to get shit done. You get it? I worked with worse than Walkers when I was walking the living lands, that's for sure. And, by the way, enough with the attitude. A simple 'yes' or 'no' will suffice. I don't need lectures from a kid barely out of diapers, thanks."

"Fine. You want an answer? Here's your answer: N-O. No. I've got my own business to attend to, lady, and if your Walkers happen to be in the area while I'm doing my thing, then that's just too bad for you."

"Oh, really?" The White Lady clasped her hands demurely together. "So that's the way you want things to be, then?"

"Pretty much."

"Fine. That's the way it's going to be. Oh-me-oh-my I do believe I've been TOLD, now haven't I?" The White Lady laughed then, a burst of racketing hyena mirth that echoed loudly.

Whoever she was before, dying made her go crazy, Wendy realized. Deep cold overwhelmed her with the thought, as if she'd dipped her hands and feet in snow; licked at icicles until her lips and tongue were numb. Wendy shivered and turned her face away from the woman, digging her toes in the sand, seeking the comforting stability of the earth beneath her feet. She took one step back and then another, when her ankle slammed into something sharp and pointed that dug deep into her skin, pricking her. Startled by the unexpected pain, Wendy yelled and fell backwards on the sand, catching herself with her elbows. Sparks of fierce tingling heat flared up her arms, stealing her breath.

The terrible laughter cut off.

"Well then, I think I'll just have to keep you, won't I?" The White Lady hiked up the hem of her robe, lifting the cloth high over knees seeping clear, whitish fluid. "If you're not going to talk business now, then we'll just have to negotiate after you've been my . . . *guest* for a while."

Sucking in a deep breath and holding one scraped and stinging elbow in the other hand, Wendy glanced around, confused and bordering on hysteria.

The open beach was gone as suddenly as it had appeared. Birds chirped in the trees and the mist vanished; the sky was a blue bowl dotted with shell-shaped clouds. The White Lady's boat was still only a half dozen feet away, moored up against a large and drooping willow tree, but they were enclosed in a large copse of trees, their branches so tightly packed together that Wendy knew she'd never be able to wriggle through.

What remained of the shell doorway was gone, but in its place was a large concrete circle marked with a hopscotch grid. At the end of the grid was a box writ with the number 13 over and over again in a chalked rainbow of colors, some faded, some fresh. A lush carpet of green grass stretched out in all directions; nearby the wind tossed the tops of trees to and fro, setting the empty swing set into a jangling metallic cacophony.

There was no path, no opening, no easy way up or down. She was trapped.

A foot or so away, where Wendy had tripped, was a cheerful red picnic blanket laid out with square white plates and napkins shaped like swans, matching chopsticks stabbed artfully into each swan's back. A bottle of soda chilled in a bucket of ice and beside it was an old-fashioned picnic basket, one corner spotted with blood. A large Chinese takeout container lay on its side beside the basket, huge clumps of white rice spilled across the corner of the blanket.

Crawling on hands and knees, Wendy approached the blanket. At first she thought it was her eyes, but the rice was indeed moving. Maggots and silverfish.

Overwhelmed, Wendy turned her face aside and dry-heaved.

"A feast for my honored guest!" The White Lady cried, approaching from behind. She stepped around Wendy's side and crouched down, the gull she'd beaned flopping from her fist by one rotting leg, and dipped the remains of its head in the puddle. "Even in dreams, a girl's got to eat, yes? Not seasoned, but we'll make due, won't we? Nothing like an impromptu BBQ, that's what I always say."

"You sick bitch," Wendy gasped, pushing away from the White Lady and wiping her mouth with the back of her hand. "You can't keep me here!"

"Tsk tsk, manners! Keeping you here, what nerve! You're my guest! My guest until we sort out some sort of truce, my most honored opponent. Yet here you are, insulting me! What, were you raised in a barn?" The White Lady threw the gull to the ground and stood. "Surely your mother taught you better than that!" She paused, tilted her head. "Or did she? Didn't teach you much of anything at all if you honestly think a mere ghost like me can *truly* trap someone who 'won't deal' with her in a little ol' dreamspace. Shame on her."

"Don't you talk about my mother," Wendy growled, staggering to her feet and balling her hands into fists. "Don't you fucking dare."

"Oh yes, Mommy Dearest is wandering our streets, isn't she?" The White Lady threw her head back and laughed and laughed and laughed. "My ears might be falling off, but they hear rumors just as well as they did before I ended up here. What you do is some kind of family business, yeah? Mother to daughter, that sort of thing?"

"Shut up."

"And not only that, but rumors say that Momma Dearest has been out of the picture for a while now. Since this summer, am I right? What happened, Lightbringer? She up and quit?"

"I said, shut up."

"Oh, I'm just fooling you! Everyone knows how you've been blowing off sending those pitiful Shades on to search high and low for her. Not having much luck, are we? How do you think dear ol' Mom feels about that?"

Wendy felt her throat go dry. "How . . ."

"I suppose it'd be a real honest-to-goodness shame if one of my Walkers found her lost little spirit before you did, hmm? If I'd, say, sent them out looking for her?" The White Lady held out one rotting hand before her as if checking her nails. A finger fell off and she tsked, scooping down to pick it up and set it back on. "'Be subtle! Be subtle and use your spies for every kind of warfare.' Sun Tzu." She chuckled. "Every leader needs a few flies on the wall here and there. Know your enemy, and all that. Even if your enemy is a snot-nosed kid."

"You . . . you . . ." Wendy sputtered.

The White Lady sighed. "Yes, me, me. Be a dear and let's make this truce work, hmm? I'll leave you alone to search for your mom's ghostie; you leave my Walkers alone when you come across them on your hunt."

"I can't do that."

"And why not? If they chase you, you run, what's so hard about that? They're weak compared to the likes of you, and it's not like they could hurt such a mighty ghost-killer, right?"

Slowly Wendy straightened, squared her shoulders, and took a long, measuring look at the White Lady. Despite the obvious instability of the White Lady's personality, something she'd just said was pinging around inside Wendy's skull. "You're trying awfully hard to keep me away from your Walkers," Wendy mused. "You start hassling me in my dreams, out of the blue, and you're making all these threats that you then claim that you can't back up if I'm really so very mighty."

"Sarcasm. They teach you all about it in school, I'm sure."

"Thing is," Wendy said, ignoring her, "it really is *my* dream, isn't it? My . . . what did you call it? My dreamspace." Wendy grabbed a handful of maggots off the ground and concentrated at them. One by one the maggots transformed into butterflies, yellow-winged and delicate. Only the centers were still maggots, wriggling and white. "You've got some control here, but ultimately . . . it's still my space, isn't it?"

Wendy flung the maggot-butterflies into the air and they massed in a brilliant golden-yellow cloud, momentarily obliterating the great blue bowl of sky. One, however, had a partially crushed wing and waved feebly at her from her palm. The wings fluttered and drew inside the body until it was just a maggot again, big and bulky and hot in her hand.

"I'm leaving," Wendy said. "And if I find out that you're stalking my mother or you know where my mother is, this conversation . . . I . . . you won't like it, okay? I'll come for you and I don't care how long it takes." She turned away.

"You can't walk away from me!" The White Lady snapped, grabbing for Wendy's arm. "We're not done here!"

"Oh yeah? Watch me." Dodging the skeletal fingers, Wendy strode to the hopscotch grid and threw the hot maggot to the concrete, grinding it beneath her heel. It bled thin, sticky ichor that seeped into the ground, obliterating the chalk outline and revealing the door of seashells. The jangle of metal chains became the hooting of the foghorn, the twittering of birds faded into the wash of constant grinding waves.

The mist was gone and with it the boat, Wendy noted, leaving only a swatch of scraped sand as testament to its appearance in her dream. A feathered gull flew overhead with a shining, scaled fish caught in its beak. The beach was beautiful once again.

The White Lady was gone.

CHAPTER ELEVEN

Friday evening found Wendy forgoing patrolling for her mother in favor of staying inside. Part of her knew this was pure lunacy—Wednesday afternoon and the disturbing dream that followed must have been some sort of delusion. But the touch of Piotr's hand, the bittersweet wariness in his eyes, and the obvious insanity of the White Lady convinced her differently. Piotr was real and so was his dilemma.

Come hell or high water, Wendy intended to help.

When they got home after school, Wendy gathered an armful of cleaning supplies from under the kitchen sink. Ignoring Chel's incredulous look and Jon's curious questions, Wendy marched upstairs and gave her room a quick but thorough onceover.

"Is Eddie coming over?" Jon asked from the doorway around the second hour of her frantic whirlwind spree. He wrinkled his nose theatrically and snagged a handful of M&Ms from the candy dish on her desk. "It smells like Mr. Clean hemorrhaged to death in here."

"Very funny," Wendy grunted, shoving the last of her (now stuffed) shoeboxes under the bed. The box slid through Jabber, who territorially hissed and took a swipe at her with his claws. Wendy snatched her hand back just in time.

"Can't a girl just want a nice room every now and then?"

Pouring an entire handful of M&Ms into his mouth, Jon struggled to chew and swallow before answering. "Using you and Chel as examples? No."

"Beat it," she replied, not unkindly, and threw him the shopping bag full of rags she'd dirtied. "And throw those in the washer while you're at it."

"Yes *mon capitan*!" Jon saluted, tapping his heels together. "Anything else your highness desires? Cake, perhaps? Possibly a virgin to sacrifice?"

"For you to stop being so nosy," Wendy said and tossed the final rag his way. "Shoo!"

Shrugging, Jon left, taking the bag of rags with him along with another handful of candy. Maneuvering around Jabber, Wendy straightened the throw pillows on her bed, made sure her abundance of ratty stuffed animals were out of sight, and turned once around, examining the room. Everything *looked* okay, but that didn't mean she hadn't forgotten something important, like panties poking out of a drawer. Piotr seemed relaxed and his clothing was very nondescript but there was no telling when he'd died or what might offend him. He could come from some super-repressed century for all she knew, and Wendy was unwilling to risk chasing him away.

The room passed inspection, however. At a loss for something productive to do in lieu of her normal routine, Wendy sat down to finish her homework early. An hour passed. Two. She completed the last line of her geography paper, stretched until her back crackled, and sighed in relief.

"I don't remember going to school. It looks tedious."

Stifling a shriek, Wendy started out of her chair like a frightened cat. Every hair felt as if it were on end, every nerve tingling with shock and surprise. "What the hell are you doing here?!"

Piotr rose from her bed, where he'd been sitting. He flushed, embarrassed, looking as if he was worried that he'd done something wrong. "*Yzveenee*, my apologies. I did not mean to startle you, but you asked that I visit you and I thought—"

Wendy held up a hand for silence, shushing him. They heard footsteps pad down the hall and a gentle tap on the door. "Wendy?"

It was Jon. He opened the door a crack, letting in a waft of sugar-scented air. "I thought I heard you yell. Are you okay?"

"Leave her alone, Poindexter!" Chel yelled from across the hall. She was breathless and the speedy beat of her feet on their mother's treadmill almost drowned her out.

"I'm fine, Jon," Wendy said. "Just stubbed my toe." She raised her voice. "And don't call Jon 'Poindexter,' Chel! It's not nice!"

The whirr of the treadmill paused and their parents' bedroom door slammed.

Shaking her head in annoyance, Wendy glanced at Piotr and belatedly realized how ridiculous it was to shush one of the dead. It wasn't as if Jon or Chel would be able to hear Piotr talking anyway, not even if he'd shouted at the top of his lungs.

Jon shrugged, set a fresh-baked sugar cookie on the vanity, and shut the door. Wendy waited until Jon's footsteps had faded to smile apologetically at Piotr. "I'm sorry, I didn't mean to be rude." Grabbing her stereo remote, she flipped it to her favorite station and turned the volume just high enough that it would drown out her low-pitched voice. "You just sort of snuck up on me. I was expecting you to come up the tree."

Piotr glanced out the window. "I can, if that would make you feel better. But the door, it is very thin, and this home is very new. Easy to walk through."

"Right," Wendy agreed. "I should have thought of that before."

Shrugging, Piotr sat on the edge of her bed again. "*Net*, it's understandable. It's not something the living must think about."

"No. We don't." Wendy hesitated beside her desk, uncertain whether he would find it weird if she sat beside him on the bed or if she should just sit back down on the chair. But it was *her* bed. She could sit where she wanted!

As if sensing the train of her thoughts, Piotr pushed further back so that he was almost resting against the headboard. "My apologies. I am stealing up your space."

"No," she said, flushing, "it's cool." Collecting the sugar cookie and nibbling on the edge nervously, Wendy drifted towards the edge of the bed, obliquely glad that she'd taken the time to neaten up. Piotr looked strange but somehow right in her room, with his dim shoulders outlined against the hot pink puffy pillows and the chipped black headboard. It was as if her life had been leading up to this moment—a ghost among her private things, as casual as if he belonged there, as if he were alive.

Wendy wondered if she were truly going crazy.

"So," she asked too brightly, searching for some topic to break the odd awkward tension. "Any word on the hat? Or the holes in it?" No longer hungry, she set the cookie aside.

At first it seemed he wouldn't answer, and Wendy began scouring her mind for some other topic, when Piotr said, "None of the others knows what it means. Lily is frantic." He reached to pet Jabber but snatched his hand back when the cat aimed an ill-tempered swipe at his wrist.

"Aren't there any, I don't know, ghostly acids or something that could have done it?" Wendy asked.

"Things, objects, sometimes pass over into the Never but I have never heard of such a thing." He grimaced. "It is possible, I suppose. But unlikely. It is a blessing, I suppose. Such an acid in the wrong hands would make . . . a deadly weapon."

His choice of words struck Wendy as strange and scary. "You know, I never thought to ask this before, but . . . Piotr, what happens when ghosts fight one another? If a Walker doesn't eat you, you can't kill each other, can you? You can only, you know, hurt one another, right?"

"That is wrong. We can destroy one another. And some do."

Gaping, Wendy pressed cold fingers to her lips. "But that's crazy. You're already dead!"

"That's what being a ghost is like. Death, existence, and death again." He smiled sadly. "Unless you find the Light. Then, salvation."

Wendy shuddered. "I'd imagine there's nothing worse than dying after you're dead."

Piotr disagreed. "*Net*. The Lightbringer is worse."

"Really?" Curious, Wendy sat up. "What's a Lightbringer?"

Standing now by the window, Piotr leaned forward and gazed out into the early evening, eyes searching and expression grim. When he turned to face her, Wendy was stunned to see how drawn his features had become, how pale he'd grown. He was still, steady, but the haze of his very essence seemed to be shaking, as if he were trembling. Piotr, she realized, was terrified.

"It's a—" Piotr struggled for the word, "a figure? A figure made of pure light, blinding light, and it sings a siren song that draws us. It's new, a snare like nothing you've ever seen." Piotr half-laughed, a broken, battered sound. "It has tentacles of light that it uses to spear us with."

"Tentacles." Wendy was starting to get a bad feeling about this.

"Thin, flexible. The light is bright. If we get too close . . ." He glanced under his lashes at her and hesitated, quieted.

The anticipation burned in her gut, a roiling mass of nerves, but Wendy didn't dare show Piotr how his words unnerved and frightened her. "If you get too close?" Wendy prompted, with a fake, sunny smile. The grin wasn't quite appropriate, but he was hardly looking at her, lost in his own dark thoughts.

"Since the light is like fire to us, if we get too close to it, the light burns us to cinders. It just starts eating away at what we are until we . . . until our very essence is stripped into nothing."

Coldness coiled in her gut. Wendy straightened, clasping her hands together to keep from shaking. A being of light that broke apart essence until it was no more. Surely he couldn't mean . . . her?

"Have you seen it?" she asked, studiously staring at a snarl of thread on her comforter. Her fingers, restless, stole out from her lap, picked at the snarl, working the knot until it had come undone. She smoothed it, pressing hard into the fabric. "This . . . this Lightbringer?"

"*Da*." Piotr shook his head, body sagging with the memory. "The other night. It was the most horrible thing I've ever seen."

As Piotr outlined his meeting with Lily and their encounter with the Walkers and the Lightbringer, Wendy remained calm and quiet. There was no doubt in her mind that Piotr had seen her on patrol that night, had spotted her when she'd been forced to reap the nosy Walkers that had scented her and tried to chase her down.

He'll never understand, she realized, sucking the ball at the end of her barbell between her front teeth. *He'll think you're after him.*

And wasn't that, in part, the truth? Hadn't she told herself just the other day that when all this was over, she'd reap him and release his soul into the Light? So who was in the wrong here? Piotr for being frightened of her or Wendy for doing her job in the first place? The job she hadn't even asked for? The job she didn't want anymore?

He thought she was a *monster*! Called her ribbons of Light "tentacles" and her glowing "horrible."

Piotr hated her. He just didn't know it yet.

Wendy felt ill.

Desperate to change the subject, she searched for something, anything to talk about. "I just realized that I forgot to tell you about this crazy dream I had earlier this week." Wendy settled on the edge of her bed, drew her legs up under her, scooted in. She could feel the coolness banking off him in waves, like the errant breeze from a weak fan. He even smelled cool—evergreens and mint and the slightest hint of something earthy just underneath. The scent of death, his death, which separated them.

"A dream?" Piotr leaned forward, curious and smiling. "Please tell. There are some that say dreams are gateways for the dead."

"So I found out." Wendy explained how she'd met the White Lady in her dream, but carefully kept their conversation streamlined, never mentioning why exactly the White Lady had chosen to single her out. "She's threatening my mother's soul," Wendy finished. "I think . . . I think that maybe she's upset that I'm meddling." It was close enough to the truth, Wendy reasoned. She *was* meddling, after all, just more than Piotr could ever know.

"This is no good," he declared when she'd finished, pounding a fist into his palm. "She cannot be allowed to do this!"

"I don't know how I'm gonna stop her from it," Wendy replied dryly. "But at least I can wriggle away if I need to."

"Spies," Piotr said softly. "This makes sense. If she had eyes and ears other than the Walkers, it would be much easier to time the kidnappings." He frowned. "I shall have to take this news to the others."

"That won't be easy. Aren't you guys spread all over?"

"*Net*, no longer. Once it was this way, but now all the Lost in the city have gathered together," he explained. "Close to the humans, safe. But this arrangement cannot last for long. Squished as we are into one little building . . . tempers are already simmering." He shook his head. "In truth, I should be there now. I've been shirking my patrol shifts and letting the others pick up the slack, trying to pick up traces of Dunn instead."

"Then why'd you come tonight?" She hesitated, tapped one finger on her temple as if searching for a memory. "I thought you wanted to bring, um, what's her name? Lily?" Wendy was proud of the way the name rolled flawlessly off her lips.

"Lily, in all her wisdom, believes I can learn more about Seers on my own." Chuckling, Piotr ran aimless fingers across her bedspread. "Besides, James arrived earlier today. Lily wanted time with him."

"Time?"

Piotr raised his fingers in air quotes. "'Time.'"

"Ooooh. Wow." Wendy relaxed, relieved. "I didn't know you still did that sort of thing."

Finding a loose thread in her comforter, Piotr ran his fingers through it over and over again. The thread wavered after several seconds of intense effort. "Why not?" He shrugged. "We're dead, not . . . uh . . . dead. *Da?*"

Wendy couldn't help but laugh. "Yeah, I think I get it. So, wow. This Lily chick sounds sort of like Eddie. She really likes this James guy, huh?"

"Indeed. Their territories are close but they can only meet infrequently. With other Riders there to watch the Lost, they can spend a while alone." He smiled. "I am very happy for her. She works much too hard and the loss of Dunn has been a blow for her. James will offer the comfort she needs."

Pausing a moment to make sure she wanted to pose the question after all, Wendy casually asked, "What about you? Do you have anyone special over there? Anyone you need to be comforting right now?"

"Special?" Piotr looked at her blankly, confused, before he understood what she was getting at. Then he laughed, flushed, and clasped his hands together in his lap. "I have in the past, *da*, but not for years. Since the early thirties at least."

"Thirties?" Wendy was stunned. "The nineteen-thirties?" How old was Piotr anyway?

"That sounds right." Piotr began tapping one finger against the outspread digits of the other hand, counting off the years. "The thirties, possibly the forties. One of the world wars had just ended. And I was with Elle for a while. Not long. She's . . . a wild child. I dated Lily as well, though only for a short time." His half-smile drooped. "James still hasn't forgiven me for that."

Amused that the dead had relationship drama just like anyone else, Wendy laughed merrily and a touch unkindly. This was something her mother's training had never even hinted at. "They'd broken up?"

"I thought seeing Lily in such a manner would be acceptable," Piotr complained, sounding eerily like Eddie for one brief moment. He waved a negligent hand. "But apparently *net*, it was not. I gave it my best, but it lasted a year. James," he grinned, "is a very persistent rival."

Hearing this guy, this boy who was her own age in physical years—if not actual years spent on the earth—sound just like her best friend, annoyed with some small fact of life, lifted an invisible weight that had been pushing Wendy down.

For the first time, she began really seeing Piotr—not just the peculiarities of him as a dead man, but as a person with quirks and foibles like herself. He was no longer simply a ghost she found attractive and would one day have to reap, but a guy near her own age, with his own problems and history, brimming with stories to tell.

Tension broken, they sank deep into conversation about the merits and perils of dating within one's social circle, what the dead did for fun, and talked the rest of the night away.

More than three weeks passed like this, each night spent deep in conversation, getting to know one another as only friends can do. After that first night, Wendy told Piotr to meet her at midnight and no sooner. Exhausted after her long nights and longer conversations, she sank easily into sleep with Piotr holding her hand. Despite his presence, her dreams grew worse.

The dreams weren't the only stressful change in her life. Determined to piss off the White Lady at every opportunity, Wendy now made a point of going out of her way to reap every Walker she saw instead of resorting to only self-defense.

At first, relaxing the personal ban on reaping ghosts had been utterly nerve-wracking—seeking them out was absolutely nothing like coming across them and defending herself. Trembling each time she dug inside herself and released the Light, Wendy forced herself to focus on taking every soul she spotted, returning to the habit of reaping with fierce concentration. She had to make up for all those souls she'd abandoned, Wendy reasoned. She couldn't let them continue to suffer.

Though she had to work back up to the regimen she'd been familiar with before, Wendy still felt a pang of fear every time she slid into the Light. Reaping ghosts was still excruciating, but dealing with the pain grew easier with every reap—as if spending time with Piotr was painting a spiritual target on her back, or as if she gave off a ghostly pheromone even when in her regular state.

Within a week, ghosts—Shade and Walker alike—sought her out at every opportunity: school, the diner, even on the bus. Since she couldn't become the Lightbringer around the living, being accosted in public was difficult to ignore. Wendy learned the art of ducking into alleys and running for the closest bathroom whenever a ghost was near. The ghosts generally followed.

Worried about what might be happening to her mother in the chaotic world of the Never, between the White Lady's threats and her Walkers, Wendy kept her searching patrols as close to home as she could easily manage. Eddie often drove her on patrol and did his homework in the car.

More than once on these whirlwind patrols, a ghost would approach, dim in the light, and Wendy would think it was her mother. She'd check her impulse to send the spirit on until it was close enough. Then, always, she'd feel the crushing disappointment.

Those reaps were always painfully quick.

Keeping to such a steady schedule soon made a major difference. In a matter of weeks, Wendy had Santa Clara swept clean of Walkers and Shades alike. There seemed to be more of the dead than ever before, and the Walkers grew crueler as the nights passed. Soon it became a struggle to reap them. The Walkers, originally loners, began traveling in pairs and then in packs. Perhaps they had other Walkers observing from the shadows, or maybe after so many encounters they were beginning to learn, but they began concentrating their attacks in the brief moment that Wendy took to become the Lightbringer. She could be wounded here, in that brief instant between physical form and ethereal. Despite their jabs, however, Wendy was still strong, even when outnumbered, and yet, as fast as Wendy was, she wasn't infallible. The smartest and quickest

Walkers would attack and run, escaping her grasp before the siren song could lure them back, returning to report to the White Lady on a semi-regular basis.

Through it all, though she looked high and low, ducking into every building she could, Wendy never saw her mother's soul.

Ironically, during their discussions Piotr worried that the Lightbringer would stumble upon the Rider camp at Pier 31, never realizing that he'd ensured its safety by letting Wendy know exactly where it was located.

"It makes no sense," he complained to Wendy. "A beast like that should be drawn to us. We are like a great feast for the likes of it! But there is nothing, not one sighting near the pier. It's all south of there. I'm starting to wonder if I imagined the thing."

These comments both pleased and hurt Wendy, confusing her deeply. Though it was her duty, the duty her mother had instilled in her from the very start of her training, Wendy was unwilling to reap the souls gathered at the Pier yet, though she knew that one day, one day very soon, she would have to. The thought of this undone responsibility pained her. Letting them sit there, still absent from the Light, went against all her mother's teaching, but Piotr, she knew, would be heartbroken at their loss.

She kept away from the nest of Riders and Lost for him.

When Dunn is found, she promised herself, *I'll send them all on*. She meant it, too. The moment the cap vanished, she'd finish them all off. But the hat was still whole, and Dunn's essence was still strong. It was a mystery.

"He must be hidden somewhere," Piotr theorized one night, almost a month after they'd met. It was after midnight and the entire house was asleep, save Wendy. Her father was out of town again. Chel and Jon had also temporarily made up, and Eddie had a new girlfriend, though he swore if Wendy changed her mind he'd dump the new girl in an instant. Wendy, laughing, declined. Life had, for the most part, smoothed out somewhat.

Except for Dunn's continued absence.

Deep in contemplation, Piotr was sitting on her bed, legs out-thrust, brainstorming out loud. It was a habit of his, she'd found. He liked to discuss what was on his mind and found her a safe reposi-tory for all his musings. After all, who would she tell?

"Dunn is being kept somewhere," he repeated, hunching over and rubbing one finger along the edge of his shoe, smoothing away a scuff. Jabber, who'd grown to tolerate Piotr over the past month, darted and dodged at the shoelace he dangled along the floor with his other hand.

"Somewhere, somewhere . . . but the North Bay has been scoured high and low! Lily wants now to search south." Piotr paused, and peered at her through a fall of his messy hair. Watching him shove the thick strands off his face, Wendy wondered if there were combs in the afterlife. "What of you, Wendy? Have you yet seen anything out of the ordinary during those walks you take?"

Only fourteen Walkers hanging out near the park tonight, she thought to herself, but kept quiet and shook her head. Wendy had three more equations to pound out before she could quit and get ready for bed. Piotr, who she suspected had never had homework a day in his life, kept rattling aloud in the background.

"This is insanity!" Piotr continued. Wendy scowled at the cracked screen on her graphing calculator and wished she had the money to buy a new one. She'd fallen hard on her backpack a week ago during the most recent Walker ambush, and had crushed it. It was a miracle the calculator still turned on. There was no way she was going to ask her father to buy her another one. Recently they'd developed a truce of sorts—she stuck to jeans and tees around the house, he pretended that she didn't stay out to all hours of the night.

"I need a job," she muttered under her breath. Jabber, ghostly bell tinkling, darted between her ankles.

"What's that?" Piotr peered over her shoulder. "You said something?"

Wendy slammed her book shut. "I said, 'I need a job,'" she grumbled, burying her face in her hands.

"I don't understand."

"My clothes are mostly ripped up, calculator's damn near broken, my bag's got a rip in it. Money's tight, Piotr, and it's a necessity for living. At least these days." She rolled her eyes and added sourly, "Not like you've got that problem."

Startled by her tone, Piotr was silent a moment, chastised. Then he brightened. "You need one of those for your schoolwork?" He pointed to her nearly shattered TI-86.

Forcing herself to keep her tone civil, Wendy sighed and nodded. "Yes. I do. But—"

She didn't get to finish her question—Piotr had dropped through the floor.

"Good going, Wendy," she groaned. "Way to scare him away." Upset with herself for her poor attitude, Wendy glumly returned to her homework, berating herself for the fact that Piotr would probably not be back tonight, if at all. So when his face appeared at her window twenty minutes later, Wendy jumped in fright, nearly falling off her chair.

"*Pros`tite*," he apologized, sliding through the wall and grinning sheepishly at her. "I was going to climb the stairs but the tree beckoned. It was fun!" Then he reached into his back pocket and drew out a package. "Is this the one?"

Wendy leaned forward, confused. "Is that . . . a calculator?"

"*Da*! Since you can touch me," he explained, setting the ghostly TI-86 on the edge of her desk, "and Dunn's cap, I reasoned that you might touch this too."

Resuming his normal position, Piotr propped himself against the headboard of her bed. "The packaging must be removed, *pros`tite*. My apologies."

"No, no, it's great. Thank you." Wendy picked up the calculator, marveling at the way one moment she could easily see through it and the next it solidified in her hand, opaque to the eye. "Does it work? Where'd you get it?"

"If it works, that is a mystery." Piotr shrugged and clucked his tongue at Jabber, trying to lure the cat to come play again. "Sometimes electronics do, sometimes they do not. Often it is not. No one knows why. I found them outside an electronic store . . . Costco? I was foraging for Dora's art supplies and learned that old merchandise is destroyed in the back. I go back frequently to check—I am the scavenger king!"

Stripping off the packaging, Wendy turned the calculator in her hands, stunned at the giving weight of it. "I wonder if I need ghostly batteries now," she joked, pressing the ON button. Slowly, unbelievably, the calculator powered on.

"*Net*, it is solar powered," Piotr said, grinning. "High tech. But which sun to work? Yours or mine?"

"This is absolutely insane," Wendy mused, turning the calculator under the light. "I thought there had to be some sort of emotional attachment for an object to pass over."

"Emotions help the process, but are not necessary. It is, what is the phrase . . . a crap shoot? Pass the cardboard please," Piotr said, holding up a hand until Wendy, still marveling over the gift, threw him the leftover packaging. He held it between his hands a moment, staring darkly down at the remnants, until the packaging wavered, shivered, and faded away.

"How'd you do that?" Wendy set down the calculator to examine Piotr's hands, turning them over in hers to make sure it wasn't some sort of trick.

"It takes practice," he said. "But flimsy things, you can make them—POOF—vanish." He shrugged. "Keeps the Never clean."

"Dead hippies," Wendy laughed. "Now I've seen everything. But thanks. I bet I can't just throw the packaging away, anyway. It'd go right through the garbage sack."

"It was no problem," he said and then lapsed into silence. They sat together, neither willing to speak, for several minutes, glancing at one another as the silence stretched longer and longer between them.

Finally Wendy cleared her throat and nervously ran her new barbell against the back of her teeth. "Look, Piotr, I'm sorry that I snapped at you. I've just been extra tired and—"

Seeming glad that Wendy had made the first move, Piotr waved his free hand. "Bah, Wendy! Go, finish your work. I will wait."

She took his hand and squeezed his fingers gratefully. "Thank you."

With the new calculator, Wendy was able to finish up her homework in less than fifteen minutes. It turned off as easily as a real calculator and stayed exactly where she put it.

Hopefully, she thought to herself, *I won't look like an absolute idiot using it in class.*

"So," Piotr said, as she joined him on the bed. "Last night I learned about the vagaries of the Internet. Tonight is your night for questions. What about the Never do you wish to learn? Pick my brain."

"Anything?"

"Anything at all." He relaxed against her pillows. "Go."

"Okay." Wendy curled her fingers in her bedspread. "Well, uh, you did promise to tell me about the Riders."

"The Riders?" Piotr smirked. "What is it you wish to know?"

"Everything."

He threw his head back and laughed. "Ask for something difficult next time?"

Wendy ducked her head, disappointed. It had taken a lot of nerve to finally work up to this subject, this deep and intricate part of Piotr's life that he constantly hinted about but never outright explained. "We could start with something else, I guess."

Shifting in place, Piotr shook his head. "*Net, net*, this is fine. It's just . . . it's fine." He cleared his throat. "The easiest explanation sounds bad, do you understand? But it is a good word to use. The Riders are like a gang. A sort of posse?"

"A sort of posse." Wendy raised one eyebrow and settled herself in for the explanation.

Sighing, Piotr adjusted his angle against her headboard and held his hands up, grasping for an eloquent explanation. "A group. A crew . . . people." He sagged. "It is complicated."

"It can't be that complicated. You all hang out, right? So what else? Who's the leader? Why do you call yourself Riders? I'm not asking you to solve the mystery of *pi* here, Piotr, just give me some background on where you go when you're not, you know, here."

"You speak . . ." he smothered a smile. "You are a strange one."

"Stalling," she replied with a wide grin. "Ahem. So, you all hang out, right?"

"*Da*," he laughed. "We 'hang out.' Infrequently. Often, though, it is a Rider and a few Lost, like a family, but there are times when we congregate. Now, for example." He smiled and his gaze was far away. "Once, before Lily and I had our time together, the Lost and Riders for miles around would gather every decade. Take trips together. Lily called these meetings *tu'wanasaapi*."

"*Tu'wanasaapi*," Wendy repeated, liking the way the word rolled off her tongue. "Fancy stuff. What was that all about?"

He shrugged. "It was a meeting of elders, I suppose. A time when we gathered and spoke, shared news and gossiped like old women. Now it would be considered . . . what was that word you used before? About flower children?"

"Hippies? New age?"

"New age! That is right! Our meeting for the *tu'wanasaapi* would be considered very spiritual; sitting in a circle and centering ourselves."

Wendy snorted. "Centering, huh?"

"You laugh," he replied seriously. "But many of the Lost were visited by the Light during those meetings. Many souls went on."

"I wouldn't dream of laughing at you," Wendy said, holding up her hands placatingly. "Not when it comes to the Light. That stuff is serious business." Moody now, Piotr had withdrawn and Wendy didn't want him to be in a huff. "Okay, so that's it then? You all just find a bunch of kids to hang out with—"

"To protect."

"To protect," she amended, "and then what? You just hang around until all the Lost have entered the Light? What then, do you get a prize? Maybe a cookie?"

He scowled. "If you cannot take this seriously—"

"Piotr, come on, please. You know me. I'm sorry. It's just . . . I don't understand why you guys would throw away your afterlives watching a bunch of kids you're not related to. Don't get me wrong, I think it's awesome; more people should take care of each other that way. But what do you guys get out of it? There has to be something, right?"

"You are not wrong. There is a reason." Piotr crossed his arms over his chest and, sliding off the bed, began pacing tight ovals around her room, stepping over Jabber as he paced. "But first, there is something you must grasp: Riders are not common. This may seem strange to you, but teenagers are new. Historically speaking."

Slightly annoyed that he was treating her like a child, Wendy rolled her eyes. "Well, duh. In the Middle Ages a girl became a woman as soon as she had her first period. You bleed, you breed, 'nuff said. No spot in between kid and adult."

"Exactly!" Momentarily taken aback at her fast understanding, it took a second for Piotr to smile appreciatively at her quick mind. "It was the same thing for boys. There was a rite of manhood—jump a horse, kill a deer and you are a man." He clapped his hands sharply, trying to explain without words the abrupt nature of the concept.

"And that 'Monday you're a kid, Tuesday you're an adult' idea bled over into the Never?"

"In a way." Piotr ceased pacing and knelt near her, the cadence of his words increasing as he warmed to the subject. "To clarify: Lily has been around many centuries. She is fond of saying that, for most people, there is defining moment when they grow up."

"Like . . . ?"

"Your heart is broken for the first time. Or perhaps you learn there is no Easter Bunny. You wake up one morning and decide there's no God. But one day, child; the next, adult. It is like a switch. In your head."

Convincing Jabber to slink near with a wiggle of his fingers, Piotr stole a few quick pets off the back of Jabber's head before the cat tired of the attention and hissed, darting away. "Elle calls it the real loss of innocence."

"How so?"

"Once you have had it, there is no returning. A seed of doubt begins to grow. You are corrupted."

Wendy could see where he was going, and thoughtfully tapped her tongue ring. "But not for everyone?"

"Not for all." He shrugged. "With some people, that switch isn't set to 'child' and 'adult,' 'on' or 'off.' There is a period of wonder . . . a middle space."

"Like a gradient?"

"You understand. These gradient-people, maybe they don't believe in Easter Bunny anymore, but they still believe in the Tooth Fairy. Or their first love burned but they are completely able to trust the next person just as much. They can separate the bad things and not grow cynical. There is still some innocence." Clasping his hands together, Piotr smiled to himself and rocked back and forth on his toes, getting into the subject now.

Wendy laughed and Piotr looked at her strangely. "This is funny?"

"No, it's not that. I was just remembering . . . when I was a kid, you could just go up to another kid on the playground and say 'Want to be my friend?' and play. Within a week, you'd have a new best friend. No worrying if they thought you were weird, you just ran off and had fun." She grinned. "I can't imagine doing that now." Wendy leaned back and thought briefly of Eddie. She couldn't remember a time when he hadn't been a part of her life.

Piotr ran his hands through his hair, pushing the long hanks off his face. "You know this, but many adults pass into the Light with no fuss. Children are the same—most of them go into the Light easily, the remaining become the Lost. But those like me . . ." Piotr's hands curled into loose fists. "We died when we were in-between child and adult. Those like me become the Riders, the protectors."

"Eternally seventeen," Wendy murmured. "Wow, suck."

"It is not so bad." He winked. "I eternally look this good."

Wendy snorted and buried her face into a pillow to keep Jon or Chel from hearing her laughter. Finally, when her chuckles had subsided, she sat up and wiped the tears streaming from her eyes. "Well how many Riders are there, anyway? Just to know what your competition is, understand."

He ignored the last. "In all the city? Perhaps ten of us, watching fifty or so Lost. Then there are hundreds if not thousands of Walkers, the White Lady, and now the Lightbringer." Piotr grimaced. "These challenges that face us . . . it is difficult to stay upbeat these days. Even together we are outnumbered."

Slowly, wanting to make sure she had all her facts straight, Wendy turned the conversation away from the Lightbringer and toward the Lost. This was a conversation she'd always wanted to have with her mother, but it had never been the right time. Piotr was filling some rather large holes in her knowledge. "If they need protection so badly, how can the Lost exist so long? Especially with the Walkers hunting them?"

Piotr gave her a look that said *come on, you're smarter than that*. "They died with much life ahead of them. The unused years sustain them, give them strength. And should they choose to share some of this life, to strengthen the will to keep going . . ."

"Share . . . oh!" Wendy understood. "You guys take care of the Lost and they take care of you. *Quid pro quo*."

Smiling crookedly, Piotr shrugged. "As I have said before, protecting the Lost has its benefits. Shaking hands in greeting will tide an older ghost over for weeks. It is a contact high. It's why the Walkers need them to exist. That energy, that will to keep going on, is what stops the Walkers from fading away. Even those completely rotten from within." He frowned. "I tire of this subject. It is distasteful. I don't wish to discuss this anymore."

"Okay." Wendy stretched out beside him and Piotr, face grave, absently took her hand. Feverish and excited after learning so much about the world she brushed only peripherally, Wendy welcomed the electric chill of his touch. It soothed her and, despite his attempt to hide it, she noted his initial wince quickly smoothed away.

"Still burns, huh?"

"Always a little," he murmured, running his thumb over her knuckles. "The calm surety of you is enough to make the pain worthwhile."

"Why do you think this is?" Without releasing his hand, Wendy indicated their joined fingers. "I mean, there's got to be some reason, right?"

"I do not know." Stretching, Piotr laid beside her, still holding her, and wrapped his other hand around their joined fists so that he was cupping her hand in his. His eyes strayed to the intricate Celtic knots tattooed across her collarbone and he winced, glancing away. "I wish I could describe what it is like."

"You could try."

Piotr's lips quirked. "I would fail. This is . . . this is different. It hurts, but it's not insistent. When I touch you everything is brighter. The grey isn't so *grey*." Absently Piotr ran his thumb over the base of her thumb, tracing the line there. "What's it like for you?"

Sleepily, Wendy yawned. She could never explain it, the comfort she got when she and Piotr lay on her bed and held hands like this, how the electric chill subsided into soothing, numbing cool. She was thrilled by the paradox of his touch, since holding his hand inevitably sent her to sleep before long. With the White Lady regularly haunting her dreams, Wendy knew she needed every second of sleep she could get.

Adjusting until she was comfortable, Wendy curled on her side and switched hands, letting Piotr caress her other hand so she could tuck her arm under her head. "It's nice," she murmured, eyes slowly closing. "I need to turn off the light."

"It's not harming anything," he said. "Stay."

"Mmm," she sighed and nodded, sinking deeper into her bed as tightly wound muscles relaxed and her light breathing finally steadied, slowed as she drifted towards sleep. "Okay."

"So this is just 'nice' then?" Piotr's voice was low, almost indistinguishable from the steady rush of blood in her veins, the soft whoosh of her own breath. She could have dreamed it; could have imagined the soft, cool press of his fingertips brushing along her cheekbone, the gentle feathering of his hair against her forehead as his lips faintly followed the line his fingers had taken. He was a perfect gentleman.

"Piotr?" she murmured, nearly asleep, not wholly conscious. "Stay?"

"*Net*, Wendy, *dorogaya*. Not tonight," he replied, as he had done every night for the past month, disentangling his hands from hers. She heard the real regret in Piotr's tone, the subtle desire to heed her wishes indicated only by a slight thickening of his accent. Piotr, she knew, rarely showed regret. "Not tonight," he repeated, "but someday."

On the edge of dreams, Wendy frowned. "Spoilsport."

The last thing she heard as she drifted into dreams was his laughter as he slid through the door and walked away.

In her dreams Wendy walked and walked.

This time she found herself not at the beach or the park but standing in the woods outside the house of her first reap. The house had begun to fall apart, the back porch spongy with rot, the lawn overgrown with grass and weeds that brushed Wendy mid-thigh. Wendy drifted closer to the house, running tentative fingers over the rusted legs of the swingset, and wondered why her dream had brought her here.

"Maybe it wasn't *your* mind that brought you," said the White Lady, stepping through the shattered patio door of the house. "Ability to blast ghosts into the afterlife notwithstanding, you don't rule the dreamspace, you know."

"You again." Wendy scowled, eyeing the backyard for potential Walker hiding spots. "Didn't I tell you that I wasn't going to call a truce?"

"I remember." She looked around the porch and tsked. "This place used to be so nice."

"Right," Wendy drawled. "I'm sure you even have a clue where this place is in real life."

"Near Middlefield and San Antonio Road," the White Lady rapped out. "Though, in the living world, I'm told those trees were torn down some time ago. Not that I'd know. I haven't been back here in a while." She rested one hand on the porch rail.

"What, did you live out here?" Wendy rolled her eyes. "I find that hard to believe."

"'When we are dreaming alone it is only a dream. When we are dreaming with others, it is the beginning of reality.' Camara. Not quite apt for this discussion, but close enough for government work, I suppose."

"You're talking crazy again. Or are you just trying to creep me out again or something?"

"I've found that 'creeping you out' is rarely worth the bother unless I want to make a point. Much to my chagrin, I see that quite clearly now. I shouldn't have bothered trying to scare you the last time we spoke. All that effort for nothing." The White Lady squeezed and the railing beneath her hand disintegrated.

"Why are you even bothering with me? I mean, come on. I know you're dead and all, but don't you have some sort of life?"

"Let's say that I have a habit of following the antics of your kind and keeping an eye on their whereabouts. It's good policy, after all, to know what your enemy is up to." The White Lady touched her throat with one hand, plucking at her stitches. "Your sort is a big deal here. You're like Bigfoot, but real." She chuckled. "You don't think about the effect what you do has on the Never, do you? How large an impact you make? Or how the Never affects the real world."

"I was taught that the Never can't influence the living," Wendy said. "The whole lot of you are just ghosts."

The White Lady chuckled. "Just ghosts. That's rich." She pointed to the swingset. "Do you remember the woman you reaped here? What was she doing when you found her?"

Wendy stiffened. "How did you know about that?"

"Answer the question. What was she doing?"

Shrugging, Wendy glanced at the swingset. "Pushing her granddaughter on the swing." She stopped. "Wait, that can't be right. She was dead. That can't happen." Wendy chewed her lower lip and tried to remember more about that day. Surely she'd imagined the old woman pushing the girl. To think otherwise was to start entertaining ideas she wasn't prepared to handle, especially without her mother to answer the questions that were bullying their way to the forefront of Wendy's mind. "Can it?"

"You tell me." The White Lady sounded as if she were smirking, but the heavy shadow of her cloak hid her face. She gestured back toward the house. "Don't you ever wonder what happened to the mother of that little girl? What sort of mother would leave her child to an abusive stepfather and a sick grandmother? Especially after that grandmother had kicked the bucket?"

"A real mom wouldn't. She'd be back home right away."

"True! 'A mother's love endures through all.' Washington Irving. So, my dear girl, why would a mother have to let someone like you intervene on her child's behalf?"

"She wouldn't. Unless she was kept away or, I don't know, was dead," Wendy said. Then she frowned, taking in the overgrown yard and rotting home. Pale white lace curtains fluttered in the windows, long white sheers hung behind the shattered patio door. Even the buckets of flowers by the patio stairs, overgrown and wilted, browned in the hot sun, had once been white. "Wait. Are you telling me that *you're*—"

"I'm telling you nothing," the White Lady interjected smoothly. "All I'm doing is pointing out that you've been taking too much at face value for some time now. Listening to one's mother is all well and good, but at some point you have to learn to think for yourself. I was watching you that day." She drifted down the stairs past Wendy and, with a slight gesture, sent the rusting swing rattling in an arc. "You were so intent on ripping that ghost to shreds on your momma's orders, you didn't even think to ask the right questions."

"Oh yeah? What should I have asked, then?" Wendy stiffened and stepped away from the White Lady. She was too close for comfort; a horrid odor of moss and rot permeated the air around her. "Let me guess. I should've made the grandma tell me how she was pushing the little girl?" She sneered. "Right."

"It would have been a good start." The White Lady caught the swing in one mottled hand. Her nails were long and yellow and curling, Wendy noted. Her bones peeped through the flesh as she slid into the seat of the swing and gently pushed off, letting the swing creak and groan as it carried her higher and higher. The edges of her hood fluttered in the breeze but didn't push back as she pumped her rotting legs harder, gaining momentum and height.

"Look, did this conversation have a point or something? Because if the only reason we're having this little chat is over something I didn't ask four years ago, well, that ship has sailed. It's not like I can go stomping into the Light, find Grandma, and ask her how she did her fancy magic trick." Wendy crossed her arms over her chest and waited patiently as the White Lady, at swing's apex, pushed off the seat and floated to the ground. Gravity was on break in this dream; the White Lady hung in the air for a moment too long and reached the high grass several seconds too late.

Despite herself, Wendy smiled. "Nice jump."

"Thank you." The White Lady wiped one hand across the hip of her pristine cloak as she passed a rotting barbeque grill. "So messy! Honestly, some people just can't have nice things."

The White Lady dusted her hands and crossed her arms over her chest. "The point of all this is that I thought that perhaps, after sharing my wisdom with you, you might actually be able to look past the terrible rumors that've been circulating about me and think for yourself for once. Make up your own mind."

"I'm listening."

"I thought that, perhaps, we trade instead of fight. A deal."

"And now I'm leaving." Wendy turned and began to head back toward the woods.

"Hear me out!"

"Go to hell, lady. I don't deal with the likes of you. We covered this already, remember?"

"Listen to me!" The White Lady darted in between her and the woods. "You're making more of a nuisance of yourself than usual. And I know for a fact that you haven't found your mother yet."

"You haven't either. If you had, you'd have let me know by now. Rub it in my face, demand something impossible." Wendy smirked. "Not really trying, are we?"

"Oh, believe me, I'm keeping my eyes peeled. All of them." The White Lady laughed darkly. "I saw her once or twice. She moves quickly. And she knows the city well."

"Oh yeah? Where?"

"That is for me to know, my dear, and you to find out. I may not have her in my hardworking but oh-so-delicate hands just yet, but I will. Mark my words, I'm closing in, and when I do you will beg me—beg me!—to have your mother's soul back."

"Getting bored." Wendy stepped around the White Lady and headed for the woods. "Good luck with all that. You just let me know if you can catch her, hmm? Until then, where was I? Oh yeah. Go to hell."

"I may not have your mother's soul," the White Lady called behind her, "but I sure as hell have Dunn's."

Wendy froze. Sweat broke out all over her body as she struggled with the urge to turn and dive at the White Lady. Knowing her, she'd vanish and Wendy would end up with a face full of dirt for her troubles.

"You. Bitch. I will *end* you."

"No, dear, you just wish you could end me." The White Lady chuckled. "Here's the deal. You walk away from my Walkers and I won't rip the boy to shreds and send those shreds to the Riders in a pretty paper package. How does that sound, hmm?"

"What are you keeping him for anyway, you horrible cow?" Wendy turned around to find the White Lady less than a foot away. The smell of rot was blinding this close up; Wendy's eyes immediately watered. "You aren't feeding the Lost to the Walkers or you would've done it by now. You're keeping him for some reason. Why?"

"That, my dear, is for me to know and you to fret yourself over. Do we have a deal?"

Wendy stiffened. "I can't do that. I can't." Her fists tightened. "But you better pray to whatever god you believe in that I don't spot your pasty ass on my rounds, lady. You've officially stepped all over my last nerve."

"Ah, yes, I think I understand now. You're trying to protect the rest of them." The White Lady chuckled. "I understand. It's a complicated choice. If you give in to me, then you've saved one soul but damned the rest. But if Dunn is sacrificed then you can still run free and attempt to stem the tide, maybe even keep my Walkers away from the other Lost. But it's already too late. My Walkers are numerous and growing by the day. I've already won, you and those pathetic Riders just don't know it yet."

"I swear—"

"You swear nothing. You understand nothing." The White Lady waved a hand. "I'm bored of this. This will take time for you to decide. I'm feeling particularly reasonable tonight. You have two weeks. Fourteen whole days, that's how generous I am. Sort out which is more important to you. The boy or," she laughed, "the Rider."

"I wish I could kill you twice," Wendy said through gritted teeth. "And if I ever get to really lay hands on you, you'll regret it. I promise you that. You'll regret it."

"Hmm. We'll see. I'll see myself out."

Wendy woke moments later, drenched in sweat and crying angry tears. She didn't know what to do. Should she tell Piotr or should she handle the White Lady alone? And, more importantly, should she sacrifice Dunn?

Wendy flopped back on her pillow, wiping her tears away. She wished her mother were there. Mom would know what to do.

"Mom," she whispered to the ceiling. "Where are you?"

CHAPTER TWELVE

K nee-deep in Walker ashes, Wendy pulled in the Light and wrestled down the heat, flickering into view. Lately she'd spent so much time as the Lightbringer that shifting back to her physical form seemed like it was beginning to grow more difficult for her as the nights wore on, not easier. Though Eddie couldn't see the monsters his best friend had battled, he could tell that this fight had been a tough one by the way Wendy trudged back to the car.

"Rough night?" Eddie held out a cup of hot chocolate laced with amaretto, just the way she liked it, and sympathized as she sank into the passenger seat in a heap. Surreptitiously he glanced at the dashboard clock. Fifteen minutes to ten. Her reaping had run over.

"A whole cadre of Walkers was waiting for me. Near a bunch of people, too, and not a one of the Walkers burned! I swear they're totally multiplying," she complained, taking the first sip and squinching up her nose. "Ugh, cold."

"Yeah, well your 'only ten minutes, I *promise*' reap took forty," Eddie chastised, finishing the last of his own coffee. He grimaced at the bitter dregs but swallowed them down. Someone around here had to show a good example. "I finished my coffee cold, so quit bitching and drink your cocoa already."

"Mm, thank you," she said. "Today sucked."

"Looks like it."

"I'm in English class, right? And a ghost walks through the wall and right up to me. How he knew I was there is beyond me but he followed me around all day, begging me to help him get into the Light. But I couldn't, right? Because, hello, I'm at *school*."

"Ouch. So what'd you do?" Eddie reclined his seat and tilted his head back, enjoying the feeling of the cool evening breeze on his warm cheeks.

"I had to lead him into the girl's bathroom," Wendy grumbled. "But it was so weird. I sent him into the Light, and right before he went he was crying. Crying and thanking me. Afterward I felt so much better, Eds. The Walkers are monsters, it's important to put them down, but actually helping regular ghosts out again . . . it's nice. I feel like an ass for quitting in the first place. This was what I'm made to do, right?"

Eddie hesitated. "Yeah. Right."

"I am so-so-so very tired," Wendy said, yawing. "On top of every-thing else, I've had nightmares every night this week. Mom, calling to me, trying to get me to find her, saying that she's trapped, that she's lost." She rubbed her eyes. "I just want them to stop already."

"Huh," Eddie said, glancing at his watch. Part of him wanted to listen to her, hug her, tell her it'd be all right. The other part knew better. He wasn't going to fall for it this time—he'd promised. "You could, uh, try some Nyquil or something."

"I don't have problems getting to sleep, it's staying asleep."

He shrugged. "I don't know what to tell you. Maybe pick up a book on dream zen or something? Learn to be one of those dream master guys?"

"Working on it," she muttered under her breath before taking a deep gulp of her drink. "So, um, Eddie? Have you noticed that my life's been sort of weird lately?"

Eddie grabbed the steering wheel in a white-knuckled grip. "Yeah. But you're preachin' to the choir there." Desperately he added, "I told you about landing a date with Gina Biggs, right? Oh, man, that girl is so smoking hot!" He forced his fingers to release the wheel and straightened in his seat. "Forest fire hot." Eddie chuckled, too loudly.

"Yeah," Wendy murmured, "you told me before." She ran her thumb around her lips, wiping away excess chocolate. "But, Gina's hotness aside . . ."

"You can't ignore how hot she is. It's impossible."

"Eddie!" Wendy ground her teeth. "Enough about your . . . whatever she is, okay? Yes, she's sexy. Go you. I'm trying to talk to you here."

"What? I'm listening."

"No you're not, you're mooning over Gina Has-a-hot-ass."

He sighed. "Wendy, just because you're jealous—"

"I'm not jealous! Why would you think I'm jealous?"

"I still love you, sweetie, you know that." He patted her hand. "It's just, you know, you said that you and me weren't going to work out and a guy can't just sit at home and twiddle his thumbs waiting for you. I mean, I would, but . . ."

"We weren't going to work out. Aren't. Whatever." Wendy groaned and buried her face in her hands. "Eddie, this isn't about Gina, okay! Just shut up already and listen to me!"

He settled back in his seat. "Fine, fine, I'm hearing you. No Gina talk. You've got my full attention. Go."

She sighed. "With me, stuff's been weirder than normal. I mean really, really weird. With the ghost stuff, I mean."

"Right-right, sure-sure," Eddie said, waving his hand. "I get ya."

Wendy took a deep breath, as if steeling herself for a negative reaction. "You know how I've been going out every night lately, right? Well, I—"

The alarm on his phone trilled a warning. Anxious that he might miss his phone date with Gina, Eddie lifted his arm and tapped his watch. "Hell, look at the time. If I don't get home soon my mom's gonna kill me."

"Oh, okay." Rubbing a hand over her eyes, Wendy gulped the rest of her drink down. When she finished, she wiped her mouth and belched. "Blame it on me."

"I have been." Eddie grimaced, now all nerves. He'd been meaning to bring this up for a few weeks now, but Wendy had been incommunicado, not up to their usual late-night texting chats, and certainly too sleepy and busy to talk with at school.

Twisting the key, Eddie started his car and fervently checked his mirrors, avoiding looking at Wendy while he said what he had to say. "Um, just to get this out there, if you keep up all this long-distance reaping, Mom says she's not going to let me hang out with you anymore. She's starting to talk about how you're a bad influence. Keeping me out to all hours on weeknights and stuff."

At Wendy's dumbfounded look, Eddie waved his hands in protest. "I tell her she's wrong, of course! But you know what a pain in the butt moms . . . are." He winced, and cursed himself for ten times a fool for bringing up his mother in particular, and mothers in general. "Sorry, Wendy. I didn't mean to go there."

"It's cool." Wendy shrugged, trying for nonchalance but clearly upset. "Moms are moms. It's not your fault, right?"

"It's not your fault either," he reminded her, getting up the guts to look her in the face. "What happened to your mother wasn't."

"Whatever." Wendy checked the time on the dash and buckled up. "Come on, Eds, let's make tracks. I've got a date with geography and you've gotta get your pretty little butt home before Mommy Dearest goes all Mommy Dearest on you."

"Wendy—"

"Move it, Jeeves, if you please." Wendy rifled through her purse and pulled out a five, slapped open the glove compartment, and dropped the money inside. "Here. For the gas."

Concerned, Eddie tried to catch her eye. "Hey, hey, you don't owe me anything, Wendy. I've never asked you for gas money."

Wendy kept her face turned away. "Exactly, you've never asked. So after all these years I totally ought to throw at least a little scratch your way. Now vroom-vroom already. The hour groweth late and crap like that. "She sounded casual, but the cup in her grip told a different story; it had gone from a *venti* Styrofoam cup to a sticky ball in her fist.

At least she finished the hot chocolate, Eddie thought to himself, and shifted the car into reverse. He'd scrub out any stains on Saturday before his Homecoming date with Gina, no problem.

A little worried but willing to let her mood slide, Eddie eyed the empty mall parking lot and started rolling toward home. He had plenty of time to worry about Wendy tomorrow, right? Truth be told, Eddie was glad to be taking her home early; the night was young and he still had a long evening ahead of him to spend flirting with the luscious little artist he intended to woo and win. Even though it killed him to be going out with Gina instead of Wendy, he had to move on. Wendy wasn't the only girl in the world. Still, the guilt niggled at the back of his mind.

With an annoyed grunt, Eddie headed home, the girl beside him weighing heavily on his mind.

When Wendy stomped into her room, she found Piotr waiting. He had a small cardboard shoebox in his hands. A swath of fabric dotted with the familiar acid-eaten holes peeked out at the top.

"You're here early." Her phone beeped. Wendy glanced down:

IKssBoiz&Grls: *Was I being an ass? U still wanna talk? I'll tell Gina not 2nite.*

Wendy hesitated then pressed *ignore*. Eddie would understand. Now wasn't the time.

"I had to see you right away." Piotr held up the box. "I did not know you would be out, so I decided to wait." He hesitated. "You were with Eddie, yes? Working?"

"Duh." Wendy eyed the box. "So this thing sounds big. What's up?"

"Another kidnapping."

"Who's missing?" she asked, dropping her bag to the floor. Jabber hissed—she'd inadvertently dumped her bag right on top of him. Head held high and tail stiff with disdain, the cat flounced through the bag and under the bed, pausing to swipe at her ankle as he departed.

"One of James' Lost," Piotr said, setting the box on her desk. "Tommy. This was his jacket."

Wincing at the thin sting Jabber's claws left, Wendy knelt down to rub her ankle, whistling at the bad news. These past weeks spent listening to Piotr's stories had advantages; she'd peripherally learned all about the other ghosts Piotr surrounded himself with, Lost and Rider alike, to the point where she felt like she could effortlessly list them off. The news struck her harder than she could ever have anticipated. She wondered again about Dunn, if the White Lady had meant her threats. "Tommy? Wasn't he once one of yours?"

Piotr nodded, lips tight. "A few decades ago. He got on better with James than he did with me. They were alive at the same time and James understood Tommy in a way I couldn't. They were friends."

"Didn't James tell his Lost to stay close?"

Piotr's fist pounded his hip. "Tommy *was* close! He was dutiful, he wasn't like the others, he didn't wander off. Do you see? Elle turned her back for one minute and he was gone. Poof! Just gone."

"And she couldn't track him?" Wendy lifted the ethereal fabric out of the box and examined it. Jacket, she noted, was too strong a word. It had probably been, in life, little more than a thin and motheaten cloak made of heavy linen. Now, with the familiar burn holes dotting the entire length, it appeared less like a garment and more like a slice of Swiss cheese.

"They hid their tracks very well. We found it torn up at the end of his trail." Piotr punched the wall and, since his concentration was weak, his arm slid through the plaster almost to his elbow, sticking deeply in the wall. He scowled and, with effort, extracted his arm. "They are angling toward the city."

Wendy sighed, nodded. "Tomorrow's a half day at school. I can take Caltrain up to the city and take a look around. See if I see anything different."

"*Spaseebo balshoye*," Piotr said gratefully. "Your aid is appreciated."

"No problem. It's the least I can do," Wendy said, folding the cloak and nestling it back in the box. Her phone beeped again.

IKssBoiz&Grls: *Hellloo? U awake? Srry bout Mom. Screw her. I'll still drive u anytime.*

This time Wendy set her phone to silent and laid it on the corner of her desk. "Is there anything else you can tell me? Anything at all?"

"Only that there was a crowd." Piotr sank onto the edge of the bed. "Walkers didn't walk in crowds before. Now they thrive on it." He buried his face in his hands. "I don't know what to do! We sit like ducks, waiting to get picked off! One this week, two the next! Even gathered together we're not safe."

The phone flashed as another text came in.

IKssBoiz&Grls: *Wendy? I'm sorry. Please call me. Please?*

"Did they take him from Elle's place?" Wendy sat beside Piotr. She started to take his hand and then thought better of it. He seemed untouchable right now and she didn't want to push their boundaries. On the desk the phone flashed again. This time Wendy set it upside down. "Did they go inside?"

Piotr shook his head. "Tommy was fond of the roof. Some clear nights, the old theater will project classic movies on the wall across the wharf."

"Was he up there alone?"

"Elle went with him but she turned to scout the far corner. When she turned back he was gone. She spotted a shadow moving south and gave chase but a block or two later she found Tommy's cloak. Nothing else. No trace of which way they went from there. Nothing."

"It's not much, but it's a start," Wendy said, guilt churning in her gut. She still hadn't told Piotr about the deadline the White Lady had set for her. He had no clue that Dunn might be in even more danger than he suspected. But it made no sense to her—why would the White Lady go to all the trouble of kidnapping the Lost and then do nothing but squirrel them away? Something about the whole mess smelled fishy. She just couldn't pinpoint what.

"Wendy, we can't take much more of this! You must help us," Piotr cried, grabbing her by the wrist. This time his touch was not just cool but frigid and Wendy, startled by the sharp chill, yanked away. She rubbed her wrist, eyes wide with shock at the pain.

"*Pros'tite*," he whispered, stunned and repentant. His own palm was dark from their brief contact; if he'd been alive, Wendy imagined it would be red and blistering. "My apologies. I hurt you. I didn't mean to."

"It's fine. Looks like I hurt you too," she replied grimly. "How's your hand?"

"I'll survive." Piotr turned away from her and stood, walking to the window. "I'm sorry."

"It's okay. You were worried, you lost your concentration and you weren't careful when we touched." Wendy laughed brokenly. "I mean, hell, it's not like there's an instruction manual for this sort of thing. We're sort of feeling our way along, right?"

"I've asked every Shade still able to talk with me if they've ever heard of anything like this. None can. Most think I am insane to even think of being near the living."

"Maybe. I wish my mom were here," Wendy said. She slid from the bed and braced her back against the mattress, legs thrust out and flexing her toes. The exercise gave her something to concentrate on besides Piotr. "She'd know what to do. She might have a clue, at least."

"Your mother?" Steadied somewhat, Piotr settled on the floor beside her. "What do you mean? How could your mother help us?"

"Mom is . . . was . . . like me. She . . . she sees. Saw. The dead, I mean."

She's also a Lightbringer, Wendy wanted to add, but kept silent on that fact. Now was not the time, nor the place. She had to think on this revelation first, to turn it over in her head.

"I do not recall you speaking of this before. So you were born this way, it was not merely your accident . . . it is inherited, your Seeing?" Piotr reached for her hand and Wendy hesitated, then drew away, uncertain if she wanted him to touch her after his outburst. He hadn't meant to hurt them, she knew, but time after time he'd told her that existing in the Never was all about strength of will and concentration. If he lost his concentration again he might do more than sting her, he might do real damage to them both. Still, despite all that, part of her was anxious to brush her fingers across his wrist, to feel that strange ethereal suppleness that existed between them.

Duty, a voice whispered within. Her duty was being denied all for the touch of a boy's hand. Wendy wanted to be disgusted with herself but couldn't quite work up to it. Touching Piotr's hand still felt too calming, too nice. Feeling like a taut bundle of nerves and emotions, Wendy gave in and brushed his fingers with hers. Now that he was calm their temperatures had almost equalized. It was very pleasant.

"Wendy?" Piotr was examining her face and Wendy, flushing, realized she hadn't answered his question.

"Sorry! Um, well, yes and no. My ability to see the dead is sort of inherited, yeah, but I wasn't born like this. I only started seeing ghosts after the accident. The one we met at."

"The accident we met . . . oh, yes, I remember now." He glanced around the room, as if looking would reveal more of Wendy's past to him. "I have asked and asked, but no one has heard of your mother. And your patrols, are they still turning up nothing?" Wendy shook her head. "Wendy," Piotr began hesitantly, "I do not mean to belittle your pain but . . . she has probably entered the Light by now. Much time has passed."

Stiffening, Wendy started to draw away.

Piotr knew that he'd said the wrong thing. Wendy's shoulders hunched and her head dipped down, her chin tucked to her chest and her eyes watering. Thoughtlessly, Piotr put an arm around her and drew her to his side, barely feeling the increase of her heat in his concern for her.

"You don't understand. Before . . . before, I didn't tell you the whole truth, Piotr. My mom isn't dead." She scrubbed the heel of her hand against her cheeks. "She's in a coma. Mom's sick."

"Oh." This changed things, Piotr knew. "Then your problem is fixed! Her soul may be where her body is and since she still lives—"

"That's the problem," Wendy whispered. Her shoulders shook and Piotr hugged her tighter, wishing that he could help. "Her soul *isn't* anywhere near her body. She's just gone!"

"Perhaps, because you are Seers, you are strange," Piotr suggested, half to assure himself and half for Wendy. "It is known that your souls are different from the rest of us. Perhaps her cord, it has grown thin and she is just traveling. Wise men, yogi, do this from time to time."

"That's what I've been banking on," Wendy admitted, "but I've scoured almost all of the South Bay and I've come up with bupkis." She scrubbed her eyes. "I hate to say this, but I've been really counting on you coming up with some sort of lead for me. You seemed to know everyone, you know? But . . . you've got your own issues. I can't ask you to keep worrying about my stuff."

"This is nonsense!" Piotr cried, tightening his hold. "I do not leave my . . . friends . . . to suffer, Wendy. I shall keep looking, I swear."

"But," she frowned, "what about Dunn and Tommy? You can't be in two places at once, Piotr."

"Shush. I am here for you." Inexperienced with this sort of misery, Piotr fought with himself over what was the best next move, what question would hurt her the least. Finally he settled on, "What do the doctors say is wrong with her?" and hoped that it wouldn't cause Wendy further pain.

Knuckling away the tears on her cheek with one hand, Wendy coughed wetly, leaned back into his steadying arm, and sighed. "That's just it. They don't know. Her condition is like nothing they've ever seen before, but . . ." Wendy wiped her eyes. "Physically the doctors don't know what happened. Aneurism, embolism . . . all these 'isms.' They can't find any actual physical damage, her collapse and the coma are a big mystery. The insurance company flew in fancy doctors from New York, Paris, London. They all want to write papers about her mysterious collapse. But I know what really did it." She pressed her lips tightly together. "It was the Lost."

"The Lost?" Piotr didn't quite understand how contact with the Lost would affect Wendy's mother that way, but after meeting Wendy, he was unwilling to dismiss the possibility so easily, unlikely as it seemed. "I do not understand."

"That night, the night of the accident, my mother was swarmed by Lost, Piotr. They . . . drained her somehow. Pulled her soul free. They had to have, because when I got there her soul was gone. Completely gone. And some of the Lost were apologizing to me. They were so upset . . ." Wendy crossed her arms over her chest, hugging herself.

"I have never heard of such a thing," Piotr murmured. "It cannot be. It is impossible."

"Is it?" Wendy studied Piotr. "You told me time and time again how unique the Lost are, how much raw power they've got. And Seers are different, right? You just said so."

"But to harm a living soul—"

"It wasn't intentional," Wendy replied firmly. "That was clear. I think it was some crazy sort of accident. I think that she went to . . . talk to them, to make sure they were finding the Light okay, and they were in a panic. They pulled her apart." Wendy chuckled wetly and Piotr realized that she'd been holding back the bulk of her tears only by sheer force of will. That will was starting to crack. "I always wondered why she wouldn't let me . . . interact . . . with the Lost before. Mom was trained by her grandmother who said that there were generations of us, Seers, stretching who knows how far back. They must have known something like this could happen."

The heat coming off her was starting to grow immense. Piotr

shifted, uncomfortable but unwilling to let Wendy go when she was hurting. "Put like that, I suppose it is possible that the Lost may have hurt your mother. But Wendy, what makes you think she hasn't simply passed on?"

"It's like that cap of Dunn's, or Tommy's cloak. If her body hasn't given up, that means her spirit's still out there, right?"

"In theory? It is possible." Piotr didn't want to offer her hope, but he'd seen his fair share of spirits that still had healthy silver cords attached. If her mother's spirit had been knocked free somehow and was wandering, there was a chance they could return her soul . . . but not if there was no body to return to. So long as the cord remained tethered, even if it were thin as silken thread, Wendy's mother might yet be roused.

Then a terrible thought occurred to him. He didn't want to bring it up, but Piotr knew he'd never forgive himself if he didn't at least broach the topic. "Wendy? There is . . . one other possible reason why you may not be able to find your mother."

"Oh yeah?"

Taking a deep breath, Piotr rolled his hands into fists, nails digging deep into his palms. He could feel himself shaking. "It is possible that she . . . has become a Walker."

Wishing Jabber were there to draw her attention away from this horrible conversation, Wendy rolled her tongue around her barbell and ran the ball against the ridge of her mouth.

"Nope."

"Wendy—"

"No, Piotr." She slashed her hand through the air, cutting him off. "If you knew anything about my mom you'd know that she'd rather vanish into nothing, okay? She's not . . . she'd never . . . look, it would go against who she *is*, Piotr. She's a *good* person. She's not a Walker, okay? She'd never hurt a kid. I don't believe it. So it's something else. Got me?"

"If you say this is the way it is, so it is. My apologies."

"Forgiven. Besides," Wendy winced, "if anyone were going to go against who they are during a tough time, it'd be me. Not her." She hung her head.

"I do not understand."

"After everything that happened—losing Mom—I quit. I started avoiding the dead, only interacting with them when I had to, because I was scared that what happened to Mom might happen to me. Or something. Maybe I just blamed myself for not getting there in time. If I'd come when she first called, when she actually asked for my help . . . maybe she wouldn't have gotten overwhelmed."

"This story is amazing." Piotr gently rubbed her shoulders and, astoundingly, Wendy felt the siren song of sleep start to wrap itself around her. She sagged against him, weary to the bone, wishing that she was stretched out on the bed rather than sitting on the floor.

"Wendy, surely you must realize that this is not your fault," Piotr added as Wendy struggled to keep her eyes open. "Had you gotten there in time, there was no guarantee that a dozen panicked Lost wouldn't have hurt you too. You are very, very lucky that they had time to calm down. Fear makes them more powerful. Trust me, I know."

"I know that now," Wendy murmured, yawning so that the tendons in her jaw creaked. "But it was hard to understand then. I'm doing the best I can on my own now, but Mom had lots of training. I don't. We were always so busy that I barely had any teaching at all. I'm not half the Ligh . . . the Seer she was. And I've got tons yet left to learn."

"Hmm. It's strange. You'd think if members of your family were there, trying to guide souls to the Light, that more ghosts would remember seeing them. Not every soul is ready for that journey so close to death, after all."

Here was the moment, Wendy realized. Sleep-ready or not, here was the moment when she would have to decide; she could make something up, could lie to him and keep him . . . or she could be honest and hope he would understand. It was all so new, so fresh and strange, and she desperately didn't want to lose the chill but comforting arm around her shoulder, the soothing cadence of his lyrical voice. She could keep quiet, or lie, or even simply mislead and let him draw his own conclusion. Or she could tell the truth. She could be true to what her mother sacrificed, what her mother was in the hospital for, and pray that Piotr wouldn't run away.

Lying, Wendy knew, wasn't right, not anymore. She took a breath.

"Well," she drawled, "there's sort of a reason for that."

Piotr's hands stilled and Wendy drew away from his comforting embrace. The moment she did, her head felt clearer, calmer; her heart rate sped up, preparing for the coming confrontation. "There's, um, well, there's something I haven't been one hundred percent, you know, open about. About me, I mean."

Slowly Piotr stood, and Wendy, feeling vulnerable on the floor, rose to stand beside him.

"Go on," he said, crossing his arms over his chest, expression guarded.

"I'm—I'm the Lightbringer, Piotr," Wendy said. "About a month ago? When you were with Lily, fighting those Walkers? It was me. I'm the monster you saw in the dark."

CHAPTER THIRTEEN

The Felix-the-Cat clock above Wendy's desk counted the passing seconds: *tick-tock-tick*. Piotr stared hard at Wendy, chest rising and falling, beads of sweat standing out against his skin. Wendy was tempted to run her thumb into the hollow of his temples, to see if those glistening droplets felt wet or if they would be made of the same stuff he was—chill, electric nothing.

"That's impossible," Piotr said with flat finality, taking a step back into her bed. From the thighs up he stood, fists resting on his hips and face set in angry lines, but from the thighs down he was gone, buried in the springs and coils and stuffing of her mattress.

Hating herself for doing this, Wendy shook her head. "No, it's not."

"Stop joking, Wendy! This is not funny! It is no joke!" Piotr was mad now and the cold came off him in powerful waves. The rapid exhalation of Wendy's breath misted in the air, turned to puffs of white. She shivered, wrapping her arms around her waist, and wished that she had pulled out her coat. There was a stained hoodie on the top of the mending pile. Wendy crossed the room and donned it, smelling the pungent aroma of tar and grass, the faintest whiff of her own blood. How long ago had she ripped this hoodie? She'd faced so many fights these past few weeks, jumped so many fences, Wendy couldn't even recall how she'd torn it.

"I'm not joking." Wendy held out her arms. "I can show you."

"This is sick!" Piotr turned his back on her. "I am leaving."

Knowing now that Piotr would refuse to believe her until she gave him proof, Wendy wavered between showing him and letting him leave. She could do it, Wendy realized, she could let him walk out the door and wait this drama she'd instigated out. He would come back; they were too close for Piotr to stay away long. They needed one another—she was helping him by destroying the Walkers, even if he didn't know it, and he had promised to find her mother. But if she did this, if she pushed the issue and showed him what she really was inside, the likelihood of him ever coming back . . .

"No," Wendy said. "I have something to show you."

"*Net*," Piotr hissed. "I do not want to see it!"

"I'm so sorry, Piotr," Wendy whispered. "But you've got no choice." Decision done, she reached inside and began unraveling the firm web of will her mother had taught her to keep tightly woven over her abilities. The heat inside grew, incrementally at first, but then with more insistence as she fed the fire of Light within. The humming, crystal clear in its clarity, heartbreakingly intense, began to fill first her mind, then mouth, then seep out of her very pores.

The air between them, previously still, began to swirl and move. Papers lifted off her desk in the wayward eddies of air, moisture pattered from the ceiling to dampen her bed and carpet; the curtains flapped wildly. Wendy knew they were creating something wrong in her room, something like a mini storm front, but couldn't help herself. The power was growing, the song rising out of her, and only when she had a reaction, only then could she feel safe enough to stop.

The shadows on her wall in the Never began to lengthen while, in the real world, the shadow cast by the light of her desk lamp began to fade. Going . . . going . . . gone.

It was the siren song that did it.

Piotr spun and, seeing the glow pulsing at the edge of her soul, hearing the sweet slinking song, stumbled back. The outline of the girl he knew, red curls brushing against her cheeks and arms outstretched, was rapidly fading under the rising wash of Light. The Light wasn't as blinding this close, though Piotr's eyes still gushed water when he gazed upon her, and he felt the song worm its way into his head. High and sharp and lovely, the song vibrated in his back teeth, turning his knees to jelly. The bones he'd long since discarded felt like shattered glass and ground gravel in their sockets and yet, despite the insistent pain, a feeling like exaltation overwhelmed him, lifted him up and made him feel obliquely, absurdly *grateful*. The Light was horrible and humbling and it was all Piotr could do not to start screaming until his vocal cords were a blasted ruin, his lungs a tattered mess in his chest.

There was a moment, just a moment, when Piotr thought he could grasp just what Wendy was. Then tentacles of Light punched through her chest in a bloodless spray of glass-green fire, leaving a wound like a lipless mouth where her beating heart should have been. The physical body he had known as Wendy was obliterated now, not a tangled hair or shred of skin left. She was Light and life and a terrible, all-encompassing *love* that filled him and stretched him and left him feeling shredded into tiny pieces. Where her mouth should have been was a smooth, flat expanse of what he could only assume was skin, her nose was gone, her ears lost to sight. Only her eyes, large and brown and warm, were the same. They gazed at him and for the first time in all his years of endless, plodding existence, Piotr felt weak.

Weighed down by her regard, he dropped to his knees and bowed his head. When he vanished beneath the top of the bedspread Wendy drew her power back inside with difficulty, forcing the banked heat inside to cool, to dim, and wrapped the unspooling ribbons of Light around herself again.

Long moments passed before she was done and when Wendy felt fully in control, felt that Piotr was completely safe from the Light side of her nature, she opened her eyes to find him mere inches from her. His expression was shuttered and she searched his face, desperately trying to puzzle out his state of mind.

"Piotr?"

"You are the Lightbringer." Flat, cold.

She swallowed thickly. "Yes."

"You lied to me," he said and his accent was so thick she had to struggle to make out his words. "For weeks and weeks, you have been lying to me!"

"I didn't lie exactly," she hedged, feeling miserable, "I just didn't—"

"You just didn't tell me that you incinerate my friends day and night!" He threw up his hands and strode across the room. "Are you the one taking them—our Lost? Did you take Dunn? Or Tommy? As revenge for your mother? The Lost took your mother, so you take the Lost?"

"No!" Horrified that Piotr would think such a thing, Wendy struggled for the right words to calm him, to soothe this troubled situation. "I would *never*—"

"Never what? Never kill one of the dead? Because you have, I've seen it!" Piotr crossed his arms over his chest and glared at her. "Or do you deny shredding those Walkers? Stabbing them with those . . . tentacles? What are they? Weapons? Knives for the likes of you?"

"They're ribbons!" Wendy snapped. "I wrap a ghost—"

"So you admit it. You strangle my kind with—"

"Strangle? Strangle!" Wendy sputtered. "I save you—"

"Is that what you were trying to tell me earlier, when you stumbled over your words time and time again? Telling me about your mother, you had such a hard time describing her as Seer. Because you are not Seer! You are more. And if you are more, then your mother must be more, *da*? Is that why you seek her so hard, Wendy? Are you lonely? Is the burden of killing the dead over and over again too much for you?"

"It's not like that! My mother—"

"TELL ME THE TRUTH! Does your mother kill my kind? Do you?"

"It's not killed if you're already dead!" Wendy yelled before she could stop herself. Wendy's hands flew to her mouth, eyes huge and horrified, but silence followed the proclamation. She'd lucked out; no one seemed to have awoken at her shout. Whispering harshly, she added, "And it's not like I knew any of you before! I was just doing what I was told to do! It's my job!"

"Your mother," Piotr snorted. "Grandmothers, aunts. An entire family of Lightbringers. Destroying souls as you see fit! Filling us with . . . that . . . making us feel small and weak and then ripping us apart! Does it make you feel big to make us feel small before you tear us into nothing with your *ribbons?*" He spat on the ground.

"You dumbass, we don't destroy anything! I reap ghosts!" Now pushed past all endurance, Wendy strode up to Piotr and poked him in the shoulder. Surprisingly, she made contact and the touch of him was like dragging her hand through dry ice. Yelping, she yanked her hand back and waved it rapidly in the air to warm it. "I don't kill you, I don't destroy you, I send you to the afterlife!"

"I am in the afterlife," he snapped.

Wendy, fuming over the possible damage to her hand, gaped at his sheer stubborn stupidity. Then, surprisingly, he added, "Did you hurt your finger?"

Subdued somewhat by the question, Wendy held it up. "I'll live." He snorted and she realized that this fight was getting them nowhere.

"I didn't mean the Never," she said dully, sitting on the edge of her bed and tucking her wounded fingers into her armpit. They stung and tingled crazily but she thought they'd be okay. "When I say afterlife I really mean *the* afterlife. I don't kill you, I send you into the Light."

He was quiet a moment. Wendy glanced up and found him standing at the window, looking out. "How many?" he asked, voice low. "How many have you sent on?"

She swallowed thickly. The tone of his voice, the low pitch, didn't bode well. Piotr had never been a shouter, but he was generally more animated than that. This sudden stillness unnerved her; his unexpected quiet set her on edge. "I've never counted. A lot. Hundreds, possibly thousands. Mostly Shades." She hung her head, for the first time ashamed of what she'd always before considered her duty, part of the natural order of things, even when she'd been avoiding her duty out of fear and guilt over what happened to her mother.

"I told you before, with my mother gone I didn't want to do it anymore, but because of the Walkers . . . I've had to get up to speed pretty quickly. So . . . hundreds. Probably more." She cleared her throat. "I've been taking out Walkers while I've been on patrol. Ever since we talked. You got me started again. I've been helping you."

"Helping me." Piotr nodded but didn't turn. "I must leave." Leading with his left shoulder, he began to phase through the wall.

"Piotr, wait!" Wendy jumped to her feet, hands outstretched, but before she could take the half dozen steps to the window, he was gone.

In her dreams, Wendy ran.

She was on the track at school, circling the field over and over again, the stitch in her side ablaze with pain, her legs trembling, the soles of her bare feet pounding the pavement in a rhythmic staccato. Stinging sweat ran in her eyes, blurring her vision, and every inhalation burned. Even her teeth ached, though whether from the cold or the exertion, Wendy was unsure. All she knew was that if she stopped running, even for one moment, she'd see that dim silver flicker at the edge of the field and she would have to follow it. She'd force her way through the woods again, nettles stinging her calves, burrs catching in her socks, branches whipping across her face, until she found the man again, still under the fall of eucalyptus deadwood.

She didn't want to see him again. She'd had enough of death and ghosts.

It was too much. She couldn't go on but she forced herself to take the next step and then the next. Wendy pushed on, pushed on, and when her leg gave out, knee buckling and calf tightening in an excruciating charley horse, Wendy shrieked, hitting the ground with shoulder and hip. She cried, writhing on the ground, hair pooling beneath her head. The pain sunk deep, angry fingers into her muscles and *twisted*. Wendy screamed and screamed and screamed.

It took a long, long time for Wendy to realize blessed, numbing cold was working its way through her leg. Her cries tapered off; sniffling, she wiped her wrist across her face and struggled to sit up.

"I'd be careful if I were you," the White Lady said, sitting back on her haunches and rising in a creaking, graceful arc. Where her hands had pressed into Wendy's leg, blue flesh rimmed in ice slowly warmed. "Push yourself too hard and you'll never catch up with me."

"Go away." Wendy flopped back to the ground and glared up at the stars above. She tried to find the Big Dipper but couldn't. The stars were different here, bigger and brighter, closer to the earth. The air was startlingly cold, especially for a California night. Wendy wished that she'd dreamed herself a jacket.

"The Rider is an idiot," the White Lady said, moving her fingers to the back of Wendy's ankle, rotating the cuff gently. "Even I can see that you provide us a good service. I don't appreciate you meddling in my affairs, don't get me wrong, but certain Shades have been clinging to the last vestiges of life for far too long. They need to be put out of their misery."

Irritated that the news of her fight with Piotr had flown so fast to the enemy's ears, Wendy gritted her teeth and feebly swiped at the White Lady's icy hands. Chuckling at Wendy's irritation, the White Lady released her ankle. "You didn't hurt anything. You'll be sore in the morning, but nothing tore."

"Didn't I just tell you to go away?"

"Would that I could. You called me here."

Wendy snorted. "I did not."

The White Lady shrugged. "Suit yourself. Feel free to leave, then. You won't see me shedding a tear. If I can still cry." She chuckled. "I haven't tried."

Sniffing, Wendy shivered. When the White Lady handed her a jacket formed of the strange dream-stuff, she took it without comment and slid gratefully into its warmth. "I have nothing to say to you."

"Don't you? Not even one question?"

"You're right. I do have one question for you." Wendy sat up, chin jutted out and glared at the White Lady. "Destroy Dunn yet?"

Patting her thighs and sitting down beside Wendy, the White Lady sighed. "Come now, Lightbringer, don't be stupid. You and I both know that if I had, you'd have heard about it by now. Your fortnight isn't up for two more days." Her phalanges scraped the edge of the track, digging furrows in the dirt. "But then again, maybe I should. I tire of our constant head-butting. It certainly would prove a point, wouldn't it?"

"I'll back off," Wendy said. "On one condition. And only that condition."

"Indeed? Well, please, elucidate. What in heaven or earth could move the mighty Lightbringer to lower herself to actually deal with me?"

"You tell me why you're kidnapping the Lost." Wendy scowled. "And quit calling me the 'mighty Lightbringer.' That shit is getting old."

"Absolutely not." The White Lady shook her head. "No deal."

"You're obviously not feeding them to the Walkers," Wendy pressed, "and you don't exactly seem the motherly type. Surely there's some reason other than just shits and giggles. Tell me why and I'll lay off the Walkers unless they attack me first."

"Why are you seeing a dead boy in your room every night? We all have our own reasons for the things we do." The White Lady tsked softly. "Kissing the dead instead of reaping them? For shame, girl. What would your mother say?"

"You could ask her." Wendy tapped her tongue ring against her teeth. "Oh, no, you can't, can you? You still haven't found her. All that bluster and you're just as lost as I am—can't find one single ghost."

"She knows the Never well," the White Lady admitted. "I'm starting to admire her."

"Just starting to?"

"Hush, girl. You'll never hear one of my kind praising one of yours." She sniffed. "It simply isn't done."

"This isn't me agreeing to a truce," Wendy warned. "Just so you know."

"The time for truce is long over." The White Lady leaned forward so that the remains of her chin rested on her knees, the rest of her face still cast in the hood's deep shadow. "You're right. I can't destroy Dunn . . . yet. I know you'll never stop hunting my Walkers. So we must agree to disagree, I suppose. No more talks of truce. No deal. Here on out, it's open war between the two of us. Agreed?"

Wendy sighed. "Agreed."

"When I find your mother—and I will find her—I'm going to obliterate her. Just so you know." The White Lady laughed and there was a dark edge to her mirth, an underlying anger that Wendy would've been deaf to miss. "I tire of this."

"You talk, but all I hear is blah, blah, blah."

The White Lady stood. "Do you even know why you called me here?"

"I didn't." Wendy closed her eyes. "Get out."

"As you wish, Lightbringer." The White Lady began to move away. "But, just a reminder, we're at war, girl. No more nice-nice. If I can, I'll have you torn to shreds."

"Bring it. You send 'em my way, I'll keep knocking them down."

"You can't keep up this pace. You've realized that, haven't you?" The White Lady chuckled. "One day you're going to reap too many souls in a row and leave yourself weak. All I have to do is wait." The wind sighed in the trees and the White Lady sighed with it. "I think I'll have you kneel before me, before I rip your soul apart. Fitting, isn't it? A simple ghostie like me destroying the mighty Lightbringer? Just the idea of it leaves me all a-tingle."

"Blah, blah, blah. We're done here."

"Yes, Wendy, I think we are. Goodnight."

When Wendy opened her eyes, the White Lady was gone. She was still dreaming, she knew, and if she wanted to, she could wake up. But waking up would mean facing the fight she and Piotr had just had; facing reality.

Wrapping her arms around her chest, Wendy conjured up a warm, sunlit beach and sank deeper into her dream. Plenty of time to be miserable in the waking, living world. Right now she just wanted peace.

CHAPTER FOURTEEN

When Piotr stormed out of Wendy's bedroom he had no idea where he was to go. Part of him knew he should head north, back into the city, to warn the others that the Lightbringer had a very good idea where they were located. Piotr had even begun the long trek back to Elle's when he realized that Wendy had known about the bookstore for over a month now; if she had wanted to tear every Rider in the Bay Area apart she could have done so already. Instead she'd held off, and Piotr had a sneaking suspicion he knew why. For him.

Unsure which option was best, Piotr skulked around town, refusing to go back to the bookstore but unwilling to head back into his own turf and hunker down at the mill. Lily might understand, but would the others? After all, it was all his fault—Wendy's words haunted him, her revelation that he was the reason she'd begun taking her duties as a destroyer of souls in earnest. He was the reason thousands of Shades and innumerable other ghosts around the city were gone. Their absence had been puzzling the Riders for weeks, but now he understood. It was all his fault.

The worst part wasn't his shame, though. The worst part was the fact that he craved the Light. Like an addict seeking that final, fantastic fix, Piotr had to stop himself from turning around and rejoining Wendy in her room, from begging her to end his existence. She had been something he'd never encountered, something terrible and wonderful, and as much as he hated her, he still yearned for her.

Stomping along the back roads, listening to the distant hammer of the train pounding on the tracks, Piotr played their encounter over again in his mind. Caught in the limbo between spirit and flesh, Wendy had never looked more painfully beautiful. As she sank back into her skin the remains of the Light played about the edges of her body, glimmering with welcome—and excruciating—heat, leaving her almost smaller than before; slighter. Though now flesh, she'd appeared somehow insubstantial to the touch and definitely weaker in both spirit and will.

Driven by instinct, Piotr had perceived the well of flowing years coursing under her fragile living skin, tempting him with its bounty of life and Light. She was fragile in the limbo between spirit and flesh—he sensed that, like a Walker, he could take her life if he wanted to.

All he had to do was strike.

Safely distant, Piotr could admit to himself that he'd hated her then, and loved her, and hated himself for loving her. The blistering cold of his fury threatened to overwhelm him. She was a monster. She was his friend.

Ignoring her pleas for understanding, he'd left. To protect her, to protect himself.

It was the only part of that whole hideous encounter he was proud of.

The touch of Wendy's human hand had been wonderful. The heat of the Lightbringer's spiritual regard had been . . . more. And Piotr knew that he wanted more from her than she'd ever be willing to give. Sickened and torn, he started to walk faster, to jog, then run. Chased by his memory of Wendy encased in Light, Piotr fled, leaving the valley behind.

Homecoming came, homecoming went, then Halloween. Wendy spent every free moment roaming town, looking for a fight with the roving dead. Sleepless and careless of her safety, Wendy burned with a furious light.

Each night Shade after Shade melted away at the slightest touch and Walkers fell by the dozens. Wendy spent every night purposefully *not* thinking of Piotr and every day drifting between classes and assignments—like a ghost, herself. When she did finally relax long enough to drift off, her sleep was rife with nightmares, some featuring the White Lady watching in the distance, most not. It was as if the White Lady saw no need to torment Wendy further; she was her own worst nightmare now.

More than once she thought she spied her mother in the distance. Wendy would speed up, hurry toward the ghost, only to find a random Shade. Her reaps were fury-driven and none-too-gentle. Wendy hated them all.

Driven now by some deep-seated urge to keep moving, to keep doing as she should have done the moment her mother fell, Wendy quit calling Eddie for help with reaping and instead borrowed her father's car without permission. Jabber stalking at her side, Wendy spent the wee hours wandering all the darkest parts of the Bay Area, seeking out the forgotten places and darkest alleys with suicidal glee.

She quit visiting her mother and deleted the calls that the hospital left on her cell. Wendy had more important things to worry about now. She didn't want to face Dr. Emma's curious concern or her mother's blank and emaciated eyes.

"When Dad comes home, I'm gonna tell," Chel declared one night when Wendy snagged his keys off the nail in the garage. Jon, sitting at the kitchen counter, took one look at Wendy's face and abandoned the area, taking his half-eaten mixing bowl full of mac 'n' cheese with him. Chel, ignoring her twin's escape, pushed on, sliding between Wendy and the door to the garage.

"Where do you go, anyway, when you take off like this? You're not visiting Eddie, I checked. Pick up a skanky boyfriend you're ashamed of, Wendy?" She eyed Wendy's bare arms, peering knowingly at the hollows of Wendy's elbows. "Or maybe got into something a little worse?"

"I go out," Wendy replied, and thrust a twenty from the grocery fund into Chel's hand. Money normally shut her nosy little sister up. "Like you can talk. Keep your trap shut or I'll tell Dad how you're slutting it up with that walking disease you call a boyfriend."

Pushing Chel easily aside, Wendy reached into her sister's purse, hanging on the hook beside the door, and pulled out a half-full bottle of Phentermine. "Or about these."

Humiliated, Chel was in tears; she snatched the bottle back. "Fuck off!"

"Go to hell," Wendy snapped back, pushing past her, and slammed the door behind.

Part of her felt bad about Chel. She knew her little sister was starting to run with the wrong crowd, starting to get in over her head both at school and after, but there were Walkers left to reap. Life, as her mother used to say, could take care of itself. Wendy just had to watch her own back. As she pulled out of the driveway, Wendy glanced up and saw Jon sitting in his windowsill, shoving spoonful after spoonful of cheesy pasta into his mouth and shaking his head. She ignored him, punched the volume on the stereo up, and spun out into the night.

Weeks passed. Wendy hunted.

Thanksgiving was subdued. Dad had left earlier; he wanted to spend the evening with Mom at the hospital, and Nana had tottered off to the guest room by eight, leaving Wendy to stuff the vast remnants of their Thanksgiving fare into her mother's weathered margarine tubs and wash the dishes by herself.

It was a dismal job. The stuffing had been soggy, the turkey underdone, and Nana's cranberry sauce had been the wrong kind, not the canned sort that you sliced in paper-thin layers but the other type, full of pits and twigs and gooshy blobs. Chel had picked at her plate—shredding her roll and feeding it to Nana's ancient poodle under the table, hiding the dollop of green bean casserole under her mashed potatoes—but Dad hadn't noticed.

Jon, on the other hand, ate more than enough for the both of them. He was starting to get round in the face and when Wendy, pitying him, had tried to convince him to join her in a pickup basketball game after dinner, he'd turned her down, preferring to mix up a batch of fudge instead.

"Fine," she snapped, irritated that he wouldn't help her take her mind off things—off having a holiday season without Mom. "It's your gigantic ass. Do whatever you want with it." Wendy stalked away, ignoring the bewildered hurt on Jon's face.

Life without Mom, she thought hopelessly, had finally begun to fall apart. In her room Wendy hid in the back of her closet, pulled Jabber into her lap, and cried herself to sleep with the ghost of her mother's cat in her lap.

Weeks passed. Wendy hunted.

Three months. It had been three months—twelve whole and seemingly endless weeks—since Piotr had learned that Wendy was the Lightbringer. Piotr haunted the trails between the city and the valley, lost in his thoughts and brooding.

To keep himself from literally haunting Wendy's home, Piotr wandered. He crisscrossed well-known trails and streets until he was not a person in the strictest sense of the word, merely a restless spirit walking; striding through the hours of the day in agony until the only face he could see was hers, his every thought tangled around the pain they'd caused one another. Time away from her had given him some hard-earned perspective. Piotr understood why she'd lied about being the Lightbringer at first, but couldn't wrap his mind around why she'd continued to do so. Didn't she trust him? Didn't she owe him that, at least?

This brooding lasted until Piotr, finally closing the circuit towards the city, found a pair of thick-rimmed glasses just outside Elle's territory. Piotr leaned down, picked them up, turned them in his hand. They were black plastic, horn-rimmed, and familiar.

The bookstore was in chaos when he arrived. Most of the Riders were gone, as were the Lost, leaving only Elle, Lily, and James. When Piotr arrived he found Lily meditating cross-legged in a corner beside James. James, battered about the head and neck, puffy with bruises and gashes, sported several even more severe wounds on his arms and legs. As Lily's hands moved over them the cuts knit closed, but they were not seamless or pretty. Lily did not have a Lost's healing touch.

"What happened?" Piotr asked, but knew it was a useless, futile question. He was a tracker and what had happened here was clear. Footsteps in the dust were marred by long, swishing swipes. Rider essence lay in puddles, silver pools that dried to dark and tainted grey. The floor was riddled with dime-sized holes, bored through in Swiss cheese patterns, and there was an unmistakable smell of wet rot in the air.

The Walkers had grown tired of trying to pick the Lost off one by one and had staged a mass assault.

"Those hoods snatched Dora," Elle told him later, after they'd gone through the remnants of the Lost to assess the damage and estimate a sort of head-count of the taken. "Specs too. The rest of the Riders are on the lam, heading east. I sent Tubs with Kurtz, for safety." Elle rubbed the bridge of her nose with one hand, filthy with dust and the day's fight. Her other arm lay in her lap, lumpy at the elbow and oozing a thin stream of essence, snapped in four separate places. Large hunks of her golden hair were sheared away at the skull; she now had a jagged cut that wound across her forehead and diagonally down one cheek. It matched his scar.

Catching him examining her face, Elle's eyes flashed warning. "I told them to pack their glad rags and get a wiggle on, no turning around. Kurtz took charge and they're heading for Nevada. They ain't ever coming back." She almost spat the words.

So that was it. They were alone. Why was he not surprised?

Piotr nodded, numb, and left Elle's side, wandering through the bookstore. He picked up an item here, an item there. Dora's sketch-book had been left behind. It was not made of the same stuff she was; he would not be able to tell if she was safe by looking at it. All the same, Specs' glasses were whole, and that indicated that Specs, at least, was unharmed. It was hope. Piotr seized on that.

Without one of the Lost there to help, the healing process took a few weeks. When James was up and on his feet again, he and Elle organized a citywide search program. "If we can't find them like this," he claimed, his dangling cornrows brushing the edges of the map Elle had scrounged from amid the rotting books, "we won't find them."

Enough time had passed that it was looking like the remaining Riders weren't going to find more than scattered clues. The Lost appeared permanently gone, but at least Dunn's hat remained solid, as did Specs' glasses and Tommy's cloak. They were still alive—at least, in a manner of speaking.

Practical by nature, Piotr set out each day expecting nothing and came back with exactly that. So it was to his great surprise when, traveling through the edges of Mountain View towards San Jose, a copy of the map with the search parameters in one hand and a flare in the other, he spotted a quartet of Walkers. One of them was struggling with a small and shrieking figure. A familiar figure.

"Specs!" Piotr yelled and, without thought or plan, dropped the paper and flare, flinging himself into the fray.

The Walkers had changed and not for the better. These beasts had faces elongated into unimaginable abominations, twisted and warped into monstrous shapes, with stitches of sinew thick as twine holding the gaping flaps of their essence together. These Walkers had been healed and then marred again. The purposeful scars were doubly hideous, lying so starkly against the fresh flesh.

Piotr, approaching at speed, drew Elle's dagger and leapt at the Walker holding Specs. The Walker went down—end over end—and Specs, yelling with surprise and glee, tugged free.

"Piotr! Piotr! I knew you'd come! I knew it!"

Mindless with rage, Piotr began slashing at the Walker. Every cut he made—shallow and deep alike—broke fragile skin and spilled a foul-smelling, noxious liquid. It was not essence; it was too thin, too runny, and when it touched his hands, it stung.

Another fine spray of droplets flew, dousing him, and Piotr felt the burn of it eating into his skin, his pants and arms. Now he knew what the holes had been—these Walkers bled something beyond mere essence. Whatever they bled was acid to ghosts, essence-burning and foul, like unadulterated death. Piotr ignored the pain and continued stabbing.

Furious or not, Piotr was still only one man, and one who was severely outnumbered. Before he could finish off the Walker, two of the others dragged him, kicking and cursing, free. The other, moving swiftly, corralled and captured Specs again. They forced him to kneel on the ground. One gripped him by the hair, dragging his head back and exposing his neck. The other wrapped powerful fingers around his wrists, locking him in place.

"Rider." Piotr was unsure which one of the Walkers spoke, as all four of them—including the one he'd attacked, which was only just now gaining its feet—nodded. "It is a Rider, yes, yes. Tough meat."

"Filthy kid-killing pigs," Piotr spat back, jerking left and right but unable to free himself. He began cursing as violently and loudly as he could, lapsing into Russian and back to English without thought, hoping that perhaps Elle, whose patrol circuit was supposed to cross his today, would hear. The Walkers ignored his tirade, seeming content to talk among themselves.

"White Lady will want him." More nods all around.

One frigid finger ran across Piotr's neck, over his chin, and pushed its way into his mouth. He could feel burning begin as the blood-flecked nail scratched the inside of his cheek. It was sharp and strong enough to cut him deeply. Specs, watching from a few feet away, moaned.

"Eat his eyes. Suck him dry." Nod-nod, agreement all around.

"Greedy Lady," one of the Walkers suggested. "All the meat for her, even tough meat. All the tasty for later. No tasty for us."

It sounded almost forlorn at this tidbit, and somewhat annoyed. The finger in Piotr's mouth withdrew, pulled back, and then stabbed him in the shoulder hard enough to pierce him through. The finger, knuckle-deep in his shoulder, twisted and wiggled, having just enough room to poke Piotr in the collarbone. The shock of its jagged nail scraping and flicking at his bone was enough to elicit a shrill and terrified scream.

"All the tasty for her plan," the Walker said again, dropping down so it was face to face with Piotr. Its tongue, obscenely long and mottled grey, rolled out of its mouth and rasped its way over Piotr's cheeks, licking away his sweat and tears. The end was forked like a snake's and flicked with eerie rapidity, sliding over his eyes and collecting the agonized tears that leaked from the corners. "No tasty for us . . . but Rider could be tasty. Tough, yes, but a tasty we don't have to share. We eat Rider instead."

The hands binding his wrists tightened and Piotr closed his eyes, preparing for the worst.

It took Eddie, waiting for Wendy by her locker the day school let out for Christmas break, to knock some sense into her.

"Hey hot stuff," he said as she spun the lock and started sorting through her books, choosing which ones would go home over break and which she'd leave at school.

"I see you're scowly as usual." Eddie waited and when she didn't answer, added, "So, is your phone broken? Cuz I've left you, like, a hundred or so texts and *someone* hasn't been returning them. I'll totally buy you a new one for Christmas if you want. I already have a gift for you but there's this sexy little black flip phone that—"

"Lay off," she said, not unkindly and, with a shrug, merely piled the whole lot into her bag. The nightmares that kept her up to all hours had long since begun to take their toll; Wendy was passing her courses but only just barely. Even math had begun to slip.

White Lady's threats or not, Wendy intended to take a few days off reaping and spend part of her holiday studying up. The ACTs and SATs were coming up and at this rate there was no way she'd get a scholarship. Not like she had much of a choice where to go to school. Until Mom came out of her coma, it was community college for her and Wendy knew it.

"You know, grumble-puss, I don't think I'm gonna," Eddie replied. His voice was so mellow, his smile so sincere, that Wendy missed what he was saying altogether.

Wendy sighed, rolled her eyes, and finally turned to face him. Unlike her, Eddie looked well rested. His clothing was neat and clean, his hair had been freshly dyed glossy blue-black, and the kohl lining his eyes was smudge-free. "Gonna what?"

"Lay off." Reaching past Wendy, Eddie shut her locker door with a sharp snap. Then, taking her elbow in one hand, he firmly guided her past the pulsing throng of other students gathering their things and fleeing the building, to a bench outside.

There he forced her to sit.

"Eddie. Eddie! Hey, let go!" Irritated with his gall, Wendy struggled, but Eddie's grip tightened and he refused to unhand her. "Eds, this is not funny."

"Never said it was," he replied as pleasantly as before. "But you, missy, and I are going to have a bit of a talk. And since you've decided texting is too *gauche*, we're gonna do it the old fashioned way. Analog style."

From the corner of her eye Wendy spotted Jon and Chel round the corner of the school, bags in hand. They spotted Eddie and approached slowly, standing just behind him, only a few feet back but far enough out of her range that she couldn't reach them without struggling free of Eddie's iron grip on her arm.

"All of you are in on this?" Bitterness crept into Wendy's voice.

"Manhandling me for whatever reason? Way to gang up, guys. I knew I could count on you three to stay classy."

Jon shuffled his feet. "Wendy, we're worried about you. You're not sleeping."

"I'm aware of that, thanks." She jerked the arm in Eddie's hand and his grip tightened firmly, not quite painfully, but close. "I'm fine. Let me go."

"You're not fine," Chel replied coolly, snagging Wendy's bag from the bench beside her where Eddie had set it. The heavy weight of the books was almost too much for her; she tilted slightly as she hefted the bag over her shoulder. "Look, you talk with her all you want, but we're gonna miss the bus. I'll drop these off in her room."

Eddie nodded. Jon moved around the side of the bench and sat beside Wendy. For the first time in weeks, Wendy really looked at her younger brother, and was more than a little horrified to see the puffiness in his cheeks, the dark circles beneath his eyes. His shirt was old and too tight; his gut was now hanging over the waistband of his jeans. Jon, realizing that Wendy was examining him closely, blushed dark red.

"Shut up," he said before she could speak, and patted his belly. "I'm working on it." He glanced over at Chel, who was patiently waiting at the sidewalk. She had a protein bar in one hand and was breaking chunks off to eat, grimacing with every bite. Her face, Wendy noted, was not as gaunt as before.

Jon gestured toward Chel. "Things have been tough on all of us, right? With Mom and everything, Chel and I sort of depended on you to stay cool and keep us sane."

Ashamed, Wendy struggled with her reply. "That's not it. I— I—there's been these bad dreams and—"

"I'm not surprised, all that stress. Look, what we've been doing to you isn't fair," Jon interrupted. "We figured you'd just keep on truckin'—at least I did—and I never thought 'til recently that maybe it'd be hard on you, you know, being in charge when Dad's gone. Then you Hulked out and got all mega-bitch and you took us by surprise. Well, you took me by surprise. I think you bitch-slapped Chel into a whole new personality."

Eddie's hand dropped off her arm. Wendy rubbed the sore spot but she no longer felt the need to flee; it was as if she were rooted to the bench, stunned speechless by her normally taciturn brother's urgent tone.

"Wendy, you woke us both up, okay? You had your say, you really hurt my feelings and scared the crap out of Chel, but you got our attention and we listened." He glanced over at Chel, still waiting out of earshot. "It may not look like it at first glance, but I promise, we're both working on it."

"I'm sorry," Wendy whispered. "I didn't mean to hurt you."

"My mouth, my body, my fault," he replied. "You're not the boss of me. Besides, I don't regret a single Cheeto." He smiled faintly, still pink from embarrassment at her close assessment, and hugged her again.

"Just listen to what Eddie has to say to you, okay? You've been a ginormous hosebeast but you've been under a ton of stress with Dad being gone. Chel's pissed right now, but she's like me—deep down all we want is for you to be happy. That and for you to quit stealing Dad's car, cause he's gonna kick all our asses if he figures that one out."

Then, hitching up his pants self-consciously, Jon picked up his things, bussed Wendy on the cheek, and left. He joined Chel at the bus stop, shouldered Wendy's bag himself, and they walked away toward the bright yellow line of buses pulling into the school's drive.

"Wow," Wendy said, watching her too-thin sister and growing-overweight brother drift into the throng of students climbing aboard their rides home. "Jon grew a pair. Big brass ones."

"Yep," Eddie agreed, "the day comes in every young boy's life when he's called a fatass by his beloved older sister. Or so I've been told, being an only child and all."

Wendy winced. "I've really been in my own world, haven't I?"

"That's a polite way of putting it," Eddie replied. "Another way is that you've been a screaming bitch, impossible to be around, um . . . almost completely irresponsible except for school and your 'side job.' And, oh, yeah, I did mention total bitch, right?"

"I think so," Wendy replied dryly.

"Because it bears mentioning," Eddie said, insistent. "Over and over again."

"I get the point, Eddie."

"No, darling, I don't think you really do. But you will. Walk with me. It'll be like old times. I'll drive you home and you, me foine girl, can listen to ol' Eddie talk."

The grounds were quickly emptying. Eddie picked up his own bag, slung a loose arm around her waist, and guided her toward the parking lot and his car.

"See, the fact of the matter is, what Jon said aside, none of us *depend* on you to be a sane and rational human being. At least not all the time. But sometimes it'd be nice. And if there's something wrong, we like to know about it so we can at least *avoid* the bitchiness if we can't deal with it."

"There's nothing wrong."

"Sure there isn't. Right. Chel's the one with the eating problem, but you've gotten werry-werry thin, me foine chickadee."

Done playing, Eddie dropped the overblown accent and brushed a tender finger across each of her cheekbones. "You've got a full set of matching bags under those baby browns of yours, and I do believe so much scowling is going to cause early onset wrinklage. At this rate, you're going to be the first MVHS graduate with grey hair."

Self-consciously, Wendy touched her head. "I said I'm fine! Drop it, okay?"

Groaning, Eddie grabbed her by the wrist, shaking it slightly. "Wendy, look, I can totally stand you ignoring my calls, not responding to my texts, deleting my emails. I get that I was the jerk first—I got totally wrapped up in a girl and forgot I had friends for a while, yeah, sure. I deserve a little no-Wendy time. But the twins, annoying as they are, didn't do anything to you they haven't done before. And with your dad gone all the time and your mom in the hospital—"

"Hey—"

Eddie held up a hand to stall her protest as they reached the parking lot. "Wendy darling, I love you, but you are going to shut up and you are going to listen to me, if it's the last thing I do in this friendship. You owe me that at least. Now hush up and let me finish."

He waited until it looked like Wendy wasn't going to respond and continued on. "Ahem, now, like I was saying, with your mom in the hospital and all, you're like, woman of the house. Hell, screw that, you're master of the house. And you, miss master, haven't been treating the rest of the house particularly well."

"I've been busy," Wendy mumbled as Eddie opened the passenger side door and ushered her inside. She turned her face to the window, refusing to look at him. "With, you know, my special stuff."

"Right, well, your 'stuff' is going to have to wait for a while, I think." Eddie shut the door, moved around the car, and slid into the driver's seat. "You get on Chel for using the Phentermine, but don't think I haven't seen those bottles of No-Doz you've been hiding."

"Hey," Wendy protested, stung, "I'm not the one abusing diet pills just to fit into some bleached-sheeple-douchebag club!" She waved her hands above her head. "Rah-rah, sis-boom-bah, gooooo bulimics!"

"No," he replied sternly, "you're the one abusing caffeine pills and chugging Red Bull so you can go and hang out with dead people all night. Which is crazier, I wonder?"

Wrapping her arms around her middle, Wendy groaned and sank back against the passenger seat. "It's not the same thing. I need the caffeine. There've been dreams—"

"Which I didn't listen to you about," Eddie said. "And I'm really super sorry about that. But now you've got my full attention. Consider me the Wendy-Wikipedia, okay? I want you to tell me all about everything that's been going on with you, especially these nightmares or whatever. Dr. Eddie is in and I'll even waive the five cent charge."

"Not now."

He adjusted the rear view mirror, and checked the mirrors on each side. "Fine, when?"

"Eddie—"

"Don't 'Eddie' me in that tone of voice, Wendy. What in the hell can be so bad that you're afraid of falling asleep? What, you got Freddy Krueger in there, slicing people up? Are you going to drop dead if you fall asleep? Because the way things are going right now, you're going to drop dead if you *don't* fall asleep."

"It's my body, Ed."

"It may be your body but I've got a baseball bat. I've got no problem letting you sleep off a concussion. Talk."

"Fine. I spend just about every night avoiding sleep and running around town reaping. I still haven't found my mom. Her soul's been threatened by a dead crazy chick with skin like rotting lettuce. I won't find her unless I keep looking so, neatly put, I have to do this, okay?"

"I get why you're worried about your mom, but last I checked you were back to reaping anyone you came across, not just the bad dudes who chased you down. Is that still the deal?"

Irritated, Wendy refused to answer.

"So it's still not just the creepy, rotting bad guys?" He waited for her reply and when it became clear that she wasn't going to give one, he groaned. "Wendy, I've said it before and I'll say it again, why exactly do you think you have to do this?"

Easing the car out of the parking space, Eddie settled into the line forming at the edge of campus. Around them other seniors threw their things into their trunks or backseats and revved their engines, lining up quickly behind him and shouting holiday well-wishes at one another. The air was cold, not frosty—not in California—but still chill enough to turn cheeks pink and make eyes sting.

"Why is it that you," Eddie continued, waving at Pete Abrahms who cheerfully leapt into his dad's van beside them, "have to go around reaping people who're already dead? I mean, doesn't that just seem a touch backward to you?"

They reached the front of the line. Eddie signaled, turned right, caught the tail end of the yellow light, and within moments they were away from the campus and heading towards home. Wendy, at a loss for words, sulked in silence.

Eddie let five minutes pass, turning left, right, and left again as he took the back streets home. "Not getting an answer, huh?"

"It's my job," she said. "It's my mom's job and it was my grandma's job and it was her grandmother's job, yada yada yada, so on and so forth. If you don't understand that, Eddie, you don't understand me after all."

They were passing a park not far from her house where a cluster of elementary kids were learning to skate on the wide paths, holding hands and following a teenage girl in a narrow V like fluorescent-headed ducklings. Watching them, Wendy pressed her fingers to the glass, yearning.

"Hey, after fifteen years of putting up with your crap I think I understand you just fine," he protested. "Maybe it's you who doesn't understand yourself. Maybe you just need to—"

"Stop the car," Wendy demanded, sitting up suddenly.

"What? Oh, no, hon, I'm not gonna let you be like that." Eddie shook his head and slapped his hand down on the auto locks. "After all this crap I don't have to put up with a temper tantrum from you. You don't get to storm off and—"

"Eds, shut your mouth for one damn second, stop the car, and open the stupid fucking door! I'll be right back!" Wendy snapped. She kicked at the passenger door, cracking the plastic, and Eddie, bewildered, stopped and unlocked the car. Without another word she was out the door and sprinting across a small local playground, fading out of sight within seconds of her feet hitting the grass.

"Damn it," he grunted, scowling. "Not again." Pulling the car along the curb, Eddie parked and waited, eyeing the cracked plastic with a scowl. This could take a while.

Piotr, eyes closed, waited for the first blow to fall. The blow never came.

Instead a slow sweep of sound broke through the clearing, sweet and high, vibrating at the top of the range with a crystal tone. Heat began baking his cheeks and face, and where the warmth touched him, Piotr felt his anxiety drain away, felt the soothing sweetness fill him and lift him up. The hands loosened their unbreakable grip on his wrists; the vile tongue slipped away.

When Piotr opened his eyes the Light was blinding.

The Walkers, lost in the siren song, held open their seeping, mutilated arms and welcomed the Lightbringer's embrace. Piotr began crawling forward, seeking the Light, and saw Specs doing so as well, both making their way as best they could towards the glorious, aching afterlife.

Before they could reach the edges of the Light, however, the song quieted, faded away. The Walkers were no more, taken with such rapidity that Piotr had hardly noticed their passing, and now only Wendy remained, the remainder of the Light glowing around her edges, eyes wary.

"Well, that's new," she said, sinking to her knees, face grave. Wendy held up her forearm. Four parallel slashes, deep enough that Piotr could see the red meat inside, bled sluggishly through the material of her grey overshirt. Wendy stripped the shirt off and wrapped the thin material around her wrist. "Ow," she complained and glanced at Piotr from beneath her lashes. "Hi," she said, tying off the makeshift bandage, "I missed you."

"You too?" Piotr held out his hand. Before Wendy could reach for it, Specs was suddenly there between them, hands outstretched and eyes wild.

"Take me home!" he half-screamed, ignoring Piotr completely. It was as if Piotr wasn't even there. "I saw it! You hid it but I saw it! I want to go home! I want my mommy! Mommy!" He grabbed Wendy's wrist with both arms and shouted into her face, spit flying, "I WANT TO GO HOME!"

A burst of energy—purple-cold and fierce—pulsed out from him in a wave so powerful it knocked Piotr a full fifteen feet backwards. It was like nothing he'd ever seen or felt before, like nothing he could have ever imagined. Wendy, trapped by Specs' tight hold around her wrist, sagged in his grip. Her face, red from the exertion of channeling the Light, bled white within moments and her lips turned bluish at the edges. She began to gag.

Horrified, Piotr struggled to his feet as Specs released Wendy's wrist and bent over her, shoving his small hands *through* the flesh of her stomach and pulling something small and round and sharply glowing from deep within her gut. "I see you," he sobbed. "Let me go home. Please? Please take me home?"

"Specs!" Piotr called, squinting to look at the intense ball of light in the boy's grasp. "Wendy cannot help you if you're hurting her! Specs! Specs! Listen to me!"

The boy didn't hear, only clutched the orb and rocked back and forth, sobbing.

Wendy, face down in the dirt, didn't move.

CHAPTER FIFTEEN

Horrified and uncertain what to do, Piotr approached Specs at an angle. Just a glance told him that the ball of light was fragile; he had a sense that if Specs dropped it, the ball might shatter. Gingerly, making sure to keep his movements slow and even, Piotr wrapped one arm around Specs' shoulders and slid the other hand around the orb. It was white-hot in his hand and he hissed a deep breath, shocked by the sheer magnitude of the pain.

"Wendy, *derzhis'*. *Ne ymiraj*," he whispered. "Stay with me. Do not die."

Carefully tensing his fingers, Piotr scooped the orb out of Specs' grip and laid it on Wendy's navel. At first nothing happened, but then, just as Piotr was wracking his brain for some other way that might return the glowing thing to Wendy's insides, it began to sink through her flesh. Piotr's other arm tightened around the boy, both drawing excess energy from him and holding him back. Specs struggled for a moment before faltering, blinking rapidly several times, and shaking his head. "Piotr?"

"*Ny ti i* idiot," Piotr said evenly, rolling and unrolling his hand as Specs' essence worked its way through his system, fully healing his wounds and numbing the excruciating blaze of pain that had enveloped his orb-handling hand.

"I don't believe that I need a translation for that," Specs groaned.

"You are okay? You are calm?"

A nod. "Yeah." Specs wiped his hair away from his eyes, licked his lips nervously. "I think . . . I think that's her soul." He glanced at the last vanishing remnants of the orb and then looked quickly away, as if not daring to stare too long lest he be mesmerized again.

"*Da*," Piotr said heavily, "I think you are right." He'd heard tales of certain ghosts being able to pull out souls before, but never imagined that a soul could come in so compact and fragile a form, or that a Lost would have that ability. Pondering over what Wendy had told him before and taking into account what he knew about her soul now, Piotr had a sneaking idea of what had happened to her mother that night. He hoped he was wrong.

"I saw my mom," Specs said forlornly. "And my dog." He sniffled. "I wanna go home."

"You and me both," Piotr agreed, hugging him gently. "You and me both."

"Ugh," Wendy agreed from a few feet away, eyes slowly fluttering open. Coughing, she patted her head, her heart, her hip, then slowly sat up, holding her head. "I feel like I just got run over by a truck."

"Sorry," Specs whispered, hanging his head. "I don't know why I did that. I saw home and I just . . . I just . . ."

Wendy laughed then, softly and sadly, and smiled. "I understand. You wanted to go home. It's okay."

Specs wiped his sleeve across his eyes. "It's okay?"

"I promise. Here." Carefully Wendy rolled over, tucked her knees underneath her, and gingerly staggered to her feet. "Tell you what," she grunted. "Give me a minute and I can totally make going home happen for you. But no more of that—" she waved her hand over her midsection, "that tuggy business, okay? That hurt. A lot."

"You remember it?" Piotr couldn't keep the disbelief from his voice.

"Sure I do." Wendy brushed the grass off her jeans and studiously avoided looking at him. "You put me back."

"Put *you* back?" Piotr swallowed. "Are you saying that you yourself . . . were the . . . thing?"

She shrugged. "I guess? All I know is that I got passed back and forth for a bit. Kind of nauseating, actually." Wendy winced. "And cold. Really cold. Outer space cold. So cold I kinda still want a jacket."

Having no response for that, Piotr sat on the grass and waited for Wendy to collect herself. Specs sat beside him and laid his head on Piotr's shoulder. "Thank you for trying to rescue me."

"*Ne bespokojsya.*" Piotr ruffled Specs' hair. "Can you tell me where the others are?"

"No." Specs' face screwed into a miserable expression. "I don't know. They always kept me blindfolded, and after the attack I was separated from the others." He sniffled again. "I don't know where they are. Only that they moved me often and kept me in the dark."

Riffling through her purse, Wendy knelt beside him but took pains not to accidentally brush against him. Popping the top on a bottle of aspirin, she dry-swallowed four, grimacing at their bitter taste. "Why couldn't you sink through a door or something and escape?"

"The Walkers," Specs whispered. "Some of them are different now." He wiped one grimy hand across his face, smoothing away tears. "When I first got taken, they made me meet the White Lady." He shivered. "She's horrible! She touched me and I was numb for days and days! Then the Walkers took me away. And every time I started to heal, when I might have been able to step through a wall and run away, they'd tie me up and take me to her again. She'd touch me and it'd happen all over again."

Wendy cursed under her breath. "Was that where they were taking you today? To see the White Lady?"

Specs nodded. "It was time for my 'treatment.'"

Groaning, Piotr flopped back onto the grass. "*Blyat*'! So close! If I'd just followed them instead of rushing in like an idiot—"

"I wouldn't have heard you if you hadn't been yelling," Wendy interrupted mildly. "And I sincerely doubt you could have snuck past all her guards to free the kids. But this is good news, sort of." Wendy held up a hand and began ticking off points. "We know that she's saving the Lost for something big and we know that she can strip ghosts of at least some of their abilities. Phasing through walls and whatnot."

Then she smiled, a dark smile that seemed very unlike the Wendy Piotr had previously grown to know and love. He was disturbed by it. "More importantly, we know that they don't keep the kids all in one place, but that eventually they all get *taken* to one place. To the White Lady."

"I see," Piotr said, growing excited, a plan beginning to form in his mind. "You want us to wait here and maybe ambush them, *da*?"

"Exactly." Wendy sat back on her haunches and nodded, pleased with herself.

"But what about the others like me?" Specs asked. "Are they going to be hurt?"

"I won't let them get hurt," Wendy promised, reaching over and brushing his messy hair away from his forehead. "I'll send them home before that." Then she straightened and Piotr knew that the moment he'd been dreading had arrived. "Are you ready to travel on, kid?"

Specs jumped to his feet, all smiles. "Really? You mean it?" Then he paused, worry flickering across his face. "Wait. Is it going to hurt?"

"Only for a moment," she promised, reaching down and taking his hands in hers. "A pinprick. Like getting a shot." Wendy closed her eyes and her hands began to glow.

"You promise?" Specs asked, but Wendy was fading away and the Light was building. Fearing that this would be his last chance, Piotr rushed over and pressed a brief kiss to the top of the boy's head. "I will miss you."

"Me too. Say goodbye to Dora and Tubs for me."

Unwilling to tell Specs what had happened to the others, Piotr chose to simply say, "I will."

It was difficult getting words past the sudden lump in his throat. Piotr nodded extra hard to make certain he got his point across. "You shall be fine?"

"Never better. Thanks for taking care of me for all this time," Specs said, his voice starting to dip and slide, sounding as if it were coming from very far away. "You were cool."

"*Spasibo*. You were cool too," Piotr agreed, feeling the tug of the Light start to interfere with his thoughts. He turned his face away and closed his eyes. If he didn't look at the Light, it was easier to handle. One note, lovely and sweetly sung, broke the silence and it was over. The warmth faded from his back, the cool returned.

Pale as parchment and shaking, Wendy slid to the ground and rested her forehead against her knees. "That," she panted, wiping away beads of sweat, "takes it out of a girl. I've got no idea how Mom could stand to do that over and over again. Reaping kids is just so *hard*!"

"It appears to be," Piotr agreed. He crossed his arms across his chest, shuffling his feet. He cleared his throat. "I am glad though. For Specs. And you. You did a . . . a nice thing."

"Sit." Wendy said. "Please? I'm not ready to be alone right now."

"Of course. How are you doing?" Piotr sat beside her, wrapped one arm around her shoulders, and took comfort from the ambient heat. Their skin steamed where they touched but neither of them minded. The moment should have been uncomfortable but it wasn't. Neither of them spoke of the fight or the empty months that lay between them, and neither wanted to. It was as if nothing had separated them at all.

"I hurt and I'm tired." She yawned, poking at her wounded arm gingerly. "Not even two o'clock and it's been a really rough day already." She started to sag against him and then straightened. "Oh! Eddie's still in the car! Wait here."

Wendy pushed up against a nearby elm to stand and staggered out of the clearing toward the park proper. Piotr watched her use several slim young willow trees for support. She passed a young woman herding a group of schoolchildren with skates toward a nearby van. Piotr spotted her friend's familiar car and rested against a tree, watching as Wendy carefully picked her way down the well-maintained path to the vehicle parked at the curb.

Though he couldn't make out what she was saying, the fact that emotions were high was obvious. She gesticulated wildly for several minutes and then, surprisingly, the boy stepped out of the car, slamming the door behind him. The trunk popped open and he drew out a small case stamped with a red cross on the cover.

Eddie, Piotr reminded himself, firmly stomping on the slight surge of jealousy he felt whenever he laid eyes on the boy. *His name is Eddie.*

Taking Wendy by the arm, Eddie stripped off the jacket and visibly flinched away. Piotr was certain that Eddie would bundle her into the car and drive her to a hospital, but was surprised when he did no such thing. Instead he reached into the first aid kit and popped the top on a bulky white bottle, pouring a liberal amount of liquid over Wendy's arm.

Piotr could hear her curse all the way across the park.

The rest of her doctoring went quickly; Eddie bandaged her up and stowed his supplies away. Then he and Wendy argued for several minutes, before Eddie broke away from Wendy and stomped up the path, stopping twenty feet to Piotr's right and pointing toward the trees, several degrees to the left of Piotr.

"Okay dead guy," he said gruffly, "here's the deal. You and Wendy have to have a talk. Well, I gotta talk to her too, and I figure I've known her longer than you, so I have dibs."

Arriving breathless a moment later, Wendy cradled her injured arm to her chest. Piotr was impressed by how smoothly wound the bandages were. Eddie appeared to have practice at this sort of thing. "Eds, stop," she protested, but was ignored.

"Wendy says this is important, and since this is the first time she's shown an emotion other than bitchy in months, I'm gonna let my chat with her slide for now. But if you piss her off or mouth off or somehow bring the bitch-queen back before I get my say, then I don't care if you're dead. I'll hunt your ass down and kill you again. You got me, Casper?"

Raising an eyebrow, Piotr glanced at Wendy. Bitch-queen? Apparently Wendy hadn't taken their fight and subsequent separation very well either. He'd become a zombie and she'd apparently turned on her friends. Wendy, noting his appraisal, flushed as red as her hair and shrugged.

"Tell him," Piotr cleared his throat, wrestling with all the things he wanted to say and finally, after much inner debate, settling on polite neutrality, "tell him I understand."

Wendy relayed the message.

"Fine. Text if you need a ride home." Eddie pointed in the wrong direction towards the woods again, growled, "I'm watching you, Casper," and stormed off.

Feeling that it was the only polite thing to do, Piotr waited until the car's taillights had turned the corner before speaking. "Bitch-queen?"

"Shut up," Wendy muttered. "I don't handle rejection well."

"You don't handle rejection well," Piotr repeated wryly.

"At all," she amended. "Cut me some slack. That was the first time I've been dumped. I could have eaten two tons of ice cream, gotten a fat ass, and whined about it instead."

Pushing past him, Wendy angled toward the clearing. The sun seemed warmer there and Wendy stretched out on the grass, tucking her good arm behind her as a pillow and squinting at the clouds above. In the distance the swingset creaked in the breeze and children jumped rope, chanting a nonsense rhyme in perfect lilting cadence.

"I think," she said musingly, "I've been here before. Huh. I can't remember when."

Settling beside her, Piotr ran his fingers through the grass and asked, "Wouldn't we have to have been dating for you to get dumped?"

"Are you kidding me? I let you in my room. I dressed up for you. We were totally dating. Or pre-dating at the very least," Wendy replied, wriggling in the grass to get more comfortable. "And you know it. Think I hold hands with every dead guy I see?"

"Hmm," Piotr agreed with mock gravity, "I suppose not." He waited for a beat and then added, "So if we were dating then does this mean we're, what's the phrase, 'back together' now?"

"That depends," she said, closing her eyes against the bright sunlight. "Do you want to be?"

Though Wendy couldn't have told how she knew when Piotr leaned over her, she sensed the movement as clearly as if he'd been alive. There was no whisper of fabric, no hush of air against her skin, but one moment her cheeks were hot from the sunlight and their conversation and the next, blessedly cool fingertips slanted over her cheek, brushed her eyes, caressed the line of her jaw. Steam billowed and fumed around them.

When he drew back they were both breathing heavily. "Is that," Piotr cleared his throat, "is that the correct way to answer?" Wendy, still fighting for breath, half-laughed.

"I can think of worse."

Even after all this time being the Lightbringer, the marvel of touching a ghost, actually feeling the cool pressure of not-skin on skin, sent shivers through her. Piotr brushed a curl of her hair off her forehead and leaned in, breath that was not-breath whispering across her cheek, the scent of him filling her world.

Once she thought he smelled like cool forest earth underlined with rot, like the Walkers, but now that she'd grown accustomed to it Piotr's scent was uniquely his own—sweet and subtle and faded, like dried rose petals releasing one last puff of sweetness before crumbling. Away from her room and amid the trees, Piotr smelled weathered, like old books and old lace and the chill clean scent of a windswept field at midnight. He smelled, very faintly, like dirt and growing things.

It was too much. She had to stand, or she was sure she'd break into a million pieces. Piotr's touch made her movements slow and languorous, almost drowsy; Wendy felt as if she was sliding into sweet slumber, a pleasant and hazy edge of sleep. In a half-dream, Wendy stood and drifted over to a tree, supporting her weight against its comforting bulk while Piotr stood before her, bathed in the sunlight of his ghostly world.

"Slow," Piotr murmured, as if reminding himself. "Slow touching."

"Slow . . . is . . . good." Wendy leaned into his touch like a plant seeking the sunlight and he chuckled, deep and low, a rumble in his chest that Wendy felt in her fingertips. With her free hand she traced the curve of his ear, marveling at the faint freckles she could see smattering across his nose. He seemed so real, so solid. Experimentally she thumbed his earlobe, flicking her nail quickly across it, but her rapid touch slid through him, meeting only air. Slowly she tried again and he hissed through his teeth, eyes momentarily closing at her touch.

"What made you change your mind?" she asked. "About me?"

"I don't know, exactly." Laughter rumbled beneath her hand as she pressed her palm to his chest. "Specs, I suppose. He wasn't scared of you at all, was he?"

"No." Wendy ran her thumb across his collarbone. "Shades aren't either. They're thrilled to see me coming now."

"It's a mercy, what you do. Sending him home, letting Specs . . . Brian, letting Brian go home to be with his real family." Piotr dipped his head down, ran the tip of his nose across the curve of her cheek, his lips brushing her skin in a cool sweep. "I see that now. And I'm sorry. About what I said before."

"Forgiven," Wendy whispered. "No more fighting?"

"No more," Piotr agreed fervently and then he whispered something, too fast and low for her to make it out, but the cadence of the words was strange, choked at the end. Pulse thrumming through her veins, Wendy licked her lips and tried to control herself.

"Wh-what did you say?" It came out a whisper.

"Oh, *bozhe, kak ya schastliv*," he repeated. "It is an endearment." His fingers traced a tingling arc across her forehead and down her temples, nails scraping lightly against the angle of her jaw. He lit momentarily on a loose curl and wound it around his finger. "It roughly translates to 'Oh, God, how happy I am.'"

His palm, deliciously cool and subtly soft, skimmed lightly over her collarbone, down the side laces of her corset, and settled lightly in the curve of her waist. He tugged her forward and Wendy went willingly into the circle of his arms.

"Are you happy? Really?" Wendy closed her eyes and relaxed into the embrace, letting him support her weight. Her head tilted back and she felt the weight of her hair slide across her shoulders, falling behind her. His breath stirred the curls at her forehead as he pressed his lips first to one temple and then to the other. Her skin buzzed faintly at the touch, like a slight current was running through her flesh, and she trembled. His lips traced the outer curve of her cheekbone.

"Happier than I've ever been. You are like a dream to me, like something I could only imagine." Then he was kissing her. "You are my home."

Once, when she was seven, Wendy watched lightning strike a tree. It speared down three times in a row, so white-hot that the world was washed of color for hours afterward; the smell of ozone stung for twice as long. The immense crack of the thunderclap cocooned her in silky silence; the static in the very air raised every hair on her body.

This was like kissing lightning.

The thrum of his fingertips was nothing compared to the persistent press of his hands cupping her neck, her jaw, her hip. The pressure of his lips, first light and then firmer, left her gasping. They existed in their own bubble of near-silence, punctuated only by ragged breaths and the hush of fingers dragging against fabric. Wendy groaned when he buried his face in her neck; she was dangerously lightheaded, gasping for air.

At first, when he finally pulled away, Wendy thought it was the mind-blowing kiss that left them both pale and shaking. And then she realized that she could barely stand.

"I . . . don't . . ."

The grass swirled up to meet her.

When she came to, she found Piotr kneeling beside her, gently patting her face and hands. The pressure from his fingers was different—warmer, stronger—and his face was flushed.

"What happened?"

"Kissing me is bad for your health," Piotr replied gravely, gently prodding her body in various places, looking for breaks. "I tried to catch you but my arms slid right through you." He shook his head. "*Prastee meenya pozhalosta*, I'm so sorry. How is your arm?"

Wendy could see the panic in his eyes and she took his hand, gently squeezing it. "It's throbbing a little, but I'll live. What are you sorry for? You didn't know this would happen." She chuckled. "That was some kiss, though."

"Amazing as it was, no kiss is worth hurting you." He stroked the hair away from her face, eyes dark with panic. Wendy realized he was shaking. "I was afraid that I had killed you. After Specs . . ."

"But you didn't." Wendy struggled to sit up, ignoring the pressure on her shoulders where he tried to press down to keep her laying still. It was harder to do than before, but she was able to rest on her elbows and scoot until she was leaning against the tree for support. She was somewhat unnerved by exactly how much support she needed.

"I drained you." Piotr held up his free hand. "Like you were one of the Lost. It's almost exactly the same. Everything around me is brighter, more colorful." He pressed his hand against the tree and, after a moment, slowly pushed his fingertips through the wood. "It is harder for me to phase, too." He frowned and his fingers clenched together in her grip. "How do you feel?"

"Lightheaded," she replied honestly, stroking his hand until the tension eased and his fingers relaxed. "Shaky. Like I just spent two hours riding the Flight Deck at Great America, or maybe the Teacups. Everything is still spinning a little." She squeezed his hand, loving the supple-cool texture of it. "I'll get over it, though. Promise. And we'll be more careful next time."

"Next time?" Piotr frowned. "I do not know how I feel about a next time. You are hurt . . ."

"Shhh," she whispered. "I'm fine. Besides, if you think I'm letting you off the hook that easily, you've got another thing coming." Wendy had lost him once already, and she wasn't sure her heart could take another beating like before. It was worth risking a little temporary pain to keep him near. She ran her fingers through his hair, thrilling inside at the touch. He even *felt* more real under her hands. Solid, almost. Perhaps him taking a little of her energy had been a good thing after all.

"I do not know—"

Viper-fast, Wendy snatched his hand and pressed it against her ribcage, where he could feel the rapid thump of her heart. Her lips parted and she leaned forward, barely brushing his with the faintest, sweetest kiss. Under his palm, her heartbeat trebled and he felt his heart answer, the electric thrumming between them spiraling into a singing haze of sensation and feeling.

She drew back, gasping raggedly, and color returned to her cheeks in a high, pink flush. "The point is," she whispered, "that, potential risks or not, I've never felt anything like that before." She eyed him critically. "You haven't either. Don't deny it."

He chuckled brokenly. "Of course not. This is . . . intense. Your point being?"

"This thing, whatever it is between us, it's new and it's special, and I'm not going to let you just walk away from it. From us. Not again."

Wendy slid forward and cupped his face, running her thumb over his lower lip. Part of her knew that doing this, chasing after those electric kisses, was courting death, but she felt fearless and wild, unbreakably young. After all, she was the Lightbringer and death had to answer to her, not the other way around. At least, not yet. For now, she was untouchable. "Come on, Piotr. 'Happier than you've ever been,' remember? I'm your home? This thing we have is like a dream?"

"Possible nightmare," he replied, but his tone was weak. Wendy knew that Piotr agreed with her. There was something about the way the world seemed to shift on its very foundation when they were together, the way the universe had neatly twisted until all there was for Piotr was Wendy, and Wendy for Piotr.

"Fine," he murmured, his lips pressing against her temple, "I will go along with this insanity. For you, and because I am a selfish idiot who can't bear to give you up. But there must be guidelines."

"Guidelines. Uh huh." Delighted with this turn of events, Wendy leaned forward and her warm lips traced fire down his jaw.

His voice cracked. "Limits. Rules."

"Limits, sure thing," she agreed, threading her fingers through his as she slowly kissed down his neck. "Rules. Gotcha."

"Stop that," he said, exasperated. Wendy leaned back against the tree and eyed him under the fall of her lashes. All at once Piotr looked faintly uneasy; it was like a rabbit being watched by a wolf. "You are . . . impossible."

Wendy gave him a twinkling smile. "Oh really? I hadn't noticed."

"Hah-hah. I mean my words, Wendy." Piotr scooted away, putting even more space between them so that he wouldn't be tempted to let her draw him in again. Firmly, he shook his head. "Rules."

"Piotr, you wouldn't hurt me."

"I might," he stressed. "I might. Or you might forget yourself and accidentally reap me. Either one of us could easily hurt the other. So . . . rules." Piotr watched her warily. "Okay? Yes?"

"Fine," Wendy huffed and crossed her arms across her chest, pouting. "Yay, rules."

He was at her side in a moment, gathering her into his arms and hugging her tight. "This is for both of us, love." He rubbed his chin against the top of her head. "I would die a thousand deaths to kiss you and never stop. But I will not hurt you if I can help it, Wendy. Let me do this. For us."

"I know," Wendy grumbled, but her arms snuck out and wrapped loosely around his waist. Piotr smiled and pressed a tender kiss on the top of her head. "So what's got you so agitated? It can't just be the kiss."

"Specs just reached inside and—" Piotr faltered. She could see that he was still affected by what he had seen; unable to describe it. "He is . . . was a Lost. Promise me you'll avoid them for a time."

"I'm sure it was a one time thing," she mumbled, but her body tensed with the remembered pain.

"*Da*, possibly, but maybe not. What about your mother?" He seemed to be about to say something, but he stopped himself, going quiet and just watching her for a few long seconds.

"This time with you is too short," he said instead, glancing at the sky. The day was fading into twilight and the first stars were beginning to glimmer in the sky above. "What time is it?"

Grimacing, Wendy checked her watch. "Late. I should get back."

"Of course." Piotr looked disappointed. Wendy was, too, but unlike him, she had a life to live and responsibilities to keep. "I should start back to the pier anyway," he said. "I have to tell the others what happened and what we discovered." He turned to go but she stopped him, wrapping her hand around his upper arm.

"You don't have to go," she suggested. "You could come with me."

"Come with you? I do not understand."

Wendy shrugged, a gesture intended to be careless, but the edges of her lips were white and her eyes were watchful. "It's not like anyone can see you; you could come right in the front door like you used to. We could . . . hang out more. In my room."

"Hang out." The emphasis she put on the words clearly left little to Piotr's imagination.

She leaned forward and pressed a soft, chaste kiss to his lower lip, drawing back the moment the electricity began to zing between them. "In my room."

"Are you sure that's a good idea?" he whispered. He still looked hesitant, like he wanted to step away, but Wendy burned brilliantly under his palms, carefree and intent on dragging him home.

"Rule number one," she reminded him, and the dangerous twinkle was back. "Call it research."

Groaning, Piotr took her by the shoulders and hugged her tightly. Her pulse rippled through him, catching and hooking into his very core. "If I weren't already dead, *milaya moya*," he sighed, tilting her head up and slowly sliding into another kiss, "you'd be the death of me."

CHAPTER SIXTEEN

Guilt warred with worry as Piotr and Wendy approached the bookstore the next morning. The sun was rather high in the sky and Piotr was concerned that he may have already missed the other Riders. He'd wanted to leave earlier but Wendy, waking early, was gone before sunrise. She'd spent the morning at the diner with Eddie and had come back both sulky and bemused. They had, she declared, made up, though for how long still remained to be seen.

After the previous night he'd decided to give Eddie a chance. Once upon a time, he reasoned, Wendy might have had a thing for this Eddie, but that time must be long gone. And there were more important things to stress about than the people his living girl-friend—his girlfriend!—surrounded herself with.

"Wait here," Piotr told Wendy, sitting her on a bench across the street from the bookstore. "I'll go in and explain."

"Good idea," she whispered, trying to appear inconspicuous. The streets, even this one, were thronged with milling tourists enjoying the holiday and doing last-minute shopping in San Francisco. Wendy, who'd brought a backpack along, settled herself on the bench and drew out a thick novel, *The Stand*. Glad that she wasn't clinging, Piotr dodged through the crowd toward the shop, wishing that he'd thought to bring her here before now. Elle was going to have a fit.

He was right.

To be fair, the remaining Riders heard him through to the end before Elle lost it. Thankfully, his reflexes were as quick as hers, and Piotr was able to duck and dodge out of the way as Elle began chucking books, bags, and whatever other refuse she could get her hands on directly at his head. She pegged him a few good times before Lily intervened, stepping between Elle and Piotr and holding up her hands to catch the missiles.

James, who'd always kept Piotr at a distance, did nothing to help the situation; he merely lounged on the stairs to the second floor and smirked as Elle ranted and raved. Piotr caught his eye once or twice with a wordless plea to step in, but James was having too much fun to intervene. When Lily interceded the smile dropped off his face and he sulked, disappointed that Piotr hadn't been injured in the barrage.

When she'd calmed enough to do more than throw things and scream, Elle (hands on hips) demanded, "What kind of balled up BS is all this? You get goofy over some hotsy-totsy jane and you expect us to just be jake with it?"

At first Piotr wasn't entirely sure he'd understood her—when Elle really got going her flapper *patois* took hold and often even Dora had trouble untangling the verbal knots of her speech—but Elle's furious expression and pointed sneer spoke volumes. "I expected you to be my friends," Piotr replied coolly, crossing his arms across his chest and resting against the counter. "The kind that support one another."

"We are your friends," Lily began, "and we always will be, but—"

"But? What but?!" Elle picked up one of Dora's abandoned sketchpads and waved it in the air, shaking it nearly under Piotr's nose. "I got a beef with ol' Pete here and I aim to have my say. This palooka's got some nerve if he thinks he can just waltz on in here and think we're gonna goosestep in time to his little suicide parade."

"Suicide? I'm already dead!"

James shook his head. "Man, there are worse things than being dead. You know that. And if this girl Wendy is the Lightbringer like you say she is, then you're not just playing with fire, you're down-right taunting it."

"Wendy would never hurt me."

Infuriated, Elle threw down the pad and began poking Piotr hard in the chest. "Listen to you! 'Wendy would never hurt me,'" she mimicked in a high nasal falsetto, tucking her tongue between her teeth on each vowel so she lisped. "Maybe not *you*, but what about the rest of us? What about the Lost? That girl's job is to exterminate our kind!"

"She's setting us free—"

Elle snorted and poked him again. "Free! Listen to yourself, Pete! Did what happen to those Walkers look like 'free' to you? They were burned up from the inside. That's sick. That's just wrong. And you *kissed* it."

"This I will not discuss with you," Piotr snapped. "It is none of your business, Elle."

"Fine, neckin' with the freakshow aside, what about the Lost, huh? You said she and the Lost have some sort of wacko connection, right? Well, you ever think that maybe your gal Friday out there was the one who took 'em? Maybe she's not killing off the Walkers, maybe she's just in league with them, had them come on down here and scoop the Lost up for her. You yourself said you told her where we all were before you knew she was the Lightbringer."

"Your point being?"

"My point being that I think it's awful convenient, her just hap-pening to hang 'round the park when you got yourself ambushed over Specs."

"It is nothing like that," Piotr protested. "She could have come and reaped all of us anytime she wanted, but she did not! She's not that sort of person."

"Sure she ain't, Pete. Sure. The glowing tentacle monster that eats our kind up like we were penny candy ain't like that. I guess that means you, Mr. Petey Optimistic, ain't stuck on her at all!"

"Do not call her that," Piotr snarled. "Wendy has a duty—"

"A duty! Hah!" Elle threw up her hands and laughed long and hard, but there was no mirth in the sound, only shrill, venomous sarcasm. "The *monster's* got a *duty*. She's all about doin' the right thing, making sure everything in the Never's copasetic, right? Sure she does! She understands all about duty, I bet. That's why she kept you, Piotr, not just any ol' Rider but the big cheese who *started* the Riders, away from us when we needed you most. That's why you, Mr. Hi-You're-Dead-Here's-How-The-Afterlife-Works himself, was off neckin' with a *monster* when you should have been here running a shift!"

"*Ny ti i svoloch'*," Piotr said flatly, slapping her poking hand away. "Insane, Elle. I have no clue what you're talking about."

"Course you don't," she spat. "Ol' Petey never has a goddamn clue 'bout nothin' these days, monsters and Riders included."

Piotr stuffed his hands in his pockets, weary now of the shouting and yelling but at a loss for how to stop it. "Elle, you're not being fair."

"I'm not bein' fair? I'm not? Fine. Fine, Petey, I'll be fair to you. I'll be fair because I'm sick of it. I'm sick of protecting you, of playin' along. You wanna drop us for some livin' dame? Fine! Then I'm gonna lay a little truth on you before you walk out that door and go back to your precious Lightbringer. I'm gonna talk and you're gonna sit here and listen! That fair enough for you?" Piotr, frustrated, turned his face away.

Elle twisted until she could look at James, still lounging on the stairs, elbows resting on knees and avidly following the debate. "Jaime-boy, tell the truth. Have I or have I not known this piker for years? Ain't we had a caper or two?"

"Long as you've been dead," James replied in his slow and thoughtful way, lifting one tightly braided dreadlock and examining the end. "Long as I've been dead too."

"Ha-ha," Piotr grumbled, "this is not the time. This trick I've heard before."

"So Pete, you've known me goin' on a century," Elle continued, ignoring Piotr's protests. "And James for almost two. If I remember right, you found me in a speakeasy and Jaime-boy hauling cotton south of the Mason-Dixon line."

Terror gripped him, set his stomach boiling with acid and anger. This joke had gone on long enough! "Elle," Piotr whispered through lips pressed tightly together, edges bled white from the pressure, "stop. This is enough."

She was on a roll and couldn't hear him, or simply chose not to. "Whether you remember it or not, you've traveled some, Pete, and you took us along for the ride. Hell, you and Lily've been dead together longer than most of the Walkers 'round this town've been walking. Ain't that right, Lily?"

The insistence Elle sank into each word chilled Piotr to the bone. Lily wasn't denying the wild claims and Piotr knew that James, infuriating as he was, had never been much of a liar. But what Elle was claiming was sheer, unadulterated insanity, and impossible to boot. Piotr couldn't remember his own death—few ghosts could—but surely he'd remember having died more than two centuries before. Wouldn't he?

"*Net*," Piotr murmured louder, shaking his head. "I don't believe you."

"She's telling the truth," James said. "You're older than Moses, Peter. You're older than anyone any ghost I know's ever met. You're damn near ancient."

"Believe me or not, Petey-boy, I think I'm tired of givin' two tin shits about it," Elle sneered, thrusting her fists on her hips and wagging her head from side to side for emphasis. "Worrying about you all the time just ain't cuttin' it for me anymore. I'm just pointin' out that you ain't exactly playin' with a full deck lately, and unless you've been lyin' this whole time then you never remember us, Pete. You never do."

"A couple decades pass and it is like meeting a new you," Lily agreed, voice pitched low and quiet, but calm and firm. She looked apologetically at Piotr, spread her hands wide, and dropped them to her sides. "Your accent and some Russian phrases remain, but the rest, your memories and recollections . . . they are new like snow, like the clear mountain stream. When I first met you, you were like the great and wise Yanauluha; you guided me in my struggles and taught me much of the ways of the Never. You were serious then, but kind, and knew how to calm the troubled waters of my mind. But years passed and with them passed the man I'd known. Who you are now is not who you were then. You are not a bad man now, but different."

Piotr groaned, rested his fingers at his temples, and massaged, hoping to drive away the tension headache that was building there. "You sound like you miss this 'old me' a lot."

Lily did not reply, but her cheeks grew dark.

"Great," Piotr muttered. "Fabulous, what a great bunch of friends you all are."

Roughly, Elle coughed, then bent over. Piotr was startled to realize that Elle, strong and nettlesome Elle, was crying. Her hands opened and closed convulsively, her shoulders shook. Lily moved as if to comfort her and was waved away.

"All that time," Elle croaked, furiously swiping the tears off her cheeks, "all that time we've spent with you, fretting over you, looking out for you and yours, all that time not knowing if or when you were going to start sliding into being someone else, and now you've thrown us over. And for what? Because you're stuck on some dizzy sheba who don't even have the decency to be dead? One you can apparently touch but, you know, just not for that long?" She sneered and spat on the floor, mere centimeters from Piotr's shoe. "Well ain't you the biggest sap I've ever seen."

"You've got a right to be upset," Piotr began tensely, forcibly keeping himself from wrapping his arms around Elle and simply hugging her. Elle rarely cried and he hadn't meant to hurt her feelings; Piotr felt lower than low for doing so. "Before the kids were taken I hadn't been around, pulling my shifts as I ought to have, you've got a point there. You and I . . . I wasn't happy hanging around. I felt I was an imposition."

"So you dumped the kids?" James asked derisively.

"*Net*," Piotr retorted, annoyed and wishing James would quit needling him. "I assumed that with all those Riders staying here I could be away more often, but I know now that no matter how uncomfortable being here made me, I could have helped. I should have helped."

"Damn right, you should've," James grumbled, lapsing into a sharp and pointed silence.

"*Pros'tite*, I'm sorry for that," Piotr continued, ignoring James. "I truly am. But the rest of it . . . this Yannihula—"

"Yanauluha," Lily corrected. "The first shaman."

"Yannihula, Yanauluha, it doesn't matter! This talk like I've been some other person, it is insane, Elle. Nothing but crazy, creepy talk. Why do you keep going on like I've been around forever? I didn't start the Riders; I haven't been dead that long!"

For a brief moment Piotr hesitated—no matter how impossible it seemed, there was a chance, slim as it was, that they weren't teasing him but in fact were telling the truth—but, try as he might, Piotr couldn't bring himself to believe it. This was his afterlife, right? Piotr was certain, he could feel it in his very bones, that if what they'd been saying was true, if he truly had been forgetting things and slowly shifting personalities over centuries of existence, that somewhere deep inside he would have sensed such dichotomy before now. He would have!

Which meant that they were ganging up on him for some crazy reason; getting together to make Piotr feel bad for not being around when the Lost were taken, and for meeting with Wendy behind their backs. This was simple, petty revenge and nothing more, and he was ashamed of them and for them that they would stoop to such lows. Lily especially. Such meanness was normally beneath her.

So long as he'd begun, he might as well finish the fight and say goodbye to these petty people who were *supposed* to be his friends. Piotr straightened and firmly said, "I'm worried about you, Elle. About all of you."

"He is worried about me," Elle sighed, and then laughed. "Petey the boy wonder here is worried 'bout little ol' Belladona Tinker. Well, ain't that the cat's meow, folks?"

"I am," Piotr said. "I'm disappointed. This joke has gone on long enough."

She nodded, the picture of thoughtfulness. "I have one thing to say about that."

Straightening to her full height, Elle slapped him.

"You worry about me and I'll worry about everything else," she snarled. "Maybe, just maybe, if you'd been really worried before, maybe you would've been here when we needed you. Isn't it funny, Pete, how the one time you run off for more than a few days they just magically appear and take us out? Like they knew one of our best fighters was gone!"

"Yeah," James chimed in.

"Or," Elle said, gaining steam, "maybe if you hadn't had your head down in your pants and your hands down hers, Specs and Dora would be a little more here and a little less gone!"

Flabbergasted, Piotr could only open and close his mouth, jaw gaping like a fish. His hand drifted to his cheek, examined the heat there, the sting and momentary swelling where her palm had cracked against his cheekbone. Then Piotr grew angry.

"*Ej! Smotret' nyzhno!* Listen to me, you—you arrogant big-mouth," he growled, hands clenching into fists. "Wendy isn't like that. She's great! She's fantastic! And unlike some of the people I know, she likes me for who I actually *am*, not who I'm apparently supposed to be. Or was. Or whatever! And as for Dora—"

"Elle, Piotr, stop," Lily said reproachfully. She stood, shifting herself once again between Elle and Piotr, and shot James a hard glance for not stepping forward with her or stopping the fight earlier. "This talk is going nowhere. You are thunder booming in the distance. Neither of you is thinking straight and you're only hurting yourselves."

"*Da*, that's obvious," Piotr said, stepping back. "Wendy's waiting outside. I think I've heard all I need to in here."

"If this girl's on the level, then she oughta prove it," Elle called as Piotr stormed away. "She oughta step up and pull her weight a little more; maybe do some real business instead of just bumping off a Walker here and there. If she's all fired up about duty and doin' her job then she ought to go take care of the White Lady herself instead of pickin' on ghosts like us. If you weren't so goofy over this dame, you'd see that."

"And if you had any faith in me, you'd trust me to know when someone's a good person or not," Piotr yelled over his shoulder. He paused at the door, hand pressed against the thick wood, and glanced back. They stood in a line in the far archway, Lily and Elle on either side of James like slim bookends leaning against one wide and battered book. The gloom loomed behind them.

"I'll be back," Piotr added, relenting at the sight of Lily's mouth tucked in at the corners and Elle's wide and watering eyes. "With Dora and the others. I promise."

"You're going to get yourself bumped off," Elle said, clear and low, as he began leaning toward the door. "Soon's you let your guard down. I'd lay a million clams on it. Two mil."

For old time's sake Piotr smiled; the expression felt brittle on his face; he half-expected the smile to crack and sift to dust before he could flee the building. "I'll keep that in mind, Elle," he called over his shoulder as he stepped through and back onto the busy and sweltering street. "Take care. *Dasvidania.*"

Picking his way through the crowd, Piotr expected to find Wendy still sitting on the bench with her book in her hands, but the bench was empty save for Wendy's battered paperback. The wind ruffled the cover back, exposing dog-eared pages and filling Piotr with a sense of foreboding. He glanced left and right, seeking some sign of her, but the sun was high in the sky and the crowd was thick with holiday shoppers using the narrow side street as a shortcut to more fashionable places to be. Wendy was nowhere to be seen.

Tucking himself between the bench and a trashcan, Piotr stood in the small pocket of safety and stared at the crowd eddying by. The heat was immense, but after spending the previous night basking near Wendy's flame, it was almost bearable. At a loss for what to do or where to go, Piotr closed his eyes and turned in place, arms spread wide. Thanks to his night with Wendy, he could feel pressure as his right wrist slid through the top of the trashcan, could nearly sense the chill of the day in the living world on his skin.

When Piotr opened his eyes the flawless sky flickered above him—grey-blue-grey—and the hazy, indistinct shapes of the real buildings solidified for one brief moment, leaving Piotr awash with vertigo at the shifting, melting world around him. Not far away, only a few miles south, the blackened ghostly remains of the Palace Hotel winked out of existence, stuttered, and returned with the wash of grey sky above. There was an ephemeral glitter, barely seen above the hulks of wood and stone, and a short flash of fierce shining light.

There. Wendy had gone in that direction.

Taking his time, Piotr gauged the crowd and the buildings around him. Most were stores full of trinkets: stepping through the walls and cutting through the buildings would be useless this time of year, every shop was stuffed with holiday shoppers and he could easily be burned by some bargain-hunting biddy diving through him for the last knickknack on a shelf.

No, he decided, the streets were safer.

Leaving the narrow pocket of safety he'd found proved easier said than done. Piotr had to wait until a hole appeared in the crowd, a six-foot space between a gaggle of giggling teenage girls and a trio of boys who hung slightly back, checking them out from behind.

Blessing his luck, Piotr stepped into this gap and traveled in relative safety most of the way to the light rail. Once there, avoiding the pulse of the crowds shuffling on and off the train, Piotr phased into a corner and prayed no one would sit where he was standing. He was lucky, the trip was short and most of the living around him were too hyped up on the season of cheer to pay much attention to the pocket of icy air that hung in the corner of the car. Any that approached were repulsed by the chill and soon, despite the crowding on the train, only Piotr's corner was free; the living sat shoulder to shoulder and hip to hip, but no one was willing to situate themselves in his frigid corner.

The light rail was swift and Market Street approached in no time at all. Piotr waited to disembark until all the living had done so before him. It was still crowded and busy here, but it was a different sort of crowded. Market Street sat near the hustle and bustle of downtown San Francisco, only a short distance away from skyscrapers crawling with important businessmen and rich gallerias. North Beach and Union Square were close but still a bit apart; nothing for someone like Piotr who was accustomed to walking, but far enough distant that most of the living preferred locomotion other than their feet to get them from point A to point B. Those who did walk were far less hurried; they milled about and enjoyed the day, tipping their faces up to the broad expanse of sky and sipping flavored drinks out of steaming paper cups. Their relaxed speed allowed Piotr the opportunity to bob and weave among them, following the sweet siren song he could now hear faintly in the distance, calling him.

Piotr found the Lightbringer on Kearny Street, reaping half a dozen Walkers in the shadow of the Telesis Tower. Though he itched to help, Piotr knew now to keep his distance, and instead settled within watching range but far enough away that he wasn't tempted to drift forward and join the Walkers on their journey into the Light.

The wind picked up her voice, tossed it so she sounded near.

"Where are they?" Piotr's stomach clenched—Wendy was asking about the Lost!

Drifting as close as he dared, observing her, Piotr's eyesight stuttered strangely again, stripping the ghosts from the scene and showing him the world as Wendy must see it, all angles and glass and hard metal stretching to the sky. In the Never, the Telesis Tower was a tall but flimsy structure, growing more stable as the years of accumulated career-oriented passion within its walls drifted higher, but still relatively fragile in the grand scheme of things. In the living world the Tower was a monstrous beast of a building, wide and tall, a peer of the realm amidst other, older structures. Piotr rubbed his eyes and the Tower he knew returned, shaped of forgotten hopes and dreams, wispy and fragile and new.

Despite himself, faced with the sight of the Tower alternately solidifying and fading before his very eyes, Piotr thought of Elle's recent accusations and Lily's lies. They claimed he'd been changing again, always changing, his memories flaking away and leaving him something new and not necessarily better. What if their claims hadn't been false? What if they'd been telling the truth? This bizarre double vision was certainly something he'd never encountered before, not even in rumor.

What if he was truly changing?

"Idiot," he muttered under his breath, shoving the traitorous thought away. "They got under your skin. Whatever this is," he glanced around and winced as the world took on a realistic edge for a fleeting second, "is just some sort of residue from being with Wendy. That's all." *But*, his mind whispered, *what if it's not?*

Lost in his thoughts, Piotr didn't notice the battle end, and when Wendy, shed of the Light, touched his arm, Piotr jumped and stumbled back, hand pressed to chest and eyes wild. "You scared me! Give a man some warning!"

"Sorry," Wendy apologized, tucking her hands behind her back and hunching her shoulders slightly. "I didn't mean to. I thought you saw me coming."

"I did not," Piotr said, forcing himself to take a deep and calming breath. "My fault."

Chuckling nervously, Piotr drew close and hugged her, marveling at the wash of sensation that drowned the initial sting of her touch. Wendy tucked her curls beneath his chin and wrapped her arms around his waist, ignoring the momentary steam that billowed around them. They were tucked off the street away from prying eyes, though to the casual passerby it might seem as if Wendy were stretching her arms oddly forward and perhaps popping her neck as she did so. Still, Wendy didn't dare stay that way more than a few moments, lest her peculiar posture draw unwanted attention.

"Wendy? What is the matter?"

"It was rough going this time," she admitted, releasing Piotr and stepping back. "You have no idea how much it hurts to hold off on a reap, but I got what we needed to know."

"You were asking about the Lost, *da*?" Deciding that she had enough on her plate as it was, Piotr declined to mention the strange stuttering his vision had picked up.

"She's at the Palace Hotel," Wendy said. "The White Lady is holed up there with some Walkers for bodyguards, but no Lost. However, some are due to come in to be drained a few days from now, so we've got time to sort out a plan and see if the other Riders want to help."

"About that—" Piotr began.

"Later," Wendy said, pressing her palm to her midsection. "I'm so hungry I feel like I'm gonna puke! Reaping's the best diet I've ever been on, I swear. I need some food, and fast. Come on, let's go this way."

As she talked Wendy reached into her bag and fumbled out a slim black headset that she tucked into her ear. A small blue light winked from one end. "I'll look like a douchebag," she explained, pulling her hair back and making sure the headset was visible to the casual passerby, "but that's better than looking crazy."

"I see," Piotr agreed. Her fight with the Walkers had drained her somewhat; her face was pale, and dark rings circled under her eyes. "You didn't wait for me."

"I couldn't. I planned to, but I saw a ghost who I thought was my mom. I went after her but she turned out to be just some Shade. I was about to turn back when that group of Walkers ran by and I had to follow them." Wendy wiped her mouth and glanced sharply around, making sure there were no ghosts of any variety near enough to overhear their conversation. "It was so weird, Piotr, they were outright booking it! I've never seen a Walker run before. Have you?"

"They can run," Piotr said slowly, taking time to think while he answered, "but they generally don't. That's why we call them Walkers, *da*? They walk, we ride." He shook his head, chuckled. "Or we did, before cars."

"Really?" Wendy chuckled, then pressed her hand to her mouth, looking green. "You know, I never even thought to ask why you all called yourselves that. So you, what, rode horses around all the time?"

"It was the easiest way to escape with a Lost. Riders still need to sleep, at least every now and then, and the Walkers—so far as we can tell, at least—don't. So you'd pile your Lost into a wagon or a buggy and," he mimed cracking a whip, "vamoose. It'd take them ages to catch up."

Impressed, Wendy whistled under her breath. "And you didn't have any problems finding transportation in the Never?"

"I wouldn't go so far as all that. Wagons were easy to find, no issues there, but locating a dead horse that stayed in the Never was difficult." He laughed, remembering, and took her hand in his as they began drifting slowly up the street and back toward the light rail. "Dogs are loyal, they hang around until their master dies. Cats like Jabber will hang about if they like a particular family member."

"Is that why Jabber's sticking around? He misses Mom?"

"Most likely. But horses? They were worth their weight in salvage; if you found one, you needed to hold on tight."

"Servitude even when you're dead," Wendy mused. "Must have sucked to be a horse."

"Of course not! We'd never force them and most were used to the work. They didn't mind helping. They kept good conversation too, if a man didn't have anyone else to talk with."

"Animals talk in the Never?" Wendy gasped. "You've got to be kidding me. Like, with words and stuff?"

Piotr looked at Wendy strangely. "*Da*. Jabber's never spoken to you before?"

"Uh, no. Not once. Has he spoken with you?"

Piotr nodded. "All the time. He's very particular about how he's petted. Behind the ears only."

"Weird! I wonder why he's never spoken to me?"

Shrugging, Piotr hid a grin. "Maybe he feels that you, being alive, couldn't understand where he's coming from?"

"Ha-ha, very funny. Okay, so if they can talk, could a horse, I don't know, tell a knock-knock joke?"

"Not exactly," Piotr drawled, looking at Wendy oddly, as if she'd suddenly grown a third eye or sprouted wings from her shoulder blades. "Words are an entirely human concept, Wendy. But the Never is different from the world you exist in. Things are far more free-flowing and open. Language exists, yes, but not exactly as you know it. Words aren't always finite over here, they carry ideas straight to the heart."

"So specific languages don't really matter once you're dead? You all can understand one another anyway? And get what horses and cats and whatnot are saying?"

"In a manner of speaking." Piotr smiled. "I am Russian, *da*? When a concept is hard to express in English, I still speak my native tongue. The gist is passed on to the others but not the exact words. But they do understand."

"So weird," Wendy said. "I guess it's just one of those things I'll have to be dead to get. Piotr, you are blowing my mind over here,"

Wendy laughed, shaking her head with disbelief. "When I get home I'm totally gonna sit down and see if Jabber will talk with me. But you! I still can't believe that you had your very own Mr. Ed."

Piotr frowned. "Mister who?"

"It was this old TV show? From the fifties?" Wendy licked her lips, feeling foolish, and shrugged. "You know, reruns? Nick at Night? No? It's not important. You were probably too busy saving the Lost or whatever to pay attention to television in the fifties anyway."

"I'm told the television set is an amazing invention," Piotr said gravely. "However, most mechanical things, unless they are very, very simple, do not work in the Never. So I've never seen one that worked. The shells of television sets, certainly. Many people pour emotion daily into those boxes, the way they are doing with computers now, so more than a few show up on our side. But advanced machines rarely work for us. They turn on but there is just static."

"But my calculator isn't a simple machine. It's got a computer chip in it, right?"

Piotr shrugged. "I do not know. I died before these computers were created. Perhaps it is simple enough in its own way?"

"Huh. Weird. Maybe it's a combustion engine thing. I mean, I've always wondered why I saw only certain sorts of cars in the Never," Wendy mused as they crossed the street with the light. She hung to the back of the pack of lunchtime businessmen so Piotr could avoid being bumped and burned. "Fancy cars mostly, BMWs, Porsches, Ferraris, and such. But they never moved."

"They wouldn't. Bicycles, skateboards, skates . . . simple machines to use and well-loved in general, especially by children. Any of them are real finds." Piotr indicated a bike messenger, whizzing by at frightening speeds with a stack of red insulated sleeves strapped to the rack behind the seat. "See how that bike glows around the edges? When he finally throws it away it will most certainly come over. It's well used and well loved."

"So if you've got bikes lying around all over the place, why don't the Walkers use them?"

Wendy stopped near a wheeled cart where a man was selling fragrant hot dogs. Piotr's eyes twitched and the cartoons on the cart popped out at him, frantic yellows and reds that screamed across his retinas in a fury of painful color. Piotr turned away as Wendy purchased her lunch, forking over neatly folded bills for a cup of sloshing soda and a long dog oozing onions and relish. They walked across the street and she settled on a bench beside a pocket park, a tiny fountain birdbath festooned with thick fronds burbling merrily only ten feet away.

Piotr shrugged. "I don't know everything there is to know about Walkers," he tried to explain as Wendy bit into her lunch. A quartet of teenagers passed the small park, singing *Deck the Halls* in four-part harmony, unconcerned with the looks they were getting or the warm gust of wind blowing their hair off their faces and billowing the backs of their choir jackets nearly off their shoulders. "But I do know that when Walkers lose their life cord they lose most memories of what it's like to be human. All they remember is what it's like to feed."

Wendy, still gazing after the fa-la-la-ing students, took another large bite of her lunch. "It still seems so weird," she mumbled as she chewed, holding up one hand to cover her mouth. "What in the hell were half a dozen Walkers doing running through town, then? Especially these Walkers. They jumped a bus to get down here, Piotr. Phased right into one and sat at the back. I nearly gave myself a hernia racing to catch the dumb thing."

"You are serious?" Stunned at this, Piotr struggled for words. For as long as he could remember the Walkers had struggled with the remnants of living society, preferring to live at the edges and avoid all mention and memory of who they'd once been. Walkers walked—that was what they did. They didn't run and they most certainly didn't *catch buses* to travel across town. The thought of them

doing otherwise sent chills down Piotr's spine. But . . . was he truly
surprised? Really? Because he'd had an inkling about this already,
hadn't he? He'd sensed that something wasn't quite right.

*I knew there was something strange about those Walkers in the park yes-
terday*, part of him triumphed. *Walkers just don't work in complex teams
like that, strategizing their attacks. At least, they never did before.*

"I bet it's the White Lady," Wendy said. She drank deeply of her
soda, pressed fingers over her mouth, and burped behind her hand.
"Excuse me," she muttered. "Anyway, yeah, maybe the White Lady
is teaching the Walkers all about technology on top of everything
else." Wendy wrinkled her nose in distaste. "And you saw their faces
yesterday, right? More and more of those sorts of Walkers are
showing up. You know, mutilated and stitched back together
somehow. It looks really sick, if you ask me."

"Specs said they were taking him to see the White Lady," Piotr
agreed. "That she had the ability to keep him from walking through
walls somehow. What if she has some way of enhancing the Walkers
around her, too? Not just mending their flesh, but their minds as
well? What if she can make them remember how to use machinery?
Or could reteach them?"

Wendy whistled. "That would be bad. Real bad. They could go
anywhere then, not just hang around the cities."

"We must stop her," Piotr whispered. "Not just rescue the Lost,
but stop the White Lady herself. Undo everything she's done thus
far. Maybe make the Walkers forget what she's taught them. Start
over from scratch."

"I agree and I'm there with you, every step of the way," Wendy
said. "But the question is . . . how?"

CHAPTER SEVENTEEN

The day spun its hours out the way days do. Twilight found Wendy unlocking her front door and stepping into the foyer. In the living room Chel was sprawled out on the couch, arms pillowed beneath her head and snoring as some reality show droned on low in the background. Wendy covered her with a light blanket and went into the kitchen for a snack.

There was a good smell of cooking there: tomatoes and garlic, onions, and a hint of something spicy and sharp. A pot squatted on the back burner, simmering, and when Wendy lifted the lid and leaned over it she was hit with a cloud scented with rich, creamy garlic. It smelled heavenly and Wendy's mouth filled with water, stomach grumbling.

"The sauce is okay, but we have to eat it over spaghetti since I messed up the ravioli," Jon said, entering the kitchen from the back yard. His basketball was clutched under one arm and he was limping, supporting his weight on his right leg. The knee of his jeans had been torn out; gravel and grass flecked the spongy, raw wreck that had been his knee.

"What happened to you?" Wendy snatched the paper towels off the kitchen counter and hurried to the sink, dampening a handful under the cold tap. Jon slid onto one of the high kitchen stools at the counter and provided his knee for inspection, wincing each time Wendy dabbed the damp edge against the bloody flesh.

"My lay-ups suck now," he admitted as Wendy flicked on the kitchen light in order to better see his wound. Mournfully he plucked at the fabric on his thigh. "Nana just bought me these jeans, too."

"Well, it's just a scrape," Wendy replied, gingerly pulling the shredded jeans away from his knee when she was done, verifying that it was the only wound on him. "A nasty one, but it doesn't look like you need stitches." Rising, she patted him on the shoulder. "Hang tight, there's some knockoff Neosporin and gauze in the bathroom."

When she returned to the kitchen, Jon held out his hands. "Give me that stuff and go stir the sauce, will you? I don't want the bottom to scorch."

"Aye-aye, Cap'n," Wendy agreed. "Anything else?"

"Turn the heat down to low. It needs to sit for fifteen or so." While she did so, Jon thumbed the lid off the antibiotic ointment and slathered a largish dollop across his knee with fussy precision. "When you're done, can you hold the gauze while I tape it down?"

"Gladly." Wendy ended up applying the gauze for him and it reminded her so strongly of the prior times she'd done this very chore for Jon that she found herself growing misty eyed.

"It's just a scrape, you big baby," Jon admonished as Wendy applied the last stripe of tape and straightened, wiping her eyes with the back of her hand. "I'm not gonna die."

"It's not that," she sniffled, ripping a paper towel off the roll to use as a tissue. "It's just, I don't know, you haven't come to me with a scrape in, what, five years? Six?"

Uncomfortably, Jon shrugged. "When he was here, Dad usually handled that stuff. You and Mom were always busy, you know, at the park and stuff."

At the park. Wendy sighed. "At the park" had been the code she and her mother used to mean "out reaping." She hadn't had to use that excuse since their mother's accident. So long as Dad wasn't around, saying simply that she was going "out" usually sufficed, and these days the few times a month Dad was home he was generally at the hospital. Thanks to their sort of truce, Wendy felt little need to explain her whereabouts to him.

"I guess you're right," she agreed. "I was at the park a lot."

Jon shrugged. "Whatever. We got used to it. Mom and Dad didn't care, so what's the big deal, right?" He limped to the stove and dipped a long wooden spoon into the sauce, smacking his lips and smiling widely at the taste. "Momma mia, the sauce, she is perfecto!"

"How are the calories?" Wendy asked and then kicked herself for asking. Jon had enough stress in his life as it was; the last thing he needed was for her to get on his case about his weight, especially since they hadn't yet talked about her bitchiness over the past few months.

But Jon didn't seem to care. He rolled his eyes and licked the spoon elaborately, running his tongue far past the point where the sauce ended. "Ish's gweate," he declared around his mouthful of spoon.

"Sorry I asked," Wendy cried, throwing up her hands and chuckling as her brother slobbered all over the spoon. In the living room, Chel stirred and sat up, her curls sticking up every which way and frizzy at the top.

Wendy affected an outrageous accent. "My apologies, good sir!"

Discarding the damp spoon in the sink, Jon wiped his mouth with the back of his hand. "Naw, no worries. It's got a skim milk base, I promise, and it's going over whole wheat pasta." He patted his gut and grinned, waggling his eyebrows wildly. "This baby's goin' away slow, but yes, ma'am, she is a goin'."

"Smells tasty in here," Chel yawned, staggering to the refrigerator and grabbing a plastic bottle filled with some thick, milky-looking liquid. Flush with sleep, Chel caught Wendy's eye and shook the bottle. "Protein shake," she said coolly. "Want some?"

"I'll pass," Wendy said, waving her hand in front of her face. "Especially if it's from Dad's can. That stuff is foul."

Chel shrugged and took a deep gulp of the stuff. "Add some fruit, it's no big deal. It stays down, too." She wiped her thumb against the corner of her mouth, checking for stray drops of shake. "I saw you go out with Eddie this morning. You done being a bitch yet?"

Amused at how casually Chel asked, Wendy couldn't help but smile. "No guarantees, but I think I'm over my bitchy phase, yeah. You done puking after every other meal?"

"Working on it," Chel said mildly and took another sip. "It's a little harder than I thought it'd be." Her head dipped down and she scowled, fingers tapping in rapid rhythm against the plastic sides of her bottle. "Okay, a lot harder."

"She quit the squad," Jon explained. Chel scowled and shot him a dark look. Jon returned her scowl with a calm smile, shrugging as if to say *she had to find out sometime*.

"But you love cheering!" Wendy protested. The idea that her bright and vivacious sister would quit cheerleading was as foreign to her as the idea of ceasing the search for their mother's soul. "What about Dad? Does he know?"

"Nana does," Chel said, belligerent. "She said she'd pay Dad back for all my gear for this year as a Christmas gift. You know, in case he flips about the money." Nervous now, Chel gnawed her lower lip and lifted the drink up once again. Looking at her trembling hand, Wendy realized that Chel's perfect nails, always manicured and glossed to a high shine, were now ragged and blunt, ground down nearly to the quick.

She's chewing on them, Wendy realized, examining her sister closely for the first time in months. Chel's nails were now too short, her hair starting to show glossy red at the roots, and even her makeup was barely there, only a one-two swipe of lip-gloss and eye shadow, leaving her forehead shiny and cheeks pale.

"You're a mess," Wendy breathed, hardly able to get the words past lips gone numb with shock. Guilt clawed at her chest, making breathing tough. "Did I do this? Make you a mess by picking on you over the diet pills?"

"I did this to me," Chel retorted, draining the last of the protein shake and throwing the bottle in the sink for Jon to rinse out. "You just gave me a wake up call." She snorted. "But don't congratulate yourself just yet; you've still been a mega bitch and if I were smart, I ought to tell you to go to hell."

"But you're not smart?"

She shrugged. "No one's smart when it comes to family. Blood is thicker than smart."

"Before we all break down and group hug like the bunch of sissies we are," Jon interrupted, "Eddie stopped by earlier, Wendy. He's going out of town for the holidays after all. He said you'd better text him back later and he dropped off a box. It's on your bed."

"A box?" Wendy straightened up from the counter and started toward the stairs. Though she'd seen Eddie just that morning, the idea that he'd taken the time to stop by her house made her a little nervous. They may have made up, but things were still tense between them and she wasn't sure what to expect.

"Probably a Christmas gift," Jon called. "Food's almost ready, though. You coming down for dinner?"

"Yeah," she called back, mounting the stairs two at a time. "I'll be right down."

The box was compact and papered in old national geographic pages. Wendy lifted it and shook. There was a small rattling noise within, albeit muffled.

Careful of her fingers, Wendy used the nail file rattling around her pen cup to slice through the scotch tape layered around each edge of the box. The lid lifted off and fluffy cotton balls puffed over the edge of the box in a white cloud. Wendy set these aside.

"What the hell?" she murmured, shaking a seatbelt buckle and a piece of folded black construction paper out of the box. Holding the buckle up to the light, Wendy depressed the bright orange button on the front but the buckle appeared stuck in its clasp. The strap it had once been connected to was gone but a tough, thick beige thread was pinned within a crack in the clasp. The end of the thread was darker, rust colored, and stiff.

Blood, Wendy thought, and thumped to the floor. *Dried blood.*

Running her fingers over the buckle, Wendy wished that she'd been there to greet Eddie when he'd brought this gift. She didn't need to be told what it meant to him, or what lengths he'd probably gone to in order to get his hands on it after the accident. Instead Wendy turned the buckle over in her hands and tried to recall Mr. Barry's face, the face she must have seen hundreds—if not thousands—of times before the accident.

"Oh Eddie," Wendy sighed, squeezing the buckle tightly. "I'm so sorry."

Eddie's note was written in his familiar looping cursive—silver ink shone bright against the black paper:

Wendy,

    I know you think it's a joke, all the times I've said that I love you or that I'd do anything for you. But the thing is . . . it isn't. I am in love with you. I have been for years. What's not to love? You're smart and funny and fun to hang out with. More importantly, you're my best friend, my amigo, the only person who gets me and doesn't think I'm some weird freak.

    I know that Miss Manners would probably frown on a missive of undying affection added alongside a Christmas gift. It's probably rude or something. But I've been wanting to say this stuff to you for years. And I have been. I've been saying it all along but you always blow me off or think I'm joking and the one time I got you to even halfway consider it, back at the start of school when I kissed you, you thought I was just blowing off steam cuz of the crap I said about your mom or the crap you said about my dad. Either way, you forgave me for the kiss. But the thing is . . . I didn't want your forgiveness Wendy; I wanted you to kiss me back.

    Because I love you.

    So a few months ago I made this deal with myself. I said, "Self, if she doesn't take you up on the next offer, say goodbye. Do your own thing for a while. See how she likes life without Eddie the Great hanging around, slobbering after her affection like a dog waiting for scraps."

Well . . . you know the rest. I started dating Gina and you started falling apart. At first a big part of me was sort of thrilled—you loved me back, you just didn't know it yet!—but then I realized that it wasn't about me. Something else was going on. But by then it was too late. You weren't answering my calls or texts and you were avoiding me at school.

I was a shitty friend, Wendy. I am so sorry about that. I decided to make up for it. I talked with the twins and we decided an intervention was in order. Obviously my declared love for you would heal you! This time I wasn't going to take no for an answer. This time I was going to honestly figure out what was going on in your head without projecting all my hopes and wants onto you. This time I'd be a friend first and a wanna-be-boyfriend second.

It worked, sort of. You'd just started to open up and then WHAM, you had to go. So I waited. And waited. And waited. I expected you to be like normal when you came back to the car—tired, cranky, maybe angry, the way you normally are after a reap—but you weren't. You were glowing, Wendy. And just like that, I knew.

You were in love . . . but not with me.

So all during that talk we had this morning at the diner, I knew. Every single time you said his name—Peter, all gooshy like—it was like you were stabbing me in the leg with your fork. Before, when you talked about your new "ghost friend" I figured you'd picked up a human equivalent of Jabberwocky, except not so grouchy, and probably around our age. But I had no idea you'd fallen in love.

Suddenly everything made sense. And I hated him. I don't even know the guy but I wished him dead . . . again!

I'll admit, Wendy, I love you but the idea of you being head over heels for some dead guy grosses me out a lot. I know, I know, it's not like that, ghosts aren't like their bodies, they're not rotted or anything unless they've let themselves go bad, but still . . . honestly, Wendy, what do you know about this guy? I mean, you couldn't even tell me when he freaking DIED. "He's Russian," that's all you could say about who he was before. Is that a good basis for a relationship? He could be, like, Rasputin's bastard stepson or something! He could have been some peasant farmer that beat his wife daily! He could have been a vodka-obsessed alcoholic . . . or worse!

I'm getting emotional. I'm sorry. Anyway, the point of all this is . . . hell, if you want to be with this Peter dude, I'm not going to stop you. I'm going to caution against it, I'm not going to like it, I might even tease you for it, but I'm not going to bother you about being with me anymore. You are my best friend. You are the most important person in my life. You were the only person who really got how tore up I was when my dad died, and you were the only person who knew exactly how much I loved Dad when he was around.

He was my hero, Wendy. And even though I'm still a little pissed at you . . . what I'm trying to say is that you're my hero too. What you do, going out and helping the dead, it's dangerous and it's crazy and it's not safe and part of me really, really wishes you wouldn't do it anymore because you're right, you could get hurt . . . but I'm also proud of you.

The world would be a sadder place without you in it, that's all I'm trying to say. You're amazing and wonderful and I'm always going to be deeply in love with you, but other than this note I'll never mention it again.

I hope you can find happiness with this Peter dude. And if you ever doubt what you're doing, if you ever think, "Huh, maybe I should stop," I want you to hold that buckle. Because I know that if Dad were around he'd be proud of you. And I know that it was Dad's death that started you down this path.

I love you, Wendy. Be happy. Merry Christmas.

Eddie

Dropping the note, Wendy wiped away the tears coursing down her cheeks.

It had been so long since Wendy had thought of Mr. Barry as anything more than the man who she'd seen die, the one whose death had unlocked something deep inside her and allowed her to see the dead. But before that he'd been a special man, her best friend's father, and one of the few fun neighborhood dads. He'd had gentle eyes, she remembered, and a slow, kind smile. Eddie didn't resemble him much, he took after his mother, but the eyes were the same, especially when something tickled him. Mr. Barry, like Eddie, had loved a good laugh.

She wondered what Mr. Barry would have done if she'd had to send him into the Light. Would he have fought it the way that girl's grandmother had?

Wendy had a sneaking suspicion that, if Eddie were in trouble, he might have.

Learning that Piotr and his kind thought of her as a monster, well, that had been a rude awakening. Once upon a time her mother had claimed that all ghosts were glad to see her coming, that they welcomed the embrace of the Light. But her own experiences these past few months with the Walkers and the White Lady had taught Wendy differently. At the end, when they were bathed in the fiery Light, the Walkers struggled and cursed and it was only the sweep of siren song that kept them at her side as she went about the deadly business of tearing their essence apart.

The Shades though, and Specs, the ones who saw it coming . . . the few who knew their death in the Never was at hand, they saw the Light as a blessing. So which was it?

Now that she'd taken the time to think about it, to get to know Piotr, reaping without consent felt wrong. It was as if she were forcing herself on the ghosts, sneaking up on them unawares and sending them on without their blessing, but until now Wendy had never really considered stopping. Staying out late, roaming around town in a ceaseless hunt for the dead—until now Wendy had done as her mother had always instructed her to do, ambushing most of the Shades in the dark, never really considering that maybe her *mother* had been the one who was mistaken, that perhaps her mother had been the one taught improperly. Maybe there could be another way.

If not, Wendy could certainly try to make another way herself.

The thought itself was sobering. After Piotr had left she'd swung from one extreme to the other, gone from reaping only in the most dire of circumstances to reaping because she felt like it.

She'd done everything but the thing that felt most natural, most right.

Did Wendy have to reap every single ghost she came across? Just because her mother had done so, as well as the countless other Lightbringers before her, didn't mean that Wendy had to follow in their footsteps. This wasn't a job she'd taken, after all; it wasn't as if she'd *applied* for it. It had been thrust upon her without her consent, a duty and a burden dropped in her lap by Mr. Barry's death.

Wendy held the buckle to the light.

"I have a choice," she said aloud. "I don't have to be her kind of Lightbringer anymore. Not unless I want to." It was freeing, admitting that fact out loud, and the stress began to drain from her shoulders, her neck, leaving Wendy feeling lightened for the first time in ages, possibly since her mother's accident. Wendy was giddy with the realization that all the horror of her daily drudgery could end as she saw fit. Once the White Lady had been taken care of, once the Lost had been freed, then she could finally relax. She could be the right kind of reaper, the volunteer kind.

She almost sobbed with relief.

"Wendy!" Jon called from downstairs. "Are you coming down to eat?"

"Go ahead without me," she called back. "I'm kinda worn out."

"Ok! I'll set some aside for you!"

Hugging the buckle close, Wendy flopped on the floor, her hair spread in a halo and her eyes drifting closed. Sleep had been a rare commodity and the subtle sounds of the house around her—the twins downstairs eating, the distant hum of the TV—soothed her to sleep. Grateful for the respite, Wendy drifted into slumber. As she slept, she dreamed.

In her dreams Wendy walked and walked. The familiar stretch of beach wavered before her, bathed in glaring sunlight and hazy from the heat. The sea murmured to her left, the craggy hillside loomed to her right. Seashell doors marched in a ragged line on the sand.

Over the past months, when Wendy visited the beach, she had
learned to glimpse the names of the dream doors out of the corner of
her eyes, to read them with a swift glance but never look at them
straight on. Sometimes the doors opened easily at her hand, leading
out of terrible nightmares and into kinder climates. Other times the
shells scattered with a touch, trapping her in terrible hellscapes that
she had to endure until morning came and brought the buzz of her
alarm clock.

Then the mist came, quenching the heat and blotting out the
fierce and glaring sun. When the first tendrils lapped at her toes,
Wendy's arm itched and burned; confused, she glanced down at the
four open slashes, surprised that she had brought her real-world
injury into the dream with her. When tiny white maggots began
squirming from the gaping holes she knew the White Lady was near.

"That doesn't scare me anymore," she called, pitching her voice
as loud as she could. "It's gross but it's not like it's real or anything.
And besides, I thought you were done with stupid shit like this. It
was too juvenile for you or something?"

"Isn't it?" The White Lady's boat drifted out of the mist,
mooring itself in the usual place. It took several minutes for the
White Lady to struggle out of her small skiff, her movements stiff
and slow. The past months had not been kind; her robes were ragged
now, worn through with large, moth-eaten holes that allowed nauseating glimpses of the extent of the rot. Where she stepped on the
sand black puddles like oil slicks formed, sticky dribbling ichor that
sank slowly into the earth and emitted puffs of scent that smelled
like rotten eggs. "You'd be surprised the things that cross over from
dreams into the real world."

"You're falling apart," Wendy noted, stepping away from the
White Lady and shifting so she was upwind. "What the hell is happening to you?"

"One of the mysteries of life . . . or death," the White Lady
replied, coughing so that Wendy could see the bellows of her lungs

fight to squeeze in and out. "Death for the dead, Lightbringer. It comes to us all."

"Not like that, it doesn't," Wendy protested. "I should know. Not that I'm complaining. I wouldn't care if you rotted down to dust after all the crap you've been putting me through."

"You'll care," the White Lady said. "One day you'll die and you'll see."

"You know," remarked Wendy, keeping her distance, "for a crazy lady, this talk's been awfully sane so far. Find a good dead psychiatrist? Freud himself, perhaps?"

The White Lady shrugged. "Eh, it comes and goes with the strength of the decay. As I said before, just wait. One day you'll see." She clapped her hands. "But enough chit-chat, I don't have time to fuss with your nonsense today. I'm here to talk about our truce."

"You mean the truce I told you to ram up your ass? The truce we agreed wasn't going to happen? Open war and all that?" Flicking her wrist until her wounds were free of squirming bugs, Wendy crossed her arms across her chest and leaned against the bow of the boat. It was like leaning against a clammy wall, and black slime from the hull worked its way down her back. Wendy grimaced and straightened, annoyed that everything even remotely surrounding the White Lady had to be so unbelievably foul. "Real or not, ugh, this is so disgusting."

"Yes, that truce. Though perhaps calling it a trade now might be more to the point." She coughed again, a horrid rattling sound that hurt Wendy's ears.

"A trade?" Wendy rolled her eyes. "Right, sure. I'm listening."

"I've got something you want, Lightbringer. You've got something I want. So we trade."

"I sincerely doubt that *you* have anything *I* want." Wendy ran her hand along her shoulder, cleaning off the clinging remains of the muck. "Unless it's a clean towel or maybe a shower."

"A shower can certainly be arranged as a gesture of goodwill," the White Lady said and snapped her fingers. "I always like to clean up before beginning negotiations."

Above the beach, forked lightning flashed and thunder boomed, nearly atop them. A two second beat passed and then rain pounded from the sky, soaking Wendy to the skin almost instantly and obliterating the chilly mist within seconds. Though the foul White Lady had called the rain, the water was clear and cold and wonderfully cleansing, raising huge gooseflesh across every inch of skin. The slime washed away within seconds and the itching eased shortly after.

"Yeah, I guess that works!" Wendy shouted over the downpour, the drumming rain filling the world with noise. She hunched over and rapidly rubbed her hands over her slick arms, seeking friction-warmth.

"I haven't many tricks left," the White Lady said, her voice pitched low but still reaching Wendy's ears, "but the ones I have are powerful."

"I can see that." Wendy straightened, determined to not show the White Lady that the chill was getting to her. "Want to turn off the waterworks now?"

"If you like," came the negligent reply, and just as suddenly as the rain arrived, it was gone. Clouds dashed across the sky, revealing the hot afternoon sun once more, and rainbows glinted all around the beach, reflecting every direction she looked.

"I've got to learn how to do that," Wendy mused. "Is that trick super handy or what?"

"Dreams are not the absolute realms of the Lightbringers," the White Lady said, reclining on the damp sand and drawing her moth-eaten shift carefully across her legs, "but they can learn a trick or two. Prophecy, a nice neutral zone for a talk, a little spying, or even a bit of glamour; your kind can become quite adept here if they need to be."

"You say that like you've met people like me before." Now that she was clean and no longer revolted by the way the dreamscape bent in horrifying ways when the White Lady was near, Wendy was back on her guard.

"I told you that I've been watching for a long time," the White Lady said, irritated. Where the hood slipped back Wendy could see long strips of essence that had been sewn together with wide, thick-stitched loops of thread. Where the strips tapered off, darker patches of skin had been carefully set with a crosshatch stitch. Examining these marks, Wendy realized that they had to have once been tattoos, but were now too badly marred to make out.

Her fingers brushed her own collarbone tats. Would the same happen to her designs when she passed over? The White Lady noticed the gesture. "Protective ink only takes you so far in the Never."

"It's worked pretty well so far."

"That's because a Walker is the worst thing you've come across. There are much, much worse things out there. Things that don't even blink at your ink."

"Yawn. Bored. Is there a point to all this?"

"My point is that your mother didn't train you well enough. In fact, she hardly trained you at all. Letting you reap only Shades for years? Until her little accident, your mother had you only reap one ghost. One. So why do you think you are coming to this talk from any sort of position of power?"

"I'm strong enough to tell you to go to hell. And I go through your Walkers easily enough. Or did you forget all that begging you were doing on their behalf earlier?"

"So you can reap a few Walkers. Yippee. I'm much worse than a Walker and I know that, for all your bluster, you've figured that out by now. And there are beings far, far scarier than I am wandering the Never." She held up her rotting horror of a hand so that the light filtered through it, casting a holey shadow on the sand. "Did I ever tell you that I knew your mother? In the living world? I knew what she was."

"Shut up," Wendy whispered through lips gone numb from shock. "That's impossible and I don't have to listen to this bullshit."

"It's not bullshit if it's true." The White Lady clenched her fist, skin flaking down. "And you? You are really starting to irritate me, Wendy."

"Good!" Wendy snapped. "Anything that gets your panties in a twist is fabulous!"

"Stupid, idiot child," the White Lady snapped. "Normally the ones like you, the Lightbringers, are sent on their first dream-walk at seventeen. But your mother was gone by then, wasn't she? She never even bothered to tell you that you woke too early. Just thirteen," she sneered. "It's a miracle you didn't go insane from the shock."

Shoving against the sand for support, Wendy started to rise. The White Lady waved a hand. Hard pressure pressed against the tops of Wendy's shoulders and she toppled back down, her tongue ring popping smartly against the back of her teeth when she hit the ground.

"I said, *sit down*."

Pressing her hand to her mouth, Wendy drew back fingers dark with blood. The sudden jolt had ripped the hole in her tongue wider open. It would heal by tomorrow but until then her mouth would be filled with the copper-rust-salt taste of her own blood. Wendy leaned to the side and spat a wad of bright red that sank into the sand. "Haw doh yah now all thish?"

"Oh for god's sake," the White Lady groaned, exasperated. "You just had to get a tongue ring, didn't you?" She crawled to Wendy's side and grabbed Wendy by the face. Wendy tried to struggle but the White Lady, rotting apart or not, was still far stronger in this dream realm than Wendy could ever be. Her long and bony fingers, the last flaps of skin flaking apart at the knuckles, forced past Wendy's teeth.

Then the White Lady grabbed for the barbell and ripped it out.

Shrieking in pain, Wendy gripped the White Lady's wrists and tried to force the filthy hand away from her face. It was like trying to push a brick wall.

"Stop struggling," the White Lady snapped and pinched the tip of Wendy's tongue. Immediately an icy chill filled her mouth, so cold her teeth ached and the molars with silver fillings began to protest the sharp shooting pain.

"To answer your question," she said, fingers probing the wet, open meat of Wendy's wounded tongue, "I just know. Do you think I was always like this? Falling apart, piece by piece? I told you that Lightbringers were a hobby of mine. I watched your mother call Walkers from three miles away. I knelt at the knee of your grandmother in these dream realms, learning how to manipulate the ether. Compared to the likes of them you are alone, a toddler wandering in the woods. You know nothing of what your kind can do." She released Wendy's tongue and crawled back, wiping her hands against her shift. "That should do it. I know that you won't say thank you, so you're welcome."

A gritty taste like rotten milk and salt permeated her mouth. Wendy staggered to the shoreline and scooped up dipperfuls of saltwater in her hands. It tasted fishy and rank but was better than the texture and taste of the White Lady that lingered foully through several rounds of rinsing and spitting.

"You bitch," Wendy gasped, spitting out the last mouthful of gritty, salty beach water. Tender probing of her mouth revealed that her tongue had closed up and the blood had ceased its sluggish flow. "You ripped out my ring!"

The White Lady, ignoring Wendy's outrage, held the hood close to her face and tipped her face to the sky, gauging the sun. "We're almost out of time. I must conclude my business."

"What business is that? Being a crazy bitch?"

"Our trade. Will you meet with me in the Never or not?"

"You've got nothing I want." Wendy turned her face away, running the tip of her tongue along the back of her teeth. Her entire mouth felt swollen and sore, tingly in all the wrong places. She just wanted this obnoxious dream to end.

"Oh really?" The whisper of her cloak was all the warning Wendy got as the White Lady snuck up behind her and grabbed Wendy by the back of her neck. "Does this look familiar to you?" She shoved an object in Wendy's face. At first Wendy couldn't make out what it was but then she gasped, both confused and furious. It was Eddie's phone.

"What the hell is this? Is this some sort of dream trick?" Then she laughed. "What the hell am I talking about? Eddie's alive. He's fine. You can't touch him."

"Oh, the things you don't know about your own power or mine," the White Lady sneered, throwing Eddie's phone into the surf where it sank beneath the surface with a quiet plop. "I was quite surprised when my spy reported in last night. Despite how badly you were wounded, you simply bandaged your arm and didn't think twice about it, did you? Even after what I told you at that decrepit old house. It didn't matter what your memories told you; you brushed off my words just because they came from me."

"Last time . . ."

"I can't touch your friend Edward? Oh really? If I can't touch your dear Eddie, how could my Walkers have harmed you? You're alive, after all."

"But when I'm like that . . . I'm not exactly alive," Wendy protested. "I'm in between."

"Even in between, it shouldn't hurt your physical body as deeply as it did," the White Lady chuckled. "Poor, poor lost child. So very ignorant, even after I warned you, even after I damn near handed you the answer at that house. Some spirits can reach into the living world, Lightbringer. Some spirits can interact with the living. The Rider does. My Walkers did."

"When I find my mom—"

"Enough of this. Your precious mother? She's with me," the White Lady snapped.

"No." Wendy shook her head. "No-no-no."

"I warned you what would happen if you mucked around with my plans and my people, didn't I? And I always keep my promises. Always." Her hand on the back of Wendy's neck clenched tighter, bone tips digging in. "I finally caught her last night. Trapped her not four blocks from your school. While you were busy with *him*." She waved something in front of Wendy's face. It took her several long seconds to comprehend what her eyes were showing her and when she did, it was the most horrible thing she'd ever seen in her life.

A flap of essence with tribal tattoos carved into it; ink that matched Wendy's own.

"No!" Wendy shrieked and struggled in her grip but the White Lady was impossibly strong. Raising Wendy high, the White Lady shook her by the back of her neck like a kitten until all the fight drained away. Wendy hung loosely, weeping silent tears.

"There's still a way to get your mother and your boy Eddie back," the White Lady said, her voice dim and quiet behind the ringing in Wendy's head. "I'll even show you how."

"You're lying," Wendy whispered. "You always lie."

"I'm not," she replied. "I want your mother back in the land of the living almost as much as you do. Think I want a Lightbringer walking around the Never? Even dead, your kind is a bother. If you knew even half of what your mother knows you'd be like a dangerous wolf loose among the sheep. I can't have your mother here. So I'm sending her back . . . *if* you help me. If you agree to my trade."

"Fine," Wendy whispered. "Anything. What do you want?"

"Bring the boy," the White Lady said. "Piotr. Tomorrow night at the park. You know the one. Around midnight. I'll take care of binding him, just bring him. Alone, if you please."

"What are you going to do to him?"

"Do?" The White Lady threw her head back and laughed. "What do you think I'm going to do? Serve him tea and cakes, of course. Impress him with how my watercolors have improved. Maybe take in a show." She shook Wendy again, lightly this time, and Wendy moaned. "It doesn't matter what I'm going to do. If you ever want to see Eddie's soul again, or see your mother out of that bed, you'll do as I say. Do you understand me?"

"Yes."

"Good," the White Lady snapped, dropping Wendy to the ground in a tangle of limbs. "Now wake up." She reached down and before Wendy could react, the flat of her palm cracked against Wendy's cheek, snapping her head to the side.

Wendy awoke on the floor with a stinging cheek and damp, fishy-smelling hair. The sun had just breached the top of the trees and down the hall Chel's alarm blared to life. Running her tongue along her upper teeth, Wendy winced at the sudden and unexpected pain.

Her tongue had closed up; the barbell was gone.

CHAPTER EIGHTEEN

Eddie didn't answer his phone. It rang and rang and the fifteenth time it went to voicemail Wendy screamed, flinging her own phone at her vanity where it smashed corner-first into the mirror. The phone, thin to begin with, snapped in two. The mirror shattered into a thousand slivers of glass.

"Wendy?" Jon tapped on her door. "Are you okay?"

"No," Wendy sobbed, sinking to the floor and burying her face in her hands. "I'm not."

The door creaked open and Jon poked his head inside. Jabber hissed at the sight of him and slunk beneath the bed, tail puffy and back arched. "Wanna talk about it?"

Scrubbing the heels of her hands against her eyes, Wendy wiped her frustrated tears away. "I can't get a hold of Eddie," she said by way of explanation, though Eddie's absence wasn't the only concern preying on her mind. "I've been trying for hours."

"So you threw your phone? Crazy much?" Jon crossed the room, picking his way carefully over the splintered shards of glass, and settled beside her on the bed. "Maybe he forgot to charge his cell. Or maybe his mom made him turn it off. You know what a big control freak she is."

"He's super anal about charging his phone," Wendy said, shaking her head. "And his mom wouldn't be weird about Eddie getting calls over the holidays, especially around her family. Appearances mean a lot to her."

"Maybe," conceded Jon. "So what's all this about? Did you guys get in another fight?"

"No, it's nothing like that." Wendy swallowed thickly. "I had this nasty dream. Something was wrong with Eddie in it so I just . . . I just have a bad feeling, okay?"

Jon whistled. "That must have been one heck of a dream."

Wendy couldn't help but laugh. "Yeah, it really was."

"Well, I know this probably isn't the time, but Chel and I were hoping to go see Mom today. Nana said this is probably our last Christmas, you know?"

"The insurance is about to run out," Wendy murmured. "Right, I almost forgot." It was just one more terrible thing to add to the list of never-ending crap. If their mother didn't wake up soon there was a chance Dad would have to decide whether to keep her on life support . . . or pull the plug. If she could rescue her mom from the White Lady, it would be a decision he'd never have to make.

Stretching, Jon used the edge of Wendy's bed to rise to his feet. "I know you're worried about Eddie, but do you think you could chill out for an hour or two and drop us off? Dad gave us permission to use the car if we're visiting Mom."

"Let me guess: Chel wants to go to Milpitas afterwards and swing by the mall?" Wendy struggled to keep from sneering but failed. Emotionally she was wrung dry and too edgy to be fair about her sister's foibles. "Maybe catch a movie with her buds or do some last minute 'holiday shopping'?"

Jon pitched his voice low. "Actually, she never suggested it. Weird, right? She said all her shopping's already done. Internet."

"Chel turned down a chance to go waste Christmas break at the mall? I guess she's serious about avoiding the rah-rahs after all."

"Everybody changes." He shrugged. "Anyway, when we're done Nana wanted to know if we'd like to crash with her up in Oakland tonight. She was talking waffles so I'm thinking hell yes," Jon said, grinning wildly. He leaned down and offered her a hand up. When

Wendy took it his open expression darkened, eyebrows drawing in. All joviality fled. "Wendy, what happened to your arm?"

Whoops! In the recent chaos, Wendy had forgotten all about the cuts the Walker had inflicted in the park. Snatching her hand out of Jon's grip, she cradled her arm to her chest. "It's nothing. I had an accident. Eddie patched me up."

"Some accident," Jon said and then his lips pressed together in a tight line. "Wendy," he said, choosing his words with some care, "I know this isn't any of my business, but you're not taking that goth-emo thing to that wacko level are you? You know, that 'I bleed to feel pain' dominatrix crap kinda level?"

Wendy rolled her eyes. "Jon, honestly, listen to what you're saying for once. You know me. Do you really and truly believe that I—of all people—would cut myself?"

"Since you didn't just give me a direct answer, I'd have to say that I don't know," he said gravely, glancing around the shattered glass and ramshackle chaos that passed for her room. "Would you?"

"No! Jesus, Jon!" Annoyed, Wendy punched him on the bicep, not bothering to be gentle. When he yelped and rubbed his arm she waved her fist in his direction. "That's for thinking I'm a cutter, you jerk." Her thoughts flicked to the dream of the night before, the skin clutched in the White Lady's hand. She tamped down on those thoughts quickly. She had a little bit of time; she'd figure out what to do.

"Okay, okay!" he protested, half-laughing, still rubbing his sore arm. "I get the picture already!"

"Next time think before you go accusing people," Wendy warned. Careful of the glass, she reached under the bed and pulled out the Tupperware container stuffed to bursting with shoes. Selecting a sturdy pair of army surplus combat boots, Wendy flopped on the bed and began lacing them up.

"Fine. Whatever. Go get Chel," she snapped, impatience coloring her tone. "I'm tired, I'm stressed out, I'm done. You and me and Chel. We're getting this over with. Move it!"

Jon looked offended. "But Mom—"

"The drive," she clarified, softening. "I want to get the drive over with. Christmas break, remember? The 101 is gonna be total crap, and crossing the bridge isn't going to be much better. Dad emptied the change tray, so we gotta swing by the bank for cash. Any clue where he stashed the debit card?"

"I've got it in my purse," Chel said, leaning in the doorway, the cordless phone hanging loosely from her hand. Dark circles ringed her eyes and her skin was tight and shiny, white except for the hectic patches across her cheekbones. She coughed into her fist. "What happened in here? Did your reflection sass you good, or what?"

"I lost my temper," Wendy said shortly. "You look like hell. Are you feeling okay?"

"Peachy keen," Chel drawled. "I'm fine. Let me grab my shoes."

"You don't look fine," Jon protested. "You're all—"

"I know how I look, okay?" Chel pushed away from the threshold and tossed the cordless on the bed. "It's just a little cold or something. Anyway, Eddie's mom beeped in about five minutes ago while I was on the line with Nana. She wants you to call her back ASAP."

Heartbeat trebling in her chest, Wendy's grip tightened on her boot until her knuckles bled white. Beneath the bandage on her arm she felt the edges of the wound Eddie had sealed with the dermabond glue start to pull apart. Twisting so her siblings wouldn't see the dark red seeping on her gauze, Wendy asked casually, "Did she say what it was about?"

"Nah," Chel said, coughing into her fist again. Outside the window, thunder rumbled in the distance, causing them all to glance out the window at the dark clouds building on the horizon. "She said just to call soon as you can, that it's important. Anyway, since we're definitely visiting Mom and Nana, I'm gonna go throw together an overnight bag, okay? It won't take ten minutes."

"Me too," Jon said, after glancing at Wendy's face to read the emotional weather. "Lemme know what's up," he whispered as he left.

Fingers trembling, Wendy shut the door before punching in the number for Eddie's mother's cell on the cordless phone. It rang three times and went to voicemail.

"You should try again," Piotr said and Wendy jumped.

"Crap! I didn't see you there," she gasped, hand pressed to her chest. Beneath her palm her heart fluttered frantically; adrenaline left her mouth sour. "How long have you—"

"Long enough to catch you obliterating the mirror." Piotr drifted through the desk and settled on the edge of her bed, his cool hand rubbing calming circles on her back. "I was going to speak up, but Jon came and I didn't want to draw attention to myself."

"Good idea," Wendy said. She pressed the heel of her hand to her forehead. "Today has been one hell of a day already."

"Is that so?" Piotr touched her wrist. "I noticed that you opened up your cuts again."

"Accident. Look, we've got a lot, I mean a whole hell of a lot, to talk about. But not right now okay? Give me just a few minutes." She held up the phone.

Understanding, Piotr nodded and pretended to zip his lips shut, resting his head against the wall so that his touch wouldn't distract her further. This time Eddie's mother answered on the first ring. "Hello? Winifred, is that you?" Even across the crackling line, she sounded frantic.

"Hi Mrs. Barry," Wendy said, injecting what she hoped was the right amount of faux cheer into her tone. "My sister said you called. What's up?"

"Winifred, I need your help. It's Eddie."

It was as if she'd reached through the phone line and punched Wendy in the gut. All the breath went out of her; her stomach felt hollow, empty, and her heart thudded so hard in her chest that the room literally alternated dark and light with each beat of her pulse.

Yet, somehow, despite the world spinning out of control right then and there, Wendy heard herself say, voice appropriately concerned, "Eddie? What's the matter, Mrs. Barry? Is he okay?" She wiped her forehead with her good arm; her skin was oily with sweat and she found that she was clenching her jaw so tightly her teeth ached.

"You remember how your mother just collapsed last year?" Mrs. Barry sobbed into the other end. "Last night at dinner Eddie was standing up to pick up the plates and he keeled over. Boom! Just like that. We rushed him to the hospital—I thought it was one of those youth heart attacks, God forbid—but his heart was still beating, he's still breathing. But he won't wake up, Winifred!"

Honking her nose noisily, Mrs. Barry spent several seconds struggling on the other end of the line. The sounds coming out of her were somewhere between sobs and crazed laughter. Wendy recognized that sound. It was the sound her father had made when they'd brought her mother into the ER that first night. It was the cry of an anguished soul.

"Oh Winifred," Mrs. Barry sobbed, "first my husband, now my only boy? I go to synagogue, I keep the holy days, I volunteer. What did I do wrong? What else could I have done?" She broke down weeping for several minutes but the sound was thick and muffled. Hearing a steady thump-thump in the background, Wendy realized that Mrs. Barry must have pressed the phone to her chest. Patiently, she waited for her best friend's mother to calm down.

Finally the sobbing slowed, followed by a wet sniffle. "Hel-hello? Winifred?"

"Hi, Mrs. Barry, I'm still here." Swallowing thickly, Wendy was surprised to realize that her voice was level, calm even, and that at some point between picking up the phone and this moment, her heart had slowed down, the sweat on her brow had dried.

"What hospital is he at, Mrs. Barry?" Wendy asked, reaching for the math notebook balanced on the corner of her desk. The pencil cup was on the opposite corner and too much effort to hassle with;

Wendy used the mechanical eyeliner that had rolled underneath the corner of her bed.

"UCSF," she muttered, jotting the address down. Later, she wasn't sure why she did. UCSF was the same hospital where her mother was staying; she could've driven there with her eyes closed. But it felt good to keep her hands busy. "We were going to visit my mom today, Mrs. Barry," Wendy said. "Stay calm, okay? I promise you that I can be there in about an hour."

"How's your mother's condition?" Mrs. Barry asked, desperation underlying every word. "Do the doctors know anything?"

Like you gave two craps about my mom yesterday, Wendy thought unkindly, but kept it to herself. "No, Mrs. Barry," she said. "But we still have hope." The door creaked open and Jon and Chel were waiting in the hall, overnight bags at their feet. The two had been listening in; Jon's face was waxy white, Chel's eyes were red-rimmed.

"I've gotta go, Mrs. Barry," Wendy said. "I'm on my way, okay? Okay, Mrs. Barry, you hang in there; I'll be there in an hour. Okay. Okay. Bye." Pressing the off switch with her thumb, Wendy dropped the phone on the floor. Outside, thunder boomed again, much closer this time, rattling the pencils in their cup.

"Eddie's sick," Wendy said and fought not to remember that terrible night when she had to explain to her siblings that their mother was in the hospital and Dad wouldn't be home for twelve hours. "He's got . . . probably whatever Mom's got. Same symptoms."

"Shit," Chel said and slumped to the floor, burying her face in her hands. "Shit, not again."

"He's at UCSF," Wendy continued, addressing Jon because Chel was crying now, slow soft sobbing that was both heartbreaking and distracting. "Your bags packed?"

"Yeah," Jon said dully, reaching down and collecting both the bags. "Yeah, they are."

"Okay." Wendy held up her arm; let Jon see the dark splotches where the dermabond had pulled apart beneath the gauze. "I'm going to fix this and then I'll need your help wrapping it back up. Then we'll go."

"Yeah, okay," he agreed, dropping the bags again and following Wendy to their shared bathroom. Wendy spun the cap off the hydrogen peroxide with her thumb, consciously not thinking about how Eddie had done this very thing for her only two days prior. She hissed when the chill liquid bubbled across her arm. At first it was bordering on unbearable but then Piotr was there, his hands icy cold and pressed against her wound, numbing it. Steam billowed up, obfuscating the bathroom, but when it cleared he was still there, eyes searching her face, seeking the telltale signs of weakness or pain that would make him draw away.

Splashing a second dose against her arm, Wendy couldn't help marveling at the way the peroxide slipped right through his hands. She could feel the wetness but her arm was now numb from wrist to elbow and with Piotr helpfully gripping her forearm it took no time at all to pat the area dry and apply another layer of dermabond to the wounds.

"Here," she told Jon, tearing off a long strip of gauze with her teeth. "Start here and wrap."

"Let me do it," Chel snapped from the doorway, pushing past her brother and snatching the gauze out of his hand. "He can't fix a boo-boo to save his life." Chel eyed the wounds and heaved a dramatic sigh. "I always knew you would flip out one day," she muttered, wrapping Wendy's arm with an expert finesse that spoke of years in cheerleading, of countless bound ankles, wrapped scrapes, and an endless succession of hastily bandaged knees. "But did you have to cut so deep? These are totally gonna scar."

"Not that I don't appreciate the help, but why does everyone think I did this to myself?" Wendy asked, exasperated.

"I always figured your goth-kiddie thing was a big cry for attention," Chel said, taping off the end. She pulled a tissue from the box and swiped at her nose and under her eyes. "The next logical steps are emo poetry and a knife fascination, right?"

"Shut up," Wendy replied and gestured for Jon to collect the bags. Piotr was already halfway down the stairs and sliding neatly through the kitchen wall. She knew that he would be waiting for them in the car, hopefully in the back seat. "Come on, let's get a move on."

"Go cry in a corner, emo kid," Chel said, brightening and leading the way downstairs.

Wendy laughed despite herself. "Can it, buffy, before I kick your ass." They collected the car keys and locked the doors, letting themselves out into the first spray of falling rain.

Accustomed to the ebb and flow of the hospital traffic, Wendy dropped Chel and Jon off at the front door, flicking off the heater as soon as they'd gone. Piotr had ridden in the backseat the whole way, making the already chilly air bitter cold.

They had no time to talk; Wendy found a parking space almost immediately.

"Not the Lost?" he asked, keeping pace as Wendy sprinted through the stinging rain.

"No," she cried against the rising wind. "The White Lady!"

Shocked into stillness, Piotr stumbled to a stop but Wendy kept going. "The White Lady? When? How?"

"Walkers, I'd bet," Wendy gasped, dodging through the doors and out of the rain. Glancing around to ensure no one was listening, Wendy wrung her hair out over the non-slip mat and dug through her purse until she found her cell headset. Luckily Jon and Chel were nowhere near—they would remember that her cell was broken and still on the floor at home—but to anyone else she would appear to be on the phone. Rude in a hospital, sure, but not crazy.

"Look," she murmured, taking the long route to the floor Mrs. Barry said Eddie was on. "There's something I've been meaning to tell you." Then, walking at a slower than normal pace, Wendy filled Piotr in on her way to Eddie's room. This time she bared it all, outlining the dreams she'd been having for months, the major visits from the White Lady, and even the White Lady's demands of the previous evening.

"She's got my mom, Piotr," Wendy finished up. "And now Eddie. I know I should have told you we were in contact before, or at the very least about Dunn, but I guess I was hoping it was just my dreams running away with me. I think that I didn't even really believe it was really her until this morning, when I woke up without my tongue ring. See?" She stuck her tongue out. "I mean, I believed it was her but I didn't *really* believe, you know?"

"I understand," Piotr said, "and I forgive you for not speaking up before. If I were in your situation I might not have believed it either. It seems so outrageous! But . . . I have got no clue what she wants with me. Do you know?"

"No idea," Wendy said. "Maybe because you're a Rider?"

Elle spoke in his mind then, the memory of her words so sharp and cutting that Piotr physically flinched: *She understands all about duty, I bet. That's why she kept you, Piotr, not just any ol' Rider but the big cheese who* started *the Riders, away from us when we needed you most. That's why you, Mr. Hi-You're-Dead-Here's-How-The-Afterlife-Works himself, was off neckin' with a* monster *when you should have been here running a shift!*

"Impossible," Piotr murmured. "It . . . it can't be true." His vision shutter-shifted again—live-dead-live—before the world was once more washed in grey.

"Piotr?" Wendy asked, hand at his elbow, "Piotr, what's wrong?"

"I-I do not know," he whispered, but that was a lie. The fight he'd had with the other Riders had been so intense, so unlike their normal spats. Elle, he knew, was truly furious with him. Worried over Dora, feeling exposed in her own haven, and overwhelmed with betrayal that Piotr, her Piotr, had been not only spending his time with a member of the living, but the Lightbringer herself, Elle had said some harsh things.

But had she said some *true* things? That was the question.

Before Piotr would have said no. But now . . . now he wasn't so sure. His vision blinked again.

If it had just been Elle, maybe he could have forgotten the entire fight, gone back the next day and made up. But it had been James and Lily too, the three of them ganging up, all saying the same thing.

Lily: *Years passed and with them passed the man I'd known. Who you are now is not who you were then.*

Elle: *I think it's pretty clear that Petey never remembers anything, do ya Pete?*

James: *She's telling the truth. You're older than Moses, Peter. You're older than anyone any ghost I know's ever met.*

"Piotr? Piotr!" Wendy's hand was on his arm, and she was shaking him. Her eyes were wide, lids drawn back so the whites showed on all sides, her pupils only specks in the vast warm brown of her irises. The heat was baking off her in waves. "Piotr what's wrong?"

"I am fine, it is nothing," he said, pulling away. He felt shaky and scared, tottering on the edge of some very important clue that he couldn't quite grasp. It was aggravating, like having a phrase on the tip of your tongue, knowing that you knew it but being entirely unable to spit out the words. "It's nothing."

Wendy heaved a deep breath and he wrapped a cool arm around her waist. "Let's go see your friend."

Careful inspection of Eddie's body proved Wendy's theory correct. Eddie's soul was nowhere near his physical shell. A length of his cord was there, extending from his navel in a thick cable that appeared, after close examination, to have been chewed off, but the soul that should have been attached to such a vibrant, healthy cord was completely missing.

"It's just like my mom," Wendy whispered, brushing the side of her hand across Eddie's cheek. She turned away, swiping quickly at the corner of each eye.

Mrs. Barry, looking up from her place at Eddie's bedside, wiped her puffy eyes with the corner of a hospital towel. "What was that, Winifred?"

"Nothing, Mrs. Barry," Wendy said meekly. "Nothing important."

"You're such a good friend, dear," Mrs. Barry said, grasping Wendy's wrist with fingers wiry and lined with wrinkles. Losing her husband had aged her prematurely, made her bony and wan; losing Eddie appeared to have sped up the process. Though she couldn't be positive Wendy was almost sure that Mrs. Barry's hair was greyer at the temples than before, that the lines bracketing her mouth were deeper. Though she didn't voice her opinion, Piotr, prowling around the tiny room, apparently agreed.

"Something's been at her too," Piotr said, leaning into Mrs. Barry's personal space and examining her face closely. She shivered and released Wendy's wrist, reached for her jacket and shrugged it on. "My word," she fussed. "They do keep it cold in here, don't they?"

"Can't you see it?" Piotr asked, pointing at her mouth and the corners of her eyes. "That residue?"

Now that Piotr had pointed it out, if Wendy squinted just right, she could barely make out what he was referring to. There was a pale, thin film overlaying Mrs. Barry's face, a clinging mesh so fine she imagined she'd need a ghostly microscope to be able to truly examine it in detail.

"I don't know what it is," Wendy said aloud and took Eddie's hand in her own to cover the outburst when Mrs. Barry looked at her curiously. "The hospital just has to keep it frigid, I guess. Think he needs a blanket?"

"I asked already," Mrs. Barry exclaimed as Piotr dug his hand in the side of her face. "It's a spirit web, I think," he said. "Whatever it is, it's put down roots."

"But that awful head nurse," Mrs. Barry continued as Piotr

worked his hands in and out of the flesh of her cheeks, rocking his fingers under the strands to gently lift them away. "She says their linen supplier is running late with the delivery! Then she said if I were willing to wait she'd see if any of the other beds of the floor had a blanket free. Can you believe that?"

"Be careful," Wendy said and then cleared her throat. "You have no clue where those extra blankets have been, I mean. Anyone could have been sitting on them. Germs."

Nodding frantically, Mrs. Barry grabbed her free hand. "You are so right, dear! And that's just what I told that nurse. I said, 'Now you listen here, young lady, I'm not going to have my only son covered in the filth of other people, no ma'am!'"

All of Piotr's fingers were now wedged beneath the web; pulling the threads away was taking real effort at this point. Whatever it was, it had sunk itself deep into her head and cords of muscle stood out against Piotr's neck as he braced his feet against Mrs. Barry's chair and *pulled*. The film began to rip.

"Mrs. Barry!" Wendy cried. When Eddie's mother looked at her quizzically she licked her lips. "Are you okay?" she asked. "You look sort of white."

"You know," Mrs. Barry whispered, hand reaching through the web Piotr was yanking free of her skull with all his might. "I do feel somewhat lightheaded. Perhaps I should . . . sit . . . down—"

With one final mighty tug, Piotr pulled the web free. Loose all the way to the roots, the thin strands were rounded like the roots of a tree and dripping with dark silver life. Seeking any energy at all, the web waved towards Wendy the moment it separated from Mrs. Barry.

The instant it was out of her face, Mrs. Barry slumped to the floor and Wendy, crying out in disgust, dodged past the nasty thing in Piotr's arms to push the call button. The nurse was there within moments.

"What happened?"

"She fainted," Wendy panted. "She was just talking and she fainted."

In the background Piotr had drawn his dagger and was stabbing the web; each thrust of the knife caused the thing to wail and keen in pain, tendrils thrashing madly. Wendy found it immensely hard to concentrate on explaining Mrs. Barry's collapse to the nurse while the web shrieked itself to death in the background. The nurse pushed Wendy out of the room and cried for a doctor over the intercom. Wendy, glad to be free, fled down the hall.

"That was disgusting," Wendy whispered, walking briskly towards the elevators. Her mother's room was two floors up from Eddie's. Once ensconced in the safety of the elevator, Wendy leaned against the back wall, pressed her hands to her face, and trembled from head to toe. "Why?" she asked. "What the hell was that thing?"

"It was definitely a spirit web," Piotr said. "It's like a rabbit snare; you throw many in the air and go back later, see what you caught."

"It was *feeding* off her?"

"It's just collecting life from her a minute or two at a time. From the look of that thing, it's been there for longer than Eddie's been . . . gone." Piotr rubbed the back of his neck self-consciously. "When it gets full or the person it takes root in dies, the web detaches and finds its way outside. Spirit webs like to stay warm. It will crawl as high as it can—plant itself on the roof of a building if possible, to be close to the sun—and wait for someone to come along and harvest the life."

"That is horrible." Wendy pressed her hand to her mouth. "But if those things are so effective then why aren't they all over the place?"

He shrugged. "I haven't seen a spirit web in a long time, Wendy. They're extremely difficult to produce; you have to find a plant in the Never's wild and then have a ghost insane enough to be willing to gestate one in their own guts. It gives the seedlings a taste for life essence." He paused. "Wait. High places . . ." Had that been what the White Lady was doing at the airport that day? Collecting spirit webs? The air towers certainly were tall enough, and with all the living moving through the area there was bound to be at least a web or two to be harvested in the wild.

"Just when I thought death couldn't get any more gross," Wendy complained. The elevator dinged and the doors slid open. She led the way down the hall and Jon and Chel, sitting on either side of their mom, looked up when Wendy entered.

"Mom's really witty today," Jon said, scrubbing his knuckles across his face. He gestured to the television mounted in the upper corner of the room. On the screen a pregnant-to-bursting teen was pulling the hair of a skinny blonde girl with one hand and punching her in the small of the back with the other. "I keep telling her that daytime TV is the new opiate of the masses but Mom's of the opinion that reality shows are where the real money is."

"I still think Nana's 'stories' top that list," Chel added, leaning back in the molded plastic chair and crossing her legs. "You can't beat good old-fashioned soaps."

"Porn," Wendy said. "It's a growth industry."

Grinning at their groans, Wendy settled into Jon's seat while he went to find another chair. They could have sat on the opposite bed, but none of them wanted to be far from their mother. Wendy held her mom's thin, cool hand while Piotr examined the body.

"Any change?" Wendy asked her sister while Piotr probed her mother's midsection, slipping his hands deep inside her guts.

"None." Chel shook her head, looking their mother over sadly. "I feel like a jerk for saying this, Wendy, but maybe they're right. Maybe it's time to pull the plug. Mom wouldn't want to be strapped down and cooped up, some vegetable in a bed. She'd rather end it."

"I don't know," Wendy mused as Piotr's hands slipped out of her mother's abdomen and rested, relaxed, on his hips. He glanced meaningfully at her mother then at the doorway, drifting out the door a few seconds later. "Mom was a fighter, Chel. She might still be in there, you know, fighting."

"Maybe." Chel squeezed their mom's hand and rose, crossing her arms over her chest. "I've been having these crazy dreams about her. You know how bad flu dreams get—you start running a little fever and suddenly you've got Wonderland camped out between your ears."

Chuckling, Wendy nodded. "We've all had a couple doozies. Why, what happened?"

"I can't remember," Chel said, shrugging. "But I was at the park, you know, the one up the street? I was sitting on the old rusty swingset, not the new plastic one but the old one that would burn your butt in July? Anyway, it was one of those dreams you get where you can watch everything happening but you're not really there? Like you're watching a movie? You were there, talking to Mom, right? You were yelling at each other. She was saying that you had to try again but you didn't want to. And I wanted to try since you didn't want to, but I didn't know what you were trying. Then she slapped you and told you to grow up. Weird, huh?"

A chill shivered down Wendy's spine. What was it the White Lady had said about dreams before? She was so tired and stressed out about her mother and Eddie that she couldn't remember.

"So," she asked, forcing lightness, "did you ever get a chance to try?"

"Nah. My alarm went off and I woke up."

"Shame," Wendy said. She brushed a loose strawberry curl back against her mother's face. "I think I'd do anything she wanted, no matter how hard it was, to get her back."

"Me too," Chel said, skirting the edge of the bed and hugging Wendy with one arm. "We all would."

Embarrassed but secretly pleased at the embrace, Wendy cleared her throat. "Does she need her nails cut or anything? I see you brushed her hair."

"They do a good job here," Chel said, patting their mother's hand. "She looks okay overall. No bedsores or anything." She lifted their mom's hand higher and twisted her wrist gently. "You know, I've seen these tattoos before but I didn't realize until today that these are the same ones you've got all over you. When'd you get yours again?"

"About a year ago. Dad had that fit, remember?"

"Right, cause Mom signed off on you getting them without checking it by him first. He was so pissed!"

"He just doesn't want us to grow up," Wendy said. "Mom understood that it had to happen sometime." That wasn't the real reason she sported the same lines and knots her mother had embedded deep into her flesh, but Chel wasn't a Lightbringer and wouldn't understand the need for the supernatural protection the ink provided. It wasn't much, it only created an aversion at best, but every bit counted, no matter what the White Lady claimed.

"She let you get matching ink permanently poked into your skin and a dozen earrings, but freaked when I wanted to bleach my hair." Chel shook her head. "I love her but sometimes she can be such a hypocrite." Her voice dropped. "I didn't want to say this before, but I used to hate you for that. It just wasn't fair." She sighed. "I guess I got over it, huh?"

Saddened and embarrassed for her sister, Wendy shrugged, uncomfortable with the direction this conversation had turned. "I'm just different than you, Chel. Different rules apply to me, I guess."

She snorted. "Why? Because you're older?"

"Nah," Wendy said. "Because I'm Batman."

"Right, right," Chel said, laughing.

"I hear the Joker's hiring," Wendy continued. "And you do have a wicked laugh."

"Yeah, but those clothes! Not in a million years." Coughing, Chel pressed a hand to her forehead. "Ugh, I feel like crap, Wendy. I wish this fever would break already."

"I know, honey," Wendy said. "Visiting hours aren't over yet, but we don't have to stay if you don't feel up to it. You know how Nana likes to cook a ton of food for lunch—"

"Yeah right," Chel snorted. "The idea of eating makes me want to puke."

"And that's different from normal, how?"

"Haha, very funny. I'll find Jon and we'll see Eddie before we leave." Chel squeezed their mother's fingers once more and laid her hand back on the bed before brushing a soft kiss across her forehead. "Love you, Momma. I'll be back soon, okay?" Then she brightened. "Oh, I almost forgot. This got left for you. Here." She dug in her purse and pulled out an envelope, roughly folded and addressed to Wendy in neat, blocky letters. "I guess some intern on the floor worked pretty closely with Mom? Dr. Hensley? Henley? Whatever."

"Emma? She left something for me?" Wendy reached out. "What's it say?"

Chel frowned. "How should I know? I don't read people's mail. Anyway, she got transferred or something and left this. You really attract the psychos, don't you?" Wendy took the envelope and tucked it into her pocket. She'd worry about reading another goodbye later. Right now learning as much as possible about Eddie and her mother was more important, even if Emma Henley had been a truly nice person.

When Chel left, Piotr drifted through the wall and sat on the edge of the bed, expression grave. "You are right, your mother's soul is gone."

"Of course I'm right," Wendy murmured. "Souls are sort of my thing now, I'm not a total newb."

"But she's different than Eddie in one major way," Piotr added. "Look at her navel."

Confused, Wendy glanced down. It was her mother's stomach, flat and moving almost imperceptibly as she breathed slowly in and out. "So? What about it?"

"Unlike Eddie, Wendy, your mother has no cord." He waved his hand over several inches above her body, moving from ribs to pelvis in one smooth sweep. "It's gone."

"What? That can't be . . ." Wendy's protest died in her throat. He was right. Eddie's cord had looked gnawed through, but the remains of it had still been firmly attached to his body, thick and healthy and vibrant. Her mother's midriff, however, was smooth and bare. "I can't believe I didn't see that before."

"I'm not surprised. You probably don't look much at yourself when you're the Lightbringer, do you? Have you ever stopped and taken a glance at what you look like?"

"Of course not, when I'm like that I've got more important things to do than preen in front of a mirror," Wendy snapped.

"Wendy, when you're the Lightbringer, you don't have a cord either."

"That's because I'm alive, though, right?"

He shrugged. "I don't know. There's so much mystery surrounding what you do and how you do it, not to mention exactly how long your family has been this way. Maybe the White Lady is right. Maybe you really were too young to be a Lightbringer yet."

"I hate that I don't know diddly squat about how all this works," Wendy said bleakly.

"I have a theory," Piotr said. "Remember what happened in the park with Specs? He attacked you and pulled your soul out?"

"He was scared—"

"I'm not blaming him, but he did give me an idea. Wendy, I think the reason your family can do the things you do is that maybe your souls are different than other souls. There was no cord when he pulled your soul out; you were just this fragile ball of light. No, not light . . . Light. And even though your soul was yanked out, you were still conscious. You could sense what was going on around you, you even understood that I put your soul back inside your body."

"Right? So . . ."

"Both Specs and I knew that we could break you, Wendy. It was

. . . instinctual. Perhaps this is what happened to your mother? I think the Lost didn't pull her out whole. I think the reason you couldn't find your mother no matter how hard you looked is because her soul was a ball, a glowing ball of Light just like yours."

Piotr hesitated, not wanting to finish the last part of his theory but knowing that he had to, even if it hurt her. "And Wendy? I think it's entirely possible that when the Lost saw your mother they panicked, pulled your mother's soul out . . . and that they might have broken it."

CHAPTER NINETEEN

Dropping off the twins was easier than Wendy had anticipated; she'd expected Jon or Chel to protest Wendy's announcement that she didn't feel like spending the night, but neither of them said a word. They merely collected their duffle bags, hugged her goodbye, and trooped up the steps to Nana's front door. When the door shut behind them Piotr slid into the passenger side seat.

"You're quiet," he said.

"Yep," Wendy replied, pulling out of her grandmother's driveway and onto the street. Experience with the route made the return drive automatic; Wendy reached the highway in a fugue-like state. "I'm thinking thoughts."

"Would you care to share?"

"Maybe. I don't know. Not really. A little."

"That's clear."

"Look, Piotr, give me a break. You think my mom's soul got broken apart. The White Lady claims *she's* got it, and she showed me a flap of essence to prove it. I don't know what to think or who to believe. All I know is that I'm sick and tired of people fucking with me, okay?" Wendy pounded on the horn. "GET OUT OF THE WAY! FUCK! Learn to drive, asshole!"

"So what's next?" Piotr asked, keeping his voice carefully neutral. "The ball, as they say, appears to be in our court."

"We do as she said," Wendy said after long seconds of silence. "You and I go visit her at the Palace Hotel. She has this all planned out, so I don't have much of a choice, do I?"

Startled, Piotr struggled to find a reply. "You're not serious?"

"I am." Wendy floored the gas and the little sedan leapt onto the highway with a short grumble of the engine. Glancing into her mirrors, Wendy slid into the middle lane; carpooling was out now, even if Piotr was sitting next to her. A cop certainly wouldn't believe her if she claimed that a ghost was riding shotgun.

"Your big plan is to hand me over to her?" Betrayal colored the words with bitterness.

"No, my big plan was to use you as bait," Wendy replied shortly. "It's almost three. Think we should take the bridge? I'm worried about traffic."

"Take the bridge, it's not bad this time of day," Piotr agreed absently. "Bait? You really think the White Lady is going to fall for that?"

"Not really," Wendy snapped, scooting between a semi and a Honda with a severely cracked windshield. The driver was hunched over, peering between the spiderweb of cracks and the pouring rain. "But that's why I changed my plan. She thinks I'm just going to show up at midnight with you in tow, then she's got another thing coming." Wendy, exasperated, tapped the horn. "Get off the road!" she yelled. "Geeze, that's a car wreck waiting to happen."

"Wendy," Piotr said patiently. "I want you to talk to me."

"I am talking to you," she replied, picking and choosing her words with care. "I'm also driving in some nasty weather, which, if you recall, was how I met you in the first place. So if you don't mind cutting me just a little slack, I'd appreciate it, thanks." Sitting up straighter in her seat, Wendy began to haltingly outline her plan for the White Lady. They just had to make one stop first.

"Petey, you're loonier than a loony tune," Elle exclaimed an hour later as Piotr finished detailing the finer points of Wendy's idea. "If you was smart, you'd tell this dumb dora to dry up and beat it."

Wendy, who'd promised to be silent while Piotr spoke with the other Riders, stiffened at the insult, but was true to her promise and kept silent. Sensing her discomfort, Lily rose with arms outspread.

"Elle," she protested, "Wendy's plan has merit. We are warriors, are we not? And yet we have done little these past months but mourn our fallen and weep for what we have lost. There has been no counting coup! Is it not time to step forward and embrace this chance for retaliation destiny has laid upon our doorstep? Much time has passed; likely the White Lady will not expect a joining of our forces, especially after the recent fragmentation of our tribe. I say we aid Piotr and Wendy—"

"The Lightbringer," James interjected, bitterly.

"Wendy is her given name, the Lightbringer is her duty," Lily insisted, "and I agree with Wendy's assessment of this opportunity. Now is the time to strike!"

Elle slapped the wall. "Spoken like a true live wire, Pocahontas, but the thing is, I don't wanna be left holding the bag when this double-crossing tomato gets the lot of us pinched by the White Lady or her Walkers. She already told us that the White Lady wants ol' Pete in trade."

"We won't get caught," Piotr soothed. His vision was fluttering wildly and he was staring at the spot where Elle was standing, hoping against hope that she wouldn't move and leave him addressing empty air. "Wendy's destroyed hundreds of Walkers in the past three months. A few weeks ago you yourself were saying how few we've seen lately. How many could she have left? Ten? Twelve? Between your skills and Wendy's abilities, cornering the White Lady and discovering what she did with the rest of the Lost will be simple."

"Says you! You just said that all the White Lady really wants is your head on a platter. What's it to Wendy here if one more ghost goes toes up if she gets her fall guy home? Or her momma? Who, by the way, just happens to be Lightbringer *senior*."

In the corner Wendy stifled a strangled snarl; her lips were pressed tightly together, her eyes narrowed and blazing. Elle smirked at the reaction.

"Stop the insults, please," Piotr pleaded. "Eddie's . . . nice . . . and I'd like to get his soul back just as much as Wendy would. It's not just Eddie; it's Wendy's mother and our Lost too, can't you see that? There's more at stake here than just your wounded pride, Elle. We promised to protect the Lost. Let's go do that."

She snorted, turning her face away. "I've had an earful, Pete. I still think this one's taking you for a ride."

"Perhaps," Piotr said evenly. "But it may bring Dora back, and I think that's a risk I'm willing to take. What about you?"

Elle considered them in silence for several seconds before answering. "Maybe Pocahontas has a point about revenge being best served chilly. If nothing else, I ain't exactly keen on you walking into Walker central with only this piker at your back. She's likely to shiv you when you ain't looking. So I'm in. But only till we get the Lost out. Then it's back to sixes and sevens with us. You copasetic with that?"

Sighing in annoyance, Piotr threw up his hands. "Thank you!"

"You're welcome!"

"Lily? James?"

They glanced at one another. "We're in," James said, tucking his hands behind his head. "But I'm not working with the death dealer. She goes on another team."

"Great," Piotr said, almost laughing with relief. He had expected a much tougher fight from James; the fact that he'd accepted so readily meant that he saw the necessity of them sticking together. "All for one and one for all? We have but four hours until sunset. Let us figure out a game plan."

"I'll scout ahead," James offered. "Meet you at the edge of the business district in two hours?"

"Sounds good," Piotr agreed readily and stripped the dagger from his belt. "Take this for protection. Be careful."

"Always am," James said, tucking the dagger into a rough loop secured at his waist. "Keep an eye on Lily for me." Then he was gone.

"So talk," Elle commanded, jerking her chin at Wendy. "What's the plan?"

Wendy waited for Piotr to nod, releasing her from her promise, before she began speaking. "I went to the Palace Hotel two years ago for one of Chel's cheer camps. I'm not really much for the rah-rahs so I had time to explore. I took the tour and everything. The Palace is *old* and there's been more than a little emotion attached to it, not all of it good."

Wendy held up a hand and started ticking off points. "A king and a president both kicked the bucket there. A couple murders, a couple suicides, nothing any other hotel wouldn't have, but San Francisco's a mighty dramatic place. Death, excitement, romance—you name it, it's happened right there, or at least in the area. So that hotel isn't just an emotional hot zone, it's an emotional war zone."

"I am unfamiliar with this area of town. What does this mean?" Lily asked.

"It means that, since the Palace Hotel was hit by the earthquake of 1906 and the subsequent fires dropped the original building to the ground, it's been built from the ground up at least twice, not counting all the renovations. Blood, sweat, tears, frustration—emotions, Lily, and lots of them, from the residents of the area who had to put up with the noise, from the contractors building the place, and from tourists. Also, the business district grew up around it, so not only do you have the emotional insanity of all that happened inside the building itself and the layers of renovation emotion, you have all that business-related angst surrounding it. Like a big boiler, over a century of human living simmering on high."

"Yeah, so?" Elle rolled her eyes and twirled her hand in a hurry-it-up gesture.

"That means the White Lady trapped herself. Yes, she picked a powerful place to set up shop, but there's also the little fact that the Palace Hotel is still in business today. And it's popular. That means the White Lady can't send Walkers all over the building—even if they don't mind crowds anymore, they'd still get badly burned. Because the building is so old and has such an emotional history, no one—not just us, not just her, none of you—can just walk through some thin spot on the Never side. I've been down there; those walls are rock solid in the Never. No ghost could pass through. You have to take the hallways just as if you were living."

"So she must be lurking someplace in the building where not a lot of people go or would be expected to go," Piotr theorized. "The attic or basement?"

"Exactly. Which means if we can keep her Walkers away, we've got her trapped. We can force her to tell us where she's keeping the Lost."

"Holy crow, the piker's got a good plan," Elle said, stunned and musing. "I was thinking that going down there's gonna be like storming Little Bighorn, 'cept our head squaw's a pill this time around." She glanced at Lily's irritated expression and rolled her eyes. "Oh dry up, Pocahontas, it ain't like you were there. 'Sides, your guys won that one."

"Piotr and I will take the north entrance," Wendy continued, ignoring the animosity between Lily and Elle. "Elle, you should go with James to the south side, Lily, take the west. It'll be strictly divide and conquer: if you see a Walker, put them down. If there are two, try to lure one away or ambush them. If you have to, run for it."

"We are leaving the east side unattended?" Lily frowned, strapping her matching daggers to the loops she'd wrapped around each wrist. "I do not feel this is wise."

"I'll take the east," Elle said. Hopping up, she gathered a supply of ghostly weapons—her bow, several bundles of arrows, and a wicked looking dagger that hung from her hip nearly to her knee. "I'm sure baby James can handle a few widdle Walkers without me."

"It's a good plan," Piotr said when it seemed Wendy would protest. He squeezed her hand meaningfully, glancing at the vast array of weapons Elle was strapping on. "She's tiny, but Elle can

handle her own, I promise. Spare some steel, Elle?" Piotr held up a
hand and Elle kicked a much smaller dagger in his direction.

"Okay if you say so," Wendy said, accepting Piotr's advice without question. "We don't have much time until sunset. Let's do this."

Piling into her father's car accompanied by the ghosts, Wendy
had to turn the heater on full blast to counteract the frigid cold buf-
feting her. Traveling from the pier to the hotel would have taken
little time had they boarded a Muni train, but Wendy wanted an
easy getaway. It was her bad luck that rain-slick Embarcadero Street
was blocked off due to an accident. Her bad luck held: Wendy struck
west, eventually turning onto Mason, where traffic kept them locked
at a snail's pace for nearly thirty minutes. Dodging trolleys wasn't
Wendy's strong suit.

By the time they spotted James at the edge of the Financial District, standing helpfully near a miraculously empty parking spot
along the road, Wendy was frazzled and irritated—Elle had kept up
a stream of snide insults about Wendy's driving the entire way from
the pier. When Piotr's hand dropped on her shoulder, Wendy had
had it. She jerked away and glared fiercely, uncaring that it was Piotr
who was receiving her ire.

"Is it just me or are those new?" Piotr asked. He pointed up and
Wendy blinked in confusion. At first she couldn't see what the fuss
was about—part of her thought that perhaps he was having a joke at
her expense—and then she spotted the fine interlocking mesh high
above, the thin wires of spiritual energy blanketing the Financial
District in an effervescent web that filled the sky. Fear rolled in her
gut; Wendy's fury drained away.

"Spirit webs."

"Spirit webs," Piotr agreed. "Thousands of them."

"Traps for the unwary," Lily said. "Snares for the rabbits among
us. Look."

At the roof level, over two dozen Shades hung by ankle and
wrist, some twisted into mummified shapes by the essence-draining

webs, some stripped down to their very bones. All were cocooned by the webs, each one struck silent by rope-thick tendrils pushed past their lips and down into their guts.

"I think I'm gonna upchuck," Elle said, nearly breathless at the sight. "I thought you was beating your gums about that spirit web earlier, Pete. I'm so sorry . . . I know I ain't been this way in a dog's age, but those damn things aren't new. I should've spotted 'em long before now. I let us fall into this one."

"Last chance," James said as Wendy turned off the engine and pocketed the car keys, eyes steadily downcast to keep from having to look up again. Her fingers brushed the envelope still stuffed in her pocket. *Later*, she promised herself. *I'll read it later.*

While the rest of them were reeling with horror over the spectacle above, Lily filled James in on Wendy's plan. "We can still turn back and go home. There are other ways to win their freedom."

"The White Lady's set up one hell of a trap," Wendy replied, making certain her father's car was locked tight. "Spirit webs, Walkers, and now my best friend's soul. I'm not falling for it and neither should you. You want the Lost back? We're going to go get them, and this time show the White Lady and all her creepy Walkers that the Riders aren't ghosts to be messed with ever again."

"Dunn is in there," Lily agreed. Dunn's cap was tightly clenched in her fist, the bill resting against her thigh. "I would no more turn back now than turn my face away from the Light."

"Yeah, well we might get sent into the Light," Elle said. She wrapped a companionable arm around Lily's waist. "But Dora's somewhere in there, so I'm all in. Come on, you ducky doll. When all this is over we'll hit the closest juice joint that serves the likes of us. I'll line the soldiers up and you can knock 'em down. In the morning we'll swig some hair of the dog and do it all over again."

"Did you see anything?" Piotr asked James as Lily and Elle began striding almost in tandem down the sidewalk, weapons at the ready and avoiding trailing strands of spirit web.

"Only a cadre of Walkers leading some Lost towards the Palace," James said grimly. "Your lady friend is right. Looks like the White Lady is planning a soiree up at the big house." His lips twitched. "I can smell lynching in the air, Piotr. Are you certain that you truly want to go through with this?"

"Dora, Dunn, and Tommy are in there," Piotr replied. "Not to mention the others. If I have to put a rope around my own neck, I'd do it a dozen times to see them safe."

"You might have to." James glanced at Wendy. "Sunset's coming, girl."

Her stomach felt like lead. Wendy nodded once. "Lead the way."

CHAPTER TWENTY

Familiar with the Financial District, James was able to skirt the most dangerous zones, his outstretched arm stopping Wendy from walking into nearly imperceptible films of spirit web strung between buildings from roof to basement several times. When they reached the Palace he broke away from the group and headed for the south entrance without a word, dreadlocks bobbing with every step.

"All he has is your knife," Wendy noted as James' braids vanished around the corner.

"He's stronger than you'd think," Piotr replied in an undertone. "I've seen him take down Walkers barehanded before. James will be fine. Are you ready?"

Wendy glanced over her shoulder as she reached for the entrance door. The sky was a rapidly darkening grey, a mass of rain clouds as high as the surrounding mountainside gathered on the horizon. "I'm ready."

Piotr let his breath out in a gust. "This way."

The walls of the Palace Hotel in the Never were just as firm and strong as Wendy remembered. Piotr pressed one hand against the wall and was unable to push through. Satisfied, Wendy grinned. They couldn't easily get in, but then again, she couldn't easily get out. It was perfect.

Assuming a purposeful walk, Wendy kept her gaze level and her expression a touch bored. She'd learned long ago that most adults ignored teenagers and children so long as they appeared to be intent on some mundane task or otherwise occupied and didn't appear to be loitering or making trouble. It was as if life didn't really start until twenty-one. This sort of benign blindness had let Wendy slide in and out of several very important buildings during the past months; if caught, she just claimed to be waiting for her dad to get off work, or apologized profusely (dancing slightly side to side, of course) and asked directions to the closest bathroom. These tricks almost always worked.

Wendy had no way of knowing it, but she was extra lucky. The Palace staff was well trained and particular about making sure every guest who walked through their doors was seen to. On a normal day her appearance would have been noted and dealt with immediately. Today, however, was different. Not only was it the Palace Hotel's evening rush, but they were hosting a junior debate conference that weekend; the vast entrance foyer was stuffed to bursting with groups of milling students, teachers, and chaperones and their bags. Wendy was lost in the crowd and easily able to sneak through an Employee Only entrance behind a bustling pair of bellhops burdened with bags. They took the elevator up, and Wendy snuck silently down the stairs with Piotr at her heels.

"I wonder how the others are doing," he said as Wendy reached the ground floor.

"They're resourceful," Wendy said, reaching into her pocket and producing a bellboy's employee badge that she'd filched from his back pocket in the overcrowded lobby. "And so," she swiped the badge against the card reader; above the reader, the light flashed from red to green, "am I. Come on."

"Are you going to change?" Piotr asked as the door snicked shut behind them. The basement was pitch black, the dense darkness almost velvet with dust and quiet.

"I don't dare, not yet," she whispered. "Unless you're ready to go to the Light right now."

"I didn't think of that," Piotr hissed.

"It's okay, I did. Now shut up, let me think!"

After several minutes her eyes adjusted, but the darkness was still nearly complete. Wendy was able to push off from the wall and maneuver her way across the room mostly by touch, avoiding the sharp corners of neatly stacked boxes and a large plastic bin overflowing with cottony, plush fabric.

"Bedspreads," she whispered. "I think."

"Have you seen a single Walker?" Piotr asked. "Because I haven't."

"There's a reason for that," said a voice behind them and Piotr felt a sharp pinch on the back of his neck. Lights blared into existence—across the vast expanse of basement, several Walkers systematically stripped the blackout sheets away from the windows in the Never as another group flicked on the lights. Wendy blinked against the glare. Her eyes were seeing the two worlds pressed together, hotel lights brilliant in the Never but dark in the living world. The Never was stronger here, stronger than she'd ever seen it before, and the living world was fading from view fast.

"Amazing," the White Lady said, "what a little bit of time and preparation can do."

They were, Wendy realized, in a vast Never ballroom, the walls rounded at the corners and festooned with sweeps of gaily painted decorations. Here and there long, thin cracks in the walls were mending before her very eyes as the living people above went about their daily business and the multitude of students revved up for the next day's competition. If she concentrated, Wendy could just make out the edges of the real world beyond the intense brilliance of the basement, but the Never was too dazzling to ignore for long.

Dozens of Walkers lined the walls like ancient, rotting wallflowers, their hoods flung back, each one marked with long, fresh wounds, still seeping, that had been roughly sewn closed with hanks of black twine. It was the far wall, however, that caught Wendy's attention. The missing Lost—a dozen of them—huddled together, bound hand and foot like an under-aged chain gang beneath a temporary stage that winked in and out of existence as the Palace, pulsing with energy, cycled through the ages and all the renovations it had been through.

All of the Lost had been starved and drained of essence; fear and pain came off them in palpable waves that Wendy could sense in her gut. They watched her avidly, hungrily. Piotr groaned—among them were Dunn, Dora, Tommy. No recognition shone in their eyes.

Beside the Lost, wrapped in rapidly expanding tendrils of spirit web, were the rest of the Riders. Lily, face slashed; Elle, mouth bloody, and James, both eyes blackened and with one arm hanging at a gruesome angle from his shoulder. It had been an ambush.

They were trapped.

"Wendy," Piotr moaned, the strands of spirit web spinning quickly around his neck and snaking down his arms, "become the Lightbringer." Walkers held him on each side, half supporting him. "Please."

"I can't," Wendy whispered. "I can't do that to you. I'm not ready for you to go." More than Piotr's closeness, however, was the matter of the Lost. They had risen to their feet now, each straining against the bonds that held them. The Walkers on each side of the group held a long chain in their hands. All they had to do was drop the chain and the hollow-eyed Lost would be upon her, feeding.

"Winifred, not even a hello?" asked the White Lady, stepping beside Wendy. "How rude!" In her hand she held a syringe filled with a bubbling, oozing black liquid. "Spirit pollen," she explained. "And seeds, of course. You've seen my topiary outside?"

"Yes," Wendy said through lips gone numb from the intense cold emanating from the woman beside her. "It's foul."

"Briar Rose's citadel had a field of pricking rosebushes," the White Lady said, nonplussed. "European castles had moats. I thought my palace could use some protection to keep the riffraff out. It appears that I was right." She drifted across the room to James' side.

"This one," she said, ruffling his dreadlocks, "isn't as stealthy as he thinks, hmm? He's been spotted in my territory a number of times 'doing his rounds' when they were looking for the children, just never this deep in. So we decided to make it a little more challenging for him."

She gestured to the Walkers around her. "I had no end of volunteers for the germination process. I'm told it's quite painful." She laughed at that and Wendy was once more reminded how insane the White Lady really was, despite her air of rationality.

"You're sick," Wendy yelled over the tittering laughter. "Sick and twisted. Let them go, everyone here, or else."

"Or else what, dear?" The White Lady crossed her arms over her chest, her giggles finally tapering off. "You'll awaken that pathetic little ability that slumbers deep inside? I've seen how long it takes you to rouse the Lightbringer. I could have every last one of them ripped to shreds before you even unlocked your Light."

"Think so?" Wendy bluffed. "I've been practicing."

The White Lady rolled her eyes. "Please dear, you're embarrassing yourself. There is absolutely no way the likes of you has sped up in a mere day or so." Casually she reached out and took Wendy by the chin, turning her face from side to side as she examined her. "No, no, dear, my initial assessment still stands. You will never show half the power of the other Lightbringers, I'm afraid. Pity, that."

Piotr moaned and his vision fluttered; when it did so, the strands of spirit web began to smoke and burn, catching fire and puffing away in a whiff of smoke. The Walkers hissed but held on; they'd not been told to let go.

Catching sight of the web burning, Wendy shifted so the White Lady's back was to the blaze. If she could just keep her distracted long enough for Piotr to figure out a way to wrestle free . . .

"Let go of me!" Thinking of nothing more than keeping the White Lady's attention, Wendy jerked her chin away. She could still feel the press of those icy fingers, a million times more horrible in real life than in her dreams, burning against her flesh. "I swear, no matter what it takes, I'm going to make you regret—"

"Threats, threats, threats," the White Lady said, waving a dismissive hand. "All you do is threaten! In my day we didn't threaten or boast or complain, we just *did*!" She chuckled again, shaking her head. "But I suppose this was your pathetic attempt to do, eh? Shoddy work, that."

"Where's Eddie?" Wendy snapped, carefully keeping her gaze away from Piotr. "What have you done with him? And my mom?"

"Eddie's close." The White Lady snapped her fingers and two more Walkers, larger than the others, appeared from the darkness, shambling forward until their stench filled the air and they were only a few feet from Wendy's side. "But first, we have a little business to transact. A bit of a trade to handle."

"Go to hell," Wendy snapped. "I'm never helping you, and if you think you're getting Piotr, it's going to be over my dead body."

"That," the White Lady said sweetly, grabbing Wendy by the back of the neck so that smoky steam billowed at her touch, "is exactly what I had in mind."

The Walkers, one at each side, attacked.

Wendy screamed, throwing up her arms to block, but she was still in human shape and the Walkers were very quick, very strong. Drawing visible essence from the White Lady in arcs like lightning, their sharpened bones punched through the tender skin of Wendy's midsection, ripping through her skin like tissue paper and spearing the organs beneath.

Framed in curls of silver smoke, Wendy sank to the floor. Her fingers, blood-bright in the dimming light, curled around her side, pinky curving against the fine copper chain at her waist, thumb indenting the flesh just under her ribs. She was bone pale in that final gasp of day, the warm red that had leached from her cheeks now spilling slowly through her fingers.

"I did warn you that some ghosts can touch the living," the White Lady said. "You should have listened."

"WENDY! WENDY! WENDY!"

Pushing against his captors, Piotr struggled against the hands holding him, but these Walkers were old and tough, prepared for his wriggling. He could not wrestle free.

The White Lady shook her head. "Too late, Rider. Look past her."

"*Poshel ti na huj!*"

"Tsk, tsk, language! Still, I suppose circumstances are a little volatile. Look."

Despite himself, Piotr stilled and did as she ordered.

There, just beyond the curve of ballroom wall, was a shaft of light where before there had been none. At first it seemed the light was the last glimmer of the fading day peeking through some hole in the ceiling, but that notion was quickly abandoned. The rest of the building was solid and strong, both in real life and in the Never. This light was coming from somewhere else.

Piotr moaned and the White Lady sighed. The light was vibrant, shimmering, and where it struck the air, it danced with shivering, whirling motes. "The Lightbringer's time has come."

"*NET!*"

"Yes." Calm and assured now, the White Lady danced to the ever-shifting stage and settled herself on an ornate chair at the edge. She drew the folds of her robe around her, rubbing her rotting hands together until they sounded like a cicada song. "Now we wait."

For long moments nothing happened. The shaft of light—no, Piotr had to admit to himself, that glow was not light but rather Light—fairly hummed with serenity. He tested the strength of the Walkers again; still their grip did not loosen.

Then, faintly, Wendy's body began to glow. It was not her regular brilliant Light but a gentle, glimmering haze, pale green around the edges and faint white at the center. The strength flowed from Piotr's legs and he wilted to the ground, the Walkers finally releasing him as he sagged to hands and knees, only barely able to hold up his head. "No. Wendy . . . *net.*"

Wendy sat up, leaving her body behind. In her hands was a

small glass ball, shining with mindless pulsing fire. Was it her soul or something more? Piotr did not know, but the orb was painful to look at, like her tattoos; its depths glimmered with Light.

Behind her the Light grew brighter, more insistent, and a low humming, both terrible and inexpressibly lovely, began to fill the room. The volume rose in a slow, sensuous sweep of sound like a radio being gradually turned up in some distant room, until Piotr's head was ringing with the gorgeous-painful chords. If the Walkers or White Lady heard the cry of the Light, they paid no attention. The Lost were unmoved, the other Riders unconscious and cocooned with the spirit webs. If Wendy heard she paid no mind. Only Piotr, with the song of Wendy's Light vibrating his very teeth, was bent in pain.

Wendy stood and the sound, blessedly, began to subside. She held out one hand and twisted it back and forth, palm up-palm down, then patted her face, her shoulder, her hip. She ran fingers across her lips, curled her fingers into a fist, and tapped the chair beside her, the one her body still lay beside. Her hand slid through the rotting wood easily.

She nodded once, her suspicions confirmed. "Well, hell. That sucks."

"Good afternoon," the White Lady said. "How are you finding your death thus far?"

"Can't say that I like it." Wendy wrinkled her nose. "Everything smells like rot."

"It does on this side." The White Lady waved a languorous hand in the direction of the warped and splintery floorboards, the water-logged walls. "You grow accustomed to it." Then, surprisingly, she indicated the shaft of Light. "That is, unless you wish to go to your eternal reward. You have earned it, after all."

Wendy glanced at the Light, her expression calm, and shrugged again. "I suppose I could. It does look kinda nice."

"It is, in fact, very nice," the White Lady agreed gravely, then smiled. "It's the nicest thing there is. Why do you think I've been doing the things I've been doing, hmm? For kicks?"

"I hadn't really thought about it much. I always just assumed you were a crazy bitch," Wendy said, stepping away from her body and strolling casually across the room, rolling the ball of Light in her nimble hands.

Wincing, eyes never leaving the ball, the White Lady waved a hand and the Walkers parted for Wendy. She knelt by Piotr. Her hand, far from its usual warmth, was cool to the touch as she ran it across his forehead, brushing aside the sweaty strands of hair that clung to his temples. "Are you okay?"

"You're dead." Piotr laughed bitterly. "I'll live."

"I can see that." Wendy helped Piotr to his feet. Weakened, he staggered as he stood, but here she was strong and supported him easily. She handed him the ball of Light; he hissed, it was hot to the touch. "Hold this and let's get out of here before this skank causes even more damage. We can come back for the others."

"Language!" The White Lady wagged one finger in a tsk-tsk motion. "You weren't brought up to speak like that, young lady."

"Up yours," Wendy sneered, pressing one hand in the small of Piotr's back for support. "You're not my mother."

The White Lady paused, just for one brief moment, and Piotr felt a thrumming in the air. The Light, just a short distance away, began trembling, the motes within whirling wildly. The song, which had faded to a nearly imperceptible hum, rushed upon him in a wave, the exquisite melody breaking with horrible force upon him and sapping his little remaining strength in a tide of unexpected ferocity. Piotr stumbled and fell. As Wendy, crying out in surprise, leaned forward to help him, she missed the White Lady rising to her feet, the quick patter of steps as the woman hurried downstage.

"Look out," Piotr whispered and Wendy released him to face this new threat. But the White Lady slowed as she stepped off the last stair, held her hands out in supplication.

"Oh Wendy," she breathed, pale and rotting fingers lifting up the obscuring hood, pushing the fabric free so that it puddled loosely on her shoulders, revealing a last few clinging curls of strawberry gold hair and a face etched with crosshatched lines similar to those the surrounding Walkers sported, but deeper, rawer, and real.

"After all our conversations and all the hints I've dropped, I truly thought you would have figured it out by now. I *am* your mother. Wendy . . . it's me."

CHAPTER TWENTY-ONE

"**Y**ou're lying," Piotr said, but Wendy shook her head.

"No," she whispered. "She's not." Making sure that Piotr could support his own weight, Wendy approached her mother, hands clenched in loose fists at her sides. "Mom? What happened to you?"

"The Lost," her mother said, her voice see-sawing wildly, alternating between bitterness and tears. "They were scared, wild. They reached for me and broke my Light, shattered it into a dozen pieces, one for each of them." She ran a hand across her face, grimaced. "Breaking my soul apart hasn't done wonders for my disposition, I'll give you that. It's made me . . . not at all balanced these days."

Wendy glanced over her shoulder at the assembled Lost and did a rapid headcount. Twelve. "But these kids aren't the same ones. I sent those on."

"I don't need the same ones," her mother chuckled, fingers rising slowly up, the tips of the phalanx bones poking through the flesh at the end. She dug her fingers into her face, the bones parting her rough stitches, essence flowing like blood in a wet gush that pitter-pattered against the basement-ballroom floor and soaked the front of her dress. "I just need the one who called their Light. Twelve Lost—even inert, they're like gunpowder, you see—and the one who whiffed out the ones who ripped me to shreds. A match. Combine the two and BOOM, I'm back. Back to the living, back to work. Back to doing what I do best."

"Mom," Wendy protested, "but that's me. It's Wendy."

"I know," the White Lady said, sadness creeping across her face. "Don't you think I know that? But it's a sacrifice I'm willing to make—no, one I *have* to make. You don't know our ways, you haven't been trained!"

"You taught me—"

"I taught you nothing!" her mother spat. "I taught you only the basics, and that was mostly to keep you in line and safe from the Lost! You had years to go before it was your time and even then, did you honestly think it was going to be *you* who got picked to wake to the Sight? Please. Michelle has more of the Sight in her little finger than you do in your whole body. You didn't even know how to ask the right questions, Wendy, not that night at the house, not ever after that. You just did whatever I said, never questioning the *why* of it all! That's not how a Lightbringer works."

Her mother slapped herself three times across the face, until the last of her stitches parted. She grabbed the flap and tore, waving the loose skin at Wendy like a banner. "And the sight of your face when I showed you my skin flap and tattoo! You just took me at face value! Never thought to question if maybe I was making the whole thing up. If I can make maggots writhe themselves out of the ground, what makes you think that a little flesh is the real thing? Pathetic. You should have known better."

"But you never taught me—"

"My point exactly. I never taught you. If you were meant to be the next Reaper, then you would have figured it out on your own but you didn't. You, as the Lightbringer? No, darling. No. You haven't got the heart for it. Or the instinct."

Stung, Wendy shook her head. "That's not true. That first night, you said, in the hospital—"

"I said what I had to in order to shut you the hell up before you started screaming." Her mother waved a hand at the assembled Walkers. "You think I don't know how disgusting and foul they look? How nasty I look? I'm not blind, Winifred, nor stupid. A little girl facing one of those? Naturally she'll tell everyone she sees. I had to shut you up."

"That's not true," Wendy said, but her voice was weaker now. "You were worried about me. You love me."

"Oh darling, of course I do! But love doesn't matter when you're dead, Wendy," her mother said sweetly. "That was a fact my own mother drilled into me, and her mother before her. Do you think we've survived against the dead as long as we have by being senti-mental? Hardly. We do what we do because we're tough and strong. Two things you have never been."

"I'm tough—"

"Tough?! Look at you!" she laughed. "You quit reaping the minute my body hit the ground. Refused to do your duty! Refused to reap! Your grandmother is spinning in her grave! Or she would be, if I hadn't sent her into the Light. Kicking and screaming, as a matter of fact."

"Mom," Wendy moaned. "Please."

"Moooom-puhleaze," her mother mocked, and spat. "Listen to yourself. Weak. Pathetic. You were given a gift you didn't earn. And now with your entire life planned out for you, a career as a Light-bringer, your duty, and a boy who loves you, still you whine! My little Wendy-girl, she has to go and mess it all up, doesn't she? Nothing's good enough for Wendy, oh no. Isn't satisfied with just doing her sister's stolen job, no, she's got to go and reap the Lost who tore her mother apart!"

"I . . . I can't . . . ." She sniffed, trying to keep from breaking down. Her mother's words were like hammers pounding, each blow shattering a little more of her heart apart. Wendy began to shake.

"Such theatrics, Wendy! And you haven't even asked yet how I got put back together. Of course, it took you long enough—or, rather, I should say, *Piotr* long enough—to figure out what happened."

"Mom . . . I—"

"Didn't know. Yes, I sorted that part out. I assume I'd still be in tiny pieces if it had been left up to you. But there was one person who knew, one person who'd been around long enough to know a thing or two about Lightbringers." She slapped the skin against her face and strode across the room to Piotr's side. "Even if he doesn't remember it."

Piotr, horrified, shook his head frantically. "I would never help you!"

"Of course you would, Piotr," she said, and grabbed him by the back of the neck. "You've helped me all along."

Piotr screamed and his knees buckled. He fell to the ground, eyes rounded with pain, but held Wendy's Light orb tightly tucked into his chest, unwilling to drop it. Where her hand pressed into his flesh, dark essence poured into Wendy's mother until the skin healed, the flap clinging to the rest of her face by the thinnest threads. Wendy gaped; her mother'd drained him for essence, like Piotr would drain a Lost.

"So convenient," she said. "He's like a walking battery for us. Even get near him and our kind gets a boost. You get sleepy at first, but he's like good wine. He grows better with age."

"H-how . . . when . . . Piotr . . ."

"Quit stuttering, dear, it's unbecoming." Her mother smoothed her hair, noticeably thicker and less ragged now, and patted Piotr on the top of the head. "Poor boy has been following our family for centuries. None of us had a clue why, but he's awfully useful to have around. Bit crazy, though." She held up one hand to block her mouth and whispered loudly, "A few screws loose upstairs. Terrible memory problem. Of course, that's our fault too, you know. He gives up a memory for every time one of us sucks him dry. But that's all right, it's what he's here for."

Abandoning all concern for her own well-being, Wendy darted to Piotr's side and cradled him in her lap. His pupils expanded and contracted wildly, his legs twitched and jerked, drumming against the floor in a slipshod staccato beat.

"You can imagine my surprise," her mother continued, stepping over Piotr and wiping fastidiously at the front of her soiled robes, "when I discovered that you'd found our little family battery pack. And my further surprise when I learned that you were *kissing* him."

"Who was it?" Wendy asked bleakly. "A Walker? One of the Riders? Who is your little stooge, Mom? Who's been your marvelous spy?"

A warm, furry body pressed against Wendy's side as Jabberwocky pushed past Wendy and trotted across the room to twine around her mother's ankles.

"I told you, dear," her mother said, scooping Jabber up and rubbing her chin against the ghost kitty's head. "I've been watching you quite closely. Hello, darling. Did you miss me?" She made kiss-kiss faces at Jabber before setting him down. The cat vanished into the darkness gathering at the edge of the room.

Wendy blinked. Darkness? Her head felt woozy suddenly, and weary. Spots danced before her eyes.

"Oh, don't worry, dear, that's just the blood loss," her mother said. "Time passes differently here, when you're fully in the Never, in a place as strongly bound with emotion as this hotel. You've only been dying a few living seconds, but you'll finish bleeding out soon, I promise." She tsked. "Though if you want to catch your Light, I suggest you hurry. It's looking a little weak around the edges."

Wendy glanced over her shoulder and shrugged. "What's the point? I came to get you and Eddie. You've gone off the deep end, what's to say Eddie hasn't, too?"

Her mother burst into merry laughter, wrapping her arms around her waist and rocking back and forth on her heels with mirth. "Oh Wendy, you are a peach! You think I had anything at all to do with Eddie? What kind of a monster do you take me for?"

"You . . . you didn't?"

"Of course not, dear. Our job is taking souls once they've crossed, not making them cross. Other ghosts can interact with the living world, but you were right all along—I'm not one of them. I was lying to you. The only souls *I* can bother are people like us, Seers or people with one foot in the grave already. Oh no, dear, a little bird came and whispered about Eddie's condition to me. I just took advantage of it."

"What happened to him?" Wendy demanded. "What happened to his soul?"

"That, darling, I can't say." Her mother shrugged. "I wasn't there. Any number of things. Drug use, astral projection . . . anything can stretch a soul so thin it'll snap. But his cord wasn't rotted, so he's still about somewhere, possibly lost as I was supposed to be. Looking for you, I'd wager. If you don't feel like going into your Light, I'm sure you might even be able to find him. Who knows? Maybe you'll even do a better job saving your best friend than you did your own flesh and blood."

Her mother stretched and held out her hand. "Your doorway into the Light's grown thin, Winifred. It's time. Give me your Light and be on your way. Or stay here and learn a trick or two. It's no matter to me."

"You'd do this?" Piotr asked, pushing into a sitting position, still cradling Wendy's ball of Light. "You'd kill your own daughter for this?"

"In a heartbeat," she said, "if she still had one. I need it more than she ever would. All that power inside and she hardly ever tapped it. Disgusting. Now give me her Light. I'll put it to good use."

"You are sick," Piotr hissed. "She is your *daughter*!"

"Yes, she is, and Momma knows best. Besides, Piotr, you don't have any room to lecture me. Or I suppose you don't remember my mother and what she did to her own sister? It is our duty to pass on our knowledge, our teaching, and our ways. The proper ways."

"Proper ways?" Piotr spat. "There is nothing proper about what you are doing."

"Manners, Piotr. Manners." The White Lady shook her head, tsking. "See, this is exactly what I'm talking about. Wendy learned the

Sight at too young an age; it taught her sympathy for your kind. It made her think of you as a *person*. Why do you think we wait until they're eighteen to show my kind the Light? Otherwise we might think things like you are 'romantic.' We might go about *kissing* you."

"We're not yours to control," Piotr snapped, hugging Wendy's fragile ball of Light as closely as he dared. "You don't have any say over our souls."

"I don't?" She seemed truly sad at that. "Piotr, Piotr, Piotr, after all these years and you still haven't learned? The dead must be sent on—Lost, Shades, Walkers, and Riders alike. No one may stay in the Never, even if they don't think they're ready to move on. No one."

"That's not your choice to make!"

"Isn't it? Ghosts like you are like children who want to stay up past your bedtime because you fear the monster under your bed, in your closet. An adult, a person with clear sight, knows better. An adult can see what really is for the best and when it's time to move on."

"You'll be killing your own line!"

"Hardly. I still have two very smart, very dedicated children besides Winifred. I'm willing to sacrifice her in order to keep our legacy strong. *Now give me the Light!*"

Wendy wrapped her arms around her waist and ducked her head. She hated to say it but what her mother said made a sick, disheartening sort of sense to her. The pillar to the afterlife was here— maybe it really was time for her to move on. "Mom's right, I guess. Do it, Piotr," she whispered. "Do what is best."

"Listen to my daughter, Piotr." Her mother said. "Give me her Light, boy."

"*Da*? Or what?" Piotr asked, eyeing the hungry, starved Lost. Wendy was no longer at their mercy, but her mother might be. "What will you do to me if no, hmm? You feed me to your beasties?"

"Or watch as I have my Walkers rip my daughter to shreds." The White Lady held up a threatening hand, deadly calm and completely serious. "So what will it be, Piotr? Winifred? Or the Light?"

In his flickering vision Piotr heard a scream, faint and far away, and sensed a trembling as footsteps pounded up a flight of stairs. In the basement, in the living world and in the living time, someone—a maid, or a custodian perhaps—had discovered Wendy's body.

"How about you go to hell?" he said and pushed away from Wendy's lap, dodging past the White Lady's goons, and sprinting for her bleeding body. Long-fingered, bony hands gripped his ankles, pulling him back, draining him, but Piotr struggled, thrashing his legs and kicking over and over again until the hands let go with a brittle crack. Then, Wendy's body only a few feet away, Piotr shoved forward with all his might. The White Lady was screaming, the Walkers howling, but all he could see, all he could feel, was the pulse of her Light sliding out of his grip.

The orb balanced on the tip of his fingers, about to fall, about to break . . .

Piotr shoved forward . . .

. . . and thrust her orb of Light deep into Wendy's gut.

Behind him Wendy shrieked and her pillar's song cut off, the glittering ray winking out.

"You stupid boy," keened her mother. "Oh you idiot! Look at what you've done!"

Across the ballroom Wendy's soul burst into brilliant Light, filling the room like phoenix fire, and a pulse of silent white exploded through the room, rocking the ghostly Palace at its very foundation. The Light burned everything it touched to a crisp—the White Lady, the Walkers, the Lost, and the Riders—bellowing Light and heat and an immense, billowing flame.

Piotr closed his eyes as the shockwave reached him, prepared for the bitter end.

EPILOGUE

I do not love you as if you were salt-rose, or topaz,
or the arrow of carnations the fire shoots off.
I love you as certain dark things are to be loved,
in secret, between the shadow and the soul.
　　　　　　　　　　—Pablo Neruda "Sonnet XVII"

TWO WEEKS LATER

The Palace Hotel was empty for repairs. An earthquake had rocked the historical monument to its very foundations two weeks earlier, and though any contractor would have sworn the grand old hotel would have easily withstood a powerful shock, this quake apparently originated beneath the building itself. Luck was with them, however: a few plates were broken, and a maid sprained her wrist grabbing her cart to keep it from rolling over the feet of a customer, but there was only one serious injury out of all the guests. The Palace would be closed for another month, but residents of the Bay Area counted themselves lucky. It could have been much, much worse.

When Wendy opened her eyes, she found her father slouched at her bedside, head thrown back and snoring loudly, the latest *PC World* propped open on his chest. Tubes and wires snaked across her body and her sides ached fiercely, itching like fire. There was a plastic cup at her bedside, and a white pitcher brimming with water, condensation sluicing down its sides. Careful of her side, Wendy gingerly reached for the glass but bumped her elbow. She couldn't stop the curse from escaping her lips.

Her father's eyes flew open. He looked at her, saw she was awake; a long, slow smile worked its way across his face. "Hey Pippi Longstocking," he whispered, "are you up?"

"Up as I'll ever be," she said and pointed to the pitcher. "I'm thirsty, though. Could you please—"

"Right away," he said and jumped up to fill her glass, his magazine tumbling beneath the bed. "You have no idea how good it is to hear your voice, sweetheart." He brushed a kiss across her forehead. "Sip this slowly and I'll go get the doctor." He wiped a damp hand across her jeans and Wendy spied one corner of Emma's envelope sticking out of the pocket. The sight of that pristine, sharp corner brought back the dreams of the White Lady in one great rush. Wendy forced herself to stay calm.

"Dad, wait," she said and gripped his wrist with her free hand. "What happened?"

"We were hoping you'd tell us, honey." He sat heavily down in the hospital chair. "I thought you were going to stay with Nana, but you turned up at the Palace Hotel after the earthquake later that night. Six point two, they're saying, but no one was seriously hurt. Except you. It was like a miracle . . . for everyone but me, that is." He wiped the heel of his hand against his face. "I thought I lost you."

"Oh Dad, I'm sorry."

"Your mom, honey, she . . . she didn't make it." Her father took Wendy's hand in his own. "I know I shouldn't tell you this before I get the doctor, but I want you to know."

Some memory niggled the back of Wendy's mind. Something important about her mother. "The earthquake?"

He nodded. "Yeah, honey. Some tubes must have jiggled loose or something. Chel and Jon were with her though, at the end. Nana too. They said it was peaceful." He brushed a stray lock of hair off

Wendy's forehead. "We buried her yesterday. It's just that you were showing the same symptoms your mom had, before. They told me you might not wake up. But if I'd known you were going to wake up today we could have waited, or—"

"It's okay, Dad," Wendy said. "I don't blame you. Go get the doctor, okay?"

"Okay, honey," he said and quickly left the room.

"I'm glad you're awake," Piotr said. He was sitting on the empty bed beside her, one of Dora's sketchbooks in his lap, a package of Prismacolor pencils at his side. He held up the sketchbook; he'd drawn the rough outline of her face, only slightly lopsided, a brief oval surrounded with curls like red fire, tinged black at the tips. "Your soul took a long time to heal."

"Mom really was the White Lady, right?" Wendy's fingers curled into the blanket. "I didn't imagine that?"

He shook his head. "*Net*, you did not. I'm sorry."

"I'm the one who should be apologizing," Wendy said bitterly. "I should have known, but it just didn't seem possible—"

"There was no way for you to have," he said. "Wendy, it's not your fault."

She wiped her eyes. "My dad'll be back soon."

He nodded. "I know. I just wanted to let you know that none of it—not your mother, not what happened to me, and what happened at the Palace—none of it is your fault."

"The others?"

Piotr sighed. "Elle and Lily survived. While the White Lady and her Walkers were occupied with us, Dora had enough energy to crawl over and cut them loose. They were trying to free James when I . . . when I did what I did. Elle dragged Lily out a window before the shockwave hit."

"James? The Walkers? The Lost?"

He hung his head. "All gone. The explosion sent them into the Light."

Wendy nodded once. "I see." Her fists opened, releasing the bunched bedspread. "And you? You were at ground zero."

"*Da*. Somehow, I don't know know, I survived." Piotr shrugged. "The Light destroyed everything around me—even the ground at my feet—but I was left alone." He laughed. "I guess it really isn't my time to go, *da*?"

"I'm sorry, Piotr."

He shrugged. "I'm not. All this, everything that's happened, made me realize that it's time to travel on for a bit. Backtrack where I can, find my roots." He glanced out the window. "Lily's known me the longest—centuries, and centuries again. So Lily's agreed to come with me, and Elle . . . she doesn't wish to stay here. Too many bad memories. She's coming along for the ride." He smiled. "I believe she's looking forward to the adventure."

"So you're leaving."

"For a while. See what I can learn about being me. See what memories were siphoned away." He hesitated. "You . . . could come with us."

"I can't. I'm needed here." Wendy sighed. "I still don't know what happened to Eddie, and I've got a feeling that I'll be cleaning up my mom's mess for a little longer than a while."

"I understand." Piotr brushed a finger along her face. "I do not wish to leave you like this. I want to stay but . . . honestly, Wendy, I need to get out of this place. I need to give this thing—this strange thing between us—a little space. I am not being fair to you." He grimaced. "You are alive. I think . . . I think that you need to be with someone who is also alive."

"All of that doesn't matter to me. I don't care that you're dead. I mean, hell, I'm the Lightbringer often enough that I might as well be—"

"Shhh!" Piotr put his hand over her mouth gently but urgently. "Do not say that! It matters to me. You matter to me. Do you understand?"

"Yeah. It sucks, but I get it." Wendy shifted in the bed, grimacing at the pain in her side. "I'm going to miss you."

He ran shaking fingers through his hair, his scars standing out in stark contrast with the unblemished skin of his hand. "I will miss you too. Very, very much."

"I wonder how many memories I took," Wendy whispered. "While we were kissing."

"Maybe some, maybe none," he said. "But even so, I think it was a fair trade."

"Right," she said bitterly. "Sure."

Fingers, cool and strong, lifted her chin, tilting Wendy's face up. Piotr was only the barest breath away, eyes looking intently into her own. "A kiss for the road?" he asked and, before she could answer, his lips slanted over hers.

When they drew apart, the monitor at her bedside was beeping wildly and Wendy could hear the quick pounding of feet in the distance, nurses running for her room.

"I'll see you around, Curly," Piotr said, blowing her a kiss as he backed through the far wall. "Good luck finding Eddie."

The doctor skidded into the room, a nurse and Wendy's father at his heels. He found Wendy sitting up in the bed, cheeks wet and a hand pressed to her lips, staring at the wall. The monitor, which had only moments before been protesting at a high-pitched whine, was dropping its tempo into a steady, pulsing beat.

"Winifred?" he asked, approaching her carefully, worried that his sudden appearance might shock the girl into another series of heavy heart fluctuations. "How are you feeling?"

"I think I'm a little lost," she replied, eyes never straying from the wall. "But I think I'd like to go home."

ABOUT THE AUTHOR

K.D. McEntire is a mom and animal lover currently living just outside of Kansas City with her husband, son, and two cats. K.D. spends her miniscule free time reading, writing, and battling her Sims 3 addiction. She loves Wil Wheaton, Stephen King, Joss Whedon, gaming, comic books, and all things geeky.